CHIRAL MAD

READ ORDER

75	43	63	11	137
115	53	81	27	93
203 (6)	157	277 (12)	121	
185	193	243	167	
225	233	345 (14)	207	
289 (8)	257		297	
	267 (10)		313	
			329	

CHIRAL MAD

ANTHOLOGY OF PSYCHOLOGICAL HORROR

www.nettirw.com

Published by Written Backwards

Cover artwork by Michael Bailey

First Edition

ISBN-10: 1-4791-5243-9
ISBN-13: 978-1-4791-5243-8

CONTENTS

DEDICATION

FOR THOSE WITH 46 HELPING THOSE WITH 47
FOR THOSE WITH 47 HELPING THOSE WITH 46

"Help us when we need help, but only enough help so we can finish what we were doing on our own." – Annie Forts

CAUSE

Reading this page means you have either purchased this book, or it was purchased for you; either way, all proceeds from the sale of this book went directly to Down syndrome charities.

If you received this book as a gift, please consider purchasing a copy for a friend to continue spreading the love.

Special thanks are in order for the contributors of this anthology. None of the authors received payment; all stories were donated with utmost support for this cause. All publishing and advertising costs were donated as well.

Thank you, readers and writers.

WHITE PILLS

IAN SHOEBRIDGE

THE LINE OF HILLS in the distance vanished. The roadmap beside him showed the corresponding area blank. When Jeff tried to visualize his destination, his mind couldn't find it, as if components of his perception were being erased.

He handled the car as smoothly as he could manage, though it was also flickering with insubstantiality. He followed his mental recollection of the shape of the road and parked on the gravel. His hands shook as he turned off the engine.

Time for another.

He scrambled for the bottle. The road, and now even the frame of the car, were starting to fade. He quickly swallowed a pill.

The whiteness of his surroundings receded, as well as the confusion. The forest and hills gradually returned, their clarity increasing unevenly, like pixels forming a digital image. The full map was again legible.

Immediate relief.

Attempts to drag out the time between doses had proved ineffectual. He couldn't stand more than a few minutes of these horrendous withdrawal symptoms.

The new pills weren't enough, though they had held off the withdrawal effects at first. Perhaps he had developed a tolerance. Clearly he had to get back on normal medication.

The white void was new, much worse than anything he had experienced before.

He counted the remaining pills. Maybe by doubling the dose he could hold off the effects, at least until he got home to the regular meds. He grimaced at the irony of the red warning label: *This medication may be habit-forming.*

Jeff started the engine, tense and impatient.

He felt listless and annoyed at the failure of his meeting with Dr. Aspeth, but he'd known it was a desperate last shot. The new drug classification system, prompted by media hysteria surrounding the psychoactive ingredients in *Amylx57*, had stirred the pot. It wouldn't be long before the laws in other states changed to correspond.

The doctor's disquieting words replayed in his mind: "*Some* patients have exhibited unusual personality changes after cessation of their medication. Often it is not the patients but their partners who notice, reporting loss of interest in old hobbies and seeming somehow different. Unfortunately, without patient cooperation, we can't conduct a proper study..."

Unusual personality changes.

Was that the real reason the trial had terminated?

The nothingness, the taste of the white void… even its memory left him on the verge of panic. It took all his effort to steady his nerves and concentrate on the road.

He had piled three boxes in the backseat, which contained copies of the trial notes he had obtained. This had earned the attention of Everetts Infinite, the company behind *Amylx57*. At times, he wondered if they were influencing doctors to cut off his supply, but of course he'd think that; paranoia and delusions of reference were symptoms of his illness. And yet, amongst the case files were suggestions that Everetts Infinite had attempted to influence the results of the trials, to prematurely establish the safety of the drug to gain quicker approval for a broader release. Their research had originally been influential in establishing the new diagnostic criteria. When this had backfired, ostensibly the 'abuse potential' of *Amylx57* forcing the termination of the worldwide trial, Everetts Infinite had gone into damage control.

Once he had sufficient evidence, Jeff might be able to go public, but doctors were becoming more reluctant to assist him in the current political mess.

The trial documents he had collected made for disturbing reading. The withdrawal effects were diverse, and occasionally invoked what could only be described (and *were* described, by patients) as supernatural experiences: divine encounters with 'beings,' spirit possessions, out-of-body experiences, terrifying accounts that rivaled the subtle psychotic symptoms of the treated illness.

Evidence that patients reported similar dreams had shocked him most. Their descriptions were consistent, as if referring to the same place: a stained, gray, concrete building, hundreds of stories tall, but without windows until the top floor, where a series of arches looked out from the concrete shell, the interior lit red and magenta from a light source within. The building was crowned with a semi-circular dome with wrought iron spikes, giving the eerie impression of an inverted carnivorous mouth. The significance of the building was unclear. Some attributed to it an ominous foreboding.

Sketches by children—the company had, unusually, gained approval to test the psychoactive drug on preteens—fit the same description, as though the children were drawing the same physical landmark.

Only one group of experimenters in the worldwide trial had looked into this, testing patients before, during and after withdrawal, properly allowing for the drug's short half-life and taking care not to implant suggestions of dreams. They found that patients reported dreams *during* withdrawal, but after the sixty-two hours it took the body to eliminate all traces of the drug, they denied ever having such dreams. Their memories had altered.

"Consider our position," Aspeth had said. "The drug is eliminated quickly, which poses problems in making sure patients maintain the correct levels; otherwise results were extremely effective: total cessation of psychotic and behavioral symptoms, both reported and observed. To come so close to a cure! But we couldn't develop a workable version of the drug—the brain and body flush out the active ingredient so quickly... so the ethics committee decided that we must cease experiments and terminate the trial."

There was a long bridge over a ravine where a muddy river channeled through the hills. It might have been picturesque in less dismal weather. Climate change had wreaked havoc with the country, making the southern highlands prone to extreme storms. The transformation of climate had temporarily rendered the landscape of dry vegetation, skeletal gum trees, and savannah grass—all struggling to adapt to the freezing temperatures—a bleak vista akin to muddy, frozen tundra. Still, it had a forlorn charm.

Jeff climbed onto the bridge and sat, watching the river. He decided to take two of the pills. Intended for use when tapering off, they had a lesser amount of the active ingredient. Clearly, one hadn't been enough.

It was an eerie thought, Jeff mused, idly fingering the bottle. They had come to define reality for him. More than define, they enabled him to perceive reality correctly. So reality was not the default state. Arguments about psychoactive drugs being unnatural didn't hold up. Reality as he knew it would gradually disintegrate without dosage. And that was not an experience anyone was supposed to endure.

What had he been living in before?

A murky, distorted realm.

Nothing was clear. Nothing could be grasped without severe perceptive bias. Such drastic distortion constituted an alternate reality. Without the drug, he'd return to that half-reality, or be stranded somewhere worse.

He swallowed the pills and looked out over the river. A calmness settled over him. The scene reminded him of one of the holidays with Kathryn only a year ago. It seemed another lifetime. Kathryn, who he had met in the clinic, had terminated their relationship first by giving the excuse that it was inappropriate, later elaborating with more personal reasons. She spoke to him occasionally, mainly to remind him that his research on the original trial was more important than the two of them staying together. Sometimes, though, it seemed—

Jeff, someone called, but no one was around. A new side effect.

Sometimes he wondered if her interest in him had only ever been part of a plot to discredit Everetts Infinite. That was a paranoid thought, unfair of him, but—

Rising from between the hills was a tall, stained, gray, concrete building, with no windows except at the top, crowned with a dome of iron spikes and barbed wire to deter vandals and wildlife.

Had it been there a moment ago?

To get a closer look, he followed a rough trail alongside the ravine. The rocks were slippery, and Jeff had to move carefully. Soon he rounded a corner and faced the building directly. It stood on the crest of a bluff. Lines of power transmission towers connected to it, so it was probably an older substation, possibly part of the hydroelectric system.

How and why would this tower feature in the dreams of patients worldwide? Surely this was merely perception, applying personal significance to an ordinary building—yet the resemblance to the sketches in the case files was uncanny.

Jeff found handholds in the rocks and began to climb. And then his hand slipped, and his body slid down the mud, grazed against the rocks. He landed upside-down and watched helplessly as the bottle of pills rolled out from his pocket and over the edge, vanishing into waters far below. There was no time for investigating the building. He had to get home. Scrambling to his feet, he hurried back along the muddy trail.

It was as hopeless as poverty, he decided—metering out his sanity, pill by pill, knowing it would never be enough.

Jeff couldn't deny that his life had improved because of the drug. He had noticed a gradual discontinuity between his thoughts, emotions and actions, witnessed himself becoming angrier, violent and abusive, all the while feeling like he was observing from the corner of the room, sometimes unable to comprehend the internal sequences that constituted his own behaviors.

It hadn't started with the violence; it had ended there.

Years were lost, incoherently filtered through his dysfunctional brain. He regretted it all, for whatever it mattered now. Looking back, he was appalled, but only because he could look back on it from a different perspective. Before? Just blurred chaos; there was no morality because there was no rational judgment. This later, sober realization resulted in suffocating, inescapable guilt, and an inability to understand his prior behavior.

There was controversy over the legitimacy of his illness, with some popular discussions derisively calling it 'Conspiracy Disorder,' partly referring to its more intangible symptoms (circular and irrational thinking, denial of personal responsibility, difficulty perceiving causation, paranoia and persecution mania, fog-like emotional state, psychopathic tendencies), but also alluding to the increasing collaboration between the pharmaceutical industry and psychiatry in pioneering new illnesses. Matters were not helped by cases of wrongful diagnosis in which patients were informed that their behaviors were symptomatic of their illnesses. Symptoms were identified by gradations of severity rather than phenomena distinct from everyday experiences. This labeling debate was unlikely to be resolved.

The particular incident that had prompted new legislation involved a tragic case of murder linked to delusion and drug abuse. A man in the trial group had assassinated a public figure, claiming the victim was an imposter. Media had given inadequate discussion to the complexities of the case, such as the perpetrator's self-medication with illicit drugs, deviation from the prescribed dosage of *Amylx57*, the preexistence of psychotic symptoms, and numerous other contributing factors. Jeff wondered if the patient had overdosed or tried withdrawing too abruptly, but never found reliable information. The case was too recent, emotions were still highly-charged, and investigations were ongoing. The public debate had implicated and condemned all the correlations, and reactionary legislation had followed, despite the protest of medical experts.

Contemplating whether his condition was a convenient label for behaviors that fell outside social norms, or an artificial demographic created to market more pills, left him bewildered. Jeff preferred to regard the diagnosis as a frame that encompassed particular experiences, a mechanism for achieving objectivity. After years of struggling, he was not willing to think of the illness as a fictional label. The problems he fought could not merely be phantoms of the imagination.

The doctor who had supervised the local trial had been in a good position to speculate about its unusual properties.

"*Amylx57* was intended to suppress certain unconscious behaviors," Dr. Aspeth had explained. "Conversely, cessation appears to temporarily dissolve the barrier between the conscious and unconscious mind, leaving some patients with chronic feelings of unreality. We define normality by continuity. If our dreams were consistent day to day, we would be unable to dismiss them as dreams. What withdrawing seems to do, for certain people, is to disrupt this continuity, making reality feel *un*real. As a consequence, patient' personalities—their orientation in the real world—can become unstable."

Aspeth assured Jeff that no one had died from withdrawal—this was not a toxic or addictive substance—but Jeff remained concerned. *Something* was happening to the trial patients. Perhaps Everetts Infinite was trying to erase evidence of a tampered trial by introducing a personality-erasing substance to patients.

A far simpler explanation could be that, if *Amylx57* had personality-erasing properties, it would automatically erase evidence without a need for elaborate conspiracy.

Jeff occasionally passed through towns more desolate than the surrounding wilderness. A rainstorm drenched the highway, rendering his windshield a ruined watercolor.

The phone beeped, although the display denied coverage. It was a text message from Kathryn: *How did the trip go? Success?*

He typed with one hand, asking her to break into his flat, find the meds, meet him on the highway. She would probably tell him he was being paranoid. It seemed to send, despite the lack of reception, but there was no immediate reply. The phone wouldn't connect a call, so he put it aside and continued driving. The only thing calling was his medication.

His thoughts roamed ambivalent memories. He regretted letting her go, or perhaps chasing her away. Kathryn was so self-assured. Only through threats and manipulation was he able to hold any ground with her. How much could he blame himself for his inability to get his life under control before this medication?

Didn't that prove his powerlessness?

The scar ran deep; the memories provoked a special kind of pain that made the rest of his life seem meaningless and mundane. But it was too late now. He had no one to blame but himself.

Flashing police lights blurred through the rain. An alcohol checkpoint had been set up beside the highway. *Let me pass*, he thought, but one of the cops waved at him to pull over.

"Have you had any drinks tonight?"

"No."

The officer stared at him for a moment.

"Can I see your license?"

Jeff handed her the license and she examined it closely.

"Do you have any other forms of identification?"

Jeff searched his wallet but couldn't find any.

"What's your date of birth?"

Jeff answered apprehensively.

"Must be your haircut. You look like someone else."

It was dark but for occasional lighted signs on the highway. The windshield wipers smeared spots of rain. White spots. Perhaps light reflected from the water.

Jeff stopped for coffee at a gas station, too tired to notice the early effects of withdrawal: pulse racing, hands beginning to shake. Being on edge made his body work harder, might make it absorb pills more rapidly. He had about two hours left before he was in trouble, he supposed, depending on traffic. He could see the neon smog haze of the city in the distance.

"You look like you've seen a ghost," said a truck driver, "or a UFO."

"I'm just tired."

"Lots of people see them in this area. You believe in UFOs?"

"No."

"I didn't used to, either. I'd seen weird things in the sky before, but never thought much about it. But then it happened to a friend of mine—abducted, I mean."

Jeff nodded noncommittally.

"He was shaken up like I'd never seen him. Had scars, burns across his chest. I saw them. Wouldn't leave his house, couldn't hold a normal conversation. Now, I've known him for years. He's a big fella." The driver indicated an approximate size. "It'd take a lot to scare him. And when I heard his story, I believed him. *Something* happened to him, I'm sure of that."

Already the world, including normal conversations, seemed distant, unreachable.

He recalled cases in the files of patients undergoing fugue states—wandering away from their lives, embarking on dramatic life changes upon withdrawal. His thoughts turned to the files boxed up on the back seat. Whatever was about to happen to him, the files had to be preserved. Earlier, he had scribbled on the box lid in red marker for his future self to read: THIS IS IMPORTANT!

And underneath, thinking that someone might find him unconscious or his car abandoned, he had desperately scribbled:

> *Refer to 5015, pp.56-68. This is happening! Withdrawal symptoms described (personality changes) after withdrawal will be denied!!!*

He knew it was futile. Either his future self would care or it wouldn't. If anyone else found the papers, the 'evidence' of his conspiracy theory was insufficient and inconclusive.

Returning to his car, Jeff sighed, climbed in the front seat and reached for the ignition, but the keys were gone. He looked on the floor, beneath the seat, and felt his pockets. Nothing. Climbing out, he searching the ground. There was a flashlight in the back seat, he remembered. He reached for the door handle and—

The car disappeared.

He shut his eyes and tried feeling for the door, felt the cold handle. He concentrated, mentally willing the world back into existence, into his subjective perception. He opened his eyes. The car was there. The door was open. Everything restored. The keys were in the ignition. Carefully, he climbed inside and started the engine and—

The steering wheel disappeared.

No, no. Not again. Come on. I'm nearly there—

The gas station disappeared.

This isn't happening. The real world still exists, whether I see it or not. Unless, when it returns, it will be slightly altered rather than me. There will be slightly less compassion, more crime, more hatred, new kinds of prejudice, control and propaganda, and I *will be the only one who notices. While everyone else thinks* I've *changed.*

Jeff shut his eyes again, felt for the car.

Nothing.

He opened his eyes.

The white was everywhere; it was everything.

It's really happening. Maybe it will pass.

He hadn't expected it to come on so suddenly. A ferocious, static-like sound resonated, the white becoming more blinding.

Jeff found himself in one of several interlocking rooms. Arched windows and red and magenta light identified the interior as belonging to the mysterious building that had so often appeared in trial patient dreams. The view from the windows seemed to be obscured by fog or an indistinct dusk. Various objects were scattered on the floor, political posters plastered on the walls, which seemed, as Jeff looked closer, to represent thoughts that had occupied his conscious mind lately. The boxes of case files were stacked clumsily in the center of the room. There was also a bottle of pills, but it was empty.

He wandered the cluttered rooms, finding lost thoughts, unfinished impulses and abandoned sentiments, all stored carelessly in boxes or stacked in secret crevices and hidden shelves behind faded curtains.

He was not alone.

A figure materialized in the farthest corner. Perhaps it had been there all along. Jeff walked toward the shape and it moved toward him at the same deliberate pace. As he drew closer, he recognized his own features.

He was staring at himself.

The two beings stared at each other. Jeff moved an arm, expecting the figure to mirror-mimic his movement, but it didn't.

"I'm *you*," it said, tonelessly speaking Jeff's own thought.

But this was not the case. This version of Jeff emanated *evil*. The eyes were ruthless, greedy and desperate, possibly insane from being cooped up in these rooms all this time, suppressed and powerless.

"We differ some ways," it continued, observing him. "Tastes, temperament, choices, judgment. That's how *I* came to be. Different choices you might have made... you are, after all, a manifestation of identity. *We* started to think things could be done better."

At these words, Jeff broke into blind panic. He backed away and searched the rooms for something he could use against the figure as it followed him at a gradual, unhurried pace.

"There's no point in running. I am you. I know everything you know. And you know this is inevitable and not unnatural." The figure spoke in a calm, androgynous drone.

This thing was not him.

"A person is, after all, not a dictatorship," it said. "It is a democracy. I have a right to oppose you and earn support for my chance, my vision. For *us*."

Jeff laughed from fear. He stepped into the adjacent room, then through the curtain into the room beyond that, but the figure advanced at a quickening pace.

"You can't stop me. I've been waiting a long time... for you to slip."

Jeff attempted to keep a safe distance, but it knew these rooms better than he did, and was faster at stepping around the erratic architecture. Jeff kept stumbling on boxes of ideas or extraneous architecture that linked the rooms. He soon found himself cornered.

"Don't feel sorry. You had a good run. You had *years*. Now it's my turn."

The figure seemed to be a projection of his unconscious. And the unconscious mind had difficulty with logic, math and language, and supposedly struggled with left-brain tasks. If he could stump it on a problem, he might demonstrate his supremacy over this bizarre leadership threat.

"What is the similarity between the following three words," Jeff said, trying to keep his voice steady. "Fish. Venus. War."

The figure hesitated. "They are related to mythical gods," it said vaguely, but from the sound of its voice, it wasn't so sure.

Jeff tried to think of another question as he backed away. He was becoming confused, too. He had forgotten about the complex use of symbolism in dreams.

"Multiply 1,878 by 1,889."

Jeff didn't know the answer. He had pulled the numbers randomly from his head; probably not the best approach under these circumstances. He just hoped to confuse it and buy time, but he also felt that the strange atmosphere of this dream-place was affecting his mind.

His adversary appeared confused and hesitant.

Jeff quickly threw it another.

"What year did Joseph Stalin die?"

"Stalin never died," the other Jeff said. "These questions are not important."

Suddenly the figure was upon him, throttling him, squeezing cold, pale hands around his burning throat.

"You need me!"

The other Jeff shook its head.

"We don't need you. Look over there."

A doorway appeared in the wall, revealing a larger chamber beyond. A dozen more clones, motionless, colorless and translucent, were arranged in rows.

"These are the others, in case *I* don't prove up to the task. In case I slip. But I won't slip. I won't make your mistakes."

The figure drained him. It turned to the boxes of files on the floor.

"We can't have *these* lying around."

The other Jeff found a lighter and set fire to the papers. Once they were fully alight, the figure strode away. A new door had opened, revealing a stone stairway, but it closed behind the figure.

Jeff fell against the wall, too exhausted and defeated to move. He watched the boxes burn until only smoking ash remained. His thoughts turned to Kathryn. Perhaps ruining his chance with her was the reason these other versions of Jeff hated him. Probably it was the display of manipulation and paranoid treachery—of which she had so frequently accused him—that brought her to mind now. Perhaps it was the other Jeffs sabotaging their relationship, motivated by irrational jealousy or fundamental contempt. They would never allow him to be happy.

Jeff gathered his strength. He felt defeated, but forced himself to rise from the floor. He explored the layout of the rooms and the items available to him. There were tools he could fashion into weapons. He peeled back the secret curtain leading to the store room. Some of his doubles, featureless and unformed, were nonetheless alert. He addressed them:

"He hasn't beaten us. Understand? He can't stay vigilant all the time. Sooner or later, he'll let his guard down and we'll be waiting. And when he is most vulnerable—sleeping, eating, intoxicated—we'll take him out. There is only one of him, and a lot more of us. We'll all get our turn and we'll all get some of the glory. Things will be different. Are you with me?"

Slowly, the faceless forms nodded.

LOST IN A FIELD OF PAPER FLOWERS

GORD ROLLO

"Whenever evil befalls us, we ought to ask ourselves, after the first suffering, how we can turn it into good. So shall we take occasion, from one bitter root, to raise perhaps many flowers." – Leigh Hunt (1784 - 1859)

A TEENAGE BOY lies in a coma.

Fell down the stairs, bumped his head.

Ask his father, standing by his bedside. He's telling everyone that's what happened.

Don't ask the poor boy's mother, though. No, not her, she's far too busy crying.

EXISTENCE #1: DREAMLAND

"Can anyone hear me?"

There's fear in your voice. No panic, yet, but definitely a hint of alarm. At first this strange dream had been thrilling, running and playing in this massive field of orange-red dirt; something you'd never have been able to do from the seat of the wheelchair in real life. The euphoric freedom of standing, of *running* on your own two legs is a joy you'd nearly forgotten. Two years have passed since the accident left your spine twisted, legs withered and useless. But in the dream you're running full out, pumping arms, and chasing your shadow across the unusual colored soil with the exuberance and energy of youth. It feels great to be healthy again, to be *whole*.

It isn't until your feet slip and you roll, laughing to a stop in a swirling cloud of dust, that you begin to wonder about your surroundings. What kind of field is this, anyway? A farmer's field, by the looks of it, the soil cared for and plowed in even, parallel grooves. But if this is a farm, where are the barns, crops, animals, or the farmer for that matter? Standing up, you slowly turn round, trying to spot something familiar. Surely there's a fence line, a pond, or a nearby road. There's nothing, just an endless expanse of flat, orange-red dirt for as far as the eye can see.

You strain to hear any of the normal everyday sounds like birds, airplanes, insects, wind, laughter, but this field is void of those things—a dead place that, despite its vastness, begins to close in on you, the dusty air tickling your throat, making you dry-swallow your first taste of fear.

"Is anyone there? Where am I? Please, somebody answer me!"

Inside your head you hear a woman's voice, tiny and faint, as if spoken across a great distance. You can't make out the words.

"Momma?"

No, boy, I'm not your mother. I'm a friend.

"What do you want?"

To help you get back home.

"I don't know what you mean. Where are you?"

A long way off, but closer than you think. Don't worry about it right now. Stick out your arm, then turn around and walk. I brought you something.

You're more confused than ever, but at least you aren't feeling as scared. Even a phantom voice is welcome in this desolate place, better than being alone. You do as instructed, and are soon walking in a new direction. You walk for ten minutes, not at all sure why you're doing this.

"Where am I supposed to be going?" you finally ask, but there's no reply.

Silence, inside and out.

You stop, unsure what to do next, considering retracing your steps—

Something green stands out in the orange-red distance.

"Is this what you brought me?"

A whisper: *Yes.*

You run, excitement and curiosity propelling you toward the small green dot on the horizon. Slowing your pace, you walk the final thirty feet. It's a flower! A light green carnation growing out of the otherwise barren soil. The stem reaches past your knees, its flower round, symmetrical and in full bloom. Beautiful, sure, but it looks so strange and out of place growing on its own in this massive field that you don't know what to make of it.

"You brought me a flower?"

Silence.

EXISTENCE #2: REALITY

"Stay cool, Sally. I told you ten times already, I got it covered. You don't need to say squat to anyone."

The tall man spoke softly, checking over his shoulder down the corridor as he led his wife firmly by the arm into their son's private room.

"But, Paul, I'm just—"

"But nothin', Sally. Let me do the talking and everything will be fine. Understand?"

Sally nodded, but Paul wasn't looking at her anymore. She followed his gaze to the foot of their son's bed, where a small woman leaned on a wooden cane. Even before the woman turned to face them, it was clear she was old and obviously quite frail. Her left eye was completely white, no iris or pupil, her vision clouded by a thick milky cataract. When she lifted the corners of her mouth to smile, it seemed to take a Herculean effort, depleting her limited energy. Sally felt pity for the poor woman.

"Who are you?" Paul said. "What are you doing in Robbie's room? This is a private suite."

"Is it? Forgive me, Mr. Moore. I just came to see how Robbie was doing and to bring him a little flower to cheer up the room. I meant no harm."

The blossom lay at her son's feet on the bedspread. It wasn't a real flower, but one made of paper, intricately folded using several layers of green onion paper.

Paul, not even noticing the flower, continued on. "You a nurse or something?"

This caused the old woman to smile, her face lighting up and revealing some of the beauty she'd possessed in her youth.

"Good Lord, at *my* age, I sure hope not!"

"Who are you, then?" Sally said, trying to diffuse her husband's anger.

"The doctors and nurses call me Aggie."

"Yeah, well, nice to meet you, but my wife and I would appreciate it if—"

"Did you make that flower, Aggie?" Sally interrupted.

"Why yes, I did. It's called Origami. Learned how in craft class down on the ground floor."

"The assisted living center?"

"Yep. That's where I live, you know? Been there…well, seems like forever."

"Then maybe you'd best get back," Paul said. "Robbie needs rest and I'm sure the nurses will be wondering where you are."

"Heavens! You're probably right." Aggie nodded and shuffled toward the door, leaning heavily on her cane for support. "Can I come for another visit tomorrow? Don't like to brag, but everyone says I have a special way with children. Maybe I can help?"

Paul was about to object, but Sally beat him to the punch. "Yes you can, Aggie. Just make sure the people on your floor know where you are, okay?"

"Sure will. Thanks."

Halfway out the door, Aggie stopped. "Hospitals are strange places. Buildings made of concrete, glass, brick, and steel; built strong enough to withstand years of pounding from wind and rain, but they're helpless to contain the surge of pain and suffering emanating daily within their walls. All that suffering… it has to go somewhere, don't you think?"

The tiny old woman left without another word, leaving Paul and Sally staring after her in stunned silence.

What do you think that was all about?"

"Nothin', Sally, just a crazy old fool who likes to hear herself talk. Probably out of her freakin' mind, and you're gonna let her visit Robbie."

"She's harmless."

"I don't care. Tell the nurses that Robbie has no other visitors, especially nutty old bats from downstairs!"

EXISTENCE #1: DREAMLAND

"Are you still there?"

You wait a long time for the phantom voice to answer, standing ramrod straight, eyes closed, hoping the woman will talk and not leave you alone in this bleak place. Well, you aren't completely alone. You have the flower.

Feeling frustrated and lonely, you sit in the dirt to study the green flower. It looks like a normal, everyday carnation, only slightly bigger. Leaning in close, your nose almost touches the delicate petals. You inhale deeply, and again, savoring the sweet fragrance. It smells wonderful, reminding you of your mother and the small garden she lovingly tends in the yard back home.

Back home—

You shut off that thought immediately, not willing or able to go down that dark road just yet. A tear runs down your cheek, a tiny drop of loneliness escaping the raging river of self-pity building steadily within you. The tear curls around your lip, dangles from your chin, and then drops silently into the center of the carnation.

The flower begins to grow.

You watch in awe, the stalk, as well as the bloom, growing in front of your eyes. The story of Jack and the Beanstalk pops into your head and for a moment you think this is how the mysterious woman plans to help. Unfortunately, before you can envision the carnation growing through the clouds and climbing it to find your way back to your family, the flower stops growing, leveling off just under your chin, the bloom a full eight inches in diameter. A huge flower, the biggest you've ever seen, but still no help as far as you can see.

Disappointed and angry, you reach to rip the mutant flower out of the ground. You grip your hand around the thick stalk and…

…look down upon yourself. Not here and now. Has to be several years back. You're younger, smaller, dressed in a blue baseball uniform: knee-high socks, cap, and glove. You are hot and sweaty, the uniform stained with dirt, a huge contented grin on your face—

You shudder, realizing there is no wheelchair… yet.

Your father's shiny new Mazda RX-7 roars into the scene, skidding to a stop in a shower of dust and gravel. From above, you can see how drunk he is as he climbs out of the car and waves for you to hurry and get in. Back then you hadn't been able to tell, hadn't had a clue your father had taken the afternoon off work to tie one on with a few buddies down at the local pool hall. Now you know better. Horrified, you watch yourself climb into the car, fully trusting your father to take care of you and get home safely.

The Mazda squeals out of sight, and you know that three intersections away your father will run a red light and a yellow Ryder rental truck will t-bone the car on the passenger side, tearing the small foreign car nearly in half, ending your baseball playing days forever…

The strange vision fades, like water down a semi-clogged drain, and you stare at the green flower gripped in your closed fist. Your hand is sore, fingers cramping, so you let go of the carnation, only then noticing the thin ribbon of blood running the length of your palm and dripping steadily onto the parched dirt below. Seeing the blood triggers pain and your hand burns. It doesn't appear to be much of a wound, hardly a scratch, more like a superficial paper cut, but it hurts badly and bleeds as if it were a gash cutting to the bone. You reach for the flower again, to carefully check for hidden thorns on the stem. Your finger barely caresses the smooth stalk when you wince in pain and pull back to find yet another paper-thin cut. Blood runs freely from both wounds now, and no matter how hard you think about it, you can't understand why touching the flower is cutting you. It's as if the flower is coated with invisible razor blades.

While removing your t-shirt to wrap your injured hand, something incredible happens. The bleeding stops on its own. The thin wounds begin to heal, the torn skin knitting together as the pain diminishes. Within seconds, your hand is fully healed and the only sign that you've ever been bleeding are the scattered crimson stains on the ground at your feet.

You don't understand what's happened; don't understand any of this, in fact. The only certainty is that you desperately want to go home.

But for seemingly hours you roam the barren field, at times calling out for the phantom woman to speak again, sulking around depressed and afraid you'll be left here in this awful place forever. No matter how far you walk, or which direction you choose to step, you never allow yourself to lose sight of the green carnation—your anchor in this wasteland.

The sky begins to darken. Spending the night in this field, alone in the dark, is a terrifying prospect, but staying near the mysterious flower gives you some comfort, some sense of protection, even if it's only in your head. You curl around the base of the giant carnation and soon fall fast asleep, oblivious to the fact that all around you the field is livening, the flowers finally starting to grow.

EXISTENCE #2: REALITY

Paul and Sally Moore made it home from the hospital in record time. Paul had bitched about the downtown traffic regardless of their progress, but that was just the way he was and Sally was used to it. Climbing out of the car, she stood by the front door of their Cape Cod home, waiting for Paul to unlock the door. For some reason, he was still sitting in the car. When she went back to check on him, he was wiping tears from his red-rimmed eyes.

"Why are you crying?"

"I'm not," Paul said defensively. "I'm just, you know, upset about Robbie. He looked so small in that bed. So...*fragile.* Is he gonna die, Sally?"

Tears filled Sally's eyes too. She was thrilled and a little shocked at her husband's unexpected show of emotion.

"I don't know, honey," she said. "The doctor said it could go either way. Come on in, let's have a nice supper and we can talk about it, okay?"

When he finally joined her on the porch, she noticed a red

stain on the collar of his shirt.

"You're bleeding, Paul. What happened?"

"Where?" He looked at his hands and down at the rest of his body. "I don't see anything."

"Your neck. Come here. You must have scratched yourself."

Sally took a Kleenex tissue out of her purse and began cleaning the mess. Fortunately, there were only two small wounds, one long thin cut and one nothing more than a scratch, neither very deep. As she dabbed, a tiny brown spider dropped onto his shoulder, startling her.

"What's the matter?"

"Nothing. Just a little spider on your—"

"Where?" Paul beat his hands over his head, chest and back.

"Relax, Paul, it's long gone," she said, trying to calm him. Sally knew all about her husband's lifelong fear of spiders.

She returned to checking his cuts, but Paul pushed her hands away and stomped off into the house. Two Band-Aid's later, the matter was forgotten, and Sally went to fix Paul's dinner. He wasn't the kind of guy that liked to be kept waiting, especially after his little freak-out on the porch. He'd be mad at himself, feeling silly, and Sally knew from experience that he'd be looking for any opportunity to prove what a *real* man he was.

Back at the hospital, Aggie had spent the rest of the day in her room, refusing to even eat dinner. She was busy making flowers, dozens of them, her knotted old hands twisting and folding the thin colorful paper hour after hour, carnation after carnation, until the nurses came to shut off her light and gently force her into bed.

Her body was exhausted and she quickly fell into a deep but troubled sleep. Aggie dreamed about a horrible car accident and of a young boy dressed in a blood-drenched baseball uniform trapped and screaming within the wreckage. The dream played over and over, the boy's pain-filled screams haunting her throughout the long night.

When she finally woke, covered in a fine sheen of sweat, the digital clock beside her bed read 4:58 a.m. The sun wouldn't be up for at least another hour, but Aggie didn't care. She couldn't stay in bed another minute. She swung her feeble legs onto the floor, using her wooden cane to climb shakily to her feet. Middle of the night or not, there was work to be done.

EXISTENCE #1: DREAMLAND

Wake up.

You stir, hearing the voice, but ignore it.

Come on, time to open your eyes.

This time you recognize the woman's voice and bolt to your feet, your heart trip-hammering inside of your chest.

"You came—"

Your words are lost as you open your eyes to something truly amazing. There are flowers everywhere! An entire field, no an entire *world*, filled with huge carnations—a kaleidoscope of color spreading out from the small circular clearing in which you've slept, for as far as your eyes can see. It's an incredible sight, taking your breath away.

Are you with me?

"Yeah, I'm here. Where did all these flowers come from? Did you bring them?"

You hear chuckling.

Heavens, no! Some of them, sure, but I think your mind did a lot of this planting on its own. That's good; it means you're ready.

"Ready for what?"

Ready to come home, of course.

"But how? I don't even know where I am, never mind how to

get home! What good is a field of flowers for finding—"

Run, boy, the voice interrupts. *Trust me. Trust yourself!*

You look across the endless expanse of flowers, not sure what to do. Then you remember what happened last night when you touched the original green carnation. Twice you'd come into contact with the flower and both times it cut you open and made you bleed. Would these flowers hurt you as well?

Run!

"I can't!" you cry. "I'm scared. They're going to cut me. Please, I don't want to hurt anymore!"

I don't want you to hurt anymore, either. That's why I'm here to help you.

"How?" you ask, frightened. "How can you stop the flowers from cutting me?"

There's a pause, then: *I can't. The flowers are made of paper...and they* will *cut you. They'll cut you bad!*

"Then why would you want me to run? Who are—"

Think about what happened to your cuts.

"They healed."

No. They didn't heal; they just went somewhere else.

"I don't understand."

In the real world, pain has to be suffered by those who receive it. Not here. Here, pain can open doorways all on its own, and can be shared by those who truly deserve it.

"My father?" A tiny flame of hope ignites within you.

Silence.

Tears run freely down your face. You let them come this time, let your pent-up river flood out in twin torrents.

"I hate him. Always have. And not just because of the car accident. Not just because of my legs. He... he still hurts me. Me and momma both."

You sob into your hands, unashamed of your tears. No, the tears give you strength, give you courage, help wash away the wall of fear your abusive father has helped to build.

And this last time?

"I was listening to my stereo up in my room. I didn't know he was trying to sleep, didn't even know he was home. He came upstairs and he was so damn mad. I tried to say I was sorry... tried to explain, but he had this insane look on his face. He smashed my radio against the wall then grabbed my wheelchair and shoved me out into the hall over to the stairs. Then he... he—"

I know what he did, boy, knew as soon as they brought you in. You don't deserve to suffer anymore. Neither does your mother. That's why I want you to run, Robbie. It's going to hurt, but you need to run.

Your tears are gone. So is your fear. Your mind made up.

"Bastard!" With that single word you're running like you have winged feet.

The flowers make you bleed with every step, the stems, leaves, and pretty colored blooms slicing and ripping open your tender flesh as easily as barbed wire. Not all the carnations have grown to the same height; some tear at your knees, others at your thighs, hips, throat, ankles, chest, and face. It's like being attacked by a nest of angry hornets, with no way to avoid their single-minded fury. The pain is excruciating, a monstrous all-consuming inferno, and you run open-mouthed, screaming in agony, but it doesn't slow you down. Your clothes tatter and shred, your momentum flaying the crimson-soaked rags free from your body, taking away strips of your skin too, but still you run on. Nothing can stop you now.

The blood drains down your forehead, stinging your eyes, threatening to blind you, to force you to stop, but it's through this red-blurred vision of the field that you finally spot the door. It's just a dance of light in the shape of a doorframe, a slight shimmer of motion like the heat haze coming off the road on a hot summer day, but you recognize it for what it is. You lower your head, pump your arms, and run flat out, fully aware you're likely using your legs for the very last time.

You don't care. All you want is one simple thing: to go home.

EXISTENCE #2: REALITY

Sally would have preferred to skip breakfast and head straight to the hospital, but she knew better than to suggest such a thing. Paul would hit the roof. No, it was better to just put on some coffee, scramble a few eggs, and keep the peace. The sooner her husband ate, the sooner she could go visit Robbie again.

"Your eggs are ready, honey," she shouted from the foot of the stairs, knowing Paul was in the bathroom shaving. "Best eat them while they're hot."

It was as close as she dared at telling him to hurry up.

Paul responded with a series of escalating screams.

Before Sally could react, he appeared at the top of the stairs, naked, his body bathed in blood. He was still screaming, his eyes tightly closed, his crimson-streaked arms flailing around in panic. Sally screamed too, grabbing the banister for support, her legs threatening to collapse out from under her. Myriad cuts ravaged his body. She nearly went to him, but hesitated, instinctively knowing her husband was already beyond help.

Paul stumbled, rolling head over heels down the staircase, blood splashing everywhere. Sally backed out of the way as Paul's progression, and his screams, came to a sudden, sickening halt when his head connected with the newel post at the bottom of the staircase. A brutal *thud*.

Sally couldn't bring herself to take a close look at his body, much less touch him to see if he might be okay. Instead, she took a moment to compose herself, then went to the phone and dialed 911. By the time the paramedics arrived, Paul was still alive, but in critical condition with a massive dent in his forehead where he'd struck the post. There were no cuts visible on his body, and not a trace of blood anywhere in the house.

Robbie woke at the hospital, gasping for breath, fragments of a bad dream lingering in his sleepy thoughts. He was covered in sweat, and was so tired that he felt like he'd just run a—

Run! a familiar voice echoed in his head.

His eyes snapped open to a collision of thoughts, sensations, and vivid memories invading his consciousness. He remembered everything at once.

Robbie immediately noticed the old woman standing at the foot of his bed, but then his eyes moved down to take in the colorful paper flowers strewn on the covers at his feet. His wheelchair leaned against the far wall—that old enemy—yet his eyes were drawn to the woman. She hadn't spoken a word to confirm it, but Robbie already knew who this frail little woman was.

"Thank you," he said.

The *how* and *why* could be dealt with later.

"You're welcome, sweetie," she said. "Everything should be okay now."

"Is my father dead?"

"No. Not fully."

"He's in the field, isn't he?"

The woman looked at her feet, neither confirming nor denying it. She shifted her weight onto the wooden cane. "Your father can't hurt you anymore."

Robbie thought about that for a moment, his eyes roaming the room and finding his wheelchair again. A dark and vengeful anger built inside him, and then an idea so sweet it brought a smile to his pallid face.

"These flowers you made me," Robbie said, sweeping his hand across the pile at his feet. "Can you teach me how to make them?

How to deliver them?"

She followed the boy's gaze to the wheelchair.

"You want to send your father flowers?"

"No, something else."

A middle-aged man lies in a coma.
Fell down the stairs, bumped his head.
Ask his wife, standing by his bedside. She's telling everyone that's what happened.
Don't ask his son, though. No, not him, he's far too busy making giant paper spiders.

THE PERFECTION OF SYMMETRY

ANDREW HOOK

VERMILLION CHANDLER looked at her agent over her grilled-chicken salad and avocado. "Why that's great," she said. "That's really great."

She took small mouthfuls while Diana ran through a list of upcoming work, nodding appropriately. "I can do that. I can do that. I don't think I want to do that. You'll have to persuade me to do that! I can do that, yes, I can do that. Is that next Friday? Yes, I can do that."

It was all artifice. Vermillion knew Diana would have already confirmed appointments and her acquiescence was but shadowplay. Not that it mattered; she trusted Diana. They had worked together since Vermillion first started on the model circuit and had mutual respect. Many other girls were in worse positions and many wanted to be in her position. She was Diana's sole client.

She bit into a piece of avocado, taking it between her teeth before closing her mouth. Although they were in a secluded section of the restaurant, there was always someone with a camera wanting to make a buck through an indelicate photograph. Preserving her image preserved her image. And it was an image that needed to be preserved.

Diana smiled and said, "Well, that's it." She looked down at her own plate, which she hadn't started, then put her diary to one side and dug in.

The smell of hot juices running off the steak on her agent's plate made her stomach flip. She forked some grilled-chicken into her mouth. It was excellent, but she missed the taste of red meat. Her dietician approved of red meat, but to Vermillion it was a slippery slope; like bacon to a vegetarian. Her figure—her entire body—was her fortune. She was twenty-two. It wouldn't last forever, and she needed to milk it for as long as she could.

Vermillion had been an ordinary child. Then, around the age of thirteen, her physiogamy kicked in like hot plastic poured into a showroom dummy mold. Her body perfected itself. Complete symmetry from head to toe.

"Who are you seeing, Vermillion?"

"No one, currently."

It was an ongoing joke. Vermillion's contract made it quite clear she couldn't have a partner for another couple of years. *Men mucked you up*, Diana said; and she had the lines on her face to prove it. Beneath the rhetorical question lay the veiled threat. Despite the joke, it was a serious business. Diana's income depended on Vermillion, which depended on her looks.

She smiled, rashly, her fork on the way to her mouth. A piece of avocado slipped back to the plate. Diana shrugged and whispered: "It'll be okay. It really will be okay."

After the swimsuit photo-shoot, Vermillion made her excuses and journeyed home. She preferred to take the wheel; there was power in the physicality and she didn't want everything done for her. At red traffic lights, she watched the faces of male pedestrians. She hadn't kissed a boy since she was eighteen: wayward, disinterested, unassuming—she had tasted fame and it bored her. But her pushy mother's death had changed everything. Money came her way out of the trust fund and she became used to a certain standard of living, and appreciative of the effort it took to maintain it. There was little point in spoiling herself while filling the bank. Other pleasures would come later.

Even so: men walked in suits that fit snug, Hawaiian-shorted guys looked like grown-up kids, others were less attractive but were no doubt great in other ways. Despite her looks, Vermillion knew the adage of beauty being skin deep was a truism. She had known enough models—male and female—to be sure that looks didn't matter in relationships.

Back in her apartment, she drank coconut water and cooked an egg-white omelet on whole-wheat toast. She was twenty floors up. Wide floor-length windows fronted her view of the city. Sun poured naturally out of the sky, creating a paler blue near its edges. She pressed her hands against the glass and leaned forward, buoyed by her reflection doing the same. She looked down at the street far below: the cars like colored boxes in a square slider game, the roads cubing the buildings in a way that you couldn't tell from the street. Vermillion allowed herself a smile. She enjoyed the height. She craved the perspective.

A loud bang shook the glass. She gasped: her mouth forming a perfect O. The seagull disappeared as quickly as it had arrived, leaving a feather glued to the other side of the window by a drop of blood.

Vermillion realized she was shaking. Her reflection did the same. The feather waved like a fascinator before the breeze took hold and it slowly descended toward the dead bird on the street.

Vermillion slept fitfully. In a dream, she heard a sound under the floorboards and eased them apart to find a deep well beneath. There was someone at the bottom. She squinted, but couldn't quite make out a figure as the cylindrical brick walls tapered to a point. Almost-words drifted upward. She woke from the dream with a shivering sensation that someone had been behind her, about to push.

By the breakfast bar, she juiced beets, spinach, ginger, carrots, orange and some celery while waiting for an egg to boil. The egg itself contained symmetry, she realized through the noise of the food processor. She remembered someone at High School telling her they had once cracked open an egg and a half-formed chick had fallen into the frying pan.

It was only after breakfast and after her bath that she stood in front of her full-length mirror.

Before she became symmetrical, before all of this happened, she had asked the typical child's question: *Mirror, mirror on the wall, who is the fairest of them all?* She was just an ordinary little girl, although an uncle, on her father's side, once said: *Do you realize you have the most beautiful face?* In Tianna's bedroom after school, they lay on the duvet and held mirrors up to their half-faces. Tianna's nose was slightly crooked. With the mirror vertical, her nose bent in on itself. Vermillion's nose looked like Vermillion's nose. There was no distortion. The only time she looked any different was within the travelling funfairs' Hall of Mirrors.

She allowed her silk dressing gown to slip off her shoulders. Naked, she was perfect; clothes only served to rumple her image. The symmetry of her body had long been documented, as had the correlation between symmetry and beauty. A combination hardwired into the public consciousness. Many models had fairly symmetrical faces, a handful had *perfectly* symmetrical faces. Vermillion's symmetry was such that she didn't need to wear make-up. But more importantly, where Vermillion differed was that she had the perfectly symmetrical body to match.

From her smallest toe, through to her knee caps, through to her buttocks, through to her vertebrae, through to her shoulder blades, through to her breasts, through to her cheekbones, eyes, ears, nose and forehead: Vermillion was perfect. The symmetry only ended inside her body, where the organs lay in the usual lopsided places. But no one was interested in her interior; it was the exterior which brought the money.

She smiled at her reflection, which smiled back. The smile mirrored itself, left to right and right to left, as it mirrored in front of her. Sometimes she wondered if she were simply one-sided, if her right half was a hologrammatic representation of her left. But this was not so. The match was complete down to the tiny light-brown birthmark on her right hip and the tiny light-brown birthmark on her left hip.

Not only was her visage perfectly symmetrical, but she had the optimum ratio between her mouth, eyes, chin and forehead.

For the avoidance of any doubt, and to accentuate the fact, Vermillion opened her mouth and said: "I'm perfect."

"Hold it, hold it, hold it right there."

Vermillion held her gaze as the camera flash fluctuated like strobe lighting. Behind her, a white backdrop caught the glare. Diana stood beside Gee, the French cameraman working for *La Femme Actuelle.* In the pit of Vermillion's stomach, a knot of hunger gnawed at her concentration. She tried to push it aside, but remembered the dead chick when cooking that morning's egg, and in turn, the seagull slamming into the window. She had called the building's maintenance to ask them to remove the blood smear. Nevertheless, like the ache in her gut for a tuna sandwich, the remembrance of the smear was dogging her day.

In truth, she had forgotten about it until she had dressed and was ready to leave the building. With one hand on her door handle, she glanced back into her orderly and well-maintained apartment and a shaft of sunlight had shone through the smear like stained-glass.

"Smile. Smile. Smile!"

The camera clicked.

Diana ran a hand through her hair; like a lion's mane, it held shape while remaining wild. Vermillion had the sudden urge to touch her own hair, its Louise Brooks bob being the best design to accentuate her looks. Hair was one thing she couldn't control. Nail growth, another. A charge of irritation ran through her at the duration of the shoot. Gee had enough shots. She stuck to her pose as though frozen. Then her hunger got the better of her and she threw the soft teddy bear she had been holding to the floor and stormed off the set.

"Wait. Wait! Miss Vermillion. I just need a few more. Wait."

The walk to the dressing room was a short one, but Diana made it there first.

"What do you think you're doing?"

"I'm hungry. I can't concentrate."

"You're not in love?"

She laughed. "No! What makes you say that?"

"Because love is the only thing that will destroy your beauty."

Vermillion held up her hand.

"Woah. We're talking about you, not me."

Silence.

Then: "You're right. You're right. Of course. Gee's taken enough photos. I'm starved, too. Let's go get something to eat."

The restaurant manager welcomed them both with open arms, managing to acknowledge the pair of them while not taking his gaze from Vermillion.

"Come, come. Your usual table is free. The quail. You will have the quail, yes?"

They sat. Vermillion pressed her knees together. She watched as Diana folded and unfolded her napkin, the edges never quite returning to their pre-folded state. Vermillion had been described once as having perfect symmetry like a paper chain person, as though she had been folded in half and cut from only one side. She had liked the metaphor until she thought of a linked procession of such figures. She had been petulant in her early days as a model. She wanted to believe she was unique.

The quail arrived: lightly grilled, sprinkled with lemon juice and served on a bed of arugula. A spaghetti side dish with sausage and peas in a creamy sauce accompanied the meal. Vermillion knew she would eat it all. That she *should* eat it all. Diana sometimes disapproved of the restaurant, but she could never fault Vermillion's determination to remain true to her cause. Slips in diet were regulated; slips in diet were necessary.

Sometimes, when both of them felt like it, Diana would regale Vermillion of her own time in the trade, when models weren't expected to be perfect and discrepancies could be airbrushed without legal scrutiny.

"Sometimes I look at those magazine covers and I don't see the person I was," Diana said. "I mean, I always expected my pigmentation to be whitened, whether through make-up or digitally, but when I saw how far they had zoomed in on my eyelashes and lined them up like soldiers, I couldn't quite believe it!"

Vermillion nodded. The quail tasted good. Juice from the cooked bird mixed with a little blood, creating a pale red lake on the plate. She detected a slight pepperiness that sat on her tongue and pinpricked it; smooth, it felt like it was absorbed into her mouth, rather than consumed.

"Your mother was against all that, of course. But she had a secret weapon; she had you."

Diana touched her lips with her napkin. "I mean, it's not as though she led the lawsuits against airbrushing, but she was pretty verbal. She paved the way for you, but you know that. And it was the right thing. It enabled true beauty to come to the fore, once again, even if some people didn't like it and got pushed aside."

"You're not much like her," Diana said. "Well, apart from your determination. She lived her life through you. That much was obvious. But again, this is what you know."

The arugula had a slight bite to it, which matched the pepper in the sauce. She rolled one of the leaves around with her tongue and for a moment it stuck to the roof of her mouth. She sipped lemon water and dislodged it.

"Vermillion?"

"Yes?"

"Are you happy? Would you say that you're happy?"

"Yes, Diana. I would say that I'm happy."

Even after the meal, the ache in her stomach didn't go away.

If there was much store to be had in the meaning of dreams, it wasn't a philosophy that Vermillion bought into. Some believed they were a subconscious reflection of the conscious, like an alternate world with just as much a right to exist as the real world. Some would say that the dream world and the real world were reversed, that *real* was the dream, and the *dream* was real. Vermillion awoke from a dream where a man had clutched himself between her legs, his hand moving forward and backward, as if he were immediately about to push.

She wrote her name in the steam that formed on the glass in the shower.

In her dressing room mirror—there was no mirror in the bathroom, no chance for her image to be distorted through condensation—she stood full-length naked.

It was rare that she let go to admiration. Despite the scientifically proven assertion of her being, she was constantly looking for the blemish, for the shock that would cause the image to shatter. It was there; she knew it. One day it would fly in on the wings of age and her uniqueness would be destroyed. She wouldn't be able to continue her career as an almost-perfect model like the other girls. The only option would be to retire and to... what, see the world? But she had already seen the world. She had seen the world on a red carpet. Once that carpet was pulled away, the protection she was afforded would be gone. Magazines would no longer need to court her, they would send their paparazzi to photograph her diminishing looks in poor-fitting swimsuits, she would be plied with drink and captured falling out of taxis with the white V of her knickers on display, she would be the trophy-fuck of the first man who charmed her. She would be nothing—one hundred percent zero—without her body.

Regarding herself in the mirror, she saw that the fall from grace had yet to happen. There was no more or less to her than yesterday. Another day of smiling and posing; another day of loneliness surrounded by people.

They hadn't cleaned the blood on the window.

She woke with that surety.

She strode into the living room, her soft pajamas swishing like whispers. It was still dark. She hadn't checked her clock, but judging from the lights in the surrounding buildings, it couldn't have been much after two in the morning. Night-owls played cards, drank, made love: with her hands pushed against the windowpane, she envisaged it all—a whole world waiting to be discovered, a world that would be soiled once she found it.

She pressed the right side of her face to the glass, closed her eyes, and imagined the window giving way, of falling toward the ground like a wingless angel, a cloth in a final flutter over a table. She saw her body, broken to pieces on the ground: her limbs at wrong angles, her face twisted, a pavement Picasso. Residue of a dream seeped out of her and pooled around her body. Then she snapped her head away from the window and out of the reverie. Goosebumps ran uniformly along her arms and at the base of her neck.

Vermillion walked through the darkness of her apartment, lit only by the moon and the soft hues of the building's security lights. Her cast shadow bent against the side of a table.

Her shadow wasn't symmetrical.

It came down to light. That was it. It all depended on the light.

When she moved, her shadow lifted itself from the sofa, ran along the floor, and then up the side of the doorway. Half of it fell through the open door, the rest hung against the jamb. She raised an arm to her head; the shadow did likewise but in a jerk as it ran over the light switch. Vermillion held her breath.

Was this what it was like to be normal?

In her dressing room, she stood before the mirror with the light off. Her outline was indistinct, the edges blurred. She looked like a smear, as though viewing her reflection through condensation or through the blood on a windowpane.

When she disrobed and turned on the light, she knew something was different.

She watched her reflection watching her, scanning her cheekbones, shoulders, arms, hands, legs, hands, knees, hands, hands, hands.

Her arms hung at her sides, the thumbs of her hands facing inwards, almost touching her thighs. Within the reflection, her thumbs were opposed; they faced outward, *away* from her body. The palms were hidden, her arms as they should be, but the fingers… the fingers were all wrong.

Symmetrically, she was still perfect, yet the mirror lied.

The mirror *was* lying.

She raised her hands to the glass and pushed them flat against the surface. Her middle finger touched her middle finger, but her index finger touched her ring finger, and her thumb touched her pinkie.

Breath caught in her throat as she stepped back. She watched her reflection for some time before snapping the light off. The sudden absence of light created blackness and dizziness, as though she were falling—falling into a well littered with broken eggshells and bloody feathers.

And within that blackness she twisted. She rushed toward the mirror. Glass shattered and her reflection held her, vertically, in a position that remained until she was found the next morning.

Almost in a pose.

SOME PICTURES IN AN ALBUM

GARY MCMAHON

THE BOOK is a slim faux leather photograph album.

The front cover is dusty and stained, and scratched crudely into the material is a circular design that matches the birthmark behind my right knee.

The very edges of the plastic pages are crumpled and torn. It's an ordinary album, something that might be stored in the loft spaces of a million family homes around the country.

Nothing strange. Nothing unusual.

Now that my father is dead, it is just another item found among his belongings… but for some reason I'm drawn to this particular album as I sort through his stuff to box it all up and send it to the charity shop.

I sit down on the bed in my old room and open the book.

Each of the seventeen photographs has its own page; every white-bordered Polaroid image is positioned perfectly at the center and covered in a thin plastic protective flap. Someone has taken a lot of time to put the album together. A lot of love went into the preparation.

I always called him father, not Dad. He was never that… he was always just a father. I can't imagine why he would take so much care in the preparation of this album, or why he would have wanted to keep the pictures I find inside.

▪ The first photograph shows me standing in front of a high redbrick wall. I am six years old. I recognize myself, but it's like looking into a mirror at a reflection that isn't quite right. I'm holding above my head a small silver plastic replica of the F.A. Cup with red and white ribbons tied around it. There is a long, thin shadow on the wall beside me. It is 1973; the year Sunderland beat Leeds in the cup final to produce a now legendary example of "giant killing." My face is joyous; my rosy cheeks are soft; my reddish hair almost matches the color of the bricks behind me. I am wearing a light blue shirt that looks like it has lighter blue flowers on it. My entire chest is hidden by a red and white rosette and a knitted red and white doll, both pinned to the shirt.

▪ The next photograph, on the adjoining page, shows simply a black door. It looks like the front door to a normal terraced house. The bricks around it are of the same shade of red as those in the previous photo, but they are more weathered. The edge of a window frame can be seen on the right of the shot. The door itself looks old, beaten. Paint is flaking off to expose patches of the cheap pale timber beneath.

▪ Over the page is a photograph of me on one of those mechanical animal rides that used to be outside shops on the high street in most English towns. Put in a couple of coins and let your kid ride for a few minutes. This one is a cartoon elephant. I am clutching its ears. My smile is huge. I am wearing a blue woolen hat. My mother—looking so young, so pretty—is standing to the side, smiling shyly. The arm and leg of what I assume to be my father can be seen next to her, the rest of him just clipped out of the frame. My body is slightly blurred because of the motion of the ride, but my face is perfectly still. I seem to be glimpsing something incredible. There is a light in my eyes that is difficult to define. A question occurs to me as I stare at the image: If my parents are both in the shot, who is that taking the photograph?

▪ Next up is the outside of a shop: a corner newsagent, Moses & Sons. Faded posters stuck up with tape in the window, a man in a white overcoat can be glimpsed behind the glass, standing at a counter. The window display is mostly sweets, with a few piles of comics and magazines. I am standing with my back to the camera, looking through the window. My face is reflected in the glass; I am not smiling. At first glance it appears that I might be crying, but it isn't clear. Perhaps I am simply concentrating on all the sugared treats in the display. There is another figure reflected in the glass window beside me, this one tall and thin, but whoever it is cannot be seen.

▪ The door again—at least it looks like the same one. A little older, maybe. More worn. This photograph is darker than the last one, so it could have been taken at a different time of day. Later. Closer to dark. I begin to suspect that each photograph represents a new time frame. Perhaps a year has passed since the last one.

▪ Over the page there are two blank sheets. No photos here, just the empty clear plastic flaps. It's as if a year has been missed, or deliberately excised.

▪ Me, nine years old. I know this because I can recall the scene clearly. My birthday. In the photograph I am surrounded by crumpled balls of wrapping paper and presents. A cowboy rifle, an Action man tank, several cars and an assortment of books. My father's foot can be seen at the bottom left corner of the frame. He is wearing the worn brown slippers I always remember, the pair with the hard rubber soles. The ones he used to like beating me with. He never wanted to hurt me, or so he said at the time. He always gave me a choice: the slipper or an hour spent locked up in the cubby hole under the stairs. I always chose the slipper, because it was over quickly and I didn't like the dark under the stairs—or the thought of what it might contain.

▪ The door again. This year it is cleaner, as if someone has given it a lick of paint. The handle has been replaced. The letter box shines. Sunlight is reflected off the golden knocker, making bright patterns on the camera lens.

▪ The next photograph is disturbing. It shows me sitting on the lap of a man I do not recognize. His eyes are large and empty; his creamy-white hands are massive as they drape over my shoulders, and at least some of the fingers are resting at a weird angle, as if they are in fact boneless. I look… well, my expression is unreadable. I am staring directly into the camera, but not smiling. There could be an element of pleading in my eyes, but that might just be the current me reading too much into a blank expression. My mother, dressed in flared pants and an ugly tie-dye blouse, stands to the side, leaning in the doorway that leads into the kitchen. She seems worried; her eyes are dull and she is biting her bottom lip. Her shoulders are slumped. I cannot remember ever seeing her look so deflated; she was always such a happy woman. The man whose lap I occupy doesn't look quite right. His hair is odd. His face is a different color to his elongated hands. Is he wearing a wig? Is that a mask?

▪ The door. Soiled. Burn marks across the kickboard. The knocker is removed. The letterbox is stuffed with dead leaves.

▪ In the next one, I'm ten. I'm sitting on a red Raleigh Chopper bike in the street, my legs too short to allow my feet to properly touch the ground. I'm balanced on my tiptoes, the bike leaning slightly to the right and toward a low garden wall. It must be cold because I'm wrapped up warm: a thick coat, a matching Sunderland AFC hat and scarf, woolen fingerless gloves on my hands. My smile is awkward, as if it is forced. Again, I have no recollection of this photo being taken, but I do remember the day my father brought the bike home after work—it was stolen later that same day, taken from outside our house when I left it leaning against the wall to pop inside for dinner. I got the slipper for that, too. My father carried on longer than usual, and he was crying when he finished. I have the uneasy feeling that there was someone else there, in the room, when my punishment was meted out; an unseen audience, watching silently from a corner of the back bedroom. Afterward, I couldn't sit down for hours because of the pain. I remember that part most of all.

▪ The door. Hinges rusted. Wood blackened. This time it's ajar. I can see the gap, only blackness visible. I wish I could remember this door, where it was, what it led to. It certainly wasn't the door to our house: that was green, and had a lot of glass panels. The door to a family home. This door is different; less welcoming. Nobody would willingly knock on this door or want to see who lives behind it.

▪ Eleven years old, in the back yard. I'm turned away from the camera, pinning young Shelley Cork to the wall with one arm on either side of her pretty face, the palms of my hands pressed hard against the bricks. We're kissing. My eyes are closed; hers are open. She looks panicked, but she doesn't seem to be struggling. I do have a memory of this, but it's much different. We were necking against the wall at the back of our house, practicing kissing like grown-ups, testing boundaries. She rested her hand against my crotch; I stuck my hand down the back of her knickers and groped her ass. There was nobody else there, so I don't know how this photograph exists. It should not be here. In my memory, Shelley wasn't panicked at all. She was excited, exhilarated. Her breathing was heavy against the side of my face; her eyes kept blinking and she pulled me tightly against her warm, soft body. The whole thing was her idea; I was the one who was afraid. I didn't want my father to come out and catch us in the act. I remember feeling a similar kind of unreasonable guilt later that same year, when Shelley Cork went missing.

▪ Again, we have the black door. It's half open, and this time a thin, pale hand can be seen gripping its edge. The fingers are too long, and there are only three of them but with too many joints. The knuckle bones jut out unnaturally. The skin is a sickly yellowy shade of cream.

▪ I'm twelve years old, sitting down by the river with my legs dangling over the rocks, the soles of my running shoes hanging mere inches above the water. Along the riverbank, on the opposite side, people are fishing. I'm not watching them. I'm staring down into the black water. My posture is strange, strained, as if I'm poised to jump. I used to go down there a lot, but this photograph seems alien, as if it isn't me there by the river, but someone else imitating me. A freakishly tall figure in the bushes directly opposite me, on the other side of the water, stands and stares.

▪ This time the door is wide open. The wood is rotten and splintered; the door hangs askew in its frame, the hinges damaged. Beyond the angled wooden rectangle, there is visible the rear view of someone walking along a scruffy hallway and into the interior of the house. The wallpaper is hanging in strips, the bare boards are warped and stained, and the figure is fading into the dark at the end of the hallway. The figure is naked. Its skin is the color of curdled cream. The bones of its spine stick out like a line of pebbles. The figure is tall and terribly thin, like a prisoner in one of those concentration camp photographs from WWII. Its legs are bent in the wrong place; its arms are so long that its three-fingered hands almost touch the floor. Its head—or what little of it can be seen—is smooth and almost hairless, like that of a baby.

▪ The next photograph is a close-up portrait shot. My face is framed nicely, centered on the page. The background is blurred, out of focus, so it could be anywhere. I am screaming. My eyes are so wide that at first I don't recognize my own face, and my mouth is stretched open to the limit. My face is pale, but my cheeks are red. I don't seem to be wearing a shirt. Someone's fingers, from the top knuckles upwards, are visible just below my neck, but the rest of the hand is cut off by the bottom edge of the photograph. The fingernails are torn and dirty. There are only three fingers on the hand. Upon closer inspection, the wall behind me is not blurred: it is ruined, the paper torn and dirtied, the uneven plaster beneath lined and raked as if by something sharp. Like nails. Or claws.

- Another blank page. But this one has small bits of adhesive dotted on the paper, as if whatever photograph was there has been hastily removed.

- The final photograph is perhaps the most disturbing of all, yet the least clear in terms of what is going on. The photographer has stepped forward, must be standing on the doorstep, so only a part of the doorframe is visible. At the end of the grimy hallway, there are two figures. Both are facing away from the black door, and from the camera. One of the figures is the familiar, thin, lanky creature from one of the previous shots. Its shoulders are hunched; its lean thighs are clenched, as if it's been caught in the act of taking a step. Holding its hand is another, smaller figure. A scrawny boy, aged perhaps fourteen years old. The boy is naked. I recognize myself from the birthmark behind my right knee: a small, dark, circular stain. The muscles in my body are tensed. I can see that even from the grainy, unfocused shot. Beyond the two figures, just about visible in the darkness at the end of the hallway, is my father. His nude body is a vague pinkish blur, but his face is a little easier to make out: a small, hazy oval in the shadows. His arms are crossed at the wrist over his pelvis. He is gripping something in his fist but I don't know what it is. His eyes are small and mean, and he is grinning.

I close the album and put it on the bed. Get up and walk to the mirror. Reflected there, in the glass, I see something other than the familiar room where I spent my childhood evenings fighting back nightmares.

I see a black door in the wall, its letterbox stuffed with dead leaves and its gold handle and knocker slightly tarnished. As I watch, the door opens. A long, thin, pale three-fingered hand bends around the frame. I stare at the ragged nails, the blood and dirt I know is crusted beneath them, and I remember.

He was always there, in my life, ever since I was six years old. For most of the time he stayed in the background, but sometimes he put on a mask and entered the frame, unable to stay out of view. I'm still not sure who he was, but my father brought him into our home, and some kind of transaction took place. My birthmark is a stamp, a barcode; it marks me out as belonging to him. Bought and paid for long ago, before the first photograph was even taken.

Each time I was taken there, to the house with the black door, I came out with something missing. The memory of what happened inside, yes, but also something else: a small part of me, sliced away. I think Shelley Cork got to see what was in there, too, but she never came back out. I suspect that my father led her through that black door and left her there, a plaything for whatever resides at the end of that dirty hallway.

I shift my gaze and stare at the door in the mirror. My face resembles that of my father, at the age that I am now. A non-identical reflection; like the left hand swapping places with the right. It does not fit. It should not be there, where it does not belong.

I glance again at the black door. It has always been waiting for me to return. The long, thin hand slips away, retreating back inside, but the door does not shut. It will never shut, not until I go back inside to take back what is mine.

To reclaim the things I left behind and stick those missing photographs back in the album.

FIVE ADJECTIVES

MONICA J. O'ROURKE

ASSIGNMENT: *Using five adjectives, write a 350-word essay describing your father.* [Eds. Note: Miss Maginty verified that of nineteen second-grade students, seventeen had a surviving father. The other two children were asked to write about their favorite pet.] *Give examples.*

My dad's name is Ken. He is kind, smart, funny, fair, and happy. Those are my five adjectives. An adjective is a word that describes a noun.

My dad is kind. He is good to me and my brother, Aaron. Aaron is five years old. I am two years older than Aaron. I am seven. He can be a pest. My dad is kind because he knows privacy is important to me.

The grass outside Nadine's bedroom window sprouts patches of brown. The blades bow respectful of the wind, reaching in unison toward the ground as if a single blade. Nadine is hypnotized by their rhythm and tries to count them. She loses track after fifty-seven.

Nadine pokes her head out of the bedroom door a short time later. Being punished. Nadine had been bad. Again.

"Dad?" she whines, knowing it annoys him. Doing so seems silly, but it attracts his attention. Which is what she craves.

He responds to her plea for clemency with a shout from the sofa downstairs.

She whines louder. He threatens a spanking.

Nadine pouts. "Can I come out of my room now?"

When he doesn't respond she creeps down the stairs and stalks into the living room. Shakes his shoulder. "Can I come out now?" she whispers, not realizing the irony.

His eyes gleam open, blinking back crocodile tears that had formed during his nap. Cold dark pupils glare at her under the dim lighting. "Dammit, you woke me up."

She steps back, but she has no reason to fear him. He has never struck her, no matter how many times he's threatened.

She leans forward and clings to his arm. Smiles charmingly. Disarmingly. Hugs his arms, the hairs tickling her cheek.

"Go back to your room."

"But can't I—"

"Back to your room." More slowly. Teeth clenched.

She doesn't relent, wants to spend time with him. Even time fashioned in anger.

"I'm hungry. Can I just get a snack?"

"I won't tell you again."

Nadine stares at him, willing him to change his mind, trying to control his thoughts. It isn't working. But she practices and waits and stares and hopes he will suddenly say the opposite of what he had moments ago, but he gets angrier for some reason, some stupid reason, and she sees tiny red dots on his cheeks.

After a minute that feels like an hour, Nadine's father slithers around in his seat and shifts one eye toward her. Finally. Not directly at her but it's close.

She smiles, wonders if she has succeeded in changing his mind.

"Go to bed."

"But I—"

"Now! Move! Bed! And don't leave that goddamned room!"

Somehow the words comfort. She feels a connection.

She runs away, crying, wishing Mom had stayed home that weekend, or wishing she'd gone too.

She wishes she could travel back in time and reverse the events from breakfast, the reason for the exile: a glass slipped through her soapy fingers and shattered in the sink. She yelled sorry as she tried to clean up the shards, placing them inside the shattered bottom. She should have been more careful—it was his favorite glass.

He snatched the glass corpse from her hands and examined it. He didn't check her hands for signs of damage, but the glass he cradled. "My crystal scotch glass."

"Sorry," she muttered again, eyes downcast, dismayed by her clumsiness. She often broke glasses and dishes. He accused her of breaking it intentionally and told her to go to her room, to stay there until he says she can come out.

And there she has been ever since, realizing of course that the punishment fit the crime, knowing it could have been worse. She sits in her room, waiting since breakfast for a parole that never seems to be granted, knowing her stay of execution might expire before Mom returns from Aunt Kathleen's.

She sits cross-legged on her bed and scoops out a handful of cereal from the box of Cheerios she's stashed.

Mom and Aaron come home around two the following afternoon, and Nadine is allowed out of her room.

My dad is smart. He tells me I should go to college one day because I'm almost as smart as him. He knows all the capitals of all the states but won't tell me any answers and says I should look them up.

Nadine's class participated in a spelling bee and Nadine came in third. Mrs. Fisher gave her a Third Place Award Certificate and a ribbon. Nadine spelled *rabbit, maintain, battery,* and *justice* correctly. She misspelled *tomorrow* because she forgets if there are two Ms or two Rs. Sometimes she spells it tommorrow, but that never looks right.

Everyone congratulated her, even Jeffrey, the boy who had the abominable habit of flicking spitballs at her.

Nadine races home, flushed from the heat, sweaty from running. The corners of her award are damp and wrinkled from her moist fingers.

She bursts into the house.

Her dad's already home because he'd had a client that he'd taken to lunch and finished work early. Mom won't be home for another two hours.

Out of breath, grinning like a Cheshire cat, Nadine waves her paper in front of her chest, dangles it beneath his nose, rocks excitedly on her heels.

He reaches out and accepts the paper.

"Third place?"

She nods, her smile faltering the tiniest bit, still hopeful that—

"What word did you miss?"

"Tomorrow."

He grunts, and she doesn't know why this noise disturbs her so profoundly. He hands the paper back without saying a word and returns to his newspaper.

She stares, again trying to read his mind... trying to change it, make him attentive, make him like her... make him love her. But still, she hasn't figured out how to do this. So she waits for a response, waits for him to say something. Waits for his congratulations. Waits for a hug that will never happen.

She swings her arms, and he finally responds. "That was a stupid word to miss. You should've won."

My dad is funny. He tells good jokes. He makes me laugh when he tells me jokes. He tickles me and makes me laugh. Sometimes I laugh so hard I pee my pants. That only happened one time. That one time he stopped tickling me after I peed, and after tears started to come out of my eyes. I don't even remember crying, I just remember my eyes being wet. He laughs and laughs and finally stops tickling me when I think I'm going to throw up. He tickles me sometimes when he tucks me in at night.

And he smiles, wrapped around his daughter's still form, tears drying on her cheeks, her hair a tousled bird's nest piled on top of her head.

Nadine pretends to have fallen asleep, but he knows she hasn't. Nadine knows this because she sneaks a peek and can see the expression on his face. He can tell by her breathing that she is still awake, can tell by the darting movements beneath her eyelids. She realizes she has to learn to pretend better.

Nadine's mom tiptoes into the room, wanting to not disturb her sleeping child. Nadine peeps at her mother through slits, still trying to pretend sleep, believing she has fooled her parents but knowing her dad probably knows the truth.

Dad plays along with it for some reason. "Shhh," he whispers, nodding his head toward the door. "Don't come in. I'll follow you out."

Mom smiles at the sight, the beautiful and perfect sight, daughter entwined with daddy, Giotto's *Madonna and Child* fashioned in masculine arms and Barbie pajamas.

Mom leaves. Dad pulls his arms away from Nadine so he can rise from the bed. Nadine's mother has left and has not seen where Nadine's father's hands had been. Her mother probably wouldn't have liked it.

Nadine drifts off to sleep for real after her dad leaves the room. She buries this memory along with every other she doesn't want to acknowledge.

My dad is fair. My brother, Aaron, and I fight sometimes, and Dad makes us stop. He yells at us both and says we shouldn't fight. I think my dad is fair because even when he punishes us, he does it fair. Some dads are very strict. My friends say their dads are strict, but my dad says he's not strict, not at all. My dad punishes me, and Aaron, but I think he's fair when he does it.

Nadine's friends have come over for a pajama party. Three girls from her class: Rachael, Emily, and Sarah. They've decided to camp in the living room because Nadine's mom said they could. Nadine's room is too small to comfortably fit four girls. Besides, Nadine wants to use her sleeping bag like her friends do.

The girls giggle about the boys they like, and they gossip about their classmates. Nothing out of the ordinary for a pajama party, and Nadine is excited that she's making new friends, something that doesn't come easy for her.

Dad trudges into the living room with a towel wrapped around his waist. "Shut your mouths and go to sleep," he says. There's no other warning, just a final decree. He disappears down the hall and closes his bedroom door behind him.

Nadine snuggles into her sleeping bag and closes her eyes, prepared to sleep, expecting the other girls to do the same.

Emily turns on the flashlight and shines it down the hall. "Grump," she says with a giggle. Rachael and Sarah titter into their fingers. Nadine pulls the blanket up to her nose. Her heart beats a little faster.

"Grump," Rachael echoes, which cracks up the visiting girls and terrifies Nadine.

"Shhh," Nadine says, but the girls giggle even more.

Her parents' bedroom door is flung open. A chunk of light fills a black section of hallway.

Again draped only in a towel, her dad storms the room. "Goddammit," he says. A shocked Emily gasps at the curse word. "I told you girls to shut up. I mean it!"

Nadine's mom calls from the bedroom. "Everything okay?"

He stands in the center of a circle of girls. "Not another sound," he warns and disappears down the hall.

The girls remain quiet for several minutes. Nadine is relieved they have fallen asleep, and the tension in her body, which begins in her toes and works its way up her legs and torso and fingers and arms and neck, relinquishes its stranglehold.

But a sudden flashlight beam pierces the darkness like a laser. Emily aims it at Nadine's face. "What's wrong with your dad?" Her voice is twangy, nasal. She says the word as "dah-aaaad." "He's creepy."

"Yeah," Sarah adds. "He scared me."

"Please," Nadine begs. "Be quiet." She squeezes her eyes shut and wills the girls asleep. Tries to control their thoughts, to tell them that her father isn't kidding. But they don't get her psychic message. Nadine has failed once again.

"Big dopeyhead," Emily says, her voice deepening, her girlish impression of Nadine's father: "Goddammit." Her cheeks puff out and her head drops against her chest. For some reason she believes this makes her look something like Nadine's father.

Rachael and Sarah think that this is one of the funniest things they have ever seen and burst out laughing, holding their noses to quiet the laughs, burying their faces in their pillows.

Nadine flips over on her side and pulls the blanket up to her ears. She pretends she is asleep.

This time, when she hears the bedroom door open and sees the light once again fill the dark corridor, she can pretend to sleep through it all.

The other girls realize he's coming. They drop into supine positions and try to burrow into their sleeping bags, but it's too late.

He sees them.

He stands in the center of the circle of girls.

Emily starts to cry and buries her face in the crook of her arm.

He stands over Nadine. "Let's go."

She looks up at him. "Why?" she says. "I didn't do anything."

"*Now*."

"But I was sleeping."

The three other girls stare in silence.

"I said let's go."

Nadine jumps up. She scoops the sleeping bag in her arms and follows him to her bedroom. He stands in the doorframe and waits for her to pass.

"But I didn't do anything," she cries, her voice hitching, tears pouring down her cheeks. He doesn't seem to notice her tears. Or if he does, he doesn't seem to care.

"Stay in your room. Don't come out until I tell you to."

"Can my friends—"

"No."

He pulls her door shut and leaves her standing in the dark.

Sobbing, Nadine climbs into bed. She cries until she's weak and exhausted and a short time later she's asleep.

Nadine wakes to the sound of laughter and the smell of coffee. She climbs out of bed and bounds down the stairs. Dad is cooking breakfast, which Nadine's friends appear to be enjoying.

Dad looks up from the waffle iron. He's laughing, probably telling them jokes. She catches his eye and his face hardens. "Why are you out of your room?"

This question barely registers. How could he ask her that? How can she still be punished? Especially when her friends were still here.

"Get back to your room."

She waits for the inevitable laughter, certain this is a joke. A cruel joke, but a joke nonetheless. Any second now he's going to laugh—might even flick waffle batter at her.

"But—" She doesn't finish the sentence because she can tell by the expression on his face that this isn't a joke at all.

She backs away from the table, from the girls staring with dewy doe eyes, forks suspended in midair. Nadine's cheeks burn with embarrassment.

Nadine runs up the stairs and sits in the doorway of her bedroom, listening to the sounds of breakfast: the clinks of forks and knives against plates, the giggles and laughter from the girls, who have no choice but to pretend everything is fine, to continue as if nothing has happened. Girls who have no clue what injustice is but feel strangely grateful for their own parents, who aren't as strict as they had once imagined. Girls who only want to finish eating and hope this pajama party ends sometime soon.

By lunchtime, Nadine is allowed out of her room.

By then, her friends have already gone home.

My dad is happy. He smiles a lot. He's always in a good mood. I'm sad when Dad doesn't smile. I wonder if he's upset with me, if I've done something else wrong. I do a lot of dumb things. I try to be good, so he'll stay happy.

It's Saturday, mid-August. Nadine and Aaron get dressed early because Dad says to get out and enjoy the sunshine.

The heat is sweltering, oppressive, the humidity almost a life form. The children play outside for a while but it's just too hot for any real enjoyment. The water in the kiddy pool is hotter than bath water. Splashing around in it isn't fun, it's painful.

The rubber bicycle tires ooze into the tar melting on the 101-degree street. The metal seats on the swing set are untouchable.

The children return to the house and go into the kitchen in search of a cold drink.

Mom has gone shopping. Dad's sitting at the kitchen table reading a newspaper.

Cheeks are red from heat and from the beginnings of sunburn. Nadine and Aaron collapse onto the cool linoleum kitchen floor.

"Why are you back already?"

"It's so hot," Nadine says, waving her hand in front of her face like a fan, her tongue lolling out the side of her mouth like she'd spent a week traversing the Sahara. Her halter top slides on her slick skin, refusing to stay in place.

"Go back outside," he says, although he allows them a drink of water before they go.

Outside again, and somehow it's hotter. The trees droop, succumbing to the weight of the onerous air, branches sagging with the burden of humidity.

They find the garden hose and turn on the tap. Icy water gushes out, and she runs it on their faces and arms. She wets her brother's head and thinks she sees steam rising from it.

They relax in the shade beneath a birch tree and peel the bark off in strips. She thinks she's pulling off the tree's skin and feels sad yet excited. She wonders if she is hurting it but continues to strip away its bark anyway.

The wind evaporates the moisture on their skin but stops cooling when their flesh is dry, a strange and inconvenient magic.

Mosquitoes buzzing about their ears are not a problem, something tolerable if somewhat annoying. But then the black flies come, and black flies tend to swarm, often in the hundreds, biting and stinging in unrelenting attacks.

They run to the house and manage for the moment to outrun the black flies. Their small porch is screen enclosed and offers asylum from the attack, but there is no room to maneuver.

Nadine grabs the doorknob. It refuses to turn; the door is locked. Perplexed, she knocks. After an interminable wait, their father opens the door but blocks them from entering.

"Stay outside," he tells them.

"But—" Nadine licks her parched lips. Aaron is crying. His cheeks are the color of brick.

"I want a quiet and peaceful house for once. You and your brother stay outside."

"But the bugs—"

"Swat them."

He shuts the door.

And right before he does—she notices he's smiling.

My dad is a great man. He's kind, smart, funny, fair, and happy. The end. [Eds. Note: Nadine's grade for this paper was a B-. Miss Maginty thought the adjectives used were weak. She later pointed out that adjectives used by other students in the same class included *compassionate, jocular, intelligent,* and *equitable.* She conceded that these students might have had parental guidance when writing their papers. Miss Maginty later confessed that another reason for the B- was that Nadine's life didn't seem to have the hardship or stress that the other children seemed to be experiencing. Miss Maginty thought Nadine was experiencing a rather simple and mundane childhood. She said that that might not have been a fair way to grade, but that after forty years of teaching, she knew a thing or two about human nature and graded accordingly. Nadine has since said she wishes she had chosen a different set of adjectives to describe her father.]

ENCHANTED COMBUSTION

AMANDA OTTINO

DADDY SPEAKS SOFTLY to Lillie so that I can't hear. He's eating cereal and there aren't any cartoons on the TV, just the ugly-haired news lady standing in front of a fire. Saturdays we usually wake up and watch cartoons and eat junk food, but this morning Daddy's different and ignoring me. He sounds like last year when the doctor told us the balloon in Mommy's brain was bleeding. I'm squeezing the butterfly I picked for Daddy so tightly that my hand's sweaty.

My first butterfly was green. Mommy had cut it out of construction paper during an art project. She hung it above my bed and said it would keep the nightmares out of my head. She promised to teach me to make one once I was old enough, but she made me wait. I ripped it off the wall because I was mad and tore a hole in its head. I taped it back together, hoping she wouldn't notice. That was the last thing she ever gave me.

Daddy says she's like the butterflies now, the ones I keep pinned to my bedroom wall. I started collecting the still ones from the backyard the day she ran away to heaven. Some have holes in their wings and I make them pretty again. I keep them pinned around me to protect my dreams. I like to go out for adventures in the field behind the house to search for the fluttering ones. I can make them stay still for me.

Why couldn't Mommy take me with her to see the butterflies in heaven?

She visits me while I sleep sometimes. I try to tell Daddy about her visits, and what she teaches me, but he always stops my story to make me get him one of his silver cans from the fridge, especially when Lillie's around. He doesn't like it when I talk about Mommy. I think she hurt his feelings when she left. Maybe she visits him in his sleep and isn't so nice, or sees him when I'm away at school. Maybe she doesn't visit him at all.

Other kids make fun of my looks and how I speak. I don't form sentences out loud like they do. That's why Mommy waited until I turned seven before putting me in kindergarten. Maybe now that I'm older, they won't throw pencils at me and call me *retard.* Daddy says it's because I have an extra chromosome. He thinks it makes me better than the meanies at school and that DNA can't change how pretty I am on the inside. The other kids only care about my outside.

I'm smarter than kids my age, but I learn differently. Miss Lillie tells Daddy that I'm *brilliant.* I don't know what that means, but she might be making fun of me.

Miss Lillie helps my daddy with chores, keeps him company when he drinks his silver juice, and reads me books before it's time to sleep. She's the only one who understands my words and listens to what I say. She fills my backpack before bed and places a clock next to my head.

"This will wake you in the morning to remind you to go to school. You push *this* button and then get up to go potty. Don't forget to brush your teeth and comb your hair. Your dress is ready for you in the bathroom. Don't forget to put on your undershorts."

"Yeth mith Lee Lee."

I have trouble forming some words. My tongue hangs out of my mouth and gives me a lisp, but Miss Lillie helps me with that. I like when she comes over. She always kisses me on the nose like my mommy used to do. Before she leaves, she helps me count the butterflies pinned on my wall. I never make it past twenty-nine without her help.

The alarm sings, but I am already awake and dressed. I am ready for my daddy to tie the laces on my butterfly shoes. He walks slowly in the mornings. I skip while he keeps hold of my hand and pull him to school, too excited to walk. The kids at school will be impressed when they see what's in my bag.

I already know who's in my class this year: the same kids from first grade, the ones who made fun of my lisp, and my hair, the way I walk. The same kids who chased me in the hallway and filled my desk with dirt last year. When they see what I brought for them, they'll learn to like me.

Each desk has a folded piece of paper with a name. The smell of mildew and wood chips fills the air. It makes me think of the field behind our house while I walk to my chair at the back corner of the room. The teacher sees me pulling out my butterfly box and walks toward me. He presses his finger to the middle of his glasses, making them closer to his eyes. His dirt colored hair is pulled back in a ponytail, but shorter hairs sprout above his ears, down his jaw and meet in the middle around his mouth. His white teeth are crooked like mine when he smiles.

"I am Mr. Papilio. You must be Daisy." He bends his knees to get closer. "You are very early, young lady. What do you have here?"

"These are my friends," I try to tell him, "they match my classmates."

I point to a still butterfly and lay it in my hand: Billy Arnold, whose real yellow hair matches this butterfly's body. I pull a *blue lacewing* out of the box: Sarah Brown, whose eyes are as blue as the wings.

He is quiet for a while, rises, and pats my shoulder.

"They are very pretty, Daisy."

Those are the only words I hear before the other kids arrive.

Tommy is the first to come in, head down and arms crossed. He looks at me in silence and with his unchanging expression walks to the other side of the class to find his name written on a card. Anna walks in with Macie and Claire. They giggle and find their desks all in a row, just like the butterflies.

I lay out the rest and place the box under my chair.

The butterflies are spread so prettily on the desk.

Josh sits down in the chair in front of me. He's fatter than the other kids. His tummy presses against his desk and his back hangs over the chair and onto my butterflies. I try to keep the wings from getting crushed. Instead of a fat Josh butterfly, I have a plump caterpillar to match his rolly body, which I had put in a jar until it stopped moving.

Joy, Stan, Lexi and Justin walk in last, together. They all act the same, always copying each other. I wanted them to like me, the way they like each other. Lexi points to my desk and smiles. Excited, I straighten in my chair, lining up all of my friends for them to see. I wave them over and then Stan wipes all of the butterflies to the floor.

The class laughs while I pick them up.

At first recess, Mr. Papilio tells me to keep my butterfly friends in the box.

I meet a new boy named Charlie on the playground. He's in first grade. He's small like me and his eyes are similar. He giggles a lot with his tongue hanging out. He's the only kid who has ever smiled at me. I wonder if he has an extra chromosome. While other kids play in the sandbox, we run for the meadow and I drag him along, like my father earlier.

At recess, we find the Charlie butterfly.

Not all days will be this easy.

I go home every day wet, either from tears, paint, water or ketchup. The second day, Joy puts finger-paints in my hair and Lexi puts paste in my ears. Justin pushes me around in the meadow on the third, making my tights green on the knees. Josh, the fat one, pees in his chair the next day, the puddle making my shoes smell like moldy bread to go with the ketchup and tots Stan sticks in my hair. The five of them find me in the girls' room the last day and pour water over me while I'm *going*.

Who knows what Charlie is going through.

Mommy visits. She tells me to be strong, to use my butterflies to protect me from *the evil doings of others*. I trust her. The butterflies make me feel strong, so the next time I see the bullies, I'm no longer afraid.

I wear my butterfly shoes. Daddy helped me tie them.

Mr. Papilio stands at the front of the class. Nobody else is in the classroom. Mr. Papilio follows me to my corner desk, straddles Josh's chair and asks if I'm happy. We're alone, but he speaks softly. After nodding, he tells me I'm different than the other kids—not *special*—and says I should ask my daddy to change my class.

He doesn't want me anymore.

Mommy always told me it's better to smile than to cry because it keeps me beautiful, but I can't stop crying, even when the other kids come to class. I can't remember the last time I cried in front of other kids. Eventually, my daddy's called and he takes me home.

The next day I smile to keep me beautiful. The mean kids can't hurt me if I don't go to school. Daddy wants to keep me home until Mr. Papilio is punished for what he said to me.

Now I have lots of time to play with my butterflies.

I separate them into piles: five butterflies and a caterpillar to represent the boys and girls at school who pick on me, and one small pile for the pretty ones: Mommy, Daddy, Lillie and Charlie. I want to rip the wings off the bad ones. I want to stomp on them until they're flat. I want to drown them in water.

Daddy barbeques lunch in the backyard and leaves me alone for a few minutes so he can get another silver can from the fridge. I remember the kids, the butterflies. Drowning and squishing and ripping their wings off is not enough. To protect me and Charlie, I burn them instead.

I turn up the volume on the TV in time to hear the ugly-haired news lady talking about the fire at school. Five kids and a teacher were inside.

Daddy no longer speaks softly to Lillie.

My sweaty hand drops the butterfly I had picked for Daddy, the one held so tightly in my fist. It falls to the floor, and that's when I hear the *thud.*

Daddy's soaking wet and red on the kitchen floor.

Still.

THERE ARE EMBERS

CHRIS HERTZ

"WHEN ALL LOVES DIE, there are embers," Charlie said.

And I believed her.

I believed her because the Waterfront Arsonist loved his work. Like God loves creation. Even now, as he cools in jail, he burns for it—a trick candle, blown out, reigniting.

The first fire thrilled like a first kiss. Pulsing, searing and exciting, if a bit reserved. Felt so fine, he went in for another. Confident and controlled. The third go round produced a real taste for it. The fifth triggered addiction.

Why? Because fire is a living thing. Moving, jumping, dancing. Lighting up a room. It's born. Has warmth. Grows and reproduces. *Breathes.* To create fire is to create life.

It's hard work. Creating life requires a mix of spontaneous combustion and planning—right down to the letter. The five P's never fail: proper planning prevents poor performance. You can never over-plan. Planning keeps you loose, ready and one step ahead at all times.

Next comes the act itself. No one is more fired up than the serial criminal on game night. The plan is set and it's all about execution. Bring your A-game and go home a champion. Screw up and it's prison or worse. You and you alone know the plan. Knowledge is power. The omniscience of God.

Trailing behind, but gnawing away at the back of your mind, is concern. One day the police will wise up and the fun will be over. You don't want that to happen. You want to keep going. To avoid capture. But you become sloppy. It's a vital dichotomy.

Your concern is slight, simply because you're too clever. But on some level—maybe the only part remaining that's human—you want to get caught, or else it will never end.

I speak of these things plainly and with some degree of certainty because I knew a serial arsonist—the Waterfront Arsonist—intimately before his arrest. I have scars to prove it. Burn scars, seared skin on my arms, legs and back, covering my head where hair no longer grows, warping my face.

Yes, I knew the arsonist well. I helped catch him. I'll tell the story, but don't expect me to *explain* it. I can't. What follows is the inside scoop—a real exclusive—about a girl named Charlie and her father. The conviction of the Waterfront Arsonist is as much their story as my own.

The arsonist struck for the tenth time the day Charlie told me how her father died.

"There was a fire," she said, as if speaking of trivial things—the weather or an old scar. "He died saving me."

I didn't respond, but waited for her to go on in her own time. It was late—after midnight. We had spent the evening drinking Firewater and igniting body heat. We lay in the living room of my house near the Waterfront. The house my own father left to me. The house where I grew up. Charlie's head rested on my shoulder, the rest of her naked in my arms. Our legs intertwined, fitting like puzzle pieces. I stroked her hair, admiring the stunning array of colors.

Black roots sizzled into orange and red streaks that licked her neck like flames.

I was drawn to it like a moth when I first saw her. I had just filled up my tank at the Waterfront Pump-n-Go. Charlie worked the register. Flaming hair crackling, beckoning. Deep brown, penetrating eyes studied me as I handed her the change. She smiled a thank you, and I couldn't help myself.

"I'm sorry," I had said, "I never do this." It was my voice, but I couldn't feel my jaw move. I couldn't feel anything. Suddenly, I was in the middle of it. "I'm usually never like this, but what are you doing after your shift?" And it worked. What can I say? I had more confidence before I became a disfigured burn victim. Charlie and I were... mutually exclusive, and starting to click. She told me after consummation that her dad had died when she was six. When I asked how, she said, "Some other time."

I peacefully breathed deep—apple conditioner, pollen scent of semen, and something else: the sweet and pungent mixture of sweat and soap, kind of like gasoline.

Those almost-red eyes held a silent blaze that consumed me.

"There was a fire," she said again, and told me the rest of the story.

Her father didn't know she had come home. That morning, before he took her to school, little white bugs crawled out of a floorboard in the living room. *What if the bugs were causing them to be poor?* Her father told her once that they were poor, and if something didn't happen soon, he could no longer afford to buy her clothes or send her to St. George's. *What if the bugs were dangerous? What if they* got *him?* So she walked the mile or so home to warn him—to watch out for him like she had done for the last year since her mother left.

When she opened the door, she smelled the smoke. She called for him, but he didn't answer. Thick clouds filled the kitchen. She went in anyway. She had to find him—to take care of him because she was the only one who could do that now.

Burning black air blurred her vision and stuffed her lungs. She squinted and her eyes watered. She hacked, wheezed and coughed, but she made it down to the basement.

Flames were there now. Loud cackling, orange-glowing heat. It danced on the floor, climbed the walls and clung to the ceiling.

Her father was there, too—bent over a box of dolls. Her dolls. He picked them out one at a time and squirted them with a clear liquid that he squeezed from a small square can—a kind of sweet-smelling water to protect them from the flames. Then he tossed them gently into a corner where the fire was lowest. But for some reason the water didn't protect the dolls. Instead, it made the fire jump and roar each time a doll landed in the mouth of the blaze. Charring their synthetic doll-clothes. Melting their vacant doll-faces. Pooling in grotesque puddles of plastic doll-flesh.

He squirted another doll, tossed it to the far corner.

The fire raged.

"Daddy?" she said and chased after it.

The flames reached out, snapping at her jumper. A chunk of ceiling crashed and knocked her back. Arms engulfed her, and the smell of gasoline. Her father.

He scooped her up—tiny in his arms—and carried her up the steps. Her watery eyes closed, but she envisioned each step crumbling beneath their weight, splintering to firewood. They were two steps from the top when he flung her out of the basement.

As she flew forward into the kitchen wall, she heard the crash. Even at six years old, she said, she knew what had happened. She knew that when she looked back she would no longer see stairs to the basement, or her father, but a gaping hole where the living room used to be. She ran out the back door and watched her house crumble to the ground.

Her daddy didn't know she had come home, but he saved her anyway. Later, a man in a fireman's hat said her daddy didn't know about the termites, either. They had eaten away at the hardwood floor in the living room for years—weakening it. The basement ceiling collapsed much sooner than he could have ever expected.

The story finished, I kissed her softly.

Charlie responded with a deep, passionate kiss that didn't break as she straddled me—streaked hair flaming. I smiled because of her hair. I smiled because of her story. I smiled because she was good at sex. I smiled because it was the first time I thought she could be the Waterfront Arsonist.

The Waterfront lies on the cold, muddy banks of the Monongahela River, but fire runs through its blood. In another life, the Waterfront housed the most productive steel mill in America—the Homestead Works. Men died there during a strike in 1892, and fifty years later it helped win a world war. When the mill closed in the mid-eighties, seas of molten metal and pillars of acrid, black smoke transformed into a quaint town square filled with pleasant shops, condos, a movie theater, chain restaurants and blue skies.

When a wave of cheap foreign labor finally extinguished that Homestead blast furnace, the fire literally went out of the region. The Waterfront was the retail phoenix that rose from the ashes. The Waterfront Arsonist was the spark that reignited the blaze.

Fear followed fire. You could sense it when a homeowner glanced over their shoulder before putting key to lock. Hear it when a fire engine screamed out of the Number Two station on West Street. See it when nervous eyes peeked out from behind living room curtains.

Charlie wasn't afraid. I found that trait strangely endearing. She relished each headline about the fires, lit up at each newscast. In truth, the stories fascinated her.

So it was no surprise the arsonist struck again the day Charlie moved in. The story broke the next night. I sat in the living room watching the eleven o'clock news while Charlie washed up in the kitchen. The anchors—a suited man wearing a burnt orange tie, and an auburn-haired woman—solemnly greeted the audience.

"Good evening," said one.

"A fire last night in the Waterfront," said the other, "is believed to be the latest in a string of local arsons."

Flames engulfed a black silhouetted figure in the background.

The caption read: THE WATERFRONT ARSONIST.

"The arsonist again," I called to Charlie.

She ran in from the kitchen. Her red tank-top clung to her moist body, flaming hair wet at the ends where it licked her skin.

The camera switched to a live feed of a brunette with bright red lips.

"David and Susan, I'm here on Sarah Street in Homestead where local police and firefighters continue to investigate another alleged arson in Pittsburgh's Waterfront."

Queue 9-1-1 tape of a screaming woman.

The reporter interviewed incomprehensible but highly entertaining neighbors. Charlie and I laughed at that part.

"Victims were taken to a local hospital," the reporter said, "treated for burns and smoke inhalation, and are in fair condition tonight. The cellphone used to call authorities wasn't so lucky. Police found it scorched in the fire—an all too familiar calling card of the Waterfront Arsonist. Susan."

The camera flicked to the auburn anchor. "Police are urging all Waterfront area residents to report missing cellphones."

By this time, it was well known that the arsonist stalked victims, stealing their cellphones and calling the fire department after setting the blaze. The evidence inevitably burned to cellular cinders.

"Pretty clever," I said.

Charlie tickled me. "You think so?"

"Absolutely," I said and kissed her.

***

We showered together and got ready for bed. The room was dark and I was half-asleep when Charlie felt like talking.

"I'll go down to the post office tomorrow," she said, "and change my address. Make this official. I love this house. The old wood frame. The hardwood floors. The smells. It reminds me of the house we had, my dad and I."

I lay with my back to her. She leaned over and kissed my ear. I mumbled groggily.

"I saw something in the basement," she whispered, "one night when you were out."

I didn't respond, but I was wide awake.

"Actually, I *felt* something—a presence. The air became heavy and I smelled gasoline. Like the day my dad died... I was warm, not cold like in ghost stories. And I felt safe. Protected. I know it sounds silly, but I think it was my father."

She paused, but my breathing was even. As far as she knew, I was asleep.

"Probably imagination or an old memory. But when someone you love dies, there are embers. Don't you think?"

I moaned, feigning sleep. She kissed me again.

"I guess I still miss him," she said and lay quiet.

Her breathing became calm and rhythmic. She snored softly in my ear.

My own breathing changed to short and rapid. My heart pounded against my ribs. My eyes darted around the room. My mind racing.

The arsonist struck for the last time the day police came to the house. Charlie was at work. I was walking home from the grocery store, lost in thought. I didn't notice the black-and-white as I turned down the front walk.

"Afternoon, sir," an officer said. "Didn't mean to scare you."

I must have jumped. Not a good start. There were two of them, both dressed in midnight blue. Both slightly overweight.

"Not at all."

My heart was in my throat, but my hands were steady.

"Do you mind if we ask you a couple of questions, sir?" the woman said.

"It'll only take a few minutes," the man assured me.

I acquiesced and excused my rudeness. Two things that don't pay: crime and copping attitude to the police.

"Are you Mr.—?" the woman said my father's name.

I said I wasn't.

"Do you know Mr.—?"

I lied and told them I didn't.

"Do you have identification, sir?

I told them I had unfortunately left it at home. This was true.

They asked about Charlie. I denied knowing her as well. The officers stood perplexed. If I didn't know the people they were asking about, why was I delivering groceries to their house?

"Is this Gehenna?" I asked.

The woman shook her head. "Four blocks over."

I must have turned a deep red. How embarrassing to be on the wrong street!

The cops offered a ride and I declined. They offered directions and I accepted. I felt their eyes on me as I walked away. On Gehenna, I waved to them as they drove out of sight.

I hurried home, placed the groceries on the counter, and reached for my cellphone. It *could* have been my phone. It had the same shape, same color. But it definitely wasn't mine.

I felt suddenly hollow, like termites had chomped their way through the solid oak floor of my life. How could I have been so sloppy?

Thoughts pounded through my head: cellphones and newscasts and a dozen burning buildings. But I thought calmly, clearly. I thought of Charlie. How she fit the profile of a serial arsonist—the flaming hair, the tragic memories of deadly fire. How easy it would be for her to steal my phone and lie about it.

Charlie was the answer. She blamed herself for her father's death. She had failed to warn him about the termites and he had died because of it. Over time, the burden of guilt intensified until one day she snapped. Warped logic. She had killed her father, and she desperately needed to change that fact. She last saw him in a fire. Maybe he was still there.

And so it began. House after house burned to the ground.

But her dad never returned.

Investigators eventually profiled the arsonist and deciphered the cellphone diversion. Time had called for drastic measures. She needed to burn down her own house to free her from suspicion. She'd become victim twelve instead of suspect one. And now she had moved in with me and *my* cellphone was missing.

The arsonist never waited more than a day after stealing a phone, so I set my plans: proper planning prevents poor performance.

Charlie would find her father, or die trying.

Fire raged across the basement floor. Charlie must have smelled the smoke as soon as she came home. I was in my fireproof gear—heavy boots and coveralls, the stuff I stole from the local firehouse one night almost a year ago. I strolled through the flames with a small tank of fuel in one hand and that strange cellphone in the other.

"Danny?" Charlie said.

"Yes, sweetheart," I said, grinning. "It's daddy."

"Danny, what are you doing?"

The smoke thickened.

"It's time for you to save your daddy, sweetheart. Why do you look so surprised? Shouldn't you be happy to see me after all these years?"

Charlie crinkled her eyes and shook her head, but didn't speak.

"I guess it doesn't matter. Take the phone, call me, warn me about the fire."

"Danny, we need to go."

She waved a hand at the flames.

"No. You're the arsonist," I said and presented the evidence to her as I had done so craftily in my head earlier.

Pain welled in her eyes.

"How can you say that?"

I burst out laughing.

"Because *I'm* the arsonist and it was all going so well until the police showed up. I couldn't figure it out either. Then it hit me. I've become sloppy. The system was simple: steal a cellphone, call 9-1-1, throw the phone into the fire. Imagine my horror when I realized I made the last call from *my own phone*."

Charlie looked stunned as I continued the confession.

"Police were here today. They asked about my father because the house is still in his name. The phone was in his name, too. They asked about you because you recently changed your address. They don't know enough about me yet, but they will. I don't want that to happen. I'm having too much fun. Your flaming hair, the flames around us. It's what keeps this relationship going for me."

She began to dry heave.

"You have to sacrifice yourself, Charlie. You'll be the arsonist tragically killed by your own dementia. I'll be heartbroken, but I'll recover. I'll go to the police and tell them why you did it. I'll tell them how your mind was sick, how you thought you could still find your dead father. The case will close, and I'll be free to move on to bigger and brighter things. So, save me, Charlie. Save me the way you couldn't save your dad. I promise that you'll be at peace with him." I held the phone out to her. "Make the call."

Charlie hesitated. Our eyes met—tears filled hers, fire fueled mine. Suddenly, her face distorted, and she finally saw me for who I was—a desperate man trying to kill her.

I had planned for this reaction.

All the planning in the world couldn't have prepared me for what happened next.

Charlie raised a fist and pummeled my shoulder. I grabbed her arm and flung her. The blaze was all around us and she passed through the inferno like a deranged firewalker, hit the wall and bounced back. She fell at my feet. Blood trickled from her nose. Tears streamed from her eyes, but they weren't enough to extinguish the fire crying around her.

I put the phone to her ear.

"It's ringing."

"White bugs… termites… Daddy," Charlie said in a daze.

"Your dad's dead. That *presence* you felt in the basement? That was gasoline fumes from my tank."

"He'll save me," Charlie said.

"He's dead. He can't help you."

And then he *did* help her. A cold, angry draft knocked me back and in the same moment lifted her off the burning floor. In a dozen fires the cops knew about, and a few others they didn't, I had never felt cold.

Charlie had called it a presence—the embers of dead love.

I say the fire was alive.

The cold blast swirled around us. Invisible hands swept Charlie onto the stairs and out of danger. Her feet, moving under the force of the unseen power, thumped against each step as she ascended, an eerie, hollow *thud, thud, thud.*

She reached the top and paused—half-conscious.

"Danny?" she said in a voice barely audible over the cracking.

The walls and ceiling were in flames.

I stood flatfooted, too astounded to chase her.

"Yes?"

"I never told you about the white bugs."

"Yes you did. You saw them years ago, when your house burned down."

"No, the ones I saw this morning…"

BRIGHTER HER AURA GROWS

DAVID HEARN

I LOVE YOU.

Her words are soundless; they pierce through me like daggers. Her love is pointed, intense.

Do you love me?

I'm thrusting against her, absorbed by the feel of her glistening, sweat-slicked skin moving against mine. Drowning in my senses, I fail to answer.

Do you love me? She calls again, more fervently.

More than anything, I think.

So close now. She lies passive, waiting for me to complete—for her the pleasure is in the seduction, not in the act itself. I close my eyes, concentrating on the intensity of our combined heat and smell; it's an almost feral odor, animalistic, and beneath that, something else, something base and lurid—intermingling raw aromas of both life and death.

Dark thoughts rise, but I push them away. I immerse myself further in her shimmering red glow. The humming sound again—it fills the air around us, a vibrant, seemingly electric charge that fills my head as I grow nearer, clouding my senses.

They wouldn't understand, she pleads. *They would take me.*

I open my eyes to find hers staring through me, drowsy from lust. And then I'm there. I buck against her fiercely, locked in our tangle of ecstasy, all sounds and smells of us amplified in my head as I empty inside her, pulsing, convulsing.

When I'm through, she releases me.

I climb up weakly, the exhilaration of the moment already fading, not bothering to dress but padding immediately across the cabin floor. My normal senses are returning, and already I feel the familiar pang of nausea and growing revulsion—the dawning realization of what she truly is—as I hurry to escape her presence.

(*come to me never leave never—*)

She's probing, tendrils of thought creeping out, grasping urgently at mine. But as I reach the porch, moving into the purifying wash of afternoon sunlight, I feel her retreat. Her pleadings grow distant before fading away altogether.

Blissful silence.

It's sweltering outside, but the faintest summer breeze helps to clear my head as I gaze through the deathly stillness of the forest around us. The stir escalates, a welcome breath of relief that washes over me. My own thoughts return, even as the last evidential moisture of us slowly evaporates away from me, cleansing. She can't come here, I reassure myself, *never* into the openness of daylight. Admittedly, the thought gives me some small sense of satisfaction.

It gives me hope.

This semblance of escape is only temporary, though. She bides these moments of my release safe in the knowledge that I'll return—that I'll *always* return to her—and she knows this with absolute certainty. As do I. Because I *do* love her, you see.

And because true love never dies.

How long have we been here?

The question comes to me as I stumble weakly up the path, a deer trail possibly, made more prominent by my recent days of travel. The path meanders ahead through thick underbrush, beneath a continuous canopy of vine-choked pines and oaks. *So fucking hot!* There's an alarming sense of heat radiating from me, and the erratic drumming of my heartbeat in my head only adds to the dizzying sensation.

Alone, surrounded by miles and miles of endless, uninhabited nothingness.

My inner voice: *You'll die here.*

Strangely, I feel detached from the notion. It's as if my mind refuses to fully comprehend what's happening; I'm starving—no, *ravenous* is a more accurate description—considering I haven't eaten anything of real sustenance, not since she abducted me into this Godforsaken wilderness. Lately, the only thing I can think of (aside from my relentless thoughts of her) is food. Every shitty on-the-run meal I can ever remember now seems like a feast.

The trail ahead grows steeper, a sudden escalated pitch that threatens to drain what little energy I have left. *Almost there.*

Pushing forward mechanically, I ignore the faltering weakness in my legs. Occasionally I swat at some obstructing vine with my rusted machete. I salvaged it out of the rotted shed behind the cabin days ago, and carry it with me wherever I go, my own little totem. Wasted energy to swing at vines, probably, but I'm already in over my ahead, so what's the difference? On the path ahead, two dragonflies pace ahead of me, darting and spinning about in courtship or battle, their buzzing drone flickering through the otherwise stillness of the forest.

Who knew that such isolated places could still exist?

Hunger resounds again, this time as a sudden, sharp cramp that wracks my sides. It's serious enough to cause a hitch in my breath. I consider stopping for a moment, but if I do I'm afraid I won't find the strength to start again.

How long have we been here?

Still no answer.

Time has become abstract, hours and days blending together immeasurably. Every night with her is an eternity.

A week, maybe more, although I can't honestly say.

More alarming than the food shortage is the lack of water. I'm down to seven bottles. I've been keeping an eye out for a stream or brook, *any* source at all, but so far all I've found is one small pool at the base of a ravine off the main trail, mucky warm and stagnant. The smell of it is God-awful, like swamp water, most certainly diseased. Hopefully, something more promising will turn up. These are mountains. Aren't there supposed to be streams?

You could find the car, my inner voice reasons. It's barely a whisper, but with the passing days it's become more frequent and pleading. *Chances are it's where you left it, tucked away out of sight, not two miles from here. Keys still in the ignition! You go and you find it, you drive to the nearest store. Hell, you passed half a dozen mom-and-pop convenience stores on the way—*

I shrug the thought away. No good. She'd never allow it.

The summit appears, and just in the nick of time as both of my calves are cramping fiercely. I reach the top and catch my breath, gazing out over the treetops to a miasmic sea of green that rolls forever into the horizon. Nothingness so far as the eye can see.

I'm the last human alive.

Enough with dire thoughts. I glance around for the stone that I've set as my marker, and eventually spot it—a large, weathered chunk of dirty white quartz jutting from the forest floor several yards away. I move beyond it, finding the thin indentation in the forest floor of what I hope is a rabbit trail, to where I've set the spring trap. Nothing.

I push carefully through the underbrush, stooping for a closer look. The leaves I'd spread over the trip wire are undisturbed, same as they were before. Maybe the design is wrong, which is altogether possible considering how little I remember about this sort of thing;

it's been more than a few years, admittedly, since my scouting days. I tug gently at the small bowed tree attached to my tripwire, testing—it feels okay, so far as I can tell. The sapling end, which I've notched and connected to a fitted stake, seems okay, not so tight that it won't trip. Even the snare, cut from a roll of mesh wire I'd found at the cabin, seems adequately set. Everything appears fine.

Everything *is* fine. Only no animals.

There's got to be something I can do. Anything...

She'll let you go; she *has* to.

An unsettling vision: her lying naked in the sweltering darkness of the cabin, eyes fixed catatonically on the ceiling above, waiting...

I struggle to shake the image from my head. Got to concentrate on the moment, figure out exactly what the hell I'm going to do. Honestly, there's nothing that I can do, except hope for the best and check again tomorrow.

Hope seems to be the only asset in abundant supply, but the way things are going, that may soon be gone as well.

Dusk is setting in by the time I arrive back at the cabin. I rummage through the meager stock of supplies—cans of soup, corned beef, tuna, and sardines, a half-eaten bag of salted jerky, plus an array of various condiment packages. The jerky looks inviting, as does the rest of it, and the crazy itch to dive in—fuck rationing, just eat everything now in one great, small feast—is more than a little tempting. In the end, though, sanity prevails, and I settle for the can of sardines, along with the few remaining packs of stale crackers.

I eat on the porch and stare out into the dusk-darkening woods; all linear, crooked shadows on this empty border of God's vast creation. Cicadas hum, a symphony that appropriately marks the solitude. Under different circumstances, it might seem peaceful here. A serene sort of beauty.

My Love, she calls.

I ignore her, continuing to eat, and secretly relish the control. The taste of food has given me enough energy to push her out, but only for so long.

I toss the empty sardine can on the porch, a dull metallic clang that jars the silence. An idea occurs to me: I could use the sardine can as bait for the spring trap. Fish oil is fairly pungent stuff; it's bound to attract something.

My stomach churns. The sardines barely whet my appetite—hardly an appetizer under normal circumstances—but already that discomfort fades. There's another craving building in me now.

Come to me. Her call is urgently growing, a hypnotic chant that silently dances interlaced between my own thoughts. *Come to me, my Love, come to me, come—*

After a moment, I stand—mindful to retrieve the sardine can, lest it be scavenged in the night—and look out into the darkening forest. I'm slipping into her world again. I can feel her aura, a powerful and brilliant red burning behind me through the walls of the cabin, grasping at mine, urging.

There'll be no escape, not for hours; but even that fear dissolves as her thoughts—narcotic and oddly blissful—invade.

She's still calling as the last rays of the day shimmer away. Eventually, I return inside to the mindless comfort of her embrace.

Inside her—absorbed by her—once again.

Her eyes devour me while glazed in fathomless thought. Her blonde hair cascades in streams of shimmering gold. I'm thrusting violently against her, repetitively, thoughtless, wishing desperately for it to end, but I'm still rock hard and brutish.

She grips me like a glove, teeming, sucking at my very soul. Wispy curls of light emanate from her and dance on the outskirts of my lesser field of blue, fingers of mist reaching in for a taste, leaching life from me for her own renewed, fantastical brightness.

Do you love me?

I do, God, yes! Tears well, clouding my vision, both from fear and pain, but also from this enormity of truth: because I do love her, more than anything. More than life itself.

The intensity of the moment pushes through me, surging forward in an unstoppable wave. I withdraw at the last moment, convulsing uncontrollably, locked in contortions of heaving climax as she waits, silently accepting.

I lower myself onto her, pulling her close. It's nighttime now, no daylight in which to escape—we're in her element, and so I remain. I can feel myself, still inflamed and throbbing, between the sticky pressing of our flesh. Her possessing aura scorches me.

Do you love me?

More than ever, I want to reassure her, despite the dreams that will no doubt come, as they do every night at her bidding. Dreams that will vaguely be remembered but prove to be no less unsettling—visions of darkness and pain and death. And suffering, such supreme suffering. She'll be there at my side, of course, her hand clasped around mine as she ushers me through, whispering cold truths in my ear, helping me to see...

The dreams will be later, though.

Her thoughts carouse inside my head, echoing the same insistent question over and over, whispers that won't fade: *Do you love me? Do you love me? Do you—?*

The night is still young. If previous evenings are any indication, I'll answer her many times before morning.

Another day. And the trap is empty. Yet again.

It's been two days since rigging the sardine can to the snare line, but still no luck. *Something's* been curious here, though; the can's been licked clean, and now lies upended, stretched to the end of its tether—just not far enough to have allowed success.

Not a particularly welcome outcome, considering the last of my food stash is gone this morning. I'd saved the jerky for last, eating the scant remaining pieces slowly, savoring their flavor before digging out the shredded remnants and salty residue from the bottom corners of the bag, sucking my fingers zealously like some crazed, unweaned infant.

And now my next meal—if there is one—will come from the trap. Do or die, that's the motto now. Although the latter is beginning to look far more likely.

She's not with me now, at least there's that. She lingers in the back of my thoughts, though, like some dark, malignant pulse. I picture her surrounded in her blood red brilliance, her aura reaching out to smother me...

How did this happen?

Why me?

A fragment of memory: that morning at *Sammy's* café on the corner of Fifteenth and Union. A morning indistinguishable from any other, with the usual sea of anonymous suits and soccer moms and others biding the morning rush, waiting for their morning fixes of caffeine and sugar before scurrying off into oblivion. Through that sea of monotonous faces she'd appeared out of nowhere, brushing past me close enough to smell the faintest trace of her perfume, a fleeting, almost unobservant gaze thrown at me—her sultry eyes being what I remember most clearly—followed by a polite, almost dismissive smile that tugged at something within me, beckoning.

And then she was gone.

In that glimpse, I'd felt something subversive: an eerie, almost electric sense of raw power that was both unsettling and arousing. Days passed, and still I couldn't shake the thought of her. She was with me constantly, this stranger from nowhere. I'd gone about my life, but I felt her presence throughout the city, like a treasured riddle's answer waiting to be discovered, obscured amongst the hundreds of thousands of nameless faces.

She called to me, waiting for me to pursue. Which, of course I had. All the way to this empty corner of the world.

What is she?

Such dangerous questions. *You know what she is,* I think solemnly, pushing the thought quickly away. Some things are best left unnamed. Some riddles best left unsolved...

I'm prodding the can with my finger, *clink! clink!* The frail noise radiates through the surrounding silence. Not that there's anyone to notice. I'm running out of ideas, and not sure how many more days I can survive at this rate.

There is one final option, one that I've tried hard not to think about. My gaze falls to the machete clasped in my hand, glimmering sunlight.

I can envision pulling the blade across my throat—the initial wall of shock and crisp, overwhelming pain—before blissful nothingness...

Not just yet.

Tomorrow, I think. *Please, God. Tomorrow...*

There's a man at the cabin when I return.

I stand frozen at the base of the trail, watching him with dumbfounded amazement. It's been so long since I've had contact with any living person.

As I watch, the figure—very real, I've decided, and oblivious to my presence—knocks loudly on the cabin door. The rapping echoes through the surrounding emptiness. When there's no answer, he wanders to one of the cabin windows, cupping his hands to his face to shield against afternoon glare.

A wave of panic—hers as well as mine—surges through me

(NO DON'T LET HIM DON'T—!)

and then he turns and notices me. His face blooms a hearty, cherubic smile as he ambles down the steps in easy strides, hollering greetings.

Her screams in my head are disorienting. All I can do is wait like a deer in headlights. Through her panic, though, comes my own sense of overwhelming elation. *Saved!* I'm thinking.

Thank God, Oh thank God—!

The name's Dan Haverty, he introduces himself, extending a hefty hand. Hesitantly, I shake. His grip is overly strong. I hear my name, and realize that I've spoken aloud—my voice weak and broken, but irrefutably mine. How long since I've heard myself speak?

It occurs to me how I must look—unshaven, emaciated physically to nearly nothing, my clothes ragged and stained—but, if this stranger (Haverty, I remind myself) notices, he doesn't let on.

He's too busy rattling on about how friggin bad this heat is, can you believe it? as he shakes his head in good-natured disbelief. He's continually blotting his reddened face with his sleeve shoulders as he drones on endlessly. The knee-length khaki shorts and hiking boots don't have much wear, and his green chambray shirt is a poor choice, much too bulky given the current conditions, as evidenced by the impressive sweat stains across his neck and chest. Judging from his impressive girth, shortness of breath, and the overall paleness of his arms and legs, it's a good bet Dan is not an experienced outdoorsman.

She's still screaming inside my head, and I struggle in vain to push her out. The elation has dissipated, though, replaced with a sense of danger, an instinctive urge to protect *her*.

Haverty is telling me about his week-long vacation and the cabin he's rented, which isn't two miles from me, and isn't it beautiful here, even if it is too friggin hot to enjoy a simple afternoon walk, which sucks because he's trying to get out and lose some weight, a little vigorous exercise like the old days, don't you know? Meanwhile, the whole time he's babbling, I'm fighting against the thick pounding pulse in my throat.

She's building inside me, frantic, overpowering.

(—LET HIM DON'T LET HIM DON'T—!)

Coldness settles through me. I understand what I must do.

The machete hangs at my side and I grip it tightly, my fingers writhing anxiously across the handle, wanting to react. Too many loose ends, though; if he were to suddenly disappear, who's to say someone wouldn't come looking for him?

But then there's an awkward lull in his monologue, followed by seconds of silence. I see the dawning expression of someone considering something that's not quite right. His gaze has wandered back to the cabin, to its warped porch and sagging roof, to the rotting piles of debris and straw clogging the corners of the porch, and across the dusted, no-longer-opaque window panes. His brow crinkles in concern.

(NOW NOW DO IT NOW!)

He's turned back, that offset expression aimed at me, and my pulse escalates, my heart drumming in my ears.

Who am I renting from? he asks. I recognize his tone: not a question borne out of suspicion, but one of neighborly concern.

It takes a moment to utter some fictitious name. I tell him it's a small agency outside of Atlanta. He shakes his head, gives a knowing laugh, tells me I don't have to tell *him* about friggin slumlords, he knows the deal, which leads him into an enthusiastic sales pitch on what an unbelievable place he's scored: a full mahogany bar, flat screen televisions in every room including the john, an outdoor Jacuzzi, the works. And all very affordable. He can drop a business card by another day if I want, no problem, he assures me.

That would be fine, I hear myself say, even managing to force a smile. The unspent adrenaline coursing through me has left me trembling. My grip on the machete is loose, like it might slip.

Our conversation has reached its end, and even Haverty seems to know it. Two miles back, he tells me, squinting eastward, and lets me know that 'back' is the hardest leg of the run. I nod agreeably, give him a parting shake.

Halfway up the slope, he hollers back an invitation for me to stop by his place sometime, to come check things out. I assure him that I will. And then he's huffing away. I study him until he crests the hill and ambles out of sight.

I consider chasing after him. What if he discovers that there's no rental in this vicinity? That would undoubtedly cause problems.

So what? Most likely he'll assume you're a squatter, some homeless person taking advantage of an abandoned dwelling. Which isn't far from the truth. All the more reason for him to avoid me in the future.

She's fallen silent now, I realize, but she's been watching—fearful, childlike—through my eyes. *Everything's all right,* I think to her soothingly. Our intimate universe of two has been restored.

Coming, my love.

As I climb the cabin steps, it dawns on me that my last chance at salvation has just walked away from here, most likely forever.

I'm poised above her, bathed in the basking glow of her brilliant color as we entangle. The room hums with her presence. I can feel myself dissipating, her tentacles of red enveloping me, penetrating. There's no pain, though; she's taken that from me as reward—no hunger, no dread, no fear of death or of missed opportunities.

Her embrace is bliss.

I am sedated.

It's the middle of the night when I awaken.

By the pale moonlight that bathes the interior of the cabin, I can make out her nude form on the mattress next to me. Her eyes are open—catatonically fixed on the ceiling above.

Off in other worlds.

Her complete absence, the sudden empty chasm of my own unadulterated thoughts, crashes through me so forcefully that for a moment I can hardly breathe. This is my chance.

I rise stealthily, making my way toward the cabin door. Every fiber of my being is screaming for me to run, but I fight the urge, forcing myself to move slowly. Despite my efforts at silence, each step sounds sharply beneath me, amplified pops and creaks that cause my heart to climb into my throat. I'm still nude, I realize halfway across the room, but there's nothing I can do. There's no turning back.

And then I'm outside, racing into the forest, racing to freedom through the barrage of sharp, stinging undergrowth. The brush is so thick that moonlight is of little help. Branches slice at my face, lash across my arms and legs as I surge forward blindly. My left heel slices open on something—a rock, or an edge of stump—but I don't stop. Pain is secondary to desperation, this hope of escape.

I'm heading east, that's all I know, toward the highway. Somewhere nearby, my late-model Lincoln Continental awaits, abandoned beneath a pile of branches well off the main roadway. If I can make it before she realizes I'm gone...

How far can she reach?

I'm barely aware that I'm sobbing as I tear through the underbrush. Already it feels like I've been running for hours. If I can just find the main roadway—

My Love?

Her waking voice flutters through me. Panicked, I freeze. The ensuing silence is deafening, as if silence would ever be enough to conceal me from her. And then I feel her tentacles probing, reaching across the vast distance, reconnecting to me, and her realization of what I've done—

MY LOVE!

Her scream wracks me over in pain. I collapse to my knees onto the forest floor, sobbing openly now. *Please,* I plead silently, *please don't—*

No my love never leave me never...

She isn't capable of love, not in any human sense.

I push her away, determined not to answer. While most of my mind is engaged with hers, there's still that small voice in the back of my mind—weak, but still alive—screaming at me to get up, to get up and run, keep going—

Do you love me?

A familiar tightening in my groin. I'm swelling to life again at just the thought of her.

—never won't leave me you won't—

I can't, I think to her, *PLEASE I CAN'T! NO...!*

She's miles away, and yet I still feel her fingers brushing against me, delicate as butterfly wings, coaxing me into this agonizing frenzy. I'm reaching down, rubbing at myself, more to appease the painful throbbing than for pleasure. *Please, no please—*

Do you love me?

No time to answer, because already I'm there. I cry aloud, jettisoning across the prickly bed of wet rot and mulch, silver flits in the moonlight, my entire body writhing and contorting uncontrollably.

Come to me.

I finish and fall to the ground, curling into a fetal position. Even with my eyes clenched, her aura overwhelms me, a kaleidoscope of twisting brightness. I'm painfully hard, and it pulses with some seemingly maddening, resilient life of its own, impossibly engorged and ready again, craving her to no ends.

Come to me, my love.

My body is a tapestry of lashes stinging with sweat. I look up through a thick canopy to the moon overhead. Her image is there, faint but irrefutable: a gleaming, iridescent skull, hauntingly beautiful. Ever seeing. Ever watchful.

The small voice of inner reason is gone. Numbly, I turn toward the cabin, stumbling through the darkness to return to her.

Days now...

Or has it been weeks? Not sure anymore. There doesn't seem to be much left of me, in either a physical or mental sense. I feel like a hollow shell, dissipating, sinking slowly into the depths of some dismal, groggy sea.

I stumble up the trail in what's come to feel like my own personal recreation of the Bataan death march. Every step is a small miracle at this point; it's all I can do to keep my legs from faltering. In the days following my attempt at escape, she's refused to let me leave, kept me with her constantly. Finally—albeit reluctantly—she's let me go, no choice on her part, really; it's simple logistics: if I die, she dies.

A choir of whispering phantom thoughts fill my head at times. Sometimes I catch myself answering them. Time also seems to be slipping away, disappearing in inexplicable gulps. I'll snap to, startled out of a daze, wondering where I am, and then the reality of it all comes crashing in again.

Is this insanity? If not, then I'm dangerously close.

My ribs have become so tightly stretched against my skin that there's chafe marks in places where my shirt has rubbed me raw. I've been running a high fever for days, a nagging, constant chill I can't shake, despite that it's a hundred fucking degrees. I ran out of water two days ago. I think that's affected me more drastically than the lack of food. I can't think straight. I feel constantly flushed, my skin sinisterly warm, like dry paper left too long next to flame.

I returned to the stagnant pool this morning. Brushing a thin film of scum and leaves away from the surface—tiny wiggling bodies, thousands of them, mosquito larvae—and without thinking, like a stupid brazen dare you just hope to get through, I'd cupped my hands together, lifted the water, drank. The taste was indescribably foul. I got down about a dozen handfuls but can't say I feel much better.

My ankle suddenly falters—a misstep on some obscure piece of debris in the path—and I flail forward, arms windmilling, barely avoiding a face-plant on the trail.

Watch where you're going! Concentrate!

The near miss snaps me back to reality. I'd hate to imagine what a broken bone or a concussion might mean at this point. A game-ender, that's for certain.

The summit of the peak lies ahead, and relief floods through me. *Not there yet, pal,* I warn myself. Got to keep focus. One foot in front of the other, steady as she goes.

Why me?

And then the memory: her fleeting glance through the crowd, eyes so innocent, and the alluring, lingering trace of perfume.

You know what she is.

I *do* know. The truth sits in my subconscious like some lurking beast slumbering in shadow on the verge of revealing itself.

You know you know what she is you know—

A high-pitched chattering ahead.

The trap!

I scramble up the remaining trail to see an enormous raccoon hanging tethered from the snare by a single hind leg. It arches up at my approach, tiny black eyes absorbing me, before thrashing about in renewed panic.

Howling in triumph, I rush forward and I'm met by a whirlwind of vicious swipes. I stumble back, ribbons of red blooming across my forearm, but I'm too elated to feel any pain. I charge in again, this time swinging. The raccoon stiffens at the initial blow from my machete, stunned, and then amazingly, despite the fact that I've nearly sheared it in half, it begins to flail about wildly, screaming now—God help me, it sounds like human screams—but I don't care, not any more. I swing again, and again.

With a shuddering spasm, it finally goes limp.

I'm laughing madly as I rush in, scooping up the dangling carcass, its liquid warmth cascading down my arms. The matted, bloody fur up close is nearly overwhelming, but not enough to stop me from eating. I'm tearing at the flesh, swallowing in huge greedy gulps, the rancid, coppery taste nearly gagging me, but I can't stop, not now. Despite the inner feeling of revulsion it's the best goddam thing I've ever tasted in my life, and all I can think of is killing the hunger, this insane feeling of hunger, and I realize that I'm no longer laughing but crying, huge sobs that come between choking breaths as I continue eating—only they're tears of relief, tears of joy...

I *will* see another day.

For her, of course.

All for her...

Several hours later, and I'm almost back to the cabin.

It's amazing how much difference a single meal can make, especially to a starving man. The shakes are gone, and I actually feel an emerging sense of new energy. Still not out of the woods yet, by any means (make that literally *and* figuratively, haha) although I'm leagues beyond where I was this morning. Even though I'm on the final upward ascent of trail before the homestead, I keep focus—one wrong step might still prove to be my *coup de grâce.*

I saved something for tonight. The remains of the raccoon hang across my shoulder, flopping lifelessly with my stride.

My stomach still lurches a bit uneasily at the thought of how this recent sense of fullness has been acquired. What is it I'm feeling, exactly? Shame? Guilt? Fuck all of that. There's no shame in survival. I've only just learned the enormity of that truth very recently.

You ate too much. That's all. My stomach does feel painfully distended, but Christ, all arguments aside, doesn't it feel good to have energy again! More importantly, I can actually think now.

Which brings me back to other issues...

I've crested the final hill, and below I can see the roof of the cabin through the dense tree line. As if on cue, I feel her thoughts reaching out, trying to meld into mine.

Not too hard to push her away, though, not at this moment. I'm too absorbed in anticipation of tonight. A second meal, only this time done right. Plus I've reset the trap, so who knows, if my luck holds—

I freeze when I reach the edge of the clearing, my pulse climbing into my throat.

The cabin door is open.

And at that very moment, a high-pitched scream.

The piercing cry unlocks me. Flinging the carcass from my shoulders, I bolt in panic across the clearing, leap the porch steps in one adrenaline-filled stride, and nearly collide with him as he's scrambling from the cabin—it's Haverty, my friend from the other day, the one with the overly assertive handshake, only he doesn't look too capable of one of those power shakes at the moment, oh not at all. His cherubic expression has been replaced by one of disheveled, whitened shock. He goes rigid at the sight of me, eyes swimming with terror, and I don't need to hear her screams to know what he's seen.

I swing the machete, burying it solidly in his neck. He emits a hoarse grunt, begins to keel drunkenly to one side. His eyes, still fixed on me, hold a stunned look of disbelief even as he collapses lifelessly onto the porch. Silence.

She's silent, too, I realize with growing horror. Her absence claws through me like some inevitable blunt force of truth

(*no oh no NO—!*)

and as I stagger into the sweltering stench of the cabin, I know her spell is broken.

I can make out her lifeless, bloated form in the rank darkness, arms and legs splayed as if in some mock crucifixion, or of some lewd invitation of embrace. The thick, droning buzz of flies clouds the air around her. As I stagger nearer I can see the rigid, gaping O of her mouth—those precious lips that I've kissed passionately so many times—now a frozen scream of overflowing pale, wiggling flecks that cascade down her blackened face and body, a million singular dances that collectively seem to make her shimmer.

I collapse at her side, suffocating in terror and realization, fighting to take a breath that won't seem to come. I look pleadingly to her, to those eyes—or to where they once were; only jutting, empty sockets of blackness now.

I remember those eyes—that loving gaze, and how they once shined.

Oh, God, I remember—

those eyes, staring up at me.

I'm pressing against her warm, supple flesh, moving against her with quickening urgency. The faint thumping of bar music plays distantly, marked by the occasional loud banter of college kids escaping into the night. I'm slick with sweat from this god-awful heat, but mostly from the adrenaline, and from the thrill of the moment.

Streetlights in the alleyway illuminate the interior of the Lincoln backseat with a pale glow, enough to reveal her shocked expression as she stares up at me, doe-eyes frozen in terror.

Despite her drowning look of fear, I see the potential in those eyes. So innocent and beautiful and vibrant, so full of life.

You could love me, *I want to tell her.*

She begins to moan. It's a guttural, rasping sound, terrified, on the verge of growing into a scream.

My hands are fumbling to enclose the soft, delicate skin of her neck. I can feel the muscles of her throat convulse as I begin to squeeze. Her eyes widen with realization, searching for answers. Why? *they seem to ask, pleading, but the futility of it only makes me squeeze tighter.*

It's okay, *I whisper softly to her.* Everything's okay. I'm here—

I can't help but be distracted by a growing sense of anger. Anger from seemingly nowhere, fury and love intertwined. Bitch! Fucking BITCH! *My hands are vice-like around her throat, shaking with rage. Doesn't she understand the lengths I've gone to, watching her for days on end, craving the feel of her, to know the smell of her? Doesn't she understand something has inexplicably drawn her to me—has drawn us together—and that I'd do anything in the world for her? That I would protect her at any cost. Can't she see—?*

Life—so slowly—dissolving from her gaze, smoldering away like the last flickering rays of daylight over a distant horizon.

The intensity of that moment, that balance on the edge of life and death, pushes me to climax, and I arch against her viciously, my hands releasing her. The ecstasy seems to last an eternity, never ending, but for her it's too late.

You could love me. You could love me YOU COULD—!

And then the memory slips away, hurtling me back to grim reality.

Oh dear God! What have I done?

I flail at the mattress, panicked and screaming, tearing at everything around me, fighting the smothering void closing around me. She can't be gone. She can't—!

My love… her voice echoes from memory.

It's too late, though, the illusion is broken.

"OH GOD!" I scream uncontrollably. "I'M SO SORRY!"

I fall to the floor, gasping, choking for breath in the growing, stagnant blackness.

Do you love me?

Even now I can hear her voice, the one that's played inside my head for so long—only a memory now—but it seems too strong, too real...

Do you love me?

Slowly, bewildered, I raise up to look at her.

She's here again, not some imagined remnant from the past, but *her*. She greets me with a knowing smile, eyes as radiant as ever. My look of terrified and overwhelming confusion seems to amuse her, because she crimps her mouth in that pouting way, that little intimate gesture of hers that I've come to adore; it's a combined look of pity and involuntary laughter, almost as if to say *you silly boy.*

I thought you were gone! I break into fresh sobs, only now they're ones of relief. I pull her to me, hugging her close. I can feel her warmth, the soft beat of her heart.

Her wafting words: *I'll never leave you. And you'll never leave me?*

No, I promise. *Not ever. Not EVER!*

Silently, she urges me to her. Her body tenses in anticipation of my touch. Her perfect breasts are bare, ripe and sun-kissed golden. Her taut stomach ripples as her hips move in that rhythmic, undulating way. Her fragrance, delicate yet powerful, so sensual and animal-like, wafts over me, through me. Oh God, anything for her!

Come to me.

I slip once again into her embrace. The warmth of her is blissfully familiar, like being home. And at that moment, I know what she says is true. I will never leave her. I will always protect her. We will always be together.

Always.

Because true love never dies…

UNDERWATER

BARRY JAY KAPLAN

IT WAS MY IDEA to drive down. Doctor Berman was against it, said maybe I wasn't so ready yet, said it maybe wouldn't do me any good but I said Doc it's their anniversary Doc, I said. I gotta, right? I pack smart: a couple of shirts that's easy to drip and dry if I stay in motels on the way which is kind of inevitable, a pair of jeans, a pineapple shirt straight out of *Hawaii 5-0*, a fave, and a pair of sharkskin slacks I lay out neat on the back seat so the crease stays sharp in case I'm ever in the position where I have to look like someone who knows the difference between a glass of beer and a Stoli on the rocks, not that I do but it's the look that counts. I've been working on my pecs too, so an open-necked shirt really shows off the goods. I see myself walking into a bar a Tiki bar a bar with a palm tree décor and mai tai cocktails and ceiling fans and tight skirts slit to…

I'm holding a little umbrella between my teeth as I drive and I belch the sour taste of rum… A mai tai? Probably 'cause my pants pocket's lumpy, as when I jam in loose bills with a damp fist and don't iron and fold them later but who was the skirt…?

I take the main roads, the route mapped out with a phosphorescent marker so I can see it in the dark since I plan on driving till my eyelids droop. I told this to Doctor Berman and he was against that too. I said: Doc, you're discouraging me and I'm in a position I want to be propped up, I want to hear you say I'm on the right track going to see them and however I go is the way to go, see? So? DB laughed at that, I could always make him laugh, told me not to forget to pack my pills and here's one scrip extra especially if you're going to make the visit longer than a week or so which is the outside edge of what I have in mind. There's only so much contrition I can take before things start cracking with me and them.

Why you driving? It's dangerous. You still got a license? They didn't take it away? What if you get stopped? What if it starts to rain? What if the radio says tropical storm Marvin? What if when they pull you over you get one of your headaches? You have extra pills? Your doctor knows? What's that shirt supposed to be? What if they call me? What'm I supposed to say? You hopped up, sonny? You on something? I'm not covering for you. I'm through with that. How much you think I can take? You're on your own this time. We don't know you.

The damned radio doesn't stick with its signals. It's the wind it's the rain it's the damp it's the car. Rented. Fuck it.

They have a little condo on an artificial lake just above the Keys. Those condos kill me. No basement because of how all the building's done on coral reefs and if by chance there's heavy rain, there's a foot of water to slog through in your slippers. Last time I helped with the grunt work. He just sits there, man he's fat. She does the grunt work, crying half the time, him slapping her when she walks past, half the time half looped on lager. Place stinks like bleach, she's got a thing for germs or something. I bet she puts it in his Sanka. Her hands're red and raw. Hey, the condo's theirs so what's it got to do with me? They bought it when I was away. I wasn't part of the real estate consultation.

I'm doing 75, 80 without even thinking about it. When it's this dark you don't feel your feet or your hands, you don't hear anything, you're moving through space but you don't feel anything, next thing you blink and you're fifty miles from where you were the last time you looked and what the hell, what was I just thinking about? Blank. Another one. It's like being underwater. Can't wait.

This time's not going to be any different from last time but my scrip's new see, so things will be at least different on my upper end. When I get there, they seem glad to see me. *Seem glad* because they have a way of making me guess what's really up. Both of them have droopy eyelids, her from drink, him from fat, and sometimes it's hard to tell if they've even registered I'm present. Neither of them wears their glasses. Or their hearing aids. Or makes much use of the walkers I spent good money on time before that or time before that. Gratitude's not something I expect but would it be too much for her to run a church key around a can of beans or for him to offer me one of his unfiltered cigarettes like any buddy'd do? They both know what I like and the fact that it doesn't happen, that time stands still while we're looking each other up and down, that my needs aren't met even now, even after all this time, says to me they don't care even if they seem glad to see me.

The sun's setting red as blazes. Even dark glasses my eyes hurt. Route 1, right but how long have I been on it? I check the map and I'm much closer than I thought though still plenty far.

…I'm in the shower at a Motel 6 on a strip mall next to a Mobil station and it's raining and the television's on and where was I when all this happened? I use a generous amount of nasal spray and watch *Law and Order* to clear my head. It's where there's a double murder in an upstate condo. Blood blood blood. It's a rerun. I've seen 'em all half a dozen times apiece but these shows are worked out so even if you did see it before, you never know how whoever did it did it and how the *Law* part finds him and solves it.

I must have drowsed off because I just saw a sign for the scuba shop and hey right yeah, my mitts're on the wheel! Ten miles to the water!

When I'm in the water deep, deep in, and there's no sound, just blue, just warm…

Ever since I was a kid it's where I feel the most comfortable. Mom, I used to ask her, can anyone breathe underwater? No, she'd answer, so sure of herself. What about Mark Spitz the Olympic champion? Thinking I had her on that one. Uh uh, she says. What about Esther Williams the swimming movie star? I've seen her last ten minutes without coming up for air! No can do. Yeah, okay, but wouldn't it be great?

I can imagine what they'd say if they knew about scuba, how you put a tube in your mouth and a tank on your back and then, yes, you're breathing, ma. Breathing underwater, see? I'd like to see the look on her face. I'd like to stretch that smile right on her, slit the corners of her mouth so she's always smiling, so she quits with the uh uhs and the no ways and smiles at my questions and promotes my good will. And him, smiling from the shock of it, me, it, the news, the blows, the blues, the blood. Him too.

I'm at the Keys. Unbelievable. Five minutes ago I was sucking a mai tai… in the shower… watching *Law and…*

No that was yesterday or…

I pull over onto a gravel patch and check the pills because I'm a little confused and Berman says if confusion was to cloud my jungle I should make sure to take the blue lagoon and even that I should never let things get to that point but to keep track, to be a good boy and take my hydro regular so I don't get the headaches and so my eyes don't burn and so I can keep on track and not forget. The whole thing about not forgetting is that it involves remembering first not to forget in the first place which is like someone or other says, a challenge.

Davey Jones Locker, Cap'n Mike, Prop. That's a laugh. Such a cornball name but hey it's his boat and his equipment he rents out so as long as I'm wet and all tubed up scuba-wise, he's good old Cap'n Mike to me.

The water is clear as no water. I'm sinking very very slowly, not even trying to go under, just letting air out of the tube and feeling myself sink. Down below me there's coral and flanks of fish banking left and right, flicking gold to green, up then down, coming at me veering off. It's very quiet. It's really quiet.

Jesus Christ holds up his arms to me. Whoa! I jerk back. Bubbles pour out of my tube, my legs are cycling but I'm getting nowhere, I'm drifting down to Jesus with his arms outstretched like he's asking for a favor, like he's begging for air. I touch his hand then I'm screaming, then I'm streaming up, then I'm on the boat, then I'm being slapped, then I'm in a bar, then I'm in the car, then I'm at their house and there's police cars there and someone opens the door of my car and says who are you. I'm the son I'm the son. And I'm crying because I don't know how'd I get here, I'd like to know.

I'm standing in the doorway. The sun in the room is very bright. Your parents have been slaughtered. I see blood on the rug. I see blood splattering the walls and a familiar suitcase in the corner. What happened, I want to know.

Is this your knife? someone says. It looks familiar. Maybe I possess some passing knowledge, I say and he says he found it in the back seat of my car lying on a pair of sharkskin slacks and there's blood on it. I look back at the room the rug the splatters. I'm sinking again, the air's rushing up beside me and I'm just letting myself go. I wish I could tell you what happened. It would be a fun thing to remember.

EXPERIMENTS IN AN ISOLATION TANK

ERIC J. GUIGNARD

HE FLOATS *on the ocean surface, limbs splayed like a pinwheel. The water is cold, but the clear sky above him is hot. His back shivers while his chest burns. He rolls over to reverse the sensations. The current of the sea is slight, and he drifts. There are no waves. He is simply carried along by the lazy whim of the flat tide. Looking down through the purple water, he sees gigantic shapes that swim beneath. They are monsters, but they are far below. He can only discern blurry shadows darting past, larger than anything he has ever seen. One shape in particular sails under him, then circles, repeating the path, again and again. At each return, it seems to rise ever so slightly from the ocean depths, closer to him. The shape looks like a whale, but it has three long horns protruding from a head, like the barbs of a trident spear.*

The man is uncertain how long he has been in the water. The sun never goes down, never moves. It simply hangs in the sky like a golden eye staring in judgment upon him. The eye is ceaseless in its vision, and there are no clouds to cross over it. He remembers nothing before the ocean.

Looking at his own body, the man wonders how he came to be in this vast expanse. Curiously, he examines himself. He is light-featured and aged in mid-years and wears print shorts. There are no scars or other markings to give away stories of his life. He wears no wedding ring. He is alone.

The purple water sparkles and shimmers around him. It would be a beautiful sight to behold, were he not trapped in it. He drifts for a long time, rolling from his chest to his back, alternating between floating and swimming. He has no destination, but thinks the greater distance he travels, the increased chance he has to discover an escape from the frigid sea. His tired arms splash rhythmically and his legs kick like a sluggish motor. He swims, then he floats.

The black shadows pace his progress far below.

"The theta state of mind is one in which your consciousness is greatly expanded. You are completely relaxed, as if floating, untethered by the senses which so often betray us. You should feel inspiration and understanding and recall long-forgotten memories."

Chris gasped and opened his eyes, frantically splashing in ten inches of water. The lid of the tank was open, and Dr. Edwards spoke in a loose, monotone voice. He did not look at Chris as he spoke, but gazed down to a clipboard encumbered with stacks of loose notepaper and official-looking forms. Chris sat up and clenched at the sides of the isolation tank for support. The sea-smell of Epsom salt hung thick in the office like rotten brine.

Dr. Edwards turned to look at him over the top of delicate-rimmed glasses. "How do you feel, Chris? Refreshed? I know it may take a moment to acclimate yourself back into the real world, but the benefits of treatment should remain with you."

"That was horrible." Chris stepped out from the fiberglass-shaped egg, splashing water across the gray shale floor.

"Wait, let me get you a towel," Dr. Edwards said.

"What did you do to me in there? It feels like you left me in that thing forever."

"The treatment is only for one hour. See, it's four o'clock."

Looking up across marbled walls to an iron clock, Chris confirmed the time. He shook his head, flustered, and took the cotton towel, rubbing it through his hair. "I was floating in the ocean."

"Yes, people liken the sensation of the isolation tank to exactly that of floating in the ocean," Dr. Edwards said.

"There were things swimming below me. I don't know what

they were, but they were terrible things. Things that could swallow me if they rose from the depths."

"Oh, I see." The doctor turned back to his clipboard, bearing shambles of papers, and began scribbling frantic, looping notes. "Would you call them *formless* things? *Nameless* things?"

"I guess. I just knew I didn't want them to get any closer."

"How do you think that relates to why you're here?"

"Because I'm scared of something. I have this constant fear all the time. I still don't know what it is or why I feel this way."

"You fear something so great that you have submerged it deep within your subconscious. However, it is now leaking out and manifesting itself into phobias, imprisoning you alone in a life of insecurity and fright. What do you fear, Chris?"

As Dr. Edwards spoke, water pooled at Chris's feet and rolled across the floor. He noticed it first as runoff from his own soaked body, dripping where he stood. But the puddle grew, and it poured out over the edges of the isolation tank. Neon purple lights looped inside the rim of the tank in fluorescent coils, so the water spilling over appeared as a violet waterfall.

"Your tub's overflowing," Chris said.

The doctor looked to the tank and his face turned sour, as if moldy milk curdled in his mouth. "When you climbed out, you must have knocked something loose. Wait here and I'll turn the water off. The main valve's in the other room."

Edwards scurried through a plain door. He was a small man, wiry and bald, with thick bristling eyebrows like speckled caterpillars crawling above his eyes. He wore a yuppie's uniform: white slacks and a lemon-yellow cardigan, with the open collar of a peach shirt flowing out. When Chris first met him, he thought the doctor dressed like a meringue pie.

The purple water streaming from the tank increased in pressure like an uncapped hydrant. It shot at Chris, and he flinched.

"You turned it the wrong way, Doc!"

Christ on crutches, it's righty-tighty, lefty-loosey, Chris thought. *Everyone knows that.* The water quickly flowed to each wall of the room and began to rise, pooling over his ankles. *It isn't possible for water to rise so quickly in such a large space. It would take hours for that kind of build-up.* He splash-stepped to the door Edwards had hastily exited and found it locked.

Chris pounded on the door. "Hey, you locked me in here! Turn off the water!"

The water quickly filled the room, rising up his legs. Chris stumbled about, banging on each wall in turn and yelling out curses and pleas. The incandescent lamp in the center of the ceiling grew brighter. His towel floated past, mixing with medical charts and glass jars and photographs of his life. After scrambling through the rising tide, he stopped to stare in shock at the pictures as they drifted to him, pooling like flies swarming upon festering flesh.

The pictures were of him at all ages, candid and furtive. There he was as a boy, curled up under bed covers, staring one-eyed at the shadow creeping from his closet. Older, now a teenager, cowering in his doorway, afraid to cross the threshold. Early adult, an image revealed him sobbing in the bathroom, hands tightly pressed over his mouth to muffle cries. Scores of pictures floated past, each a portrait of his phobia or terror.

One picture edged above the others. He was a child, lying in the basement of his home, pins pushed through his chest, his fears bubbling out in release. He was being crushed with stones. He was being told to *be strong.*

The medical charts and glass jars began to sink through the water, falling below the surface to become blurry shadows. The office walls sank in on themselves, sliding so placidly under the sea that they left behind only ripples. The photographs remained. His father was in each one…

***

The man blinks. He is back in the ocean. He flails and swims a few strokes before lying prostrate in the purple water, allowing himself to float freely once again. The sun hangs motionless in the clear sky.

His name is Chris, and he wonders about his strange thoughts as he looks below.

The blurry shadows move beneath him. They have increased in number. The one with three horns circles higher now. Peering down through the murky depths, he can faintly make out markings upon its hide. It has the black-and-white coloring of an orca whale. Instead of a tail fin, the monster trails long sinewy tentacles, like those on a giant squid. Another shadow has risen as well. It is tubular and somewhat translucent, like a cavernous worm, with two separate heads that move in unison. The two heads morph into massive claws then back to heads again. The creatures do not threaten him as he drifts, but they rise, and Chris feels a foreboding take hold, like icy fingers choking him.

He does not want to see the blurry things swimming beneath, so he rolls onto his back. The warmth of the sun upon his chest is pleasant after the chill of the water. His back cools in the refreshing sea. Soon his chest will sear and his back will turn frigid. There is no respite but to turn over and over. Does everyone float alone in this great ocean?

Why is he here? What has happened to him? The man grapples for any fleeting clue. He knows nothing but his fears and the dream of a doctor. He floats on the surface and examines the horizon. It is a perfect line, encircling him like the rim of a bottle. Above the line lolls the clear sky and below is the purple water. He thinks of his mind, floating free like his body, and a rising image of a face comes to him, ascending from the depths.

"Sensory deprivation is the removal of stimuli that could otherwise mislead you. The sense of sight, sound, even gravity, are subjective perceptions which are shed in order to engage the clarity concealed within one's brain. This is achieved through the isolation chamber."

Chris gasped and opened his eyes, frantically splashing in ten inches of water. "Let me out of this damned thing!"

Dr. Edwards looked at him over the top of his glasses. "Is something the matter?"

"Jesus, yes! How'd you get me back in there?" Furious, he scrambled out of the fiberglass tank, stumbling to his knees and spilling purple-hued water.

"Back in there? It's only our first treatment. We've just begun."

"That's bullshit and you know it. I got out of there already and you locked me in here and I—I..." His voice trailed off as he looked around the room. There was no sign of any flooding, aside from the water he dripped onto the gray shale floor.

"Let me get you a towel," Dr. Edwards said.

"How long was I in there for?"

"Not long. The treatment is only forty-five minutes. Your brain slows while in the theta state of consciousness. Neurological activity is heightened to peaks you are not used to. It is an extraordinary realm to explore, your mind. The isolation tank allows you to live as if in a waking dream."

Chris wrapped the towel around his torso in a tight embrace, and glanced at the clock. "Screw me on Sunday, it was so real..."

"Tell me what you saw." The speckled caterpillars above Edwards's eyes crawled closer together in fascination as he wrote into his bound stack of papers.

"The monsters were getting closer. I was helpless."

"You are never helpless. Remember that."

Chris shivered and clenched the towel tighter as if to hide inside its cotton folds.

"I saw my father."

"Yes, Chris, yes!" Edwards's tone changed like a burst of orgasm. "We are making progress now!"

"I haven't thought of him in years."

"You have repressed memories of your father and he is the source of your fears, the monsters rising to you."

"He died when I was seven."

"Your father was a great man. Many people sought him for his wisdom."

"What are you talking about? My father was an asshole. I remember that he beat me every day. He—he experimented on me."

"You were too young to understand. He taught you strength, but you have since forgotten it. You hide your fears below a gruff exterior. You do not face your fears, and so your fears swim deep within. Inside, you are still a seven-year-old boy."

"I don't have to listen to this crap. You don't know what it was like with him. You don't have any idea what you're talking about."

Edwards's voice changed: "Gawwdammit, Chrissie, after all these years you haven't learned a thing, have you?"

Chris shrieked.

The voice was of his father: "You're scared again, aren't you?"

He knew he had been caught. He was a little boy again, cringing and wet under his father's shadow. "I'm sorry, Poppa, I'm trying to be strong!"

"Your lesson's not over yet." His father, in the lemon-yellow cardigan, hauled Chris up and pushed him back into the isolation tank. "Face your fears or they will swallow you!"

Chris wailed, and the clear lid crashed down, slamming his head forward into the water. He sobbed into blackness, choking on the salty brine…

The man lifts his head from the ocean, coughing and gagging and screaming. Salty tears fall from his eyes and mix into the salty sea. The salt is the same, he thinks. The ocean is made of his tears; a collection of lonely laments pooled to form his very own prison. Chris realizes he fell asleep in the calm purple tide. He had been lying on his chest, swallowing the water, while the sun cooked him from above. His back feels bright red and blistered. His chest is pale and soggy like a dead fish. He rolls over.

He dreamed of the doctor again, and also his father. He barely remembers his father's face, but the voice haunts him. The voice once spoke of many things, cruel things that he shudders to remember from boyhood. He tries to push those things back into the darkness, but they have grown too great to hold within, and the cobweb-covered fears of his father pours out.

Memories, like photographs, float upon the ocean of his mind.

A creature with horns and a tail follows him as a boy through the halls of his house, stalking. It is his father in costume. He slashes Chris across the arm with a knife. His father, now as tall as the ceiling and with many arms, holds a whip and whispers words like an old woman. Later, a formless shadow falls upon Chris as he sleeps, a germ borne upon the wind that places his hands around Chris's throat.

"Be strong," his father tells him. More words are spoken, indecipherable in ancient tongue, as if several voices converse at once from the same mouth.

He weeps in reminiscence, and the sun stares upon him, watching, judging, calculating. The blurry shapes below swim faster, excited.

One night Chris visits his father as he sleeps…

"Fear is the sensation induced by a perceived threat. It is innate and controls one's behaviors. Irrational and delusional thoughts fill the vessels that are built of fear. Only when fear is conquered will your brain blossom from a small seed of potential into the beautiful rose of self-realization."

Chris gasped and opened his eyes, frantically splashing in ten inches of water. Shivering and panting, he rose. The tank was like an enclosed bathtub and he stood, back pressed against the open, hinged lid.

He wrapped his arms around his chest, staring at the doctor in a wide-eyed plea. "No more, no more, please don't put me back in there—"

The speckled caterpillars on Dr. Edwards's face wriggled in concern. "Chris, therapy should be gratifying. You are being cured of an imbalance, a predilection for phobia that is not natural to you. You must free your mind to rediscover the strength that is your birthright."

Chris shook his head. "You've left me in there for years."

"I assure you the session is only for thirty minutes. Come on out of there and let me get you a towel. Remember, you once compared your life to being adrift at sea, surrounded by faceless fears?"

"The fears are inside that tank," Chris said.

"Your senses are isolated inside that tank. You see what your life is. You must put a face to your fears. That is how they are defeated!"

"I killed my father."

Edwards froze at the abrupt announcement. It hung between them, and Chris quivered at the cold sound of his confession. The coils of neon purple lights glowed brighter. Blurry moments swam past, and each man pondered what words to speak next.

"Yes, I know. We have known all along," the doctor said. "Your father perfected a practice to eliminate fears, to rise up and own this world. The strength of mind is invincible. People live their lives amongst unnamed terrors that hold them back. Who is not afraid of embarrassment or of failure or of loneliness? Who can defeat the fear of death or damnation, let alone the fear of earthly reprisals, of laws and norms? We are taught these fears from infancy, taught by our parents, customs which weaken us, defeat us and lead to the shackles of subservience. Only men who are strong take what they want. Only men without fear live forever."

Chris's heart pounded in a rapid rhythm as he listened to the doctor. Memories of his father pounced anew, the panic that crippled him in life and left him in tears, catatonic on the floor, unable to function. He could not remember why he came to visit Dr. Edwards, or having ever met him before, but the doctor struck him as familiar. His voice and the things he said mimicked the man he knew last when he was only a boy.

"Your father taught you pain and fear, and he taught you the means to defeat them. He taught you power. You conquered your greatest fear when you were only seven. Such a remarkable feat! Why, Chris—why are you still scared?"

Softly, Chris spoke. "I can't give up my childhood with him, even if he was a monster. All I have left of my father are the fears. It's all I remember. But I don't want to let him go, I don't want to forget him."

"He *wanted* you to kill him, to prove yourself worthy. Your father taught you strength, and his greatest pride was the night you embraced it; the night you crept into his room and placed your hands around his neck. Child hands that wielded the magnificent strength to crush his larynx and strangle him while he thrashed in tears beneath you. You defeated your greatest fear, the fear of your father. You were ready, Chris."

"I killed my own *father*. He's dead, don't you get it? I've had to live with that my whole life."

"You killed your father, but he is not dead. Who do you think brought you to me?"

More tears. Chris again shook his head in denial.

"It's time for you to face your fears," the doctor said.

The words lashed at him. There would never be an escape; he knew he was trapped in that prison. If it was a dream, he would never wake, and if it was a nightmare, he lived his life within it. Chris wiped his eyes and ceded. He lay down in the isolation tank.

Edwards lowered the lid and his lemon-yellow cardigan glowed under the lights.

"A famous man once said, 'There is nothing to fear but for fear itself.' Remember that, Chris."

***

The man wakes and splashes and chokes again. He knows the end will arrive soon. He falls asleep more often now, and the dreams rolling in his thoughts are more vivid, sapping his strength and sanity. He cannot determine where he belongs or if it even matters. If he cannot stay awake, he will drown in this ocean. If he does not drown, he will be swallowed by the things below, or worse. The sun still has not moved in the sky, and he tries swimming closer to it.

The propulsion of motion sails under him. Panic floods him at this new sensation, and Chris rolls onto his chest to gaze into the water. The blurry shapes have risen much closer from the depths. It is their swell he feels as they swim past. He is tiny—insignificant in size—compared to their enormity. Each of the shapes is terrifyingly long, stretching as if fifty isolation tanks were laid side-by-side.

Closer, he now sees the orca with trident-shaped horns and trailing tentacles has an open gash along its back, pink and frothy and filled with teeth. It is nearest and rising quickly. The two-headed worm has spiny humps like a camel impaled with cacti. There is a gelatinous blob of many colors that ascends, and also something resembling a crocodile, covered in scales and electrical surges. They swim faster now, their circling formation tighter. Chris is at the epicenter of their spiral, as if at the tip of an inverted funnel.

They are all *his father. He is immersed in his father.*

He is *his father.*

He rolls onto his back. The sun blinds him. The sun is his father, too. He cannot escape the eye that sees all.

They are his fears, and Chris must conquer them. He feels their torment, the way he did when he was seven. The anger burns, its rays cooking his chest. He feels the forgotten strength—his father taught him to harness it, to use it. His father taught him well, but he was so young, and he cried out in remorse. It was his father, and Chris killed him, and the fear of reprisal and regret had washed over his waning strength, drowning it. The memory returns, the burn, the strength. His father was right—he can conquer anything.

The man drinks deep of the purple water…

***

"Your father was heralded as a savior. He was our light and the prophet. You, Chris, you are to take his place. It is your thirty-third birthday, the day of awakening. Long have you lived imprisoned, but now it is time for your father to be free. Come forth, in peace and in strength, and be anointed."

Chris gasped and opened his eyes, frantically splashing in ten inches of water.

Dr. Edwards looked over the top of delicate-rimmed glasses. "How do you feel, Chris? Refreshed? I know it may take a moment to acclimate yourself back into the real world, but the teachings of your father should remain with you." He paused, and then stared sternly at him. "Are you ready?"

"Yes, Doctor," Chris said, calm and confident. "Yes, I am."

Chris rose from the water and stepped forth, dripping onto the gray shale floor. A towel was offered, and he refused. He embraced the ocean and grasped his own neck between his hands, squeezing, feeling his larynx tighten.

The speckled caterpillars leapt on Edwards's face. "Congratulations! Your progression is remarkable. I never thought we could have brought you back in such a short period of time. Your father said you could do it, but I just didn't believe. Only one session in the isolation tank and fifteen minutes at that! Truly amazing. You *are* your father's son."

Chris interlaced his fingers and squeezed tighter around his throat, choking himself. Changes began to emerge on his face. It aged and grayed, features sharpening. Wrinkles grew on his brow, and crow's tracks strode across his temples.

"Yes, Chris, yes," said Dr. Edwards.

Chris's chin grew broader, dimpled, and he staggered from his feet as the room grew hazy and lopsided. His father's features overlaid his own, like a dark cloud floating over the sun. Ears shrank and scars appeared on his cheeks, erratic and twisting to the corners of his mouth. His lips thinned and paled and trembled, and he watched from faraway as Dr. Edwards gazed upon him, his own face brilliant in rapture.

"Remember, there is nothing to fear but for fear itself."

From deep underwater, Chris shrieked in denial. Something snapped in his brain and, like flicking a switch, he released himself. He lunged instead at Edwards and latched around the man's neck in a flare of clarity and rage. The doctor spasmed like a puppet. His clipboard flew through the air, spraying the room in pages of notes and forms and photographs. Chris's hands clenched, squeezing, and the doctor's windpipe constricted.

Edwards tried to cry out but instead his tongue unfurled, lolling swollen and extended between flapping, hissing jaws. Confusion washed over his face, and he sank to his knees, clutching frantically at Chris's hands. Tears glistened around bulging eyes, and his delicate-rimmed glasses shattered on the floor.

Face blank, Chris bore down on Edwards, tightening his grip. Fingers dug into doughy flesh, crushing the fragile cervical vertebrae. He stoically watched as the doctor fell limp. Edwards's meringue face darkened, and Chris knew he had defeated his father.

The purple light of the isolation tank still shone bright, and Chris laid the doctor's body to float freely inside it. Grimly, he closed the lid over him. He sat in the office, embracing the adrenaline rush he had not felt since he was seven years old. He felt no remorse, no fear of reprisal.

Chris felt no fear at all.

He quietly walked out of the doctor's office and locked the door behind him. The office was tucked away in the back of a small strip mall at the side entrance to the main boulevard. The parking stalls were directly in front, christened with signage that read PATIENTS ONLY. There awaited his BMW. He may have lived in fear before, but he had done well in the world. Now he was unstoppable.

He entered the car and flipped down the visor mirror to stare at himself. Roaring in triumph, he pounded on the steering wheel. A new life fell into place. *Thanks to Poppa*, he realized. Chris pulled out onto the street and slammed down the accelerator, racing away, his heart revving like the car. He felt invincible.

The doctor was right: therapy *was* remarkable; his fears were gone; the black depression and mutilating self-doubt were removed, like shitting out bad food ingested the night before.

The sun fell, and traffic on the streets was sporadic. He barreled into the oncoming lanes so others had to drive wildly to get out of his way. Chris could cause the fear now; he would never be a victim again. The light at the intersection turned red and he drove through, laughing. He drove with no destination, but the greater distance he travelled, the increased chance he'd have to discover an escape from the frigid sea. Letting the current of the highway carry him along, he drifted until the coastline shimmered in the distance under the setting sun. The sky turned from blue to indigo, darkening in thythmic hues.

He drove and left the highway. He drove down the street, drove through the iron chains signaling the end of the road, drove onto the pier.

The land fell dark as the last of the sun's light cast onto the ocean. The darkening color of the water turned *purple, purple, purple.*

Chris had nothing to fear but for fear itself. He was invincible.

He drove on until his car floated freely in the air, off the pier and, in a burst of glass and rent metal, the BMW smashed into the deep sea below. Sinking fast, Chris struggled in the driver's seat, kicking against the door. He tasted the familiar salt. The visor mirror fell open and Chris saw himself in the reflection.

The blurry shadows surrounded him.

***

The man opens his eyes, gagging on the choking water, but he feels strength now. He feels determination. He envisions the face of his father on the blurry shadows and knows how to defeat them.

The horned orca rises and swims to him.

Chris watches it approach and, in sudden revelation, screams. It does not have his father's face after all. It wears a lemon-yellow cardigan and has rows and rows of speckled caterpillars crawling upon its brow. Its mouth opens wide, a horrible cavern, like an isolation tank with no escape.

He remembers: He has nothing to fear, but for fear itself.

But Chris does fear it, and he knows it is coming to swallow him.

NEED

GARY A. BRAUNBECK

"One can go for years sometimes without living at all, and then all life comes crowding into one single hour."
– Oscar Wilde, *Vera, or The Nihilists*

THE LETTER, written on official department stationary, tumbles across the autumn sidewalk, skimming the surface of a puddle (soaking only the middle of the page, smearing certain portions of certain words) before the wind propels it against the base of a lamp post where it flutters, trapped, neither the wind nor the puddle nor the letter aware of their part of this brief mosaic nature is forming to amuse itself. A nearby rat, searching for nest material, sits up on its hind legs and regards the paper, then slowly moves toward it. The rat doesn't care about the needs of wind or paper, it is not aware of its own determined part in this mosaic, it only cares about its own need; for which this sheet of paper will do very nicely…

"I've got a special dessert for you guys tonight."

The two children look at each other and smile. It's been a long time since they've had a meal this good—hot beef tacos and now Mom says she's got a "special" dessert.

When the children don't say anything, their mother shakes her head and laughs. Now the children are very excited—Mom hasn't laughed in a long, long time.

"Well," she says to her son and daughter. "Aren't you even going to ask?"

"What're we having?" says the little girl.

Mom leans back in her chair and folds her arms across her chest, then looks at the ceiling. "Oh, Jeez, I don't know if I'm going to tell you or not, seeing as how you weren't interested enough to ask me in the first place."

The children give out with groans of disappointment and frustration—groans they both know Mom is expecting—and their mom laughs again.

"Okay," she says, leaning forward and gesturing for them to lean closer.

Mom whispers—like it's some kind of a big secret—"Chocolate mousse."

"*Chocolate mousse!*" they both shriek, delighted. This is their absolute, hands-down, no-question-about-it favorite dessert in the whole wide world.

"But only," adds Mom, "if you guys have another taco."

The children tell her how much they love her, grab up another tortilla, and spoon them full of the sliced beef for the tacos.

…now Charlie's going on and on about how no decent woman would whore herself out like that because that's what it amounted to and how that spineless scumbag was more concerned about his parents' money than he was about being a man and owning up to responsibilities so as far as he's concerned you don't talk about it with him, not ever, and Henrietta nods her head and smiles at him but not too widely, too wide a smile and he might think she's humoring him (which she is but mustn't let him know it) and get even angrier, and Charlie, you never have to do or say much to get him started on one of his rants, like today, all it took was Henrietta's letting slip with a mention of "the whore's" name (Charlie only calls her that, "the whore") and off he went, asking how could she still *talk* to that whore every week, and he was still going on, so Henrietta nods again and waits for him to storm over to the other side of the room (Charlie likes to cover a lot of ground while he's ranting), and when he does, when he heads toward the other side of the living room, Henrietta sits forward to look like she's really paying attention, like she's really interested, and as she does she slips one of her hands down into the space between the sofa cushions because just maybe Charlie or her lost some change down there, and it won't kill her, walking to the Bridge Club meetings instead of taking the bus for a week, she could use the exercise and at least the weather's been nice and as Charlie turns to make his way back her fingertips brush across the surface of something that might be a couple of quarters, so she continues smiling (but not too widely) and nodding her head because as long as Charlie makes eye contact he won't be paying any attention to her hand…

Inter-Office Memo
From: Paul Gallagher, Principal

Darlene:

I know you meant well, I really do, but several of the other teachers have expressed concern to me over your actions during 2nd Grade Class pictures last Tuesday. You did not have permission to take that girl off school grounds, let alone to the mall. We have a lot of children from poor and disadvantaged homes in this school, and anything that even remotely smacks of favoritism is frowned upon, not only by myself and the other teachers, but the School Board as well. Your actions—caring though they might have been—can be looked upon as "playing favorites". It is not our responsibility to make sure the poorer students have decent clothes to wear for their class pictures, and it is certainly not your responsibility to buy them (though I've seen the pictures, and the little girl looks like an angel).

In the future, please keep your more dramatic humanitarian impulses in check. You're new here, and I'm sure you'll learn how things are done in due time.

Albert Morse sits on the front porch of his house on Euclid Avenue. He's enjoying the warm weather and thinking that he needs to trim the hedges this weekend. Just because the house isn't in the best neighborhood is no excuse to let it all go to hell. The house is paid for, and Albert takes a lot of pride in that. He and Georgia have made themselves a nice home here, one that the kids and the grandchildren love visiting. At the end of the day, what more could a man ask for? Work your whole life away on the factory line, retire with a good pension and good insurance, own your own home, have the family over for dinner and holidays.

Why the city decided to build those goddamned government-subsidized apartments across the street was a mystery to him, and an even bigger pain in the ass some days. Not a day goes by when someone who lives on Welfare Row doesn't drag their business into the street.

Like now, for instance; that young girl at the row of mailboxes, screaming "*Fuck!*" over and over again because of something she just read in a letter. Can't take your drama inside, no; you've got to play it out here in front of God and everybody like your problems are so much bigger and more important and painful than everybody else's.

Albert watches as the young woman continues screaming "*Fuck!*" over and over, louder and louder, until finally she breaks down into violent, wracking sobs. She wipes her arms across her eyes, shakes some hair from her face, reads the letter again, and then just tosses it away before starting in with the "*Fuck!*" and the sobbing again, right there in the middle of the damn sidewalk. She continues screaming and sobbing until a school bus stops at the corner; as soon as she sees this, she turns around, pulls some tissues from her pocket, wipes her face and nose, and turns around, puffy-eyed and smiling as a little boy and girl run from the bus to her side. She kneels down and hugs them, then holds their hands as they make their way back inside, behind closed doors, where any decent human being ought to damned well keep their troubles.

Georgia comes out and hands Albert a glass of fresh iced tea. "Just got off the phone with Cal. He and Rhonda are bringing the kids over for dinner Friday night. Cal says he wants to take us all out to see the new Disney movie."

"That sounds like fun," says Albert, taking the iced tea but staring at the letter the young woman had tossed away.

"What was all that racket a minute ago?" asks Georgia.

"Some gal over there," replies Albert, nodding toward Welfare Row. "I swear, honey, some of *trash* they allow to live there…"

"Don't get yourself worked up," says Georgia. "You don't need to go and get all upset about the way they act."

Albert shakes his head. "It just… it just makes this seem like such a rotten place to live, and it isn't, you know? Or it *shouldn't* be." He discovers that he can no longer see the letter; the wind must have blown it somewhere. "I swear, the *trash*…"

"I tried so *very hard*," says the drunk as he's escorted from the bar by Sheriff Ted Jackson, who's been through this routine enough to know that this particular drunk doesn't require handcuffs.

"I *tried*, I really did," says the drunk.

"I know you did," replies the sheriff, as he always does. He looks over his shoulder and sees Jack Walters, owner and proprietor of the Wagon Wheel Bar & Grille, standing in the doorway, shaking his head in pity. Jackson nods to him that everything is all right, just business as usual, and Walters gives the sheriff a mock salute before turning around and going back inside.

The drunk stumbles, almost falling, but catches himself on the trunk of Jackson's car. "It wasn't my fault. It wasn't." He reaches out and grabs Jackson's collar. "You know that, right, Sheriff? You know that it wasn't my fault."

Jackson removes the drunk's hand from his collar, and gently guides him into the back seat. "You need to sleep it off, Randall. We've got your usual bed ready, and in the morning, we'll get you fixed up with a nice, hot breakfast, okay?"

"Nobody calls me that," says the drunk. "I mean, she used to, once… like it was a pet name, you know? But nobody calls me 'Randall.' I always hated that name. I should have said something once I was goddamn old enough. Fuckin' sissy-assed name like that." He curls up into a fetal position on the back seat and begins sobbing. "I should've said something about that. I… I should've done a lot of things, you know? If I'd've stood up to my folks, then maybe…" He leans over the seat and vomits into the plastic bucket Jackson had put there earlier, in anticipation of the usual pattern. Once he finishes vomiting, he wipes his mouth, sits up, and hands the bucket to Jackson, who empties it in the gutter.

"I'm gonna quit wasting my time and get on with my life," says the drunk.

"I know you are," replies Jackson, as he always does, as he always has every few weeks for the last couple of years after Walters calls to say, "Same old song and dance, my friend."

Jackson closes the door, stuffs the bucket into a plastic trash bag, then, as always, tosses it into the trunk of the cruiser, thinking as he does that all the money in the world—and God knows that the drunk's got enough money, having inherited it from his parents—can't do a damn thing to make the nights less lonely.

From the back seat the drunk's sobbing grows louder and more violent; the spasms wracking his body shake the entire cruiser, and Jackson cannot help but feel a morbid kind of awe. While there is the usual excess of self-pity in this puking, slobbering booze hound, there's also a depth of genuine anguish that Jackson cannot ignore—which is, he supposes, why people put up with this sort of behavior from the drunk.

There is some grief you never recover from.

to inf-rm you that, up-n revie-, the Cedar Hill Dep—tment of -ealth and H-man

Having completed the required six weeks of training, this Wednesday is Daniel's first night working the Cedar Hill Crisis Center phone lines without backup. It is a little before eight p.m. when his phone rings for the first time. Taking a deep breath, he answers, and after identifying himself and telling the caller whom they have reached, listens as the voice on the other end says: "How can you go on living when all there is to look forward to is more yearning?"

The caller hangs up before Daniel can say anything.

He notes the time in his log, and in parentheses adds: *probable crank call.*

Still, the question finds him again, as it will continue to do over the course of the otherwise uneventful evening, as well as a few mornings later when he happens upon the article and photos on Page Two of *The Ally*; it comes back to him again and again as it will for the rest of his life, never leaving him, never losing him, no matter how much he tries to hide from it.

Detective Bill Emerson stares at the stack of mail on his desk, none of which is addressed to either him or anyone else at the Cedar Hill Police Department. There's the usual monthly detritus you expect to find in the mail—phone bill, gas bill, electric bill—only all of these envelopes are emblazoned with the words FINAL NOTICE stamped in bright red ink.

Emerson cracks his knuckles, then runs a hand through his thick gray hair, noting that he needs to get a trim. Between his bushy hair and equally bushy moustache, it's no wonder some of the other officers call him "Captain Kangaroo" when they think he can't hear them.

He riffles through the mail once again, tossing the bills to the left, the junk mail to the right, and everything else in the center. He's been doing this off and on for the last two days, his variation on walking a labyrinth for the purpose of meditating on a problem, and, as always, he comes back to the business-sized brown envelope that weighs more than all the rest and has way too much postage on it.

They should have used Priority, he thinks. *Four bucks and it's there in three to four days.*

He checks the postmark date against the report. Five days. Even with all the extra postage, it had taken this letter five days to reach its addressee. If they had used Priority, it would have only taken three to four, and that might have made all the difference in the world.

He drops the letter on top of the center stack, unconsciously wincing at the muffled *thump!* it makes when it lands, and stares at it.

He's still staring a few minutes later when his partner, Ben Littlejohn, comes in with dinner in the form of four cheeseburgers and two orders of fries from the Sparta. It smells great—The Sparta makes the best cheeseburgers in the free world, period—and Emerson looks up as Littlejohn sets the food on the corner of the desk.

"Still haven't opened it?" he asks Emerson.

"And your first clue was…?"

Littlejohn wags a single finger back and forth. "Ah-ah, save the snappy banter for the rookies, not me." Littlejohn looks at his partner for a long moment, then says, his voice softer: "You want me to do it?"

"No. I was first on the scene, I found it. It should be me."

Littlejohn parks his ass on the edge of Emerson's desk and starts removing the cheeseburgers from the bag. "So... *when* are you and Eunice going to take that vacation she's bugging you about?"

"To London? Don't start, I'm warning you. She has talked about nothing *but* going there since she saw that damn *Notting Hill* movie. I rue the day Julia Roberts and Hugh Grant were born, because it set into motion the events that would lead to the making of that movie. My life has been endless misery since. Did you know they serve their beer room temperature there? Can you imagine that? No wonder we broke from the Crown."

"Uh-huh. Open the goddamn thing already, will you?"

Emerson picks up the brown envelope, noting again its weight, then looks at his partner. "You're a radiantly compassionate fellow, you know that?"

"I'm an intensely *hungry* fellow who's not going to be able to enjoy his dinner until whatever's in that envelope is out of our lives, and since that isn't going to be anytime soon—seeing as how you've put off opening it for almost two full work days—I'll settle for our knowing its contents."

"You should have seen it," whispers Emerson.

Littlejohn leans forward, rapping his knuckles on the desk to break Emerson's morbid reverie. "I *did* see it, Bill. I was only two minutes behind you."

"I know that, I'm not completely dim." He taps the envelope against his hand in a soft, steady tattoo that after only a few seconds annoys even him, but he doesn't stop. "Have you ever heard of something called 'The Observer Effect'?"

"That's a physics term, right?"

Emerson nods his head. "If I understand it correctly—

Einsteinian whiz-kid that I am—it says that a person can change an event just by being there to watch it. They don't have to take any kind of physical action or what we think of as active participation, just *being there* changes it."

Littlejohn's expression grows concerned, albeit cautiously.

"Okay…?"

"It was *different* after you came in. When it was just me, there was a… I don't know… almost a *peacefulness* there for a few seconds. But then you came in, and I saw your face and you saw mine and when we looked at it again, it was just… ugly and pathetic and sad." Emerson feels that last word fall from his mouth and land at his feet like a dead bird dropping from the sky.

"Bill," says Littlejohn, "I'm asking you now as your friend, not your partner. I'm asking you to please, for everyone's sake, open it."

Not taking his stare from the cheeseburger bag, Emerson picks up the letter opener, slips it under the flap of the envelope (Scotch-taped, three times), slashes open the top, and removes the two sheets of paper inside.

The first sheet is blank, a twenty-pound standard weight of recycled typing paper that has been used to make sure someone couldn't hold the envelope up to the light and discern its contents.

You used a brown *envelope; no one could have seen through this, anyway.* The second sheet, he watches as the bills tumble down on the desk: two twenties, a ten, a five, and three ones. He reaches down with his other hand and arranges the bills side by side.

He looks at the letter, reads what it says—words written in a slow, unsteady hand (*probably arthritis*, he thinks; *a lot of older folks have trouble with that and can't write as neatly or steadily as they used to*)—but it's not the words that cause his throat to tighten, though they are bad enough, no; it's the two quarters, three dimes, one nickel, and four pennies that are taped across the bottom of the page (three pieces of Scotch tape, just like the envelope).

He blinks, pulls in a breath that is heavier and thicker than it ought to be, and hands the sheet to his partner.

"Fifty-eight dollars and eighty-nine cents," he says. "Who the hell sends someone fifty-eight dollars and eighty-nine cents? *Eighty-nine cents?* Why not just make it sixty dollars even?"

Before Littlejohn has a chance to finish reading the letter or respond to the question, Emerson speaks again:

"I'll *tell* you who sends someone fifty-eight dollars and eighty-nine cents, someone who only *has* fifty-eight dollars and eighty-nine cents. Someone who has to go through their purse or wallet, and then the pockets of their coat—hell, they probably even pulled the cushions off the sofa to see if any loose change had fallen down there, just to make sure they could send every *penny* they possibly could. *Anybody* could send you sixty bucks, but only… only someone who *cared* enough to scrape together all the money they possibly could would send you fifty-eight dollars and eighty-nine cents."

He realizes that he is almost on the verge of tears but doesn't care. "*Eighty-nine cents!* I'll bet that old woman had to walk to the store instead of taking the bus to make sure she could get that eighty-nine cents in there. Jesus H. Christ, Ben—*why* didn't she use Priority? That might have made all the difference in the world!" Emerson presses the heels of his hands against his eyes, takes a deep breath, then releases it slowly before wiping his eyes and lowering his hands, which aren't shaking nearly as much as he feared they would be.

"That was very moving," says Littlejohn. "Look at me—I am visibly touched."

"I'm turning into an old woman, aren't I?"

"No, you're just maybe possibly arguably a little too you-should-pardon-the-expression human for this job sometimes."

"And my cheeseburgers are probably cold."

Littlejohn shook his head. "Nope. I had them wrap everything in heavy-duty aluminum foil, just in case we didn't get to the food right away."

"I really *am* predictable, aren't I?"

"Let's call it 'dependable' and remain friends, shall we?"

"You're too good to me."

"I get a lot of complaints about that."

Emerson unwraps the first cheeseburger, starts to bite into it, then pauses and says, "Why didn't she use Priority?"

It is a question that will find him again and again throughout the rest of his life, even when he tries hiding from it.

Edna Warner stands in line at the grocery store and thinks to herself, *The damn meat's gonna start thawing if she takes any longer.*

The young woman in front of her is riffling through a small stack of food stamps. The cashier exchanges a quick, exasperated glance with Edna, one that says, *I'm really sorry, ma'am, but there's nothing I can do.* Edna smiles in understanding, though it's a forced smile. Why did it seem she *always* picked the slowest line in the store? Just her luck, getting stuck behind a welfare case who doesn't have the sense to have her food stamps out and ready.

She takes a tissue from her purse and blows her nose, quietly, as a courteous lady is supposed to do. *Why* she felt compelled to stick her head in the pet store earlier would probably always remain a mystery to her, but that puppy in the window had been so *cute.* It never occurred to her that the pet store would also have cats. Edna was severely allergic to cats, couldn't even be near someone who *owned* the terrible things because people who owned cats always had at least a *little* shed fur on their clothes, and that's all it took to make her allergies go crazy.

Luckily, that was a few hours ago, and she's had a chance to take some non-drowsy allergy medicine, so now she's feeling much better, for which she is grateful. The last thing she wants is to be all stopped-up and red-nosed when Joe gets home from work. He always says it's hard for him to eat at the same table with her when she's like that, eyes all puffy and nose running like it was trying to win some kind of race.

Sometimes, her Joe can be awfully high-maintenance.

Edna busies herself with looking over the headlines on the tabloids in the rack by the checkout lane; this star has gained weight, another one has entered Betty Ford, someone else is having an affair. It's actually quite funny, when you think about it, how these newspapers try to make stars' lives seem even more dramatic than the characters they play in the movies; as if by splattering all their troubles on the front page will make them seem like regular folks. *We have problems just like the rest of you*, these stars' faces seem to say.

Sighing, Edna checks her watch and sees that she's been standing here for almost five minutes. The young woman in front of her hears Edna's sighing, and smiles at her in apology. Edna is at first embarrassed to have been found out, then struck by how sad the young woman's smile is and—*Lord!*—how tired she looks. There are dark crescents under the young woman's eyes that stand out against her pale skin and make her smile seem even more cheerless. For a moment, Edna almost feels bad for having drawn attention to the awkwardness of the situation—*the poor thing looks like she hasn't slept in days*—then thinks again of the pot roast in her cart and how she hopes it doesn't thaw too much before she can get it home and into the freezer. If it thaws too much, she'll have to make it tonight, and Joe wouldn't like that; it's only Thursday, and Joe likes to have pot roast on the weekend. Feed him a too-heavy meal during the week, and he complains about how it keeps him awake and feeling tired all the next day.

Still feeling the young woman's eyes on her, Edna busies herself with the contents of her vinyl coupon holder, making sure that all the ones she'll need are in front, ready to go so that the cashier can scan them without delay. When she's sure the young welfare woman is no longer looking at her, Edna sneaks a peek at what she is buying. Edna's father always used to say, *You can tell a lot about a person by the contents of their shopping cart*, and over the course of her fifty-six years, Edna has found a lot of truth in that observation.

So she looks.

There is a coloring book with a torn cover and a bottle of over-the-counter sleep aids (both of which the young woman pays for with a handful of singles and change from her pocket), six cans of cat food (sliced beef in gravy), a quart of milk, a box of instant pudding mix (chocolate mousse, actually), a packet of taco seasoning (mild), and some frozen tortillas (corn).

The first thing to cross Edna's mind is that she's not sneezing.

The second thing that crosses Edna's mind as she stares at the items is a commercial from the nineteen-seventies with that old gal—what was her name? *Clara Peller, that's right!*—where three old ladies are looking at a hamburger that's mostly all bun and Clara Peller starts squawking, "*Where's* the beef?"

Edna doesn't know why that, of all things, crosses her mind at that moment, but Clara Peller's famous question will find her again, during dinner, as it will find her again and again, for the rest of her life, never losing her, even when Alzheimer's Disease begins fragmenting her mind in another seventeen years: to the attendants on the ward at the nursing home where she'll die quietly in her sleep, Edna Warner will always be known as the Where's-the-Beef? Lady.

*Serv-ces has, aft-r conside—tion of yo-r individ—l case (***AB765-L7) determi—d*

In the basement of St. Francis Church on Granville Street, the Monday night Alcoholics Anonymous meeting is winding down, and Chet Beckman—twelve years sober, known to his friends as

"No-Skid" because he's got the best record of any bus driver for the Central Ohio Transit Authority—is adding an extra spoonful of sugar to his coffee when one of the other fellows in the group says, "Where's that guy who was here last week? That fellow whose family… oh, what was his name?"

"Randy," says Chet, sitting back down and stirring the creamer until the coffee takes on that soft golden color that means it's just right. "And they weren't his family except in his head, and my guess is he's down at the Wagon Wheel getting stewed to the gills."

The fellow who'd asked the question seems genuinely disappointed. "How can you *know* that?"

Chet sips his coffee and smiles; it tastes perfect. "I can know this because Randy comes in here about—what?—every three or four weeks after he's gone on a real bad binge, and sits there and says 'I'm gonna stop wasting my time and get on with my life.'" Chet takes another sip of his coffee. "He's been doing that for damn near two years, and the pattern never changes, no matter how many sponsors we sic on him or how many quit or how many he fires. Hell, *I* was his sponsor for a while, when it looked like he might actually get past what happened."

"It sounded to me like it wasn't his fault, hear him tell it."

"That's what he keeps telling us when he bothers to show up. 'It wasn't my fault. It wasn't my fault.' You ask me, he keeps repeating that because he's hoping that if he says it enough, he'll start to believe it." Chet shrugs. "Hell, maybe that wouldn't be such a bad thing, you know? Him starting to believe it."

The fellow who'd asked about Randy leaned forward. "Sounds to me like maybe you don't agree it wasn't his fault."

Chet sits back in his chair and regards the other fellow carefully. It doesn't do to get tempers flaring at these meetings; a bad argument's all the excuse someone needs to fall off the wagon, and this other fellow, the one who asked about Randy, he's only been sober five weeks and has got that desperate, anxious way about him that says he can go either way in a heartbeat. The first six weeks are always the hardest, and that sixth week is always the killer. Half the people AA loses they lose during the sixth week of sobriety, so Chet considers his words very carefully as he replies.

"Did you see that news story the other night about that avalanche they had in Colorado? The one that killed them two skiers?"

The other fellow nods his head.

"See, here's the thing about assigning blame to anyone or anything," says Chet, taking another sip of his perfect, golden-hued coffee. "I kept wondering—I wonder about shit like this sometimes when I can't sleep—I kept wondering, what if the snow itself could think like we can? I mean, imagine that every snowflake in that avalanche was able to think. Do you suppose any one of them would feel responsible for those skiers' dying, or would they just tell themselves 'It wasn't my fault'?"

The other man thinks on this for a moment, then shrugs. "I don't guess I see your point."

"So what's responsible for that?" asks Chet. "Is there any one word that I just said that's responsible for you not understanding me, or was it *all* the words?"

The other man shakes his head. "You're fucking with me now, aren't you?"

Chet shrugs, deciding that he's had enough coffee for tonight.

> *that you no longer qualify —r ben—ts as outlin— under O-io Co-e —— and*

"Would you look at *this?*" shouts Steve over the roar of the garbage truck's compactor.

His partner, Marty, pulls the wax plug out of his left ear and shoots back, "What?"

Steve points to the contents of one of the trash cans they're emptying along Welfare Row. "This one bag came open. Take a look at this."

Marty peers over the edge of the trash can, looks at Steve, then back down at the contents.

The compactor finishes chewing up the last batch of trash, and howls loudly as it moves back into place for the next load.

"Looks to me like somebody's got insomnia."

Steve shakes his head. "That's more than insomnia, bud. There must be—what?—forty empty bottles in here. Fuck, that's enough to knock out Godzilla for a week."

"Is there anything else in there? Anything that might be salvageable? A busted radio or something we could maybe hock?"

Steve rummages through the rest of the contents. "Nah, ain't got shit."

"I guess that DVD player yesterday was a fluke, huh?"

"We were in a better section of town."

"Oh."

They toss the contents into the back of the truck, toss the cans back to the curb, and run to grab the next ones.

> *all mon—and oth— —— of ——— sha-l be immediately discontinued. If you h-ve*

The rat finishes shredding the paper for its nest, not caring that a large section of it has been caught by the wind again and is tumbling its determined way toward another role in a different mosaic that nature will soon form because of the need to amuse itself. The rat carries away the last of the shreds, knowing now that its nest is complete, is warm, is safe.

"So… how was dessert?"

"It was really *good,*" say the children.

"It was different than last time," says the little boy. "It was kinda…"

"…kinda *crunchy,*" says the little girl.

"Yeah," says the little boy. "Like there was sand in there. It made it a lot thicker."

Their mother brushes some hair from their faces. "But it was good, wasn't it?"

"Oh, yeah!" they cry in unison. "It was yummy. And we at it *all!*"

"We sure did," says their mother.

"And you made so much of it!" says the little girl, laughing and yawning at the same time. "You never eat dessert when we have. You're always saying… oh, what do you say?"

"That chocolate goes right to her hips," says the little boy, who's also laughing and yawning at the same time.

Their mother laughs, as well. "Well… tonight was special."

"…sure was," says the little girl, fighting to keep her eyes open.

"That was the best dinner yet," says the little boy.

She kisses them both on the forehead, then the cheek, then hugs them and tucks them in for the night. She turns off the lights and sits on the floor between their beds, her right hands stroking her daughter's cheek, her left hand touching her son's shoulder.

She remains like that until they are both asleep.

She lowers her head and pulls in a deep, wet breath, then listens to their breathing.

She sees the coloring book lying on the floor at the foot of her daughter's bed. The two of them had been coloring in the pictures. They hadn't finished the last one.

It looked very nice. They played well together. They were each other's bestest friend.

They had loved the coloring book.

She listens to their breathing as she studies the colors, how well both of them stayed within the lines.

Later, she goes into the bathroom and runs hot water into the tub, lights a candle, unfolds the plastic bag, and measures out the duct tape.

"Good-night," she whispers in the direction of her childrens' room. "Sleep tight. Don't let the bedbugs…"

She begins to undress, feeling groggy.

NOT THE CHILD

JULIE STIPES

HER WINGS WERE SHARP and shimmering white and four times her size. The faerie was no more than a foot tall, and naked, her skin also white and translucent. She flew in spurts and eventually perched on the traffic signal, wings outstretched.

I watched this creature from my downtown apartment while pregnant. I assumed it was all in my head at first, something fantastic my mind had conjured to transport me away from the thought of carrying a child.

I was wrong.

She tucked her wings and fell onto a businessman waiting to cross the street, fluttering as she landed on his shoulder. Curious hands played with his ear while she looked inside his head. Tiny fingers pulled at something dark inside. The man was oblivious as she pulled out a smoky substance that pooled on the concrete.

An ethereal body materialized from the ground up: feet, followed by legs, a torso, arms and a head, all of which she tugged out of his ear. Soon the man had a ghostly twin.

When the crosswalk light changed from an amputated hand to a walking man, the faerie flapped her wings and hovered. She held onto what I thought was his soul with both hands. The man's body stayed behind and walked in the opposite direction while his shadow walked in place, gripped by this beautiful thing with wings. A thin line of dark matter reeled out of his ear.

Despite thinking a person's soul would be weightless, she carried it with burden, the way I'd carry a suitcase made for giants if I had wings and could fly. She was quite beautiful with the early sun casting light upon her body.

The faerie struggled outside of my window as the gray line, anchored to the man on the ground, pulled taut. She looked my way for a moment with her glowing eyes, but she couldn't see me.

I followed the trailing substance back to the man on the ground as she pumped her enormous wings, stretching the cord, and then it snapped and she flew out of sight, a length of gray trailing behind her.

The soulless man on the ground staggered a few steps before collapsing.

Moments later, he was surrounded. A woman on a cellular waved frantically for help as a man in a suit passed undisturbed. A young man with scraggly hair let his bicycle crash as he jumped off from it and knelt next to the fallen body. The cyclist searched for a pulse as spectators amassed.

Like a silent film, I watched from my apartment.

I reached for my phone, but realized a few on the street were already calling for help.

The cyclist performed compressions and mouth-to-mouth resuscitation until the ambulance arrived. With exception to the medics, he was the only one who offered assistance.

A dozen others surrounded this poor fellow.

They all wanted to watch.

The ambulance left with its lights flashing and sirens blaring. Show over, the crowd dispersed—all but the cyclist. He sat on the sidewalk and stayed awhile, exhausted, looking in the direction of the ambulance. He finally rose, retrieved his crumpled bike from the curb, and rode away.

The child inside pushed against a rib.

I wrapped myself in a blanket and held her close.

I awoke to a disturbance outside my window later that night when I got up to pee. Tire squeals brought me to the window, as well as the rev of an engine and a glimpse of taillights dissolving into the street.

Two women argued over whoever had sped off in the black sports car. A lonely streetlight illuminated the two women in dim orange. The smaller one held a knife. They exchanged rapid Spanish, but I only understood two words: *puta* and *dinero*.

I suddenly craved Mexican; that's pregnancy for you.

Two glowing embers from the other side of the street watched a reversed image of what I could see. The faerie. I saw only her eyes. She perched on the ledge of the building opposite mine. She waited, I knew, for the chaos of life to give her work—to take one of these women if the fight between them worsened. To *where* was the mystery. She'd swoop onto one of their shoulders and pull out the darkness.

Swearing led to slapping led to hair-pulling led to wrestling led to the larger of the women choking on blood with the hilt of a knife sticking from her chest. She wheezed from pierced lungs, holding her stomach, trying to cover more stab wounds than she had fingers. The other woman rambled off a string of words not in my vocabulary before getting into a beat-up Nissan Sentra and driving away.

I called 911.

The holey woman moved onto her back, her panicked face searching for air like a bloodied trout slapped onto shore. She tried to sit upright, but collapsed as the faerie descended from her hiding space across the street.

"What's your emergency?"

Under the streetlight, the creature's eyes lost luminescence. White wings fluttered as she landed on the woman's chest. Outstretched, the wings were nearly the length of the dying woman's body from head to toe. How the faerie's small figure supported such a weight had my mind reeling. The uneven and bloody surface under her feet rose and fell as the woman under her tried to breathe. Erupting wounds spattered the small body red.

"I need to report a—"

The creature stood over the dying woman, looking into her mouth, reaching into it with delicate hands, pulling.

"Miss?"

Little did the faerie know, I watched from my window.

An assault, I wanted to say, but that wasn't the right word.

From the woman's throat, the creature slowly pulled out something the size of a garbage bag. It lay next to the lady in a lump, like a giant, black, cancerous lung, and it took a while to realize I was staring at a shadowy replica of the dying woman. Holding an end of it with her delicate hands, the faerie pumped her wings, rose into the air and flew away with a line of black trailing behind her. It was taut for a moment, and then snapped near the stabbed woman's mouth. The woman convulsed and her life ended.

"A murder."

The naked white faerie with the bat wings flew away, body splotched in the blood of the dead, clutching the black mass that had once lived inside the profane woman's body. She faded into the night with the shadow of a kite string trailing behind.

I explained what I had seen: two women fighting, one pulling a knife on the other and stabbing, the other driving away.

Yes, the woman was dead, I said. Yes, I was sure. No, I wouldn't go down to check, and yes, I would stay in my apartment. The car was a silver Nissan Sentra, I told her, but I couldn't recall the plates.

A police cruiser parked a far distance away from the dead woman. It had taken nearly thirty minutes. Two officers inspected the body with flashlights and spoke into radios on their collars. A crime scene unit arrived to take pictures, followed by a van. They bagged her up and drove away.

This was the city in which I lived.

This was the city I so desired to leave.

As a soon-to-be single parent, I didn't have much of a choice but to stay.

Something the size of a crow hit my window months later, but I knew it wasn't a bird of any sort. My previous tummy bump resembled a basketball shoved under my blouse, and I supported that extra weight as I admired my semi-transparent reflection. I looked through myself to the white smear the faerie had made.

She hit the window a second time, wings fluttering against the glass. Like a moth's phototactic attraction to light, she frantically struck the window over and over again, wanting inside. It was the middle of the day and she wanted inside. She managed to grasp the bottom frame of the window with clawed toes, her hands slapping the glass and staying there, wings pumping just enough to hold her body upright. Up close, she was both beautiful and terrifying: smooth white skin, thin, ill-proportioned wings too big for her body, an angelic face, small jagged teeth and wide scarlet eyes. Definitely female.

Her small lungs panted.

I put my hand against the glass so that our hands met—her entire hand smaller than my thumb—and noticed her glowering at my stomach.

No.

As I moved, her eyes followed the hand supporting my belly.

I smacked the glass hard and she fluttered away, only to return, slapping against the window. Clawed fingers created four parallel marks on the glass.

Not once did she look at my face.

I stepped back as she repositioned, gripping the top of the window with her tiny hands, her feet pushing off, body swinging, feet slamming against the window.

"Stay away from my child."

She flew away, as if adhering to my words.

"That's right."

She slammed into the window again.

No!

I hit the glass with a balled fist and that's when she noticed me. She cowered. Something about me had scared her, maybe an aura of color I had released—like the smoky substance escaping the bodies of the souls she took—for I could tell she didn't see me the same way I saw her. Jerky eyes searched the room for what had pounded against the glass, head swiveling rapidly. She knew I was there, but I was invisible.

Her work was the child and only the child.

The child inside doubled me over in pain and whatever color I projected scared the creature enough that it flew away.

"Not the child."

The woman in front of me in the checkout stand turned her head and admired my stomach and the items in my cart before minding her own business. I couldn't blame her for the curiosity; what I had said sounded strange coming from the mouth of a pregnant woman.

"How far along are you?"

"Thirty weeks."

"Boy or girl?"

"A girl, I think."

She left it at that and I was relieved she didn't ask about the man in my life, since the man in my life had left the same night he'd put this new life inside of me. I was thirty weeks along and hadn't returned to the doctor to determine the sex of the—

"My god," said the woman. She said it casually, and so she said it a second time dramatically and with a hand to her mouth; the other hand pointed to the rose blossoming from the middle of my sweatpants, blood running the length of my legs.

I saw the faerie creature as I fell to the floor. She admired the mess from atop a pile of paper bags, wings folded behind her back.

The checker said something into the phone mounted on the pole next to the register, but I couldn't decipher the garble over the loudspeaker. The woman in front of me opened a roll of paper towels she planned to purchase and wadded them around me, afraid of touching my blood. She shoved more toward me and then stepped away to make a call, like the woman I had seen in the street. Others in the store scrambled to my aid but stayed far enough away, afraid of what they were seeing. My eyes stayed on what they *couldn't* see.

"Everything will be okay," said the woman on the phone.

Nothing would be okay.

"Not the child," I said again. "Please, not the child."

The child pooled around me.

My child's white faerie glanced to the rafters where a second creature had perched, waiting patiently for fate to unfold, like her wings, which disentangled. Side by side, the two were identical, twin-like: one to take my child's life, the other to take mine.

I felt *my* life draining my child's.

The second faerie flapped her wings, body outstretched. Dainty feet touched down beside me.

The other joined on the opposite side.

No!

I managed to kick the one on my right, but the other jumped onto my legs and held me down and I lay paralyzed, her clawed feet somehow holding me down without piercing my skin. She stood on me as if I were nothing more than a ledge from which she perched. Her touch kept me immobile. She bent over the red mess between my legs and pulled out the gray. I watched her pull out the child, my nameless child, with delicate infant features periodically showing through her soul cloud.

And then the faerie flew away with the life of my unborn child.

"Have some water," said the checker, holding a bottle in front of me.

"I called for an ambulance," said the woman who had placed the call. She took the bottle from him, kneeled next to me, unscrewed the cap and lifted the back of my head. Water poured over my mouth and down my face.

I was the only one who saw them.

The second faerie eagerly advanced.

I zapped the hell out of the little white creature with my Taser before she could lay her claws on me. I'd kept it in my purse since becoming single. Her body went into spasm and curled into a fetal position. I held her scrawny neck to the floor and smashed the Taser against her skull, over and over again. To those around me, it must have looked like the woman who'd just miscarried took out her frustrations on the first thing she found in her purse. Gray leaked from the mess of a once-beautiful being and evaporated. Her white body started to darken, still writhing—convulsions, really. I grabbed each of her wings and ripped them from her slender body and it was like tearing at tissue paper. The best way to describe the texture is cotton candy dissolving against wet fingertips.

That's when I noticed the moth. The common insect fluttered toward the dying faerie and landed on her shoulder, there to take her away.

***

I don't remember the ambulance ride to the hospital, nor much of anything after the moth, but I thought about the paralysis and whether or not the first faerie's touch had put me there, or fear. Either way, I was unable to save my child, only myself.

Never had I bled so heavily. To think that it was the life of either my daughter or my son spilling out of me...

The doctor smeared cold ultrasound jelly over my swollen belly to find the rapid heartbeat of a child.

"Only one child has miscarried," he said.

THE WHITE QUETZAL

GENE O'NEILL

"¡Madre de Dios! He visto El Blanco..."
El Indio, St. Elena – Costa Rica, July 1970

SIMON JUDAH first saw the white quetzal Wednesday afternoon at his uncle's funeral.

After leaving work early in San Jose, he had driven up the peninsula to Millbrae, arriving ten minutes late for the graveside ceremony. A grounds man directed him to the tiny cluster of people around the white-draped casket, listening to a minister.

Self-consciously, Simon joined the group of strangers—the men in dark suits and sunglasses; the women in dark dresses, dark hats, and sunglasses—smoothed the wrinkles from his blue polo shirt, then jammed his hands into his Levis cords. He took a deep breath and tried to concentrate on the eulogy, but the words blurred into a meaningless drone. Too hot, he thought, wiping his forehead and glancing yearningly at a nearby circle of shade, cast by a magnificent black oak about twenty yards from the group of mourners. His gaze shifted to the coffin, draped with a shawl of white linen and a huge spray of red carnations—Uncle Will had always worn a red carnation in his lapel.

Simon smiled. His uncle had been quite a character, often mentioned in Herb Caen's column in the *Chronicle*, usually connected with his gallery in San Francisco. Probably most of these people were from the art crowd, Simon thought, looking around at the group. He spotted one familiar face: Mr. Rutherford, Uncle Will's attorney… and beside the lawyer, a young man with a handkerchief to his face. Always a young man around Uncle Will, he thought, even now.

Simon let his gaze wander back to the great oak. Uncle Will had been good to him in his senior year of high school; after the death of Simon's mother, the old man helped him into Stanford, but Simon had flunked out in the second semester, and they had argued violently. He hadn't heard from his uncle in twelve years. So Simon had been surprised when Mr. Rutherford called to advise that he would be included in his uncle's will.

The minister droned on in the heat, like an old water cooler with loose bearings.

Simon felt sleepy—

Something landed on a branch of the black oak. Simon narrowed his eyes against the reflected glare, realizing it was a bird. A great white bird, dazzling in the sunlight, much larger than a seagull, long tail feathers drooping below the tree branch. He almost choked with the recognition. It was a quetzal, the rare Central American bird. But this one was unusual—the color of clouded ice. Simon clutched himself, shivering and rubbing goose bumps along his arms—the temperature had plunged twenty or thirty degrees. He glanced at the others, but incredibly, no one seemed affected by the temperature drop or the appearance of the strange bird.

The minister closed his book but rattled on.

Simon looked back at the limb, but the bird was gone, and overhead, fleecy clouds screened the sun. But it had been a quetzal, he thought, a remarkable sighting. *Quetzal blanco.* The expression triggered a memory.

As a high school graduation present, Uncle Will had taken Simon on a business trip to Costa Rica. Will's friend, Miguel, only slightly older than Simon, had accompanied them on the trip. They landed in San Jose, the tiny capital of about three hundred thousand, where Will spent the day with an art broker, securing items for his gallery. Left on their own, Simon and Miguel roamed the narrow streets of the busy city, buying mangoes, unusually sweet bananas, and delicious green oranges from street vendors. In the afternoon they escaped the din and diesel pollution of the city by taking a bus tour of Irazu; but they saw little, the famed 11,260-foot volcano shrouded by an icy curtain of rain. After returning to San Jose that evening, the boys looked over Will's new acquisitions. The colorful *molas* of imaginary creatures caught Simon's eye—the unique reverse appliqué stitchery was made by the Cuna Indians of San Blas Island off the coast of Costa Rica in the Caribbean. After dinner at the Amstel Hotel, they all fell into bed exhausted.

Early the next day, they traveled five hours by jeep, northwest of the capital up into the Cordillera de Tileran, to Monteverde, an isolated community settled by Quakers from Alabama in 1951. While Will negotiated with a young woman for watercolors of wildlife, Simon and Miguel hiked the narrow trails of the nearby cloud forest, a jungle without stifling heat. The boys saw numerous rare amphibians, including the poison dart frog and the beautiful golden toad, a local species only recently discovered in 1964; they saw huge beetles with varnished ebony armor, and many, many brightly colored birds, including the famed quetzal—emerald and azure cloak, scarlet chest, long tail feathers elegantly iridescent. At noon they ate lunch at a cleared spot on the continental divide, *La Ventana*, catching glimpses of the Caribbean Sea to the east between clumps of cloud mist blown in by gale like winds.

Tired but happy, the boys joined Will later that night at a cantina in the nearby village of St. Elena. Over his first legal drink—*guaro*, the local equivalent of rum—Simon described their adventure to his uncle. But their celebration was disturbed by an old man who sat at a corner table, staring up toward the cloud forest, moaning something over and over in Spanish. After consulting with the bartender, Miguel pieced the story together.

The old man, a mestizo called El Indio, had seen a mythical white quetzal in the cloud forest. The Indians, dating back to the Aztecs, believed the quetzal to be sacred and decorated their helmets with quetzal feathers. But the white one was special. It was said to be the personification of death—*El pajaro de la muerte: El Blanco.* So the old man had seen the White One.

That night at their *pensione* in St. Elena, Miguel was scratched by a cat. Twenty-two days later, back home, he died of rabies...

The draped casket had disappeared, lowered into the grave; and the people were all leaving.

Simon took another deep breath, still stunned by the sighting of a mythical creature. Of course he didn't believe in old legends, garbled by drunken Indians... still, he knew he had seen a white quetzal, a unique bird unknown to science. He forced the image to the back of his mind and followed the group to the parked cars. At his Mustang he slipped into the front seat and rubbed both arms vigorously, remembering how suddenly the air had chilled after the appearance of the bird. *El pajaro de la muerte: El Blanco.* He shuddered and flipped on the radio. "Cast Your Fate to the Wind," by Vince Guaraldi. Starting the car, Simon decided he needed a drink. As he approached 101, he ignored the southbound turn off to Sunnyvale; instead, he turned north, drawn toward the City of Guaraldi's haunting jazz piano.

The TV woke Simon.

He was disoriented, but recognized his bedroom in Sunnyvale. The digital clock on the dresser read: 1:15 p.m. Damn, he thought, rubbing his throbbing head, unable to recall much of the evening after the funeral. He had driven to San Francisco... but after that everything was vague; it was like trying to recall a dream. Simon sat up and shivered, remembering the bird at his uncle's funeral—

The TV blared, sending a sliver of pain into a spot behind his eyes. One of those stupid game shows or soaps, he thought, grimacing. He got up and stumbled into the front room. His eleven-year-old daughter was lying on the floor in front of the set. "Jenny, for God's sake," he growled, "turn—"

She shushed him, making the *Be Quiet* sign with a forefinger to her lips.

Simon glimpsed the overlay, NEWS UPDATE, before it blinked off the screen. Then a woman's voice: "...found brutally stabbed to death in Golden Gate Park... sexually mutilated. The young victim has been identified as Paul Saboda..." A photo of a young man flashed on the screen, stirring a vague recollection in Simon. He rubbed his eyes, trying to massage away the annoying pain. "Saboda was last seen leaving ETC, a bar on Castro."

"What does it mean, Daddy?"

Jenny was asking something, but her voice sounded strange, distant. "What?"

"Sexually mutilated?"

Simon shrugged. "I'm not sure." The expression was ominous, raising goose bumps along his arms. He left the room, shuffling into the kitchen. Rummaging through the refrigerator, he found a can of tomato juice, a shriveled lemon, and a tray of ice. He fixed himself a Bloody Mary, minus the vodka and spices; then he washed down two aspirins with the drink.

Still he felt peculiar, his thinking fuzzy.

Betty came in from the backyard, wearing her gardening togs: an old white shirt, Levis, and a red bandanna over her hair. Simon stared at her, as if looking at a stranger, not his wife of twelve years.

"Morning, or afternoon," she said coolly, placing several small zucchini in the sink. "You were awfully late last night and noisy."

Her voice sounded strange, too—tinny, distant, like an echo.

Simon nodded numbly. Sweat glistened on Betty's upper lip, and the sight repelled him, causing him to look away. "Sorry," he mumbled stiffly, as if he had brushed a stranger's arm. "I went out for a few beers after work."

She continued, but her words were a drone, like the minister's at Uncle Will's funeral.

"Nelson called from the plant about seven." She paused a moment, washing her hands. "He was wondering where you were."

God, he'd forgotten to go back and finish the report for the Consumer Products Protection Agency.

"Well," he began, clearing his throat, feeling like a schoolboy trying to explain an unexcused absence. "I had a couple of beers with Mr. Rutherford, Uncle Will's attorney, one thing led to another, you know."

Betty dried her hands, then wiped her upper lip with the dishtowel. She nodded, accepting the explanation. After a moment, she frowned, and said slowly, "Simon, we need to talk, about us. You and me and Jenny. It's like you've been avoiding us the past two months. Staying away from home until all hours. I know you're worried about this promotion when Nelson retires, but…"

She droned on.

The lie about Mr. Rutherford reminded Simon of the funeral and the white bird. The quetzal. Something flickered through the fuzziness: Had he seen it a *second* time, later last night? He thought so, but he wasn't sure.

Betty touched his arm, her fingers rough as sandpaper. "We haven't made love in over two months." Unable to maintain eye contact, he struggled to concentrate on her words. But it was no use. Her tinny voice sent more slivers of pain into his head. Every so often he nodded, but his thoughts drifted to Nelson, the operations manager at the plant. Nelson would be mad as hell about the

CPPA flammability report. The government agency had got several non-compliance injunctions against cellulose fiber insulation plants in the East. Jesus, what timing! he thought, ridiculing himself. Nelson retired soon, and he was being considered for the spot.

Betty had stopped.

Simon felt compelled to say something.

"I'm sorry, dear," he mumbled lamely, "it's the strain at the plant. The promotion and all."

Betty took off the bandanna and shook out her auburn hair. She flashed Simon an understanding smile. "I know," she said, patting his arm affectionately. Her hand felt hot, abrasive. "When will you know, if you got it, I mean?" Her voice seemed softer, more normal.

"Soon, I think," he answered, able to look her in the eye. "Nelson leaves at the end of the month. So it'll be soon."

The strain eased from Betty's face. "What do you think about the trip to Mother's?"

Mother's? She had mentioned something about Sonoma.

"It would be good for Jenny and me, if it's okay with you. Maybe you could drive up Sunday?"

Simon nodded, feeling a sense of relief. His head cleared and he felt better. The trip was a good idea. He needed some quiet after work. "Fine."

Betty opened the freezer and smiled. "There're several TV dinners for you."

He smiled back and left the room.

Simon took the Central Expressway south to the industrial park back of the San Jose airport.

He waved at Gavin, the security man, as he drove through the gate at *Insul-Gard* and into his parking stall. For a minute he sat in the Mustang, the pre-work tension tightening his stomach muscles.

The Feds, the State, the local planning commissions, and even utility companies: all interested in cellulose fiber insulation, requiring more testing, more controls, and *more* headaches for Simon. He sighed. Quality control supervisor was definitely the hot seat at *Insul-Gard.*

Stiffly he climbed out of the Mustang and walked across the parking lot, waving or nodding to a few of the guys on the day shift. He stopped for a moment to talk to Ed Jarecki, his day shift Q.C. tech.

"Ed, how's it going today?"

Jarecki frowned, shaking his head. "McHenry's waiting in your office."

Simon winced as if he had been jabbed in the chest with a sharp object. McHenry was their Underwriters' Laboratories field inspector, a retired army major who enjoyed the surprise monthly inspections, especially writing up variances in production or quality control procedures. Simon groaned, managing a feeble wave as Jarecki left. Dammit, he thought, two hours and who knows how much trouble. But he realized the U.L. label was *Insul-Gard's* lifeblood. Without it, they couldn't sell one bag of cellulose fiber insulation on the West Coast. Reluctantly, Simon stepped into his office next to the plant lab.

The heavy-set, red-faced McHenry rose from a chair, setting down a cup of coffee. He shook Simon's hand as if they were close friends. "Judah, how are you?"

"Good, Mac. Yourself?" Simon answered, able to mask his hostility. He spotted a note propped up on his desk: *See me after U.L. leaves. Nelson.* Jesus, more trouble, Simon thought, remembering he had left Nelson hanging last night with the unfinished CPPA report. He poured a cup of coffee. "Well, records first, Mac?"

McHenry nodded, but raised a pudgy finger. "We'll cut this month's inspection a little short, Judah," he whispered in a conspiratorial tone. "Granddaughter's birthday party tonight. Just skim the records." He opened his blue U.L. binder, paying little attention to the various records, except for the number of forty-pound bags *Insul-Gard* had received from the bag manufacturer since the last U.L. inspection. *Insul-Gard* paid U.L. for each label that stated U.L. testing data. "Ah, same formula?" McHenry asked, referring to the borates used as fire retardants in the ground newsprint.

"Yes," Simon answered. They could not change their formula and retain the existing U.L. label without going through a full-scale set of expensive tests at the U.L. lab in Santa Clara.

McHenry skimmed through the other records. "Hmmm… good." He snapped his binder closed. "Okay, Judah, let's take a look at the line. We can skip the inventory count and broken-bag count. I'll accept your figures this time."

Inwardly, Simon smiled. Happy birthday, little girl.

Before leaving the office, they put on hard hats, slipped on particle masks, inserted disposable earplugs. Then they stepped out onto the plant floor and were assailed by the din and dust of production. Simon led McHenry through the maze of pallets of finished product to the equipment line. They followed the production flow: the chemical loading station and chemical grinder, the newsprint pre-shredder, the two *Jacobson* hammer mills—Simon stopped and signaled a lineman to cut the chemical feed. After a moment, a warning light flashed over the first paper mill, indication that no untreated newsprint was being processed. The line started back up, and they moved to the bagging tank with the huge cyclone, which resembled an inverted twenty-five foot high ice cream cone—it controlled most of the dust. For a moment they paused, watching the plastic-wrapped forty-pound cubes of insulation coming off the two bagging pistons, every fifth bag manually checked on a digital scale before being stacked on a pallet: 39.8, 39.7, 40.4, 39.9, 40.1. U.L. allowed only a 0.5-pound tolerance to ensure proper chemical-newsprint mix in the final product: a difficult parameter with a low-density material.

Abruptly, McHenry walked away, hollering over the noise: "Looks good, Judah. Let's see one lab test, a basket burn."

They walked into the line lab next to Simon's office, shedding their masks, earplugs, and hats. A young man was at the lab bench, doing calculations with a desk calculator.

"Jim, pull a sample for a basket test," Simon said to the tech.

In a few minutes, Jim returned with a large basket of insulation, which looked like the gray stuffing from a soft doll. Simon watched as Jim prepared and executed a burn of the insulation—19 percent weight loss, well within the U.L. fire-retardant parameter.

McHenry nodded and scribbled a note in his blue binder. Then he turned the binder around and said, "Sign my inspection sheet, Judah."

Simon signed his name and walked McHenry out to the parking lot. He waved goodbye as the inspector left, then sighed with relief. His back was soaked with sweat, his left eyelid twitching out of control. As Simon climbed the stairs to the management offices, he looked at his watch: 5:32. Everyone would be gone by now, except Nelson. The door to the old man's office was open. Nelson looked up from his desk, signaling Simon to come in and sit down.

As Simon settled in his seat, Nelson leaned back in his swivel chair and asked, "How'd it go with U.L.?"

Simon grinned. "Okay, no variances this time."

Nelson looked back at his desk, grunting his approval, and then he burst out angrily, "Dammit, Simon! That was a fool stunt last night, not even calling after the funeral." He was staring at Simon, his bushy white eyebrows knotted in an angry, questioning frown.

Simon pressed his eyelid, trying to control the flutter. For a moment the old man's face blurred, as if the room had suddenly filled with fog. Simon blinked, "Yeah, I know, Jack," he said, his voice tight with strain. "I… ah, met with my uncle's attorney, Mr. Rutherford," he lied lamely. "We had a few beers, one thing leading to another. Finally, it was too late to call, you know?"

The old man shook his head slowly, the wrinkles in his face etched deeply. "No, Simon, I don't know. You could've called me at home." He picked up a pencil, chewed on the eraser, and stared absently out the window.

Sheepishly, Simon asked about the report.

Nelson shrugged. "I finished the report myself. T.J. read it to-day before sending it to CPPA." He looked back at Simon. "You know it could've killed your chance to sit here"—he tapped the arm of the swivel chair with his pencil—"if T.J. knew *you* hadn't finished that report." The old man glanced at the door, lowering his voice. "You've come a long way, Simon," he said, the anger fading, leaving his voice soft, tired.

Simon rubbed the fluttering eyelid again, and then nodded. "I know and thanks, Jack." It was Nelson who had taken him off the line, pushed him through promotions: line foreman, shift supervi-sor, and Q.C. supervisor; he had encouraged Simon to take busi-ness courses at San Jose City College… and now covering for him. He owed the old man a lot. "I appreciate—"

"Okay," Nelson interrupted gruffly. He looked squarely at Si-mon, the concern obvious in his eyes. "Everything else okay, son? I mean at home, the wife and kid?"

"Oh, yeah." Simon nodded. "Everything's fine at home, Jack. Ah, right now Jenny and Betty are up at Sonoma visiting Betty's mother, but everything's fine."

The damn eyelid continued to twitch.

"Good." The old man looked self-conscious. "Thought it might be home problems, guess it's just me." He turned back to his desk, rearranging papers, apparently shifting his train of thought. Finally, he asked, "What about Jim?" The deep frown had eased from his face. "Doesn't he leave Monday for school?"

Oh, Jesus! Simon swore to himself. It had slipped his mind that he needed a new swing shift tech trained by Monday. "Ah..."

There was one boy on the line. Manuel Rodriquez. He seemed bright, energetic, though for some reason, the other men shunned him. "I've got a man spotted, Jack. Thought I'd talk to him at dinner tonight. Rodriquez. He's living with relatives in San Jose, studying English at night school. Hardworking, wants to better himself."

Nelson stood up. "Good. Take care of it." The old man moved slowly toward the door. He stopped before leaving. "Simon?"

Simon stood up. "Yes, Jack."

"See a doc about that eye," the old man said. "Might be a vitamin deficiency or..." His voice trailed off and he left the office before Simon could answer.

After dinner at eight, Simon met with the shift supervisor, making arrangements to relieve Manuel on the line. He took the young man into the lab and introduced him to Jim, instructing the tech to familiarize the new man with the various test procedures and preliminary reports. Then Simon went into his office to do paperwork.

Later, after work, as Simon opened his Mustang door to leave the plant, Manuel appeared.

"Thank you very much, señor," the boy said in careful English, looking down at his feet.

Simon understood. It was more than the dollar or so an hour difference in pay. He recalled his own feelings after getting off the line: *respite*—relief from the dust; the rattling of the equipment; the never-ending stream of bags; and the other men, often rough, crude, sweaty.

In the light cast by the nearby mercury-vapor standard, the

boy's face seemed different… smooth, his high cheeks pink as if rouged, his eyelashes long, black, delicate.

A car eased by them, an old Merc slung back, low-rider fashion, just out of the umbrella of light. From the dark interior, Simon heard a low mix of English and Spanish, nothing clear except one word: *puto*. He stepped nearer to see inside but the driver suddenly gunned the car, and it jumped away, headed for the parking lot gate. Simon shrugged. Someone jealous about the promotion. He looked back at Manuel.

Simon gasped.

The white quetzal was sitting on the fence near the stall sign: *Mr. Judah*. So close. The bird stared back at Simon, its snowy feathers glistening in the eerie light. So beautiful. Almost translucent, just a hint of blue, like an ice sculpture. Magnificent.

He breathed twin plumes of steam into the night air, realizing it was freezing. Simon wrapped his arms around his body, trying to ease the chill.

"Señor? Señor Judah?" The boy was grasping Simon's shoulder, shaking him gently. "What is it, señor?"

Simon's left eyelid twitched out of control. Unable to answer, he gestured behind Manuel toward the fence; but the white quetzal was gone.

Brrring.

Sluggishly, Simon struggled into consciousness.

Brrring. His mouth tasted metallic. He took a deep breath, letting air trickle across his cracked lips. The clock read: 8:30 a.m. It was early Friday morning. He was home in Sunnyvale.

Brrring. The phone, it was the damn phone. "Hello," Simon whispered dryly.

"Simon, is that you?" The voice was distant, unreal, like a computer recording. "Simon?"

"Yes, it's me," he answered, closing his eyes.

"Simon, some son of a bitch stuffed your new tech into the dumpster behind the plant. Cut his balls off?"

"Jack?" Simon was still fuzzy, but he knew the voice belonged to Jack Nelson.

"Yeah, garbage men found him at six this morning."

New tech? Manuel Rodriquez! Finally Simon was making sense of Nelson's ranting. "They found Manuel?"

"That's what I'm telling you. *Murdered.* Cops are here now. Whoever nailed him is one crazy bastard."

Simon felt nauseated. Then he remembered the boy in the parking lot after work, and the low-rider Merc. Jesus! The bird, too.

"They'll probably want to talk to you when you come in."

"Jack," Simon mumbled hoarsely, "I'm not coming in today. Sick." His eyelid fluttered.

After a pause: "Okay, but Simon there's something else. T.J. made his decision. He's promoting Raymond when I go." The voice sounded more distant. "T.J. can talk to you when you do come in. You know I'm sorry, Simon. I guess T.J. feels Raymond has a more rounded background. Line, sales, sales manager. He finished college—"

The phone slid from Simon's hand, dropping to the bed. It didn't make any difference, he thought, but the boy.

"Simon, Simon?" Far away a voice squeaked.

Absently, Simon picked up the phone and gently dropped it into the cradle.

Late Saturday morning, Simon again awakened slowly, struggling up out of the familiar fog, his memory of the previous night a blank. He dressed and drove over to the Copper Kettle for breakfast. Brooding over his coffee, he glanced at the front page of the *Chronicle.* A photograph of a young man raised the hair on the back of Simon's neck. He skimmed the article: *...slashed to death... mutilated... linked to at least two other murders in the Bay Area...*

Heart beating rapidly, Simon stared at the photograph, and he recalled fragments of the evening.

He had driven to San Francisco, and drifted aimlessly from bar to bar, a vague blur of places and faces. Then he was on a stool, where everything seemed right—the light, dim and silvery. He ordered a stinger and sipped the drink slowly, watching couples dancing in the mirror. Suddenly, it dawned on him: the dancers were all men. He drained his drink, his gaze drawn to the golden letters over the mirror: *ETC*. He sat in place, trying to remember another time. Finally he gave up and ordered another drink.

Someone slid onto the stool next to Simon. A young man: white even teeth, fine features, short blonde hair, eyes a washed blue, a tiny gold post in his left earlobe. The young man looked at Simon and smiled. Simon shifted his gaze to his drink, stirring it with his finger, a strange sensation tingling in his chest.

"Hello," the young man said, lightly touching Simon's arm. "I'm Donel."

Simon looked down at the hand on his arm: long fingers, nails manicured, a gold ring engraved with a gothic *D*. The fingers moved gracefully, the touch delicate. Simon swallowed hard, trying to work up moisture in his dry mouth. He nodded. "M-m-my name's," he stammered, "Judah, Simon Judah."

The young man removed his hand, making a gesture to the bartender. "Jeff, give Simon another stinger. I'll have one, too, please."

Things slowed down, the memory dimmer...

They danced, Simon awkward, clumsy. Eventually they left *ETC* together, Donel's hand gripping Simon's elbow, guiding him to a nearby flat. Simon stumbled on the porch steps; he knew he was drunk. At the door, Donel paused, and then leaned close to

Simon, his warm moist lips brushing Simon's cheek. In the dim light, the boy's face made the breath catch in Simon's throat. So beautiful! He closed his eyes as Donel unlocked the door and led him inside. He opened his eyes and groaned—

Simon thought it was a painting over the table; but the chill struck him like a blow, and he knew. The white quetzal sat on the table, staring at them, its eyes glittering like two blue-white stars in a wintry sky.

"Oh, n-n-no," Simon stuttered, his teeth chattering in the freezing flat; then everything became slower, dimmer, confused.

A scream, but the sound distant, like an echo from the far end of a tunnel. Donel on his knees reaching out to Simon, his hand wet and sticky.

And the others—Manuel and Paul—had reached out, too, terror on their faces—

Simon blinked and stared at the newspaper. He rose slowly and threw a few bills on the counter, feeling numb—his mind frozen. He needed air. He staggered out of the restaurant, looking about frantically until he spotted the familiar Mustang. Ride, he thought simply, ride.

A high-pitched wail penetrated Simon's confused state.

In the rearview mirror, he saw the black-and-white patrol car closing in on him, its turret flashing red in the darkness. It was night! Panic seized him. He jammed down on the accelerator; but, amazingly, the patrol car swung out and zoomed by, as if the Mustang were crawling along. Simon stared wide-eyed as the red taillights disappeared. Then it dawned: they were not chasing *him*. He eased up on the accelerator, a squeak of relief catching in his throat. Somewhere someone was looking for him. He had been bad; he had to find someplace safe. He glanced out the side windows: colored lights dancing like a neon kaleidoscope.

Tears blurred his vision. Where was he?

A sign; he recognized that street sign. Van Ness and 101 winding through the City. He cried out with joy! Betty's mother's. They'd come this way many times—Betty's face flashed into his mind; and he mentally clung to his wife's image. Betty, Betty, Betty.

The Golden Gate Bridge loomed ahead, its burnt orange color obscured by the fog. He passed through the free side of the tollbooths, looking for the first tower; but it was gone, swallowed up in the dense mist. Slowly, he edged the Mustang up the grade of the bridge. He was overwhelmed by a feeling of aloneness. The thick fog had sealed him off from the world: no lights, no cars, no joggers, no cyclists. He was alone, following the cone of yellow light from his headlights. Suddenly they blinked out. He pulled the Mustang over, feeling panic. He had to get across the bridge, drive to Sonoma, and find… find—

He couldn't remember the name. He got out of the car, trying to recall, but his thoughts were a confusing blur. Then he glimpsed something in the mist and heard… Wingbeats? He cocked his head expectantly. Nothing. Absolute quiet. The mist blew against his face, washing his mind clear. Then, he understood. He knew *who* he was; he recognized this place, *La Ventana.*

He was home.

Quickly he stripped away his clothes. Then he hopped up and perched on the limb of the strangler fig. After a moment, he spread his wings and soared out into the cloud forest.

MIRROR MOMENTS

CHRISTIAN A. LARSEN

THE PRINTING PRESSES were hulking gray machines that blocked out whatever ventilation would have come through the open windows. Racks of trays filled with lettering lined the inside wall. It always seemed odd that the machines weren't on the inside wall, but I guess it had something to do with them overheating. I never asked Grandpa, or Uncle Harvey, who was the only other person who worked there. When Grandpa would sneak upstairs and take a nap in the vacant apartment, and Uncle Harvey would be in the office working on layout, Doug and I would get into rubber band fights or push each other around on the hand truck, zooming by the printing presses while they were grabbing, whirling, and chomping sheets of hat tags. We never thought of the danger.

We never even knew.

Still, I used to white knuckle those rides. My brother would pretend to lose his grip and, ramrod straight, I would bounce on the steel frame, gulping down my fear. The back of my skull felt like an eggshell waiting to crack open over the concrete floor. Of course, I never had the same fear for Doug. Hold it at the right angle, and you could roll a hand truck with your finger. I rolled him back to the end of the room, near the washroom nobody ever used and the back door with the St. Pauli Girl poster.

"My turn! My turn!" I said, geeked to the gills over how fast I had rolled Doug across the room on our last pass.

"Okay, Cole," he said, a sly smile creeping across his face. "I've got an idea, though." And then he added solemnly: "To make it really scary."

"What's that?"

"Stand on the hand truck, but don't lean back. Just close your eyes. I'll grab the handle and start you up real fast. It'll be scarier if you don't know it's coming. But you can't look, no matter what."

I agreed, stepping on the steel lip. It was going to be awesome. Doug said so.

"I'm going to make sure the coast is clear."

"Okay," I said, catching a glimpse of him disappearing into the hallway. I didn't mean to look. It kind of felt like cheating, but I wanted to peek at that St. Pauli Girl poster. It was the kind of picture my mom would have made me throw out. I always felt guilty for looking at it.

The lip on the hand truck wasn't exactly level, or there was a dip in the floor, because it tipped a little, clicking into the concrete whenever I shifted my weight. Doug was gone for so long, I was shifting quite a bit.

Click-click. Click-click. Click-click.

He must have gone through the storage area, where we punched the tags, all the way back to the office, or maybe up the stairs to the apartment where Grandpa liked to slip into the bedroom with the window air-conditioner and sleep.

Or maybe he was hiding around the corner, giggling into his hand, making an idiot out of me. Like his version of snipe hunting.

Something kept me on that hand truck, my eyes dutifully shut with the St. Pauli Girl's breasts burned as negative afterimages onto the insides of my eyelids. My palms were sweating, and I shifted my fingers on the frame.

And that's when the hand truck dropped low and zoomed

forward, like the luge event I had caught part of in the '84 Winter Games. Those guys looked like they were wearing full-body pantyhose with their junk all bunched up. I wore jeans and a t-shirt, and I could swear the corner of my sleeve whisked one of those hulking, industrial presses. Just a nick, almost not at all. I had heard somewhere that batters would make a noise with their mouth to fool umpires into thinking they had been nicked by a pitch. But I didn't think Doug was that good at making sound effects with his mouth.

It took every ounce of my willpower not to let go and check for a hole in my sleeve. If I shifted my weight, even a little, Doug might lose his balance (and mine) and dump me sideways into the hot, inky rollers—or both of us might crash and get flattened. My heart beat with helium, each thunk-thunk bringing it a little higher in my throat.

The hand truck slowed and wheeled around at the end of the aisle, or maybe it wheeled around before slowing. The whole thing took a couple of seconds, tops, but it seemed like forever, the way those moments can. The hand truck pitched forward, an ignominious end to the ride, but one from which I could walk away. I was fine, but there was a tiny hole in my sleeve that hadn't been there before. I had gotten my money's worth, all right.

Still holding my shoulder, I felt my heart knocking against my sternum. This was better than riding *The Demon* at Great America. This was real danger. I shuffled around to thank Doug, smiling widely.

But it wasn't Doug standing there.

It wasn't Uncle Harvey, either. And it certainly wasn't Grandpa. His distended belly was so crisscrossed with scars from cancer surgeries that he couldn't even pull weeds, much less bus a 115-pound tween on a hand truck. No, it was something else entirely.

There was a press operator named Bob Nugent, an old guy

who had played minor-league baseball in the 1930s who fell to unskilled labor the rest of his life and worked at The Shop when I was a little kid. I could only remember the edges of what he looked like—the fine white hairs on his head and a canvas apron stretched across his round middle, stained black with ink. It made him look like a butcher of demons. I couldn't remember his face, though. He was a dream person with an empty spot where his face should be.

That's exactly how the guy standing in front of me looked, even though I was staring right at him with a slash of sunlight over his face—an empty spot where his face should be.

"Who are you?"

"Helluva ride, eh kid?"

I thought he might have sounded like Bob.

"Do you know my grandpa?"

"Sure, I know him, and your uncle," he said. "I know a lot of people, really."

"Where's Doug?"

"Your brother went upstairs, kid."

"Who are you?"

"You heard of guardian angels?"

I imagined him smiling behind that empty face.

"Sure."

"I'm kind of like that," he said, stepping past the pallets of virgin paper toward the trays of lettering on the far wall.

My uncle had never used the lettering to make a forme; it was old technology even when my grandpa was a young man. But my mom's family never threw anything away, and the shop was like a personal museum, leaving detritus like lettering in trays for faceless strangers to rummage through while I stood gape-mouthed next to a furious press.

He beckoned me again with his ink-stained fingers. They were black like his apron.

The sound he made reminded me of the sound I made looking for blocks in the toy barrel when I was a kid. He wasn't searching for typeface; he was searching for a particular piece of typeface.

He didn't seem to notice or care that I crept forward, probably because he knew I couldn't resist.

He held up a wooden block with a piece of type on it.

"You see this?"

Something pushed my head forward—the vacuum where my willpower used to be. The type wasn't easy to read. There were no straight lines and the serifs were rounded off, kind of bubbly, but the answer seemed obvious.

"Sure, it's a lowercase *d*."

"Is it?" He licked his blackened thumb and pressed it against the relief of the type. "Come here."

I stepped closer.

He held my chin in his hand. Once he steadied my face, he took the piece of type and pressed it to my head, hard, three times, all in a row. I wanted to pull away, but part of me had already given in to this faceless pressman.

He let go of my chin and rocked back off his plant foot, admiring his handiwork. I couldn't see it on his face, because I couldn't see his face (that empty spot smack dab in the middle of my field of vision), but I may have even sensed a smile. There was a feeling in the air of satisfaction as thick as those slivers of cardstock that billowed in the air like primordial dust motes.

"Check the mirror," he said. "The one in the washroom."

I had to obey—it was something my college roommate would have called the 'escalation of commitment.' I was in too deep to back out now, even though I hadn't done a thing. But try telling that to yourself as a twelve-year-old. Kids are easily manipulated, as are adults sometimes.

I passed the velvet painting of the mountain lion that hung on the bare cinderblock wall, and its eyes seemed to follow, not out of malevolence, but out of a curiosity so strong it could animate the inanimate.

Where the hell had Doug gone?

One of my uncle's cigarettes rested on the edge of the hydraulic paper cutter. It wasn't much more than a butt, but it smoldered. A tendril of smoke rose to the ceiling. Uncle Harvey couldn't have been gone more than a minute or two, and Doug less than that, but it felt like the whole afternoon had passed me by. The moment stretched like the tape in a cassette, long and thin—like that tendril of smoke—to the point of breaking.

My forehead itched like a thousand mosquito bites, worse than the time I played in the attic and got into the fiberglass insulation. Maybe it was just the curiosity, but that's the worst kind of itch anyway. I wanted to scratch at it with my nails, but knew the faceless man in the ink-stained apron wouldn't want me to.

The butcher of demons.

I opened the washroom door. There was a toilet, a sink, a mirror, and four cinderblock walls—unforgiving, but direct in its purpose. I never saw my uncle or grandpa ever use the washroom, but the toilet paper didn't look old and there was water in the bowl. I flicked on the rack of fluorescent tubes over my head and stuck my face in the mirror, leaning on the sink with both hands.

The mark on my forehead read: 666.

I tried to rub it away, but it wouldn't come off. I tried water and even scraped at it with a bar of pumice soap, but it was indelible. My heart started thudding all over again, like I was about to get caught doing something wrong.

Kids see things differently; that's why they make such great victims.

I looked down in the sink and scooped up some cold water to rinse my forehead, hoping the suds lathered there would make a difference. Mr. No-Face stood over my shoulder. He might have been grinning. There was no way for me to know for sure, but it sure felt like he was grinning.

"I'm going to be in big trouble!" I said, dragging the soap across my forehead again. It was useless, and I knew it, but you only lose when you quit trying.

"Not yet, you're not."

I started to cry.

"Who are you?"

"What you said before."

"My guardian angel?"

"Your guardian, yes."

The water kept running, but my hands went still.

"What do you want?"

"I want you to understand, Cole."

I looked into that empty spot.

"The typeface I pressed into your forehead? It could be a lowercase *b*, or a *q*, or the number *9* or even a *6*, depending on how it's placed. What things are all depend on what we do with them. Time is like that. Each moment has a mirror image. An inverse. Good can happen, or bad. But it all comes with a cost. Even if you choose to do good, bad can come from it."

He put his ink-stained hand on my shoulder.

"Do you see?"

I shook my head a little, without confidence.

"You let your brother push you on that handcart, and you'll wind up in a bad way."

"I won't. I won't let him."

"Good," said Mr. No-Face. "Very good."

I heard my uncle's smoker cough down the hallway. He would be to the press room in a few seconds. I had the sensation of stepping onto the people mover at the airport, like I was rejoining real time again. The sounds around me were bending like a record or a tape gaining speed. It was a relief, in a way, but—

"Do you know how I know this, Cole?"

I shook my head again. This time I really shook it.

"Because you already have, in that other moment—the mirror moment. But I've given you another chance. I'm your guardian, after all. You said it; you're mine."

He ran his thumb across my forehead and erased the '666.'

It was gone, like his face, but it was still there.

"But it comes at a price. I may never call in the favor, but if I do, you have to pay, or the mirror moment comes into play, and everything that's happened shatters like glass. Now do you understand?"

"Yes."

"What do you understand?"

My forehead looked clean and a little red, and no longer itched, but I rubbed at it with my forearm anyway.

"That good guys can be bad guys," I said. "And people offer help for the worst reasons sometimes."

So, if you hear someone say 'the devil made me do it,' ask them to be specific. Because I'd love to catch up with my old friend, Titivillus, and see if we can't flip the typeface and forget the whole damned thing.

ALDERWAY

PATRICK O' NEILL

YOUR LAST WORDS to me, Caroline. How they haunt me now.

"Swear that you'll never go to the church at Alderway. Swear it."

For years I had assumed they meant nothing and were simply a by-product of the increased morphine dosage in your bloodstream during those final hours. They told me that the drugs would bring you comfort but all I saw was confusion and fear. I shudder to recall the desperate minutes in which I witnessed your sanity melt into a distorted grimace. You were gone far before your pulse slowed to a stop, and your hand became cold in mine.

"Of course, I swear it."

Yes, for many years, I thought nothing more of those words and focused instead on the memories that brought warmth: the way sunlight played across your dark hair in summer time; your tender lips against mine; the scent of jasmine on your skin. I had never known or even heard of Alderway, or that there should be a church there, until I found your work in the attic.

Having lived alone here for so long, I had assumed that I knew every inch of this house, but I was wrong. The sliding compartment at the bottom of the leather chest was the perfect place—just enough room for the crumpled sheets of paper—for the roughly sketched family trees and brass-rubbings. Why did you not destroy it all, Caroline? Why did you not burn everything? In the end, I cannot blame you. You hid it well. How could you have known you would become ill so suddenly, or that I would ever find it?

I had always harbored an interest in discovering my family history and I could only imagine, as I knelt in the attic with your papers splayed out before me, that—knowing this—you had chosen to find out for yourself, with the intention of surprising me at some future point.

But of course, once you had discovered all there was to discover, you hid it. And who could blame you?

As I unrolled the larger brass-rubbing, the one of the knight's face behind armored visor, I felt as you must have felt on seeing it that first time: excitement that the similarity was too apparent to be coincidental, and also the distant but unmistakable sense of dread; the fleeting chill across skin that could not be accounted for.

Do you remember, on summer mornings, how we used to watch fallow deer creep from the woodland and graze on the roses at the far western corner of the lawn? If we so much as flinched from our concealed vantage point in the sitting room, they would twitch their heads and scatter into the trees immediately. I kept a record in the hope of understanding their pattern of behaviors: how often they might visit the lawn, and at what times. You mocked me, but I would tell you, as always, that everything bears its own unique pattern, that there is always symmetry and regularity; and that you only need look for it. Even now I hold this true. I am retired, but I will always be a mathematician.

It is different now. The deer seldom come to the lawn and when they do, it is not my movements in the sitting room that startle them. They are already anxious because they sense something in the trees about them. They never stay to eat the roses anymore. Their pattern has been knocked out of kilter.

For the longest time, I resisted. But with every year that passed, with every November that dark clouds bloated in the skies above the house and cold rain beat against its windows, I was reminded of your passing; was reminded of your final words and of the secret that would always remain between us, unless I was to visit the church at Alderway and find out for myself whatever it was that lay sheltered there.

It became harder and harder as time went on to ignore that something had been kept from me, but also that I had the power to change it, and that there was no reason why I should not know.

Besides breaking my promise to you, what harm could it do?

The journey took less than an hour from the house. So strange that I should never have known of the place; although it is well-hidden. Even on ordinance survey maps, no more than a solitary black cross set in open contours with the word *'Alderway'* hanging above it, suggests its existence.

I drove through Compton and into the valley below Pangley, where the road narrowed and became a tunnel of low-hanging branches, clawing around me like skeletal fingers. But soon the landscape opened onto fields again. I passed deserted farmyards, deeply-ploughed fields where crows winged against heavy skies; and all the while, as I drove deeper into remote acreage, the distant sense of dread that I had first experienced grew closer. I brushed it aside, assuming that my guilt at breaking my promise to you was clouding my reason.

How little I knew.

A mile or so from my destination, the road narrowed again. Wild branches scratched intermittently against the side of the car and rain began to fall. There was only room for one vehicle here but I passed no one else, and knew that I would not. This place had been left to Nature. I stopped the car only because a fallen tree in the road had made the route impassable.

Beyond the driver's side window, half-obscured amongst brambles, stood a broken wooden gate, hinged in studded-iron.

The dark grey stone of Alderway was visible from here too. Once again, I shuddered as an inexplicable coldness crept through me.

I switched off the engine and sat for a moment, listening to the rain ticking against the roof of the car, wondering why I had come.

I turned to the passenger seat—where you once sat—and fumbled through the rolls of brass-rubbings until I found the family tree that you had created.

The first relatives must have been easy to source:

Simon Tacher (Father)
Geoffrey Tacher (Grandfather)
Edwin Earl Tacher (Great Grandfather)
Henry Jameson Tacher (Great Great Grandfather)

But after that, to unwind history back so far, to the arrival of a French family at Alderway in 1242, must have been painstaking.

The fallow deer came to the lawn again last week: a nervous doe and its slender fawn. They have been away for some days and only stayed a moment before something in the woodland startled them. I thought for a moment that I saw something in the trees. As I become weaker, they visit the lawn less and less. In a way, it makes perfect sense. A new pattern.

The cemetery at Alderway is unremarkable if not for the ancient yew-tree that shadows the majority of the graves and keeps the air moist and filled with the scent of damp earth. As I walked beneath its heavy branches and toward the entrance of the church, I noticed the grass was not trimmed and that many of the headstones were crumbled and dilapidated. There were no fresh flowers about the graves either; nothing to suggest that anyone had been buried here for a long time.

Before I pulled open the thick mahogany door, I gazed up at the Norman tower of the church: dark stone against amber skies.

Then, without reason, I had the strangest feeling that someone was standing directly behind me on the pathway I had walked, but when I turned to look, there was nothing—only the headstones jutting from the ground like crooked teeth, a crow cawing into the silence, and the yew tree, casting dark shadows about the overgrown grass. The sweet scent of jasmine hung in the air.

I wonder now if it was you, Caroline, standing there, willing me away from this place one final time.

Inside, the church was musty and cold, but a set of strip-lights hanging far above cast an orangey glow over the wooden pews and broke the silence with a monotonous hum of electricity.

I strolled down the south transept, toward the altar and the colossal oak cross that hung before the stained windows, conscious of the sound of my step. The flag stones were smooth from centuries of wear. As I reached the altar, I looked down to see the brass image of the knight that you had rubbed onto the tracing paper.

I knelt and gazed into the face peering back at me from behind the shining visor.

Yes, the similarity was too faithful to be anything but an ancestor: the hook of the nose and deep-set eyes, the birthmark about the right eye so keenly etched into the metal. I stood again, this time absorbing the entire image of the knight: sword at the center, clad in well-cut armor. The deep italics engraved above his head looked as though they had been impressed only yesterday:

Here Doth Not Lie

Simone le Tache

1268

The One who made Foole of The Devile

Below these words, and in a separate box that had been carved from the figure's chest, was another group of engravings, perhaps of Arabic or Chinese—more like symbols than words. I recognized them immediately from your brass rubbings. You had specifically focused on this section.

I started as a voice sounded behind me.

"Interesting, is it not?"

A chaplain dressed in black habit and dog collar smiled upon me with pale blue eyes. I took him to be around sixty and in poor health. He was overweight and his breaths wheezed as he leaned heavily against his wooden stick. When he saw the birthmark to my right eye, something passed over his face that I could not gauge. Something like fear, although it was hard to tell.

"Yes," I agreed, "but it makes no sense. Why should he *not lie* here? I don't get it."

His grip tightened momentarily on his stick as he coughed and wheezed into the silence, but then his smile returned.

"Legend has it," he said, "that Simone le Tache arrived in Alderway in 1242 having travelled from central France. He was not a man of any great wealth and at some point, it is written at least, he sold his soul to the Devil in return for riches. The Devil agreed to secure his wealth but warned him that wherever his body was buried—be it inside or outside the church—that he would take his soul to Hell. Soon afterwards, Le Tache became unexpectedly wealthy but on his death, years later, his family buried him neither inside the church, nor outside."

"They buried him here." He tapped his stick at the stony wall beside him. "Inside the northern wall. So you see, not inside the church, not outside the church. He cheated the Devil and his soul escaped damnation, hence the writing here on the brass plate."

Silence settled around us, broken only by the buzzing of the strip lights.

"That's a great story," I said, stooping once again to look into the face of Simone le Tache. "Really Great."

"Oh, but that's only the half of it; literally." He prodded his stick toward the ground. "The carpet beside the effigy—pull it up and look underneath. Well, go on."

I knelt down and rolled back the thin red carpet to reveal another brass plate.

"An exact replica," he said. "A perfect mirror image of the original. You see, even the words have been mirrored to read backwards."

"That's extraordinary," I said, rubbing my fingers across both smooth surfaces. "But why?"

"Why indeed," he said, hobbling slowly toward the altar. "Why indeed? That is indeed the question."

"There must be a reason," I said, feeling over the cold metal. "The work that has gone into this. The symmetry is perfect."

"Well, the truth is, nobody knows. It is the great mystery of Alderway and in a way it is good. The mystery keeps the place interesting. The congregation has dwindled in recent years and any interest can only be a good thing, I think."

I had stopped listening to him now and was focused only on the brass images before me, trying to find a fault in the symmetry. The wording: all perfectly reversed. The imprint of Le Tache in his armor, even the intricate flowers on his sword: all flawless in reflection on the corresponding brass plate. Even the Arabic-looking symbols in the box of their own across the knight's chest: all mirrored exactly.

"I just can't see it," I said. " But there must be a pattern. A reason."

I stood up and gazed down at the images from above, and suddenly there it was.

"The reflection is perfect," I said aloud. "The symmetry is there. But it's chiral."

"What is chiral?"

"It means the image cannot be perfectly superimposed onto itself. The images look the same, but are different when you put one on top of the other. Wait. I'll be back."

"Slow down, young man," he said, leaning against his stick. "All is well. A mystery can be a mystery. There is no harm to it. Quite the opposite, I think."

But there was no time for dawdling. I knew I was right, as you must have known. I rushed through the cemetery, beneath the yew, to the car where I found the brass rubbings and your dark-blue wax crayon. I realized then, as I huddled them against my body in the beating rain and made my way back to the church, why you had chosen tracing paper.

Once inside, I strode to the brass plates and knelt again.

I unrolled the first brass-rubbing, the one of the knight's face, then pushed it aside. Not that one. Then the next, and the next, until I found the images of the chest portion, where symbols had appeared Arabic or Chinese. There were two rolls of tracing paper, but I chose the one on which you had written, *Mirror Image.*

I set it on top of the original brass plate and lined up the edges until the square fit perfectly. Then I began to rub across the symbols with the wax crayon, and soon it became clear.

"You see," I said, as I rubbed frantically. "They're not symbols, or letters from another language, but half-letters, English letters. They only become whole when the mirror image is superimposed onto them. It's a mirror image, but you have to put them together to make them whole. Chiral. There, now you see."

I stood back and read the words that now appeared in waxy blue text:

But The Devile will take what is His
and Owne the souls of those who share the Blood Line of le Tache
And who Step upon this Place.

The atmosphere had changed now and I looked up toward the altar, at the cross. Behind me, the walking stick clicked against stone and a whispery laughter echoed into the silence.

A chill found its way down my neck, tingling to the base of my spine as his voice rasped behind me.

"I have waited a long time for you. But time is mine. I have all the time. Now who is the fool?"

The deer do not come now. I was right about the pattern. It was inevitable that my deterioration would result in their absence. The roses have died and the shadows in the trees are clearer with each day that passes. The new pattern is easy to understand.

My every weakness becomes His every strength. My every loss becomes His gain. He is coming nearer because He knows I am close to the end.

Last night, I had the dream again.

In the dream, I was running from the church, through the beating rain, beneath the yew tree to the car, not looking back. I started the engine and maneuvered a turn in the road before pulling away. I tried not to look as the old man tapped his cane at my window, but something made me look, just as it did that day, and I saw his face again—the face no one should see.

I woke to a noise outside on the lawn and went to the window. The clouds had parted and moonlight cast a silvery light across the grass. Near the rose bed I could make out the portly figure resting against His stick, staring back at me.

No, it is not long now, and He knows.

I will leave this letter by your graveside, Caroline, far from Alderway. I used to believe that, even though you were taken from me, that we would meet again some sunny day.

Now I know it can never be, because of all that we found at Alderway.

I have one last idea, though it may come to nothing.

Dear Mr Tacher,

Thank you for your letter of 19 September 1985.

May I begin by expressing my regret to hear that you have been ill of health in recent weeks. I wish you a speedy recovery and all the very best for the future.

It is my unfortunate duty to inform you that your request to be buried inside the North Wall of Alderway Church, Berkshire, alongside your ancestor, has been declined by the Council. It is worth mentioning that we receive a number of such letters each year, outlining unusual applications, and that we are not always in a position to provide consent.

You may be aware that Alderway Church has remained vacant of both congregation and minister for some years now; however, it is important to note that the church itself, dating from the early 13th Century, is of Significant Historical Interest and as such is a Listed building. It will not be possible therefore to make any alteration to the building, however small, without an application, and subsequent approval, from the High Court. You may wish to pursue this route, and indeed I enclose papers should you wish to do so; however, I would point out that I have never known a request such as this to be authorized by any Court in England.

I am sorry that we have been unable to facilitate your request in this instance. I wish you all the best for the future.

Yours faithfully,

Brian Jones
Administrative Manager
Berkshire Borough Council

SIGIL

P. GARDNER GOLDSMITH

WHAT CAN I EXPRESS about this strange phenomenon that will not inspire within you merely a subtle sense of disquiet, rather than utter, uncontrollable dread?

To you, the tale I intend to recount will seem a trifle, the most ordinary of occurrences, dismissible as a simple twist of fate or the combination of average circumstances as seen through an old man's *paranoid dementia*. But to me, the witness of these preternatural events, it is a story so horrific as to implicate the Devil himself.

In my lonely and solitary existence here in New England, I have endeavored to trouble no one. The pale and silent snows of winter blanket my surroundings, delivering peace and tranquility to my once tormented soul.

They bring to mind the deep arboreal stillness of my homeland, where a man might walk for miles and encounter no one. His companions, mute and unmoving, would consist of the majestic firs and brooding oaks, and the crisp air would fill his lungs and caress his skin. Invigorated and enlivened, he would march with a bounce to his step, planting his boots in the snow and delighting in the crunch of one against the other.

I can recall with vivid clarity the varied colors of the wood: the deep green of the pines and the pearly white of the snow, the somber browns of the shadow-filled valleys, and the ghostly gray of my own breath, billowing into the air. The frosted canopy had its own wonderful presence, and I encountered it like a subject does his king, with heartfelt and profound reverence.

Many years have passed since then, the days and trying times accruing like layers of tarnish on silver. But the brilliance of those memories remains—of a time when I was young and vital, standing alongside my friends in a great and noble struggle.

Tragically, almost all of them are now gone, buried beneath those knee-deep snows, their pale bones turning to dust in unremarkable graves. It is all too clear that I cannot return to see them, but I *do* have my memories. And although my loneliness is sometimes profound, I can relive those halcyon days by exercising my mind, and thumbing through my care-worn diary.

My recollections from that time are set down on some one hundred eighty pages in an almost unintelligible script, written with an uncooperative fountain pen over the course of three years. The sheets themselves are yellowing and delicate, like centuries-old vellum, and bound in a brown leather cover embossed with the glorious seal of my people.

It may seem to you that all of these images are rather sedate and bucolic: a cottage in the woods, the drifting snow, a cherished diary. Had I not experienced what I have, I might be inclined to agree. But such a judgment could not be further from the truth. Think me mad if you must, but it is these very underpinnings of my ordinary world that have conspired to drive me to paroxysms of fear, the sort of chill terror that is unvanquishable and unrelenting.

Winter evenings here can be very cold; the air can numb one's skin, and great harm can be dealt the delicate constitution of an old man. I, therefore, wisely retire early, retreating to my familiar rocker by the fire, where I wrap myself in homespun Yankee blankets and contemplate the leaping flames. How lively they are sometimes, rising up as if to engulf my entire world. Their lambent orange glow is more than sufficient to illuminate the cottage; the pop and crackle the only sounds in the haunting night.

On my lap rests my diary, a tiny looking glass to days gone by. As I scan the pages and remember, a curious sensation of warmth o'erspreads my aged form, bringing with it contentedness and lethargy. The scribbled words speak clearly to me from so long ago, telling those familiar stories I hold so dear, and I cannot help but feel a pang of emotion upon reading them. Occasionally, I am even driven to weep.

Perhaps it was the saltwater coalescing in my eyes, or a manifestation of my failing sight, but three nights ago, as I felt slumber coming on, something most... *peculiar* occurred.

The fire was slowly dying, its light retreating to the interior of the wood, and I sat content in my warm and comfortable chair. I had been fighting off drowsiness with an ever-weakening resolve, hoping to finish a particular chapter written in 1942. Had I been a younger man, perhaps, I would have stayed awake, listening to the howl of the frigid wind. But as it happened, my head began to nod, my chin to rest on my shrunken chest, and my eyes to close.

It was then, when I was most susceptible, that it happened.

As I tried to remain awake a moment longer, the letters on the page seemed to *move*, shifting ever so slightly.

I dazedly blinked and came back to myself. But the odd moment had passed and, there being nothing remarkable to see, my eyes quickly lost their focus. I proceeded to fall into a deep, uninterrupted sleep.

This sequence of events occurred on the night following as well, in precisely the same manner, under entirely similar circumstances. The fire had expired, the room had grown dim, and the grieving furies wailed like tormented souls outside my little cabin. But what my eyes beheld this time, as I retained that final bit of self-awareness, made me jerk awkwardly to life.

The ink had blurred and moved! As surely as I breathed!

And, most unholy of all, a *word* had appeared.

I stared at the faded script on the page, but, like quicksilver, the message was gone. I was left with only an *impression* of what had been—a fleeting impartation of something horrid and unspeakable. The diary invited further investigation, but I could not bring myself to read what I *knew* to be the simple recollections of a young man. I shivered convulsively, and, suddenly aware of my age and solitude, I sought the refuge of my bed.

When I awoke this morning, all memory of that uncanny experience had vanished from my mind. The day was bright and sparkling with possibilities, and although I first drifted about absent-mindedly, as if there were something important that required my attention, I quickly shed my listlessness in favor of a stroll through the woods and some late afternoon hours spent collecting fuel for the fire.

I returned to the cottage tired, but contented, and recalled with a smile those days I had exhausted myself in the service of my country, marching back and forth along the stark, frozen perimeter of our camp.

A hot meal of beef stew and a touch of sherry to rekindle my heart, and I was ready to recline by the hearth; my belly was full and my spirits were high.

But, as I settled into the old rocker with my diary in hand, a strange sense of unease seized upon me. It was slow to comprehend, building ever so gradually, but it palpably existed nonetheless. The twilight and the glow of the fire reminded me of something from the night previous that I should have recalled, but could not. Like a half-forgotten dream…

It was a word. A *word.*

I must have slipped into an uneasy sleep then, for when I opened my eyes some time later, the fire had died. Outside, the pale face of the moon shone just over the blackened tips of the trees, and it cast strange shadows on the floor.

Perhaps I was still in a dreamlike daze, but, looking at those otherworldly designs, I felt a peculiar chill, as if something most foul had found deliverance from the grave and touched me with its cold and lifeless hand. I rose, gripping my diary to my chest, and hastened toward my bed, where I thought I might find peace. I moved stiffly, without much grace, my thin legs weak and unsteady.

Coming to rest upon the mattress, I laid my diary down on the night table and slipped beneath the covers. I shut my eyes and for some time sought the intoxicating nectar of sleep.

It remained elusive.

The moon rose higher, and my unease grew. I felt that the letters in my diary had tried to tell me something. I knew it was a warning, a premonition of the future, of *that* I was certain.

But the meaning remained unclear.

I sat up, propped against the pillows, a weak, frightened old man staring into the gloom. My body lay before me, spent and emaciated, covered by blankets as if by a shroud, repulsing me, reminding me of *them*... Confused, I turned away. I tried to avert my gaze.

But my eyes fixed on the blanched flooring of the room as I listened more closely to the howls beyond the walls.

The howls... Like tormented souls.

And I understood.

The moonlight, shining garishly through the twisted limbs of the denuded forest, slid slowly across the old planking of the floor. And in the swirling grain of the faded pine, I saw their faces, twisted and tortured, screaming at me like inhuman beasts, their mouths tearing apart, eyes bursting with fear.

They were the faces of the past. The faces of the camp. And I had seen them all.

Before I fell asleep, I ventured one last look at my diary, at the cursed black insignia emblazoned on its cover… and I knew the word I had read.

I closed my eyes.

The word was *Hell.*

THE PERSISTENCE OF VISION

JON MICHAEL KELLEY

DILLON'S MOTHER had put the feeders up for the season, entombing them in the attic, yet the little Ruby-throats remained hopeful of their most premature resurrection.

Had they really grown so reliant? So much as to resist the pull of their southern migration? The temperatures at night had already begun dipping toward the freezing mark for well into a week now, and this species of hummingbird, he'd learned, wasn't inclined to enter torpor, a sort of mini hibernation to conserve energy, as easily as some of its cousins.

Being a rapt student of biology, Dillon made sure to always canvass his studies.

He wondered if his feelings on the matter were a standard case of 'transference,' that unconscious 'redirection of emotion' he'd once heard his mother, the degreed behaviorist, drone on about. Made sense, he supposed—then nearly winced at his own averseness to that stark and pending truth.

"That's cruel," he'd said to her the fourth day, watching the hummers dip and dart in the periphery of the feeders' absence.

"That's life," she'd said. "*Time to move on.*"

The acidic verve brought him fully around to embrace a sort of kinship to those tiny creatures, to recognize that both he and they had grown mistrustful of this season's pale and abridged light, while at the same time learned a most valuable lesson about the risks of dependence, as he too felt a desperate urge to gorge in the shortening day. To yank back the receding edges of summer and tie them to anything that wasn't also being slowly pulled toward shorter, colder days—dear old golden rule days—and that autumnal cadence thrumming in his ears like the heavy respirations of something untamed lurking around the corner.

His thin, darling mother had given a perceptible nod to the window, motioning to the less transparent world outside, implying that his long accustomed season of her apron strings was racing to its own conclusion, not so unlike another that was blazing along the distant rolling hills in ruddy and saffron iridescences. A remarkable fire, Dillon recognized, which burned with more strident confidence than the one smoldering within; awkward, insecure, But most unquenchable: the onset of his maturation. No matter how hard he tried staring beyond that adorned foliage outside, he still couldn't see the colors of his own future, those hues remaining obedient to the prevailing uncertainty. The only guarantee would be the envy he held for those residing in more equatorial climes.

His mother's insinuation that 'life giveth, then taketh away' was a sobering one, authenticated by the loss of her husband four years earlier. The passing of his father continued to slip wispily between his fingers, no matter how long or tightly he maintained a grip. As his mother had once become, Dillon was a prisoner to the memories of his father, just more subtly than she had ever been, the desperation manifested in his isolation, where he has relegated such reminiscences.

Where he clung to memories, she'd begun clinging to material things, promising to never again allow the seizure or repossession of anything that had first been hers. She was not honestly looking forward to him leaving the nest, despite her recently implied fingerprints all over his back. Her despairing moods, her admittedly fertile and increasing reveries over the true meaning of life—all were symptoms, he recognized, of profound loneliness and disillusionment.

"*...to the dreary and seemingly pointless progression of days: you still have my full attention, if not my allegiance,*" she'd articulated to a bare wall one drunken afternoon (was toasting it with a full glass of wine, as a matter of fact), not knowing he was behind her, having returned from his own awful day at school. Hers was an especially vivid rant, one that left him feeling guilty, if not distinctly doomed. It was this very dilemma that he supposed was responsible for her growing preoccupation with material things; that to embrace something was to give it necessary meaning. He figured her 'obsessed,' a term she occasionally bandied about with utter detachment, and he often wondered if doctors were less equipped, or inclined, to diagnose themselves.

If he couldn't stop the season's progression, Dillon decided he could at least taunt its determination. While his mother addressed certain laundry duties downstairs, he prepared a pot of water (short of putting it on the fire), added probably too much sugar, and headed to the storage room where he would pull down the wooden stairway that accessed the attic. A place, Dillon sagely decided, that should be well known, too, for *its* reluctance to let go.

All three hummingbird feeders were glass-blown and highly prized by his mother, passed down by *her* mother, two years deceased, their purchase allegedly from a carnival long ago in the Northern Province. A carnival, of all places—and a legendary one brought to that distinction by its ability to waver like a mirage between allegory and the horizon, as it always seemed that very little if any direct evidence existed to support its authenticity, at least in any certifiable sense (the feeders' original boxes, for instance, bore no clue or specific indication as to their *place* of creation, only relying on Grandma-ma's word). The occasional confessions heard from those alleging to have patronized that notorious locale were often filled with such absurdity as to make them seem outright fraudulent.

The carnival was one of those intriguing franchises perpetuated by enduring myth. Probably less of a disappointment, he supposed, if left to remain that way. Enchanted carnivals indeed! He considered himself fortunate to no longer be of an age that entertained such possibilities. It intrigued him to know that so many adults had reached their 'moment of truth,' as his mother had once put it, their 'crossroads,' at which time they began yearning for that lost aptitude to once again 'circumvent reality without the guilt.'

As he climbed the stairs, he thought he recalled precisely how the feeders' packaging appeared; their colorful logos of balloons conveniently contorted into a pageantry of letters that spelled out the creator's name and credentials: "Dmitry, Artisan of Glass and Stone." A glace and candied style of marketing that was heaped upon the inventor, he remembered, with just a dollop spared for the product. Certainly more optimistic than the feeders themselves. Each one was an exercise in Gothic nuance: ribbed vaulting at its rounded top, tendrils snaking downward along its gourd shape, rowed on one side by linear sequences of quills and other sharp protuberances, with a few strays poking here and there to complete a most organic effect, all having been pulled by the artisan to various lengths as the glass cooled. And it was from these spines where the hummers fed, the sweet nectar pulled to the ends not by gravity, but capillary action.

When he'd first seen the feeders two years earlier, Dillon thought their designs were coerced into resembling, if not downright mimicking, certain formidable marine crustacea.

Inside the attic, the gloom was cleaved by sunlight eking in from the only window, a multifoil of leaded glass situated forever to filter the end of the day. Hundreds of boxes were stacked neatly, each inventoried by black marker in his mother's florid hand. Keepsakes less contained huddled in the gloom, and all about this repository of ephemera, there hung in the dimness something Dillon had never noticed before: a subtle tenacity woven throughout the customary redolence, an otherworldly determination fuming to break from its state of intangibility into something… corporeal. Its present incarnation was not so unlike the one currently suspending the dust motes in the last waning rays of sunlight—only *heavier.*

The attic reminded him of an apothecary, reeking curatively of dried orange rinds, rosemary, and cedar. 'Nostalgia,' his mother had called it upon their most recent visit together. Something, she promised, that he wouldn't be able to smell for many years yet.

"I smell it just fine," he'd said, indignant. He knew what nostalgia meant.

"And what does it rekindle?" she'd asked. "Just how far back does it take you, hmm? To our last month's adventure up here in search of canning lids and paraffin?"

He'd shrugged, letting her nose dwell on whatever it wanted.

A-framed, the space was as tidy as the main structure below, and just as long, and was high and narrow enough that Dillon could stand in the middle, hold out both arms, and barely touch the rafters slanting on either side (a feat he wasn't able to accomplish a year earlier). His mother insisted on keeping the center aisle clear, as everything she'd exiled to these dusky regions was neatly tucked away, situated efficiently between the trusses. Anything that could be stored in a box went to one side, everything in varying degrees of cumbersomeness in the other: a treadle sewing machine, an assortment of wicker baskets atop a large steamer trunk (the key to which he has never located despite years of searching, although his mother maintained it being empty), a standing lamp with a miner's helmet hanging in place of a shade now long missing.

He stared reverently at the locked trunk.

His father's things were in there, he knew.

But it was the other side of the aisle where the feeders would be found. He crouched and sidled along the row of trusses, searching for three tall and flamboyant packages. He found them blooming amongst a patch of nondescript boxes labeled 'highlights,' followed by dates that clustered within a specific era, one that would have found him as less than a twinkle in anybody's eye. From the broken seam of one peeked the rim of a hat, and a wisp of dusty pink feathers. His mother's stuff. He leaned down, and sniffed.

Nothing; no nostalgia here.

This reminded him of that strangely pronounced ether he'd first detected upon entering, prompting another slow and cautious survey of these close environs. Suddenly, he focused on the rocking horse behind him: its mouth hard and forever upon the bit, its dark liquid eyes ceaselessly beckoning, its black, ratty mane hanging like Spanish moss from its thick and arching crest. A product of his father's skills—some parts fashioned by his pragmatic side, others lavishly sequined by a flamboyant one—it was as close to a carousel piece as any equine rocker could get. It reminded Dillon of a more thriving time, not only serving an example of prosperity's rewards, but also his father's extravagant creativity.

Something on its shank had stolen his attention. He initially thought the eruption was sap bubbling out of one of the many cracks upon its chestnut body, borne of the attic's aridness, but when he was nearly upon it, he had to stop. It looked like insect larvae. An egg mass, specifically, of about thirty. They had reached their advanced stage. Hatching was evident with most of the casings, the hollow majority showing pronounced ruptures.

Spider? Insect?

He ran a hand down the saddle's dangling (and more practically fashioned) apparatus: dee ring, fender, latigo, girth—they were all present, chrome and leather twinkling and glinting respectively in the growing eventide. Even at the young age of four, every time he mounted the wooden steed in his father's presence he was made to first point and shout off each part by name—from horn to stir-rup—until he had fully memorized them.

The sensation of something delicate fluttered in his chest; a moth, a fragile damselfly, and he thought nostalgia flitted on similar wings. But did it inspire the fumes of lantern oil? Did it bring back the mornings when his father, preparing for the day's work in the mines, would fill his lamp and carelessly (and, as it later turned out, prophetically) talk about the dangers of false floors and firedamp to a young boy?

Why had he suddenly thought of such specific things? By rousing one memory, it seemed he had loosed another from those fringes; one long forgotten. Had it been sufficiently long enough? That ephemeral 'yearning' one should feel when experiencing nostalgia—the *distance* between those feelings and their associative moments made the accompanying sentiment feel, in a way, compulsory, and therefore most undeserving of someone his age. Or, to use one of his father's witticisms, he didn't have enough rope down the well to pull up *that* bucket of water.

Regardless, he paid particular notice to that melancholic inkling, made even more poignant by its transitory nature.

Focusing once again on the horse's shank, Dillon concluded that the egg mass had been deposited by an insect, a common species of blowfly, most likely. But blowflies had a particular penchant for laying their eggs upon rotting meat, not wood. This was curious. Curiouser still was that strange mawkish matter he'd initially regarded as sap, the stuff holding the mass together. Too hard to be wax, he reluctantly concluded that it was the rocker's thick coat of shellac that appeared to have somehow melted in that small area, specifically into the crack, and had then re-hardened, thereby encapsulating, either partially or wholly, the already existing casings.

To see it was to be particularly reminded of insect parts fossilized in amber.

Matters became even more bewildering when he spotted the marionette across the aisle. It dangled by one arm from the open end of a tall box, its strings loosely trailing back and disappearing into the container. A puppet eerily renascent, as if it had attempted to escape its prison by going over the wall, only to lose its nerve upon discovering the precipitous drop to the ground. This initial impression was further encouraged by the startled look on the puppet's face; specifically, the high arch of its black, painted eyebrows, and the fear captured in its tiny brown eyes.

Dillon had forgotten all about this toy. The marionette's name was Alton. No, *Anton!* Expertly carved from a block of pine, then capably jointed with brass pins in all the prudent places, the puppet and its painted-on wardrobe appeared to have remained impressively intact: blue shirt, red vest, brown pants, black shoes. Back then, he couldn't wait to hear them tap across the kitchen table.

Make him dance.

His imagination was getting away from him. Someone—probably him!—had simply rummaged through that box in search of something else and had carelessly tossed the puppet aside, and left it there to contemplate its perilous position.

But, no, that wasn't true. The only reason Dillon ever came to the attic alone was to check the lock on the trunk, to see if its contents had finally become accessible, to maybe find the internal mechanism disengaged, perhaps by a reticent mother finally overcome with sympathy for her most curious and pining son.

It was even less likely that his compulsive mother, drunk or not, would have cavalierly left that box, or any box, in such a disheveled way. To learn that she had done so would disturb Dillon considerably, as it would indicate a breakdown of a serious magnitude—the collapse, finally, of an already untenable foundation.

Then he noticed another toy lying in a heap directly below where Anton was hanging for dear life. Dillon was instantly struck with the ludicrous notions that either the puppet had thrown it out just prior to its attempted escape, or had dropped it as it dangled from the edge, the thing having finally become too heavy for its scraggy arms. To have imagined one of those scenarios was ludicrous, Dillon decided, but to have so easily entertained both indicated—blushingly so—that he'd not completely outgrown a juvenile inclination to woo the supernatural.

The other toy was a thaumatrope, or 'magic disc,' as his father had called them, a thin, simple disc held on opposite sides of its circumference by pieces of string. When rapidly spun, the images on either side of the disc appeared to become superimposed. As a young boy, he'd amassed quite the collection. One of the simpler designs he recalled having depicted an empty jar on one side of the disc, and a pincered beetle on the other. When spun, it appeared that the insect was trapped within the jar. It was basic in conception, but still fun. Other such pairings were only limited by the artist's imagination.

Thaumatropes had beguiled him, garnering a more involved level of respect. His father had explained to him the principle of 'persistence of vision,' the retinal determination to hold onto the image of something for roughly 1/20th of a second after it's gone. Recalling that definition now seemed eerily befitting for the moment, and was soon inspiring him to stretch its meaning to cover peripheral aspects more internal in scope, to quaintly remind him that some untiring, unwavering things never left the mind's eye.

Like the marionette, he'd forgotten all about the thaumatropes. That relatively short span of time between then and now had him feeling unworthy of his emotions; to bridge that distance with a particular sentiment was to cheat and go to the head of a line, a line stretched by natural order.

Suspiciously, Dillon walked over to the dangling puppet, then reached down and picked the thaumatrope from the floor. The paired choice for this one was also basic; perhaps the most popular union of them all: on one side, a bird at rest upon a straight line, and on the other, a rounded cage. Spin it and you got a caged bird, perched contentedly. Dillon did just that, and was instantly perplexed by the effect. Instead of the bird's resulting incarceration, Dillon saw only the image of the cage, *but with its door open.* There was no bird, perched or otherwise.

He flipped the disc over, then once over again. There was clearly a bird, then a closed cage. He took hold of the strings and spun the disc again. Empty cage with its door open.

Dillon dropped the toy, too stunned to back away.

He stared at the marionette, as if for an explanation. But nothing was forthcoming; just that startled look, appearing even more apt for the occasion.

Directly across from the rocking horse stood his sister's large and elaborate dollhouse, one his father had built. His sister had moved away long ago, married some man of 'less than modest means,' and now lived in a town so far away that her face had all but disappeared from his memory. In fact, he'd last seen her at their father's funeral, and her visage was the only image he could no longer clearly recapture from that day.

It had been a closed casket affair, but Dillon hadn't needed that opportunity to remember his father's creased face. His sister, on the other hand, should have been so lucky.

There was a family picture album, within which he could satiate that privation of memory, but locating it would require an extensive search through these very boxes, and whatever bond he and his sister may have once shared wasn't titillating enough to initiate such a quest. After she'd left the house for good, he would sneak into her room and play with the family of whittled figures she'd properly found to tenant the dollhouse—a distinguished family made to emulate her own in both its number and wardrobe, he recalled. But his fascination had really been drawn by the structure's aesthetics: the joinery, the imbrication of the roof shingles, the stately entrance of the tabernacle frame; rather than aspects customarily doted over by maternal pretenses. Dillan was captivated by the intricacies that were so much his father, a man consumed by detail.

It bothered him, a little, to be reminded that his father had lavished just as much extravagant talent upon his sister.

And now inside the dollhouse there faintly glowed a spectral tint, just a figment of a pigment, the same sort of insinuation of light that clings to the horizon moments before the day is snuffed, a light in passive transcendence. So dim, in fact, that it was most probably lit by his own fanciful notion. To suppose anything more would be... more nonsense.

If there were intentions behind this ghostly display, Dillon didn't know them.

Outside, the sun had just sunk below the horizon, and the attic would very soon be a potage of shadows, with just enough light slipping in from the dropdown stairs to make the consommé barely negotiable.

Dillon managed to turn his attention back to the rocking horse, thinking to start there, that he must have missed a connection, however tenuous, to those other mysteries burgeoning around him. He considered each unusual instance in the order encountered, then quickly accepted that approach as disingenuous and wondered if a proper understanding could be had by knowing the truer sequence of events; assuming, of course, that such a progression existed outside his imagination.

He drew lines with his eyes, connecting first the rocking horse to the marionette, then quickly down to the thaumatrope, then back to the dollhouse—then, upon a startling notion, to the attic's round and only window, now a spectrally charged sphere between the dimming sky and the darkening interior. His interest was not the window itself, but the sill. If flies had hatched from those casings, he reasoned, it was almost certain that some of their dried remains would be resting there, having found that ingress into the wild a deadly illusion.

He considered what he might find, and made his way to the window. What he discovered, upon initial inspection, were five ordinary flies, all clearly dead. He pinched one up from the curved sill, and upon closer examination, found it exhibiting a rather distinct and misplaced morphology: its eyes were... belonging to a different species. That is to say, they were the compound eyes of an insect, yes, but each seemed especially large and displayed a pronounced 'pseudo-pupil,' characteristically seen in certain predatory insects, such as dragonflies, praying mantises, tiger beetles... Three of the four remaining flies showed these same features. Despite these peculiar nuisances, Dillon would have disregarded them if not for another modification: the flies' mouthparts, those mandibles having also assumed deviant proportions, appeared more suitable for chewing than 'sponging.'

He closed his eyes, shook his head. Again, more nonsense.

Reluctantly, he looked back to the large trunk. His father's things were in there. Of course they were.

Without any sort of describable provocation, his attention was fully and immediately diverted to the three feeders that he'd initially come to get. *Did the answer lie with them?* he wondered—and quite unashamedly, as he was allowing himself the privilege to 'circumvent reality without the guilt,' if only for the moment. Did one or all of those feeders retain some excess of magic brought over from their place of manufacture, that near-fictional carnival of enchanted repute? Did one or all possess the means to light, however dimly, a dollhouse? To alter, however vaguely, the morphology of insects? Emit enough diabolism to animate a marionette and give it the initiative to abscond, if only partially, with a cleverly deceptive thaumatrope?

Did it have to necessarily be a theft? Could the puppet have been attempting... a delivery?

He smiled, fully letting go of his momentary endorsement of the speculative. Being a willing student of biology in one classroom, and a rather reticent one of the human condition in another, he was aware that his species was powerfully inclined to recognize patterns. Preferably, more logical kinds of patterns and behaviors, but certainly willing to take just about anything, and in growing degrees of absurdness as options waned, the chief example here being that a puppet had attempted to get to him a curious toy—one obviously altered to affect upon him a profound realization.

Or, had his imagination simply become a liability? At the very least, he understood these sudden mysteries around him to be the stray and unraveled ends of a boy's once gullible imagination; at most, they were some of his childhood's favorite things having become impossibly enlivened. What was that word his mother had used? *Rekindled.*

But to what purpose?

He considered the flies and their odd modifications. What did the changes represent? Something purely biological, or profoundly metaphorical? Despite a staunch adherence to the scientific method, he went with the latter, deciding that in order to understand, he simply had to glean a simple yet poignant inference from the flies' peculiar metamorphoses. A corollary...

Then it came to him: *aggression.* The flies were turning from prey to hunter.

Strangely, that reach didn't seem so far: an allegory he easily recognized for his hormonal rage from boy to manhood.

What about the puppet, the thaumatrope, his sister's dollhouse? Where did *their* shenanigans bolster his theory? Did each tacitly imply a bold assertiveness? He met with them one at a time and imagined a correlation for each. The animated puppet, he decided, represented *initiative*; the thaumatrope, *his pending release from a gilded captivity*; the dollhouse light...?

Dillon stared back at the large trunk. His father's things were in there.

The dollhouse light: *the assurance that the finality of life is just a cruel illusion.* And the atmosphere he'd first encountered in the attic? *The effluvium of magic.* Or, more appropriately, he thought, *the residue of a fuse set burning.*

Looking closely again, then drawing back and taking in the whole landscape, Dillon had to finally accept that, yes, the feeders were influencing certain objects. The rocking horse's flank, for instance, was blatantly exposed and in direct line-of-sight to those heirlooms, as was the tall box with the fleeing puppet, as was the dollhouse. No other objects, partially or wholly, stood between these items and the three feeders.

Then again, a majority of artifacts fell similarly within the feeders' proximity, yet appeared free of their alleged effects.

It was as if these things, *these childhood things*, had been selectively targeted. Besides their magic, did the feeders also possess a kind of intelligence, one capable of wielding such discretion?

No, of course they didn't! To imagine them emitting magic was crazy enough!

That would mean more than one force was at work. A cooperation, of sorts, between forces. Indiscernible forces, he imagined, that would have to be ethereally entwined. Entities sharing the same veiled realm.

Not cooperation, he further premised, but a mutually agreed *understanding* of what was to be accomplished in this attic.

Back at the rocking horse, Dillon stared intently at its invaded shank, at the egg mass and its nest of dried resin, finally concluding that at some point during the past year, specifically when the feeders were wintering in the attic, 'something' had attempted, either intentionally or inadvertently, a change upon the very most exposed area of the horse's shank, turning the wood to flesh. Then, evidently, that 'something,' that magic, was abruptly taken away. Probably when the feeders were removed and relocated to the back porch, he reasoned, while spring was edging into warmer days. And while those feeders were absent from the attic, that patch of flesh began to rot before finally changing back to its original wooden state—but not before a common fly exploited the putrefaction, exposing itself and its offspring to that dwindling residue of magic.

Had there not been an interruption of that enchanted flow, he further suspected, Anton the puppet would have been able to complete his journey. It would have allowed the dollhouse to achieve and maintain its grand illumination.

He once again regarded the large trunk, half buried between a spillage of wicker baskets, a tattered shawl twisting between them like the sloughed skin of a paisley snake. A trunk, Dillon mused, that was like most other things: tucked too far away from any errant sources of magic, too far away from basking properly in the feeders' glow.

Well, not for long, he thought.

Dillon made a fresh batch of sugar water, and before he had the first feeder back up under the porch's eave, hordes of hummers were literally swiping his body, rushing aggressively past to get to the sweet serum. The fact that full dark had settled in made no difference to them whatsoever. They gorged, while seemingly never sating their hunger.

He watched for quite a long time.

Dillon smiled, no longer suspicious over their piqued and habituated demeanor. Most people never made it past the hummers' tiny size and adorable reputation to realize that they were predators themselves, chiefly insectivorous and only ate sugar water and plant nectar to give them the energy to chase down those tiny bugs.

He would only hang two of the feeders, as he'd already committed the third to its permanent resting place atop the large trunk, the one in the attic, having deliberately and clandestinely hidden it beneath a cluster of fraying wicker baskets.

The trunk held his father's most cherished things, his *spirit*.

It wasn't about opening the lock. Not anymore. Maybe, just maybe, those cooperating forces could reach an understanding.

In preparation of his mother's eventual questions regarding the last feeder's whereabouts, Dillon practiced an excuse that he had carelessly dropped it, shattered into unrecognizable fragments, and that he had discarded the carnage with the rest of the refuse. He would gladly and sincerely apologize for not being more careful and accept his punishment, no matter how severe, confident that it would be.

Lastly, in the warm yellow glow of lanterns, Dillon noticed a peculiar feature upon some of the hummers: a serrated irregularity along their long, thin beaks, nearly imperceptible, made especially so in the diffused light.

He smiled wider upon realizing what was happening.

The hummers were growing teeth.

Dillon shivered, an act inspired not by the culmination of bizarre events, but rather an authentic cold. The snow would soon be here, and would once again herald the start of a new cycle, just as a waning gibbous moon hangs on the edge of an early morning sky to tell of another's end.

THE BAD SEASON

A.A. GARRISON

THE WINTER WAS LONG and full of knowings, but it was ending, and soon.

Terrance Pot. The slender thirty-something sat anonymously in the crowded ski lodge, affecting health using his facemask. He was alone, as always, his little table half-empty. An amber drink kept him company, untouched, a stage prop like his fake face. Alcohol was unconscionable, especially during the bad season.

The People, red with sweaters and drink, surrounded Terrance's table, their laughter as hollow as his facemask charades. Their realities encroached his own, threatening to drown him. Small, soulless creatures, chasing their highs and serving their youth—yet vicious. So vicious. The deadliest animal, and blissfully unaware of such. But Terrance would not hate them. Could not. Because then They would see it in him, and then it would become real, and then it could not die, not from words or love or money, or the cummerbund of explosives under his shirt.

He tuned Them out, along with his stupid emotions, purifying his mind. Purity was paramount in the bad season, and particularly now, on the eve of its ultimate end. The piano was into a warm adagio, and Terrance focused on it instead, letting the notes infiltrate him. He bade his facemask smile, and it did so.

He crossed his legs, surveying the ski lodge where his parents had first met. It was storied amongst Terrance's family: 1969, his mom and dad to be, in the mountains, both single and tired of it. Dad had popped a dirty joke, their eyes had met, and the rest was history. Terrance scanned the room, stopping at the bar; that was where the fateful meeting had occurred, though his parents had never divulged this particular detail. Terrance just knew, in the same way he knew destroying the lodge would thwart his parents meeting, thus preventing his life and its uncommon wealth of pain.

The bar was lousy with People, so much in another galaxy, mingling like Terrance's parents probably had. He looked away, again tempted to hate; it was too easy to, come the bad season, with that ugly sense of contrast always knocking on his door. The shorter days were enemy, bringing with them the cycles, the heightened awareness, the questions, and, eventually, the answers—the *knowings*. The answers could be scarier than the questions, and usually were, but they were necessary. To ignore them would be suicide, though of a kind wholly different than what he had planned.

A man passed—a *Person*—and Terrance refreshed his disguise, his facemask drawing high and approachable. It was imperative to stay unremarkable, lest They see his true face, pearls before swine. The two made brief eye contact, exchanged shit-eating nods, then the man was gone to a party of similarly vacant bodies across the room. And that's just what They were, bodies, human only in the way Jason Voorhees is a hockey player. For Terrance, he was the only sentient creature in the room, the People being mere constructs, cartoons of their own manufacture. But that was okay; it made them expendable.

The latest question, occurring to Terrance at the start of this active Season, had been a tough one: how to cancel oneself completely. Not death; death was a misnomer, being only a change of state rather than a genuine end. It was also elementary, easily mastered, achieved by innumerable means. Nonexistence, however, was a whole other ballgame. Its question had been plague, but as of this final winter and its devices, Terrance knew the solution. It was quite simple: he had only to prevent his parents from meeting.

This had presented its own problems, naturally, but the answers had come, and, for all their magnificence, they too were uncomplicated. By blowing up the present lodge, at precisely the right moment, when the eleven-fold Reality Nexus was aligned and the gulf of time lay open and all became possible, the lodge would cease forever, past and present, therefore solving the quandary of his being. Terrance would disappear in the destruction's wake, he theorized, erased like a bad drawing. This was pure conjecture, but, regardless, it would be marvelous.

He checked the lodge clock with his fake eyes: five till eleven.

Eleven. The number sent sunshine up his earthly person. It jibed with him, eleven, and never more than at the peak of the bad season—which wasn't so 'bad,' given the knowings it brought. He turned the number over in his mind. Eleven parallel universes. Eleven people at the bar. Eleven versions of himself, in varying states of suffering. Eleven sticks of dynamite. He was eleven when the knowings had first visited him, during his incipient Season. Eleven letters to his name. He'd scarred himself with the characters, if counting his body as himself.

Eleven. Eleven. Eleven-eleven.

11:11. It was his one window of opportunity, he knew, when he would detonate his payload and efface the eleven Terrances from the multiverse, as revealed to him by God, or to whatever the bad season played agency. He said the number aloud. His facemask glowed. It was 10:59.

Terrance was pretending to sip his drink when doubt struck. It came with its familiar shock, exploding into mind so much like the fireworks at his belly. He raised a mental barrier, in the way he'd learned, but stray words came through: *crazy, deluded, schizoid.* He hated the last one most, for its sheer audacity—who was a paltry psychiatrist to judge Terrance's condition, to plumb his depths? Besides, there *was* no schizophrenia, not in him, at least; experience was the only thing separating him from the People, nothing more. He'd once been like Them, and now, after many bad seasons, he wasn't, by his own volition. The insanity of conventional thinking has an exit door, and he'd opened it, his enlightenment no more chemical than a rainbow was magical.

He told himself this, many times, and it slowly but surely eroded the doubt. Some lingered, of course, nibbling at his subconscious like the hate he refused to indulge, but it was contained. The bad season wrought as much doubt as it did knowings, it seemed, as though its mechanism was equal parts skeptic and believer. The conflict was extraordinary, nothing short of war, regularly driving Terrance to the brink of madness and back—why the bad season was the bad season. But he supposed it necessary; the doubt worked to keep him on his toes, preserve his integrity. The human mind is notoriously fallible, given to projections, persuasions of the ego, delusions that feed on themselves, so he was thankful for his overaggressive doubt. He feared self-delusion; it was the one true insanity, he thought.

The clock hands spelled out three after eleven, and the piano upbeat, joined stealthily by a bass. Terrance almost fell into the music, the chords visible behind his eyes, but he caught himself. He couldn't miss the window: 11:11, his one chance for salvation. He would surrender the song for that—would trade this roomful of 'lives' for that. And perhaps the People would cease to exist, simply dissolving into whatever Zen awaited Terrance. Perhaps not.

There was dancing now, couples swaying over the parquet dance floor. One couple, a tall dark man and an elegant redhead, were inching uncomfortably close to Terrance's island table, and he suppressed a snarl. If there was one thing that stabbed him more than the People, it was their illusions of love. Terrance was not unacquainted with love; he'd known it as a teenager, while still receiving the basics of his strange discipline, and it had been just enough to reveal to him its lunacy. Using his exceptional faculty of examination, he'd dissected the devious emotion, deduced it to mere hormones and selfish attachments. His insatiable doubt had a hand in this (plus several branding rejections, though he would never admit this, even to himself). The saying was all wrong: knowing is bliss. Ignorance is pitiful.

Eight after. Three more minutes in this hell.

Or was it heaven? Terrance wasn't sure. The trials of his thirty-three years had, after all, awarded him his knowings, without which he would never have reached his current pedigree, nor gained the understanding necessary for his undoing. Life is strange, he thought.

Nine after.

The dance floor surged, sending the dark man and his redhead even closer, dangerously so, enough for Terrance to suffer their conversation. He didn't want to listen, but his keen ears heard anyway: she was having such a great time, how beautiful the mountains were, is your sister all right? The words waxed vile in Terrance's fake ears, faltering his facemask so his true self peeked through. The woman went on and on, and Terrance had to resist muffing his hands over his ears.

Then he caught something in the woman's voice: the hallmark of sincerity, of warmth, of *sentience*. The antithesis of the soulless drivel he expected, in any case. He again tried to ignore it, block it out as he did when he was scared—but no, not now. He was too aware, thanks to the bad season and its voodoo. He upset further.

The doubt reared up then, perhaps scenting weakness: *Could she be alive? Could she have feelings? Could you be wrong in your meditations?* Before Terrance could tackle the first three: *Might she have a* soul?

The last pierced him to the bone, monkeywrenching his entire theory of existence—*he* was the only besouled, the only one who truly thought and felt and lived.

But weren't you once like Them, by you own admission?

No answers. Terrance felt to be sinking, the rug pulled out from under him. In his upheaval, the facemask fell completely, for one moment revealing his actuality, what might've been a twisted slab of hickory. He looked madly about the lodge, feeling suddenly naked, sure everyone would be looking—pointing, gasping, perhaps in awe. But no one was looking.

11:10.

Terrance calmed some, his facemask recomposed... until the redhead bitch reappeared, bringing up the doubt like puke.

Could she...? Could you...? What if...? Maybe...

The questions left holes in his doctrine, contagious holes, spreading through his entire house of cards, all the way to the task at hand. His knee bobbed. He ground his teeth. Ugly sweat beaded his forehead, red in the lodge's mood-lighting.

The clock clicked 11:11 as Terrance warred with himself. The couple again came very close, and Terrance had to will away violence. It was her, the woman—*her* fault for infecting him with this broken thinking. He knew she was just an empty body, *knew*... but didn't, not anymore. The bitch had hurt him, the way so many of Them did, their dirty thoughts queering his compass, leaving his processes out of true. Fouling him. *Raping* him.

Once like them... could be wrong... have a soul...*?*

The second-hand passed the one, the two, the three, Terrance's precious window evaporating before his eyes. Panicked, he activated his defense mechanisms, to parry the questions, relearn the mysteries which had seen him to this place.

He was enlightened—

Deceived.

He was aware—

Deluded.

He was pure—

Corrupt.

He was beautiful—

Abominable.

He was perfect—

Flawed.

The hand rounded the five, the six, so much the grains of an hourglass. The detonator was duct-taped to his chest and he clutched it as a nun would her rosary. How could he kill them if they weren't soulless monsters? Or, was *he* the monster, lost in some crazy, egocentric fairytale?

He had let go of the detonator, resigned to indecision—when she looked at him. The redhead, her eyes, locked onto his. Time ceased, and Terrance was overcome: by the disgust he was sure he saw there, a million pointed fingers, as he'd seen in every woman he'd ever known. It was that bitter old rejection, like knives in him, what he secretly hated more than anything and could never *ever* admit, much less confront. In that eternal instant, Terrance knew her, the elegant dancing cuntwhore who thought the mountains were beautiful and is your sister okay I hate you forever you ugly bastard jerk die.

Their eyes broke, the contact lasting just a heartbeat. But Terrance had seen inside her, and there was no soul of which to speak.

Projection... delusion...

The words murmured from his depths, like bubbles underwater, and he choked them off. There was no doubt. He was certain. Like the Reality Nexus. Like his unmaking. Another knowing. Eleven. Yes.

When the second-hand met the hour-, forming a perfect trinity of his beloved number, Terrance gripped the detonator and smiled, with both his facemask and the real thing. Tears pushed from his eyes. The button made a dull click no one heard.

STORM OF LIGHTNING

AARON J. FRENCH

YAH DID IT AGAIN, tiger. You spoilt yerself.

The voice of his old man echoed with all the redneck charm he could remember. Harry set his axe against a tree and looked around at nothing but miles of forested hills. The sun permeated through the branches while clouds puffed over the horizon. Birds sang from all corners, notwithstanding the scene of brutal violence which had taken place.

Sighing, he lit a Winston and squatted on a large slab of limestone, letting his weight settle. Betty was a ruined woman, a puddle of torn flesh, organs and bones hacked apart. Blood saturated the grass—forehead cleaved in twain, brains leaking out—and he leaned over to vomit. The smell burned his nostrils as he rolled onto his back. Leaves and morning sky filled his vision. He took a breath. Released. The sounds of the forest momentarily nabbed him. He smoked... traveling back to his Kentucky youth.

Mama knelt behind the refrigerator. She always did this after a fight. She had a blanket and a pillow back there, so she could hide with the dust bunnies and the cobwebs. She had her Bible, too.

Harry inched out of the hallway and moved across the tiles. Brown gravy stains—what had once been their dinner—covered the floor, the front of the fridge, and the counters, from when his father had dashed his arm over the table, hurtling everything across the room. Now his old man sat on the back porch, passed out in his rocker. Been there a while. Probably fell asleep with chew in his mouth.

Harry peeked around the side of the refrigerator and found his mom on her knees, the blanket tucked beneath her. The Holy Bible lay discarded by her calf. Her eyes were closed and her lips moved soundlessly while she cried. She had her fingers steepled before her chest, making what she liked to call "Jesus Hands."

"Mama?"

The sounds of the screen door slamming against the house, footsteps, grunting, labored breath.

In Jesus' name, we pray. Amen.

Mama's eyes snapped open.

Winston down to the filter, he flipped it away. Harry had the flashing image of a forest fire and sat up, a world of trees and trunks and bark swinging into view. Morning was officially here, heralded by increasing humidity. He scanned the ground, wary not to look upon the ruined woman, located the butt—no longer smoking—and after watching a moment longer, he let it be.

Murder Man stood near the bushes.

Harry ignored him at first; that is, he didn't turn and look, but his body reacted: heart doubling in pace, skin chilling with gooseflesh. He blinked. Then, slowly, he raised his head.

Murder Man resembled the creature of any child's worst nightmare—a towering hulk of leathery flesh the color of oil, a soiled mop of long black hair, and tree root arms ending in grotesque clawed hands. His face was long and sloping, almost horselike, with a snout and long, sharp teeth. The eyes, dead orange things... portals to the other side of existence, through which, Harry knew, some demon peered.

The creature did nothing. Watching. Waiting. *Directing.*

Murder Man finally said, "This one's done. But how about another?"

"I don't want to do this anymore," Harry said, cold and sternly.

He no longer felt emotions, had *willed* himself not to feel them; feeling them meant the end of the Earth, meant death. He was one tough-armored sack of two hundred fifty pounds of flesh. Fear and horror and rage were things he twisted into knots of unknowing, forcing them deep into his soul.

"You have no choice," Murder Man said. "Death is your purpose."

Harry wanted another cigarette.

"How did this happen?"

It wasn't a question he expected to have answered, but Murder Man, shambling into view, opened his horse-like mouth several inches too wide, revealing blackness and shapes and color... and Harry looked deeper.

Harry pulled his coat tighter and blew into his hands, wishing he had brought gloves. There had been a time, back when he first started this, that the fear of getting caught would have forced him to go back.

He peeked around the corner of the alley, across the parking lot where sodium lights threw a greenish sheen upon the cars, to the back entrance of the bar. The door had been left open from the cook coming out for his smoke break. Blue and green neon filled the frame, and folks dressed in black and leather, the sound of a jukebox playing Johnny Cash.

Another thirty minutes before last call. Sometimes it took another thirty minutes for everyone to leave. Good thing he was patient. Harry sat against the brick wall and smoked a Winston. The night was silent but for the last of the drunkards in the parking lot.

An hour later, they had all gone; the parking lot was clear. The neon signs powered down. Everything went silent.

Where is she?

Grinning, Harry lost his cigarette and rose to his feet.

The back door cracked open a final time and there she was—the tall blonde he'd kept tabs on for the past month, Betty Goldstein. She was a divorced, middle-aged, hot-to-trot trail-blazer who either owned the Swingin' Shack Saloon, or operated it for someone else. She crossed the parking lot toward her Dodge pickup.

Harry cautiously crept out of his hiding place and dashed across the street. He was nimble, given his size, especially in these moments when his head was full of excitement, his heart pounding, and his cock nearly bursting through his jeans. He made it to her truck and hid.

She muttered as she came around the side of the vehicle.

Harry crouched in a dark pool of shadows near the left front wheel well, a shadow himself. A sliver of moon shone briefly through the screen of clouds, and a glow appeared around the truck, spotlighting it. He froze, not expecting this.

She glanced suddenly at his bulk, eyes widened.

"What the fuck—"

Although he had the ability to throw his weight (he'd been an amateur boxer in his youth, junior varsity, back before he started gaining weight), she managed an elbow into his face, but his two hundred plus pounds forced her onto the asphalt.

"Get off me!"

Her knee met his groin, but he deflected and slammed down his fist onto the bridge of her nose where a geyser of blood erupted. She tried to scream, but Harry jammed his fingers into her throat, felt a couple of her teeth dislodge.

She started choking.

He applied his weight, pressing her against the asphalt, jamming his forearm against her head. Her eyes finally dimmed as she fell unconscious.

The parking lot was deserted.

Harry hoisted her body over his shoulder and crept back into the alley.

He left Murder Man standing in the trees and started up the trail. He had to get away from the body, needed to clear his head.

Sunlight streamed through the branches to glint on the maple and oak leaves. A few small critters darted across his path. The silence was immense—an ocean of possibilities—and he felt he could dissolve into it, as matter into matter, as the bodies of his victims had returned into the earth.

He found a towering cottonwood with a massive trunk and stopped under its umbrella of branches. He caressed the gnarled bark. It felt good against his fingers.

Murder Man's face materialized in the deeply grooved crevices running along the trunk. "Back that way," he said. A few of the branches pointed down the trail.

Harry ignored the face and kept walking.

The swath of dirt sloped up and around the side of a hill into a clearing bordered by several tall pines. A ruinous single-story shack sinking into the ground endured in the center of the clearing. Composed mostly of rain-rotted boards, the sagging structure had a caved-in roof, which reminded Harry that time was always doing its best to decay matter. The signs of age stained every splintered beam, in the blackened grooves and knots of the clapboards, and even around the empty window frames and crooked front door.

What time does to things, I do to women.

The voice of his father: *You spoilt yerself again.*

Murder Man appeared beside him, a black splotch in reality.

"How about another?" he whispered.

Harry fought a wave of emotion. His whole body tightened.

I will not emote.

When the wave passed, he released its frothy spume in the form of a sigh, and stepped through the door.

Under the bed.

Boom.

Harry winced and covered his face as tears streamed through his small hands. His parents were arguing again. It had woken him, his eyes snapping up and staring into bedroom darkness. Dad drunk, Mom scared. It was always something.

Boom.

After the hitting started, he had crept under the bed, clutching his teddy bear. He had closed his eyes, covered his ears, but still he heard it: the unmistakable thudding of flesh against flesh. Mama screaming, crying, praying to the Lord to send a storm of lightning to take Daddy away.

Harry stared out from under his bed at the yellow light beneath the door, wondering if God could really send a storm of lightning to take his father away; then that sound echoed through the house—*boom*—and his heart nearly leaped out of his—

"Harry?" his father called.

Boom.

"Rise and shine... wakey wakey."

Harry knew better. It wasn't really time to get up: the sun wasn't even awake. His dad was playing a trick. Daddy wanted to do to Harry what he had done to Mama.

Boom.

A shadow darkened the space of light beneath the door and the footfalls ceased. The doorknob turned, and then the door creaked inward—"Harry?"—and then his dad's terrifying, staggering form entered the room.

"Time to get up, Harry. Where are you?"

Harry watched his father's legs from under the bed. When they reached him, he stole a breath and shot out wildly between the ankles, scrambling across the floor.

"Git yer ass back here!"

But Harry was already down the hall. He slammed the door, sped to the staircase, taking the steps two at a time. His father's footfalls struck behind him.

Boom boom boom.

Light in the downstairs rooms hurt his eyes. He ran into several pieces of furniture. He tore into the kitchen, expecting to find Mama behind the refrigerator on her knees, making Jesus Hands. When Harry saw her, he slid to a halt.

She lay in the center of the floor beside the dining table. It didn't make sense what had happened to her, and yet he instinctively knew she was gone and never coming back. The Lord had sent a storm of lightning to take her... instead of Dad.

Her clothes were gone and her legs stretched open. Welts and scratches and wounds ran along her thighs and waist, her bare breasts, and up to her neck—Harry screaming and sobbing simultaneously—and where her head was supposed to be, there was a puddle of gore like a watermelon smashed over the tiles. Resting in the center of the puddle was his dad's hand axe, buried to the handle in flesh.

Dad bounded into the room—*"There you are, you little shit!"*—but he slipped on the blood, stumbled, crashed into the wall and sprawled on the floor.

Harry screamed and leaped over the body of his mother and out the back screen door. He jumped off the porch steps and into the grass, hurrying toward the dark wilderness beyond.

The screen door slammed again.

His dad's footfalls on the porch.

"Harry! You come back here!"

Harry screamed through the trees without looking back.

The inside of the ruined shack churned with a darkness split only in places where sunlight seeped through broken boards. Harry fell to his knees and knelt religiously in the center, the jumbles of junk and old furniture surrounding him: a rusted porcelain sink, a crumbling chest of drawers, a dusty mirror shattered like gossamer.

Harry cried, but not for Mama, not for Dad, not even for the six-year-old boy of his younger self he had just witnessed fleeing into the trees. He cried for the intensity, for the sheer shock and horror of his memories, for the bloodstained world that was once his childhood. He mourned for a life he never would—never could—have. And he was bitter that his had not been a normal, peaceful existence, that he wasn't able to go to school with the other kids and feel normal like they did—that he couldn't enjoy playing with toys as they did—and most of all that, after six, with his mama dead and his dad sent off to Remington Prison, he had no family to speak of and had to live in a foster home with Mr. Creashak, a middle-aged black man with a hair-trigger temper and an afro the size of a Buick tire, a man who listened to soul music constantly and who beat the living whiteness out of Harry on a daily basis.

Murder Man stood by the wall, statuesque. He didn't offer condolence or a single gesture of sympathy. Murder Man was a cold, uncaring creature who desired Harry to feel pain and suffering. He had no inclination to deal with Harry as a *real person.* Harry was an object to be despoiled, a tool, an animal to cage and torment. Murder Man abided in the inner sanctum of Harry's being and did what Murder Men had done since the dawn of time and had always done so well: murdered his eternal soul.

***

The sun had fallen well behind the trees by the time they returned to the ruined woman. Harry retrieved the shovel and dug. He'd wanted to be home by now. The entire day was gone.

After an hour, he had managed to carve a decent hole in the soil. Crickets and critters sang praise to the coming twilight. Harry worked while Murder Man watched from beside the trunk of an old cottonwood.

Harry scooped the woman with the shovel blade, levering her anatomy into the hole. A disgusting job. The smell was awful. Even though he had acquired a stomach for death, he gagged on the stench.

Murder Man observed silently, his oily black hair strung down over his face, looking on with the implied authority of a construction foreman. Harry hated feeling that ugly black presence at his back, and fantasized about plunging the blade through its neck.

Harry filled the hole.

Murder Man lifted his head and said, "This one's done. How about another?"

Yah did it again, tiger. You spoilt yerself.

Images flashed through his mind: his raging father, Mama kneeling behind the refrigerator, waking in the middle of the—

"No. I won't do this," he said, shaking his head. "I'm going to the police."

He tossed the shovel into the open grave and turned to leave.

Murder Man materialized in his path: a snout face exposing teeth, hair thrown back over his head, orange eyes alight.

"What?" he snapped.

"You heard me."

"They'll throw you in jail. You'll be raped by another man. You'll hate yourself and your life even more than you do now."

"Are you kidding me? How could I hate my life more? I can't stand who I've become. Do you hear me? I want to *kill* myself."

Murder Man was silent, cogitating.

"If you do this, I won't be able to reverse it. I won't be able to bring you back."

Harry fell to his knees, closed his eyes and made Jesus Hands before his chest. He thought of Dad sitting drunk on the porch, chewing tobacco and complaining about the spooks and jigaboos taking over the town. He saw a quick flash of Mama nestled in her secret place in the kitchen, drinking a glass of whiskey, and praying to the Lord to send a storm of lightning to cleanse the souls of the wicked—and in the next image she was lying dead on the floor, Dad's hand axe buried into her face.

"I've got your lightning storm, Mama," he whispered, crying again. "And I'll bring it down upon the most wicked heart of all." A pause, a sob, a breath, and then—"Mine."

In Jesus' name, we pray. Amen.

He rose and opened his eyes.

Murder Man blocked his path.

"Death *is* your purpose," the demon said.

Harry took a militant step forward and passed through its incorporeal form. His entire body shot through with horror, and when he passed to the other side, Murder Man flickered like a television with bad reception and vanished.

Harry lit a Winston and kept walking.

One step at a time.

"This is for you, Mama," he said. "A storm of lightning... a sword of apocalyptic justice."

He continued to his car, down the mountain, and back into town. He made his way to the police station as night spread its mantle of darkness over the town and its inhabitants.

There was peace, once again, for a time, in Harry's eternal soul.

INEVITABLE

MEGHAN ARCURI

"OH GOD, NOT HER AGAIN."

I am Bud. A 25-year-old white guy with long, brown hair. Sometimes I wear it in a ponytail. Sometimes I don't. I am six feet tall. My arms are skinny. My legs are long. I never grew out of that pre-adolescent, awkward phase. My mother's always called me gangly. I hate that word. It reminds me of some pus-filled skin disease. Fuck her.

I like computers. I like video games. I even like that shit they used to play with joysticks. I've played my whole life.

"That's why he doesn't have any friends," he used to say to my mother.

My dad. Arrogant prick.

The computers. The technology. They've served me well. I'm a computer programmer. I work from home. I make good money. But you'd never know it. I don't like fancy clothes or cars. I eat Dunkin' Donuts and McDonald's. I don't have a girlfriend.

I live in the basement apartment of Mrs. Jablonski's house. Wood paneling. Shag carpeting. Straight out of the 70s. I love it. I've always been an old soul.

I'm in my apartment, standing in front of the mirror that hangs over my closet door. I am Bud. I feel like Bud. I think like Bud.

But I don't see Bud.

I see a six-year-old girl. Again. Pigtails. Bows. Pink seersucker dress. Mary Janes. Mary Fucking Janes. At least they're black this time. Not that pink glittery princess shit.

This has been happening to me for god knows how long. I can't remember when it started. I wake up, thinking I'm myself, but when I get to the mirror, I see another person. And the reflection isn't the only thing changed: my body, too. Sometimes for a day, sometimes a week. But never longer.

"Shit."

I giggle. An honest-to-god little girl giggle. Hearing a little kid swear is hilarious.

"Shit. Ass. Fuck."

Awesome.

I haven't taken a piss yet. Now I gotta remember to sit.

I take care of business and head for the kitchen. I'm craving some Cocoa Puffs. Well, Pigtails is, anyway. Although I am still Bud and I still think and feel like Bud, I sometimes take on certain personality traits of those I become.

Lucky for Pigtails, I like Cocoa Puffs. I always have an extra-large box. We never had sugar cereal when I was a kid. Once a year, maybe, if Mom ever stopped worrying about what the check-out lady would think. Fuck her.

I sigh when I see the box of Cocoa Puffs. It's over the fridge. I drag a chair over and stand on tippy toes. I'm able to grab the box. I get off the chair, put the box on its seat and drag everything back to the table.

"Shit."

Another giggle.

I need a bowl. They are in the upper cabinet back by the fridge. More dragging. More tippy-toes. I get what I need, prepare the meal, and take a bite. Awesomeness. Sheer awesomeness.

After breakfast, I walk to my office, which is the dining room portion of my living/dining space. Three huge-ass monitors. One PC and two Macs. The PC and a Mac are for work. The other Mac is for pleasure: gaming, YouTube posting, and porn watching. Those girls are so fucking hot. And the shit they do. Man. When I get a girlfriend, I hope she'll do all that to me.

Not today, though. Pigtails' influence will have me at PBS Kids or Disney.com. Not that I mind all that much. *Elmo's World* can be kinda cool.

"That's because he never grew up enough to get a real job," he said to my mom, after I told them about my sweet work-from-home gig.

My dad's such a dick.

I'm about to sit on my chair, when I see the package I left on it last night.

Shit.

This changing bodies thing was crazy at first. I never knew who I would become or when. I was afraid to leave the house. I didn't want Old Jablonski thinking she was renting some clown-car of an apartment and start charging me more money. She naps a lot, though, so I learned how to avoid her.

And my job lets me stay inside for days on end if I choose. For the most part, I stay home during one of these episodes, as I call them. Most of my other forms are repeat offenders, especially the frat boy and the bodybuilder. And Pigtails. I become women, too. Like a gospel singer and a hot chick. Maybe even more often than men.

"That's probably because he's some sort of queer," he'd say to my mom if he knew this was happening to me.

Asshole.

I'm not gay. I like girls. Always have.

I did go out once as the hot chick, though. Just to see. Got all kinds of looks, from both men and women. But, for the most part, men. Even got laid. Craziest experience ever. It felt way better than when I'm home as Bud, jerkin' it.

I've never been out as the little girl, though. Way too risky.

But this fucking package. My boss needs it overnighted. Some notarized shit for the lawyers.

Mrs. Jablonski's house is two blocks from the post office, though, so I can't get into too much trouble.

I grab the package, my keys, and a twenty. Mrs. Jablonski gets up at ten, so I should be able to get there and back before she's opened her eyes and put on her raggedy slippers.

I walk to the post office. I resist the urge to skip. Pigtails isn't going to dominate everything.

No one's in line when I get there. Thank god.

I walk to the counter. It's above my head. I lift my arms and slide the package on the counter.

"Oh!" says the postal worker, peering over the edge. "You startled me."

"Sorry," I say, in a shy mumble.

"It's okay," he says, in that high-pitched condescending tone adults use with children. "Where's your mommy?"

Presumptuous idiot. I should say, "She's dead," just to make him feel bad. But I give him the party line. "Outside."

"Shouldn't she be sending this?"

More condescension.

"No, you jackass," is on the tip of my tongue.

"I'm a big girl now, and she let me do this all by myself."

A few other patrons have gotten in line behind me.

"Well, you certainly are a big girl," he says. "That'll be three dollars and twenty-one cents."

I hold up the twenty. He takes it and gives me the change.

"Careful now," he says. "Do you have any pockets in that beautiful dress of yours?"

Something about the question bothers me. In fact, the whole exchange has annoyed me. Time to fuck with him.

Loud enough for everyone to hear, I say, "Why do you care so much about my dress, Mister? That's gross!"

I turn and run. As I reach the exit, I hear him bumbling and the other patrons whispering.

Victory is mine. I run home.

When I get to my driveway, I stop short. Jablonski's outside. Of all fucking days. Housedress. Raggedy slippers. Letters in hand, heading to the mailbox.

Before I can hide behind a bush, or run, she sees me.

"Hello, there," she says. "Who are you?"

"Ummm—"

"That's Bud's niece, I think," says a voice from behind me.

I turn to see that it comes from Susie, the cute girl that lives next door. Her driveway's right next to ours.

She knows my name?

Susie's home from college for the summer. She's wearing a lanyard with a whistle on it and a white tank top with a big, red cross on it. She's a lifeguard at the nearby lake. Her bathing suit straps poke out from under her tank top. What I wouldn't give to see her in that suit. Or naked.

She waves at me and smiles.

"Bud has a niece?"

"I saw her here last summer," says Susie. "Have a nice day."

She drives off in her car.

She's seen Pigtails before? Shit. I must have been too careless.

But she knows my name.

"Daddy drops me off for a few days every summer so I can see Uncle Bud," I say, in the most innocent voice I can muster.

"Where the hell–er, heck is your uncle now?" says Jablonski.

"He let me go to the post office while he's on his phone."

"Did he, now?"

"Yeah. He had to talk to some people at work."

"Maybe I should walk you back."

"No, thanks. I'm a big girl. And he's probably still talking."

"All right," she says, suspicion in her eyes.

I skip to the door and let myself inside the apartment.

That was close. Hopefully that old bitch won't ring the bell.

I stay inside and work for the rest of the day, my internet meanderings taking me to Sesame Street and some shitty princess website, as predicted.

The next morning, I wake up and walk to the mirror. Bud is staring back at me.

Thank god. Six-year-old girls are crazy as hell.

I am myself for the next few days. Then shit really gets crazy.

I wake up and walk to the mirror. I see my bedroom. Nothing else.

What the hell?

I move to the left. I move to the right. I feel the shag carpet under my feet. I hear the floor creaking. I see nothing. No corporeal image exists in the mirror.

I wave my hand in front of the mirror. It is not reflected. I wave my hand in front of my face. It is not on this side of the mirror, either.

Holy shit.

I touch my face, hair, body. I feel my stubble, my ponytail, my tank top and the shorts that I put on for bed last night.

I am Bud, but I am invisible.

Fuck.

This has never happened to me.

My heart thuds in my chest. Sweat forms over my upper lip. I wipe it and look down, expecting to see my moist and glistening finger. Nothing.

At least with the other forms I see someone reflected in the mirror. It may not be Bud, but it's something others can see. And I know Bud is in there somewhere. But what the hell is this?

I walk into my bathroom. The mirror on the vanity shows me the same thing: nada. After these episodes started, I thought the mirrors might have something to do with the changes. I went so far as to go to Kelvin's, the local hardware store, and buy new ones.

That was three years ago.

I pick up a towel to wipe my sweaty face. After I've dried myself, I look to the mirror to see if my face is back. It's not, but the towel is reflected, floating as if by magic. Or by some sort of rigged pulley system edited out of the scene.

For kicks, I brush my teeth. The floating toothbrush is weird and cool. Foam and bubbles reveal a mouth-like shape. I swallow some, hoping to see it slide down my esophagus into my stomach. No such luck.

I pick up a cotton ball and hold it in my palm. When I close my fingers around it, it disappears.

Pretty fucking cool.

I decide to stay in for the day. I don't want to risk bumping into someone who can't see me. And I see no sense in freaking people out with random floating objects if I forget and pick up something. Although, to see Old Jablonski process a moving car without a driver would be funny.

The third day of waking up invisible, I can't fucking deal. I've gotten a lot of work done and tons of web surfing.

But I need to go out into the world. I'll have to be careful not to touch anything.

I walk to Wal-Mart. It's a couple miles away, but my legs need to stretch. The place is huge, so the risk of touching anyone is low. Plus, it's always a shit show in there. Craziest. People. Ever.

Even during the middle of the day, the store is packed. Lots of old people and moms with kids trying to avoid the summer heat.

"I want it! I want it! I want it!"

I turn in the direction of the bratty kid voice. He's about six, and he's talking to his mom, holding a Star Wars *LEGO* toy.

"For the last time, Ryan, I said no."

"I hate you, Mommy."

"That's not nice," she says, turning from him to push the cart holding squirming twin babies and a week's worth of groceries.

Little shit.

I decide to take this invisibility thing out for a ride. I sneak behind Ryan by the *LEGO* display and push a box off the shelf.

"Huh?" he says, turning in my direction.

He looks from the shelf to the box on the floor, face in complete bewilderment.

I push another box to the floor.

His eyes become saucers and he says, "Mommy!"

"What?" she says, turning.

When she sees the mess on the floor, she says, "Ryan, pick that up right now!"

"But I didn't—"

"Ryan. Pick it up. Now!"

"But, Mom—"

She rushes at him and grabs his upper arms.

"*But* nothing. Just pick it up and shut up."

I don't know what scares him more: the ghost in the toy aisle or his mom's rage. Who gives a shit, though? He deserved it.

I do a loop around the store and pass by the pharmacy.

A dude in a lab coat is in front of the counter talking to an old dude with a cane, khakis belted just below his armpits.

"The hearing aid seems to fit better now, Mr. Greene, but if you run into any more trouble, give me a call," says Lab Coat.

"Thanks, Jim," Greene says, heading toward the exit.

Something comes over me, and I can't fucking resist.

I sneak behind Greene and say, in a whisper, "How's that working out for you, Mr. Greene?"

He stops and turns his head.

Must be a pretty good hearing aid.

He starts walking and I say, in a louder whisper, "Greene!"

"What?" he says, turning all the way around.

His expression is one of confusion. He looks like an idiot, but he keeps walking.

I get as close to him as I can without touching him. Walking in tandem with him, I say, "You're not going crazy, old man. You're just old."

I swipe his cane with my foot and watch him stumble. He bumps into a shopping cart and it runs over his foot. He groans and falls, landing on his hip.

Did I hear something crack? That's gotta hurt.

The pharmacist and one of those annoying greeters run to him.

"Oh my god. Mr. Greene, are you okay?"

I back away to begin another loop.

See ya, losers.

After a couple more hours and a couple more ghost encounters, my stomach rumbles. I need to go home. Eating in public is not an option.

Back in the driveway, I'm about to open my side-door entrance, when I hear moaning.

Girl moaning. Coming from Susie's house.

The thought of Susie having sex makes me horny. I creep toward her house. I'm invisible after all, right?

The sounds come from a window at the back of the house. The shade is down, but she's left it up enough so that I can see her lithe body riding a masculine form. Her boyfriend? Who cares?

I'm hard. I touch myself, hoping to see them do some of the stuff I've seen on the Internet. They don't, but when they finish, I do, too. All over the bushes. Good thing it's invisible.

"Shit," she says, and the shade is pulled down with haste.

"What?" he says. "You worried about your neighbor?"

"Bud?"

She knows my fucking name. Yeah, bitches!

"I guess," she says. "But not just him. Anyone, really."

"Don't worry about it, Susie. Come here."

I hear them kissing.

My stomach rumbles. I go home.

After three Hot Pockets and a liter of Pepsi, not to mention a kick-ass day of being the Invisible Man, I need to sleep.

The following morning, I walk to the mirror.

I am Bud again.

Shit.

I have a regular, boring day, living my regular, boring life.

Bedtime.

I wake up and walk to the mirror.

My heart races and my upper lip is wet. When I wipe it dry, though, I see the hand pull away from my face. It is large, foreboding and familiar.

I look at the reflection in the mirror.

It's my dad.

It's my mother-fucking dad.

"What the fuck?"

The rage in that voice, now coming from my mouth, is both horrifying and intimate. My memory floodgates open to a variety of wretched childhood vignettes.

He was always such a dick.

I crawl under the covers, hoping that a nap will help me wake as someone else. Not that that's ever worked in the past.

Day four.

I am still my father. I've tried to stay calm, keep things normal. I've done some work. Met some deadlines.

But he takes charge at times. Like yesterday, when I went out and bought a pipe and the tobacco he smokes. Then spent the rest of the day watching *Judge Judy*.

He can't get enough of that shit.

Something tells me that this is going to be one of those episodes that lasts the full week.

I'm at day eight and I still see him in the mirror. The longest I've been someone else. Why him?

This mirror is crazy. Always reflecting me. Maybe not all of me, but usually the stuff that's cool.

But this? Him? I've always kind of looked like him, but he can't be in there. In me. He's such an asshole.

I need to get out. Take a walk. Clear my head.

I grab my keys and leave the apartment.

I walk around the block a couple of times. More exercise than my old man has ever done in his life.

As I turn back into my driveway, Susie pulls out of hers. Warring urges, sexual and something unidentifiable, overcome me. I need to follow her. I get in my car. She might recognize it, but the desire to go after her outweighs all other thoughts.

I assume she's going to work. Her car turns off of our street.

I'd love to see that hot body of hers again. Preferably naked, but I'll take the bathing suit at this point.

The thought reminds me of the last time I saw her on her way to work. Which, in turn, reminds me that she recognized Pigtails.

That's not good.

Maybe I need to do something about that.

I feel anger in that thought. Suspicion. The conspiracy theory crap my dad loves so much.

Shit.

Now he's infecting my thoughts about Susie.

I stay a few cars back from hers. She turns off the main road. Must be taking the back roads to the lake. That ride is prettier. Quieter. I like it better, too.

She seems clueless to the fact that I'm behind her.

Good.

That's his voice in my head. I take a deep breath.

She's cruising along, windows rolled down, hair blowing in the breeze. I see her head bopping up and down to the music.

I wonder what kind of music she likes.

Who the hell cares?

I can't seem to shake him.

My breaths are shallow. My grip on the steering wheel is tight. I put more pressure on the gas pedal. I close in on her car.

A sharp curve is ahead of us. As she begins the turn, I floor it. The front of my car rams into the back of hers. My car spins and I slam on the brakes. When I stop, I am facing the opposite direction. I look in the rearview: Susie's car has gone off the road, its front end wrapped around a tree.

Holy shit.

What the hell did I just do?

What the hell did he just do?

I open my door and hurl. I clean my mouth with my hand and wipe the puke on my pants. I close the door. My entire body trembles. From the violent retching, as well as the attempted murder.

Or was that an actual murder?

I don't want to find out for sure.

My car still runs. I step on the gas and speed home.

At home, I shower but I still don't feel clean.

This shit needs to end. He needs to leave. Now.

I open a bottle of Jim Beam and drink myself to sleep.

I spend days nine and ten in an alcoholic haze. By day eleven, I am a complete mess. He's still here.

I feel more and more like him every day. Less like Bud.

After the incident with Susie, I haven't left the house. I haven't done any work. I can hardly eat or sleep.

Is she hurt? Is she dead?

The gorge rises and I rush to the bathroom.

What are you gonna do: faint? Clean yourself up and act like a man.

I can't take it anymore. I can't take him.

I remember the gun he gave me when I moved out.

"Wuss like him has to defend himself somehow," he said to my mom.

I retrieve it from its box in the closet.

In front of the mirror, I put the barrel in my mouth. Although my dad's face is in front of me, I see flashes of myself in the eyes. I'm in there, trying to escape. But he's too strong. Always has been.

I pull the trigger.

Click.

I spin the cylinder.

Fuck. I got lucky. That was an empty chamber. The only one.

I put the barrel back in my mouth.

A tear runs down my cheek.

Fucking wuss. That's his voice. Not mine. Not Bud's.

As I squeeze the trigger, I feel faint. I'm about to pass out.

Fucking wuss.

I'll take care of this myself.

SEND YOUR END

PATRICK LACEY

THE VIDEO QUALITY was grainy at best. There was a shot of a bathtub. I opened my mouth to tell John I wanted to stop watching when a woman entered the frame. She wore a bathrobe covered with exotic flowers. She threw it aside, made sure the camera was still rolling, got into the tub and stretched. Smiling.

"I don't regret anything," the woman said. The audio was low, so John turned up the volume. "This is the way it needs to be. It's been a long time since I've enjoyed anything, and my husband's no help. I'm quite sure he's been cheating on me with my next-door neighbor. I've never seen myself as the type to see a shrink and I sure as hell don't want a long list of prescriptions to fuck me up even more so. Which is why I'm here, at this exact moment."

The woman pushed aside the hair covering her face and for the first time I saw her beauty. Her eyes were partly slanted, almost Asian. She could've been a movie star or a model. She reached into the tub, near her legs, and retrieved a knife. She slit both her wrists, first horizontally, then vertically—two mock-crosses bleeding onto the porcelain. The knife clattered.

She leaned her head back and stared into the camera.

After a while of just lying there, looking frustrated, she picked up the fallen knife and sliced her throat. Her eyes widened, as if showing regret, and then they closed and the video ended.

I looked up at John, not sure what to say.

He tried catching his breath.

Send Your End. It's a secret website with a generic black background and a single field in which to type a password. After typing in the password, the screen is filled with thumbnails of videos and an option to submit. There are thousands.

I haven't seen John since watching that first video. It's not hard to picture him huddled in front of the screen in his parents' basement watching video after video. He'd always gotten off on things like that. It'd started with banned horror movies, then snuff films he got from a 'guy at work' who probably told him about the website.

Each time I closed my eyes, I saw the woman smiling, like her suicide was the most normal thing in the world.

My father shot himself in the face when I was three, so I guess to some people it's normal. Most are shocked when I say it like that, as if it's in poor taste, but I've yet to find a nicer way. From what I've heard, he was a real asshole anyway.

After two restless nights of thinking about the woman in the video, I finally gave in. It was one in the morning and I couldn't fall asleep. My bed was an ocean of sweaty sheets. I turned on my lamp and then my laptop and searched through the Internet browser history to find the site.

I scrolled through the entries, knowing how fucked up it was to watch, but feeling relieved at the same time. I picked a video at random.

This time it was an attractive teen boy with a chiseled face. He was shirtless and had a scar on his stomach. He wasn't like the woman. He didn't talk, just stared into the camera after opening a bottle of prescription pills, tilted his head back, and swallowed hundreds of them. Ten minutes in, he started to seizure.

A tingle went through my body, starting at my feet and rising, until it stayed below my belt. I didn't want to admit what I was feeling, didn't want to admit to myself that I was watching the video in the first place. But it was hard to deny. The more the boy shook and convulsed, the more I became aroused, as if my body was in tune with the video. I felt an orgasm shutter through me as he finally fell off his chair and choked on vomit.

It took a long time for my heart to slow. My stomach churned and I ran into the bathroom, hovered over the toilet, and threw up like the boy.

Heroin addicts call it 'Chasing the Dragon.' You get this amazing high the first time, but then the next time it isn't quite as mind-blowing. So you try more, and then more, until you realize you're after an imaginary experience, a train that's already left without you. But your body doesn't care; your body's already hooked and wants more, so you end up using to keep your flesh from protesting.

That's exactly how I felt that summer.

The dragon was long gone.

At first I'd watch a few videos a week, then it turned to ten, then twenty. I was up all night every night, typing in that damn password.

If I hadn't been in the last days of my senior year when I found *Send Your End*, I probably would've been delivering pizzas for the rest of my life, which would've been preferable to all the hours spent alone in my room.

On the last day of school, Mr. Bolonsky shook my hand. "It's been a pleasure, Ms. Clark."

"Same here."

"I want you to know that you've got a future in this field. Have you given any thought to studying it in college?"

I shrugged. I hadn't given much thought to anything lately.

To be honest, Mr. Bolonsky's class was the only one I remotely gave a shit about. He was new to the high school, had more than a few jokes about his last name circling around, but he was damned smart and he didn't treat me like I—along with everyone else in my generation—was going to fuck up the world.

I remembered a conversation we'd had a few months ago. Class had been dismissed, and he'd stopped me on my way out the door. "Ms. Clark, would you mind waiting for a moment?"

He put on his glasses, thick black frames, and looked at a sheet of paper. "I have you down as choosing advertising as a topic for your term paper."

"That's right."

"Do you mind me asking why you chose that in particular?"

"Is there something wrong with it? If you don't think I'll have enough to write about, I can always choose something else."

"No, it's not that. It's just that most students choose something like Freud or Pavlov and then try to connect it to today's world, and let's be honest here," he said, looking in the hallway and lowering his voice, "that's a bunch of pop psychology bullshit."

"I guess you're right."

He nodded. "So then why choose a topic like advertising?"

"There are a lot of subliminal things going on, you know? Like there's something going on beneath the surface that most people don't notice."

"Interesting. I think you're on to something there and I think you're right. I think today, more than ever, we are being influenced by everything around us. We live in a very stimulating world."

He had written that exact comment, *We live in a very stimulating world*, on the back of my paper in red ink, handwriting so shaky it looked as though he'd been drunk while grading it.

"Is everything alright, Marissa?" he asked, bringing me out of the memory.

I wanted to tell him then. I could sense urgency in the way he'd switched from my last name to my first, like he knew I was holding on to something.

"You've seemed a bit distant these last few days."

The bell rang, ending my last class as a high school student.

I crossed my arms, my skin feeling cool, and pictured my room with the shades drawn shut.

"Everything's fine, Mr. Bolonsky. I guess being a senior was more than I bargained for."

His eyes narrowed and I knew he didn't believe me.

"I guess it is. Well, if you need anything, please don't hesitate to contact me. My number is on the syllabus if you still have it?"

I nodded.

"Then have a wonderful summer, and take care of yourself."

"You, too. Thanks."

As I was leaving, he called to me.

"Ms. Clark, there really *are* things beneath the surface."

I turned around, unable to speak.

"I'm referring to your paper, the one about advertising. I don't think I ever got a chance to tell you how terrific it was. And that you were right. There are a lot of things that we don't pay attention to, and it's not only subliminal messaging. There are things that we choose to ignore, but when we become in tune with them… well, let's just say we can lose ourselves in the process."

I pretended that what he'd said didn't chill my bones.

At home, I logged into the site and watched a video of an old man suffocating himself with a plastic bag, making crunching sounds as it stuck to his mouth.

More and more my body became less my own. That's the only way I can describe it, as if the videos were taking small pieces of me away, pieces I would never get back.

My mother picked up extra shifts for the first month of summer. She worked for twenty-eight nights in a row, sleeping through the days, which left me alone.

I tried to tell her once.

We were in the kitchen and it was evening and she was trying to find her stethoscope. She looked through cabinets, under notebooks, even in the trashcan.

I sat at the kitchen table, trying to eat the Ramen noodles in front of me. They reminded me of worms.

"Mom?"

It wasn't until she found the stethoscope, in her scrub pocket all along, that she looked at me. "What is it dear?"

"Why did Dad do it?"

"Honey, that's a question I've been trying to find an answer to for a long time, but I really don't think there is one. All I can tell you is that he was a good man once, and that he had issues."

She looked at her watch.

"Is that why people kill themselves, because they have issues?"

She sat down next to me.

"Baby, is everything alright? Is there something you're trying to tell me?"

"Nothing's wrong. I just haven't had this much free time for a while, so I've been thinking a lot."

"Thinking is good, but don't dwell on things like your father. I've done it, and trust me, nothing good can come from it."

She kissed me and left in a hurry.

I went upstairs, telling myself I'd watch only one video, one short video to make myself a little calmer. I chose one at random, twenty pages in.

This time it was a girl, probably around my age. She looked into the camera, her eyes bloodshot and distant. She mouthed the words "I'm sorry" while standing on a chair in the middle of the frame. I couldn't see the noose, but knew it was above the camera. Her feet came down off the chair and hung in the air, swaying back and forth. Somehow that was worse: not seeing her face.

I tried to stop, but the cursor moved to another video.

The sun was up and my mother was just getting home when I finally left my room to splash cold water onto my face. I lost count of how many I had watched.

Later that day, I searched my room for almost two hours for Mr. Bolonsky's syllabus before I finally saw it hanging on my cork-board. The website did that to you, made you unaware of things right in front of you because you were so preoccupied thinking about the videos.

I called him and he answered on the third ring.

"Mr. Bolonsky, it's Marissa Clark."

"You are no longer my student, Marissa. Please, call me Peter."

"I need to talk to you about something. It might sound crazy, but I think you're the only one who can help."

"Are you in some sort of trouble?"

Send Your End's homepage stared at me from the laptop.

We met at a coffee shop two towns over. I'd explained to him that I wasn't worried about people seeing us together. I just felt safer being away from home.

"What exactly do you feel safer from?"

"A month ago, my ex-boyfriend showed me a website, one where people upload videos of their suicides. He was into some pretty weird stuff and this was right up his alley. I watched a video with him. I still don't know why."

"Curiosity can be dangerous."

"Since then, I haven't been able to stop watching the videos. It's like I'm an addict or something."

"Why don't you give me the address of the site, and I'll at least have a better idea of what we're talking about. Maybe we can get it shut down. That sort of thing is not entirely legal."

"You don't want to see it."

"This isn't about *wanting* anything, Marissa. I'm trying to help you. People become addicted to all sorts of things. When I did my clinicals, I met a man who couldn't stop eating cat litter. Addiction is an odd thing, so please—just give me the address."

"You'll need the password," I said, and wrote it down.

My mother was at work and I had the house to myself. I paced: upstairs, downstairs, through the hall, around the yard—it didn't matter where I was, as long as I kept moving. I had put my laptop in the attic so I wouldn't be tempted. In the kitchen, I stopped suddenly, swore I heard a noise far away. It was scratching or breathing or both. I pictured my laptop in the attic, calling for me.

The phone rang and I startled.

It was Mr. Bolonsky—Peter.

"Ms. Clark, I've looked at the website."

He'd switched back to using my last name.

"And?"

"You were right to be worried. These videos are disturbing at the very least. Watching enough of them could be… damaging."

"So how do I stop? That's all I want."

He breathed heavily, and in the background it sounded as if a woman were screaming. "You'll hear from me soon."

He hung up before I could say anything.

Peter never called back. I tried calling him the next day at noon, but there was no answer. I tried again at three and five, only getting his voicemail. When my mother went to work that night, I broke and used the computer in her room.

The website called instead.

There were close to twenty new videos posted that same day. My heart pounded and I felt feverish. I clicked on the newest video and immediately felt trapped, like my life had become a dream and I couldn't wake up.

Peter Bolonsky stared at me from the screen, holding a piece of paper. There were red letters in his shaky script. *I'm sorry, Marissa*, it read. *There is no way out.*

I tried to stop watching as he reached for the gun.

He was my father for a moment, raising the pistol to his face, wanting to leave it all behind: his wife, his daughter—everything.

And then he was Peter again, my favorite teacher, and he pulled the trigger.

Send Your End controls me now. It's hard to deny that when you spend all hours watching the videos. The website is alive somehow. I'm not even sure how the videos make it online. I think about that a lot, about who controls *Send Your End.* On most nights, I wonder if my video—if and when it surfaces—will be grainy or clear, or if I'll have some message for whoever is watching.

The password is in here, hidden amongst these words, but do yourself a favor and don't find it. Forget all of this. Don't search for the website.

There *are* things beneath the surface, and once you find them, they grab on and never let go.

A FLAWED FANTASY

JEFF STRAND

"SO LET'S HEAR IT," said the unbelievably attractive brunette. She'd said her name was Debbie, though she looked more like a Tiffany to him. "What's your ultimate sexual fantasy?"

Blake laughed and took another swig of his beer. His buddy Carl had been right: if you looked like you were rich, the hot chicks flocked to you. Expensive clothes, expensive haircut, smile fresh from the dentist... this was going to be a very memorable night in the life of Blake Denver.

"Aw, I don't know," he said. "I'd have to think about it."

"I don't believe you. You can't tell me you don't know your own ultimate fantasy." She scooted her barstool a little bit closer to his. "What's the matter? Are you shy?"

"Nah," he said, making no attempt not to stare at her fantastic cleavage. She was jutting her chest out at him, so it was okay to stare. He'd stop staring if it started to feel creepy.

"Then why? I let you buy me a drink, so in exchange, I want to know your ultimate fantasy."

"Aw, hell, why not." Blake finished his beer and gestured for the hot bartender to bring him another. "Twins."

"Twins."

"Yep. Twin sisters at once. That's my fantasy."

Debbie's smile disappeared. Blake's own smile faded a bit, as he realized that he might have misunderstood the point of this whole exercise. She was probably asking about a fantasy that she could actually grant him. He was so dense. He should have said something about bringing a hot brunette he'd just met into the restroom of a bar... or would that have been too transparent?

"That's a flawed fantasy," she said.

"Huh?"

"It's a fantasy that you didn't think through."

"Are you supposed to think them through? I thought the whole point was to fantasize about shit that didn't make sense."

"You're cute but you're dumb. All guys fall back on the 'I want to have sex with twins' fantasy, but if you analyze it, it's vastly inferior to a standard threesome."

"I'm not so sure that it is."

"When you have two women at once, you want them to interact, right? That's the best part. If you have twins and they interact, it's disgusting and deviant. You want to watch incest in action?"

Blake had to admit that it was indeed an element of the fantasy that he'd never thought through. Two chicks had been making out at a party once and it was the hottest thing ever. Still, he didn't appreciate Debbie criticizing his fantasy before he'd slept with her.

"I don't care about the girls doing each other," he said. "In my fantasy, all of the attention is on Blake." Carl had recommended that he refer to himself in the third person every once in a while. Not every time he spoke of himself—that would be obnoxious—but maybe once every four or five times.

"Even if the women aren't bi, even if they're focused entirely on the guy, there's going to be a time when their boobs brush against each other. Do you really want to see sisters having their boobs brush against each other?"

Blake was not entirely sure that he didn't. "That's not incest, is it? I think twins are allowed to do that and it's okay. I knew these twins in high school, and sometimes a bunch of us would go to the beach, and they'd hug each other in bikinis."

"Hugging in bikinis is not the same thing. I'm talking about breast-on-breast contact in a sexual situation. It's not cool."

"I don't see why they have to touch."

"Well, you could take a magic marker, draw a line across your waist, and say 'You stay on this side, and you stay on this side,' but what fun is that? You have to make sure that everybody is properly balanced, and if you want to them to switch sides, you have to blow a frickin' whistle to make sure that one twin doesn't move too quickly, or else they might break a vile taboo. And in fact, I will state for the record that if siblings are even *watching* each other have intercourse, it's wrong. If a sister sees her sister's vagina in a locker room, that's completely fine, but if there's a penis inside of it, she flat-out should not be watching. Did you give *any* thought to your answer before you blurted it out?"

"I think you're taking this too far," said Blake. "First off, maybe in your world people are flopping all over the bed like fish, but the experience of Blake has been that people can actually avoid smacking into each other. So I reject that thing you said about how I'd have to draw that magic marker on my waist or blow a whistle."

"That was an exaggeration. But if everybody is firmly in place, balanced like the Scales of Liberty, then you're not doing it right."

"They're the Scales of Justice, not Liberty," said Blake. "So if you're going to criticize my awesome fantasy, maybe you should get your facts straight. Second off, I don't think it *is* incest if their boobs touch. I think they could rub them against each other, on purpose, for, like, fifteen minutes and it wouldn't be gross."

"I disagree."

"You can disagree all you want. And let me tell you something else: I've got a brother. We're not twins, he's a couple of years older than me, but when I was eighteen and he was twenty, the neighbor lady came over and asked if we could help her move a couch. And I'm not going to lie and say that she was hot—she wasn't—and she was probably fifty, but we went over there, and she didn't give a shit where we moved that stupid couch. It was all a ruse. And my brother and I, we seized that opportunity, and we shared her right there on that couch. It was sweet. And you know what? I'm going to tell you this next part, I don't care: she wanted to use her mouth on both of us at once. We agreed. We didn't even have to discuss it. And our dicks touched, and it wasn't the *least bit* incestuous *or* gay. So you don't have any idea what you're talking about."

"That was totally gay," said Debbie.

"I just finished telling you that it wasn't."

"That was homosexual incest. For shame."

"You know what? When you sat down and started asking me about my ultimate fantasy, I wanted to do you. I wanted to take you back to my place and pound at you like a Viking. Now I don't. Do you know how off-putting your personality has to be to make a guy as horny as me not want to do a girl as hot as you? You'd have to be like a chick version of Hitler."

"Are you comparing my nitpicking of your puerile fantasy to the extermination of millions of Jews?"

"Yes. And I'm okay with that comparison. I really am."

Debbie sighed. "All right, I apologize for being rude. When I asked you about your ultimate fantasy, I thought it was going to be about having sex in church or something. I wanted to be the hot chick who came up to you in a bar, asked about your fantasy, then immediately granted it. I wanted to be a story you'd still be telling when you were ninety."

"Well, church is up there on the list," said Blake. "I'd tell that story."

"I don't have a twin sister, but what if we found somebody who looks like me, and we dressed alike?"

"You're screwing with me."

Debbie shook her head. "I won't act like she's my sister; I won't ask her how Grandpa is doing or anything, but if you want to play out that fantasy in your head, you're more than welcome."

Blake looked closely at her. She didn't seem to be messing with him. She probably was. She had to be. But, if there was, say, a two-percent chance that she was serious about giving him a three-way, and a ninety-eight percent chance that she was going to laugh and post pictures of his junk online, it was still worth pursuing.

"Do you know anybody who looks like you?"

"No. To save time, we'd just call an escort service. Dutch treat. Ready to go? Do you want to ride with me or follow me in your own car?"

"I'll, uh... follow you."

Debbie smiled. "You scared?"

"No."

"It's okay. I won't hurt you. But maybe, when we're done, you'll grant a little fantasy of my own."

"What fantasy?"

"You'll find out."

"No, tell me."

She glanced around to see if anybody was listening. "I'm going to kill the hooker when we're done."

"*What?*"

"I've always wanted to kill a hooker, and if you're there in the room with us, I'll feel safe enough to do it. You wouldn't have to do anything unless it looks like she might get away."

"I'm not doing that," said Blake.

"Oh, really? You'll let me go down on some skank dressed like my twin sister, but when it's time for *my* pleasure..."

"You're talking about murder."

"I didn't say that I wanted to assassinate the president! It's a hooker! If we don't do it, somebody else will."

"You got all high and mighty and called me a deviant, but this is way more deviated. At least my sick fantasy was legal."

"Don't act like I said I wanted to mummify her or keep her as a pet. All I want to do is slit a hooker's throat. As soon as she bled out, we'd leave."

Blake pushed back his bar stool. "No. I'm not doing this."

"Is it because you have a tiny penis?"

"No."

"Because, I've got to say, you're acting like somebody with a tiny penis."

"Trust me, it's completely adequate."

"It curves at a weird angle, doesn't it?"

It did, sort of, but Blake had never heard any complaints. He didn't care how hot this chick was, if she wanted to commit the heinous act of murder, Blake was not going to be part of...

What if he had the sexual experience, and then stopped her from killing the hooker? She'd be mad, sure, but what was she going to do, file a lawsuit against him for not fulfilling the terms of their threesome?

"Okay," he said.

He ended up riding with her. They stopped at a Wal-Mart, where Debbie bought two identical pairs of red negligee. Then they checked into a very cheap motel, paying with cash. Debbie called the escort agency from the motel room phone. It concerned Blake a bit that she knew the number by heart, but he wasn't going to let that ruin his evening.

The prostitute arrived forty-five minutes later. Debbie opened the door and let out a groan of annoyance.

"Okay, you're at least ten years too old, and your hair was supposed to be shoulder-length. You call that a D-cup?"

The prostitute shrugged.

Debbie looked over at Blake. "It's your fantasy. Should we send her back?"

"No, no, it's fine," Blake said. He didn't want to wait another forty-five minutes and give Debbie a chance to change her mind.

Debbie and the prostitute went into the bathroom, closing the door. Blake sat nervously on the bed, listening for audio evidence that Debbie might be stabbing her to death, but heard none.

After twenty excruciating minutes, the women emerged from the bathroom. They wore the same red negligee, the same pink lipstick, and had sort-of similar hairstyles. They didn't really look like sisters, much less twins, but Blake wasn't going to complain.

Watching them pleasure each other should have been the greatest moment of Blake's life. Both of them were completely into it. Unfortunately, he kept worrying that Debbie was going to whip out a knife—even though there really wasn't anyplace she could hide it—and slit the hooker's throat.

When they beckoned for him to join them, his mind said "Yes, yes, yes!" but his penis said "No, no, no, she might slash her throat while you're over there." Though the women made a valiant effort to overcome his technical difficulties, it just wasn't working.

"You're the best sister a girl could have," said Debbie, as if to throw him a bone. It didn't work. In fact, the 'ick' factor of the comment made things even worse, and he decided that she had in fact been right—it was a flawed fantasy.

So he sat on the corner of the bed and watched. After a while, he got a little bored. He glanced at the clock a few times, wondering when the hour would be up.

When they finished, Debbie reached for her purse, which rested on the nightstand. "Let me get your money."

They'd already taken care of payment, but the hooker said nothing, probably hoping that she'd accidentally be paid twice. Approximately ten seconds after Debbie's comment, Blake would regret that his reaction had been "Wow, that must have been really good girl/girl sex if she's so delirious with pleasure that she forgot we'd already paid!" instead of the much more intelligent reaction of trying to stop Debbie from getting anything out of her purse.

A quick flash of silver, and then a thin red line appeared across the hooker's neck.

Blake slammed his hands over his mouth and tried not to scream as blood began to gush.

Debbie held the hooker down as she gasped and twitched. It had been a really effective slash with the knife, and it didn't take long until the sheets were soaked and the hooker was dead.

"Thank you," Debbie told him. "Thank you for making my fantasy come true."

"I can't believe you killed her!"

"That was the plan, right? I'm sorry that your fantasy was sort of messed up by your impotence, but mine was awesome. C'mon, we should get out of here. I'll take you back to your car."

Something bothered Blake about the whole situation, something he couldn't quite put his finger on, and he realized what it was just as she pulled into the parking lot of the bar.

"This was no fantasy," he told her. "You've done this before."

"No, I haven't."

"Bullshit. I saw how you used that knife. That wasn't your first throat-cutting. You *lied* to me. You've done that with lots of guys!"

Debbie lowered her eyes. "Not *lots* of them..."

"I can't believe this. You make me think I'm the first, but then you show that you know exactly how it's done. You *used* me."

"I'm sorry. I wanted you to think it was special."

"Well, it wasn't. It kind of sucked."

"But you got to have twins."

"You weren't twins! I won't be telling anyone about this when I'm ninety. I won't be telling anyone, ever! I'm going to go home and drink whiskey until I forget it, myself!"

"Okay. I'm sorry you didn't enjoy yourself. I won't wait for your call."

"Good."

Blake got out of her car and slammed the door shut. As he walked toward his car, he felt kind of bad about slamming her door, and turned back to apologize, but she'd already driven away.

He got into his car, started the engine, and then thought: *No. I'm not going to let her ruin this. She can spoil my twins fantasy, but not my evening.*

He shut off the engine, popped a breath mint into his mouth, and returned to the bar to see what other hot chicks might still be around.

CUBICLE FARM

R. B. PAYNE

SOME CALLS *may be recorded for training or quality assurance purposes.*

Hello, my name is Douglas, ID Number 958029 of the Interstate Collection Agency of West Covina. This call is about your mortgage with First Regional Bank and is an attempt to collect a debt.

Yes, Mrs. Wong, I understand you've been out of the country.

However, your house payment is overdue. We need you to make a payment today. You understand if you don't make a payment, the bank will be forced to turn your account over to the Collections, and this may adversely affect your credit rating or you may even lose your home.

Adversely means bad. Yes, Mrs. Wong.

Okay, to summarize our agreement, you will contact your son and call us back today with a payment of $1,845.12 before 11:00 p.m.

Thank you and have a nice day.

Doug sat in his cube.

Tossing his pencil aside and clicking his headset to *mute*, he reclined in his chair and counted the ceiling tiles surrounding the flickering tube of fluorescent light. Two tiles by three; his workspace was four by six feet. As a trainee, of course, he should have expected a shit desk. Still, according to the *Welcome* email, when his collections met management expectations, there were opportunities for a rise in pay and a bigger cube.

Rolling back a few inches, Doug stretched his arms wide and touched the gray fabric panels on each side of him while extending his cramped legs. He checked his watch. Fuck, still an hour to go before the five-minute walkabout break. Doug wiggled in the chair; his ass was half-asleep. He really needed to stand but that violated company policy. McConnell, the floor supervisor, said overactive behavior disturbed other employees who might be in a conversation with a customer.

A beep in his headset informed him he was about to be connected to a customer. Jesus, why did he have to listen to so many bullshit excuses?

Doug cringed as an already familiar sound crawled over the cubicle walls. The cough was thick and phlegmy, a moisture-filled hack-hack-hack. Next, a wet blowing of the nose, one side, then the other, and Doug waited for the thump of a foot hitting a plastic garbage can as a chair swung in a cube and a tissue was tossed.

He was tempted to stand and locate the offensive employee, but he had no idea what aisle, what cube, or even which department housed the coughing hacker. And there seemed to be more than one person. How could he find them? And what would he do if he knew who they were? Besides, the call center covered a half-acre, neatly organized into hundreds of cubicles. How would he ever figure it out?

The headset beeped in his ear, indicating he was connected to a customer. The auto-dialer turned off his mute as his computer flickered a screen of financial data. He waited while the disclosure played.

Some calls may be recorded for training or quality assurance purposes.

He grasped the edge of his desk to pull closer to his computer. A yellow sticky note lay on his keyboard.

What the hell is this?

Knife-like electricity discharged down the center of his chest.

His solar plexus burned like fire, and then the pain was gone.

Maybe he'd eaten something bad for dinner. He couldn't remember eating. That was one of the problems working swing shift. His body clock was totally screwed.

A girl's voice interrupted his thoughts. "Hel-wo?"

Doug moved the note aside and spoke, "Hi Sweetie. Is your Daddy home?"

"Mummy, it's for Daddy," said the preschooler.

Beyond the child, he heard the clinking of dishes. Dinnertime. A woman's voice. Running water.

"Mummy wants to know who it is," said the tiny voice.

Shit. Banking regulations dictated what he could say. It would be easier to lie. What he wanted to say was "Hey, this is Doug. I'm a pal from your Daddy's office. Can I talk to him honey?" What he actually said was "My name is Douglas, ID Number 958029 of the Interstate Collection Agency of West Covina, and I'm calling about your Daddy's mortgage with First Regional Bank."

He knew what would happen next. A hang-up followed by dial tone. Mom had been listening.

Doug switched his headset to mute until the next call. He read the scribbled message on the sticky note. *Welcome to the cubicle farm.*

The message wasn't signed, but he recognized the handwriting.

His own.

But he hadn't written the note.

Doug sat in his cube.

At 11:00 p.m. he checked his online performance report—slightly over a hundred and sixty calls and only three payments processed. His ratios were crapola. And Mrs. Wong hadn't called back with her payment info. Bitch, so much for promises.

He'd failed to meet quota. Again. He had to be more aggressive with these losers. Tomorrow. He'd start tomorrow. Get tough.

Fucking tough. No mercy.

Doug headed to the exit. He was alone in the building. How had everyone left so quickly? Was it a Friday? Jesus, he wasn't even sure... it might be Friday. Did he have tomorrow off? Where was everyone? Wasn't there a cleaning staff that worked nights?

He hurried along the long aisles between cubicle walls too high to see over. Somewhere he heard the murmurs of a few customer service reps trying to close out late-night calls with customers either drunk or too stupid to take the hint that all they had to do was promise they'd make a payment tomorrow and both debtor and collector could hang up.

Somewhere another cougher was hacking. Still, Doug didn't see a single soul.

At the glass-enclosed security gate, Doug pressed his electronic badge against the card reader. A red light flashed and the gate refused him.

Pausing, Doug rubbed his eyes. He couldn't focus. He'd never worked on a computer this much and everything was blurry after a couple of hours. He probably needed glasses. Still, he wasn't eligible for the company health plan until he'd been here ninety days and was off probation.

Maybe he should stop at the all-night gas station on the Interstate and buy a pair of those cheap glasses with the crazy frames. No, he hadn't been at ICA long enough to get a paycheck and when he did, he'd need every dime for food, rent, and alimony. He hadn't worked for seven months and he had to wait still a few more days for the first payday in a long time.

Doug rubbed the security pass on his pants leg. Sometimes that helped. Static electricity could really mess up electronics.

He tried again.

Red.

Again.

Red.

And again.

Doug felt faint and he dropped onto a plastic visitor's chair in the reception area. Everything spinning, he put his head between his knees and gulped air.

Doug sat in his cube.

Had he gone home? He scoped his shirt and pants. They were different than he remembered yet he had no memory of arriving this morning. Or showering. He touched his jawline. Apparently he'd shaved. But when?

A tap on the shoulder jolted him. McDonnell wanted to see him in his office. All of this was communicated with the twitch of a McDonnell's *come-with-me* finger. Logging out of the system, Doug followed McDonnell down the narrow aisles of gray.

McDonnell was an asshole, a twenty-something with permanent smirk, and a pock-marked attitude about everyone. Even though the dress code was business casual, McDonnell wore an ill-fitted suit, a white shirt, and a yellow power-tie. *The kind that real bankers wore* is what McDonnell told everyone. To cap everything off, he insisted all employees address him as 'Mr. McDonnell.'

Jerk.

McDonnell's "office" was a larger cubicle closer to the exterior windows. Doug stood as McDonnell sat and swiveled in his chair. As McDonnell talked, Doug counted the ceiling tiles. Six by eight. That would be a cubicle twelve by sixteen feet. Enough room for a real desk.

"Douglas," concluded McDonnell. "I've been looking at the collection rates for your first month and I'm sorry to say you're not really cutting it. Your collection ratios look... dismal, at best. You've got to be more persuasive. We know these people can't afford to make their payments, but we've got to extract the money anyway. Don't be soft. It's us or them. Work hard, Douglas, and you can have a great career here at ICA. Honestly, I'm rooting for you."

Doug winced. He'd been here thirty days?

His saliva was thick; mucous ran down the back of his throat. He wanted to say "Thank you, Mr. McDonnell," but all he could do was cough.

A phlegm-filled cough.

The coughing didn't seem to bother McDonnell.

Repressing more insistent coughs, Doug headed to his cubicle, passing rows of cubes filled with faceless men and women. Most were hunched over keyboards and speaking into headsets. Some were resting for a moment. A few were coughing. None ever looked up.

Back at his cube, Doug flopped into his chair and swung around to his keyboard. A yellow Post-it note was stuck to it.

Cull the herd, the note read.

Jesus, his own handwriting again. Pulling a tissue from the drawer, he wiped the keyboard clean of phlegm.

Doug sat in his cube.

An alert flashed on his screen. Mrs. Wong still hadn't paid. Fucking bitch, what good was a promise if you didn't keep it? Another day and he'd failed to meet quota.

Doug coughed. Something thick rose in his throat but he swallowed, forcing it back.

Precisely at 11:00 p.m. he logged off and leapt to his feet. Surely he could walk to the parking lot with some of the other Collection Agents.

Since starting at ICA, he hadn't connected with anyone. The workers walked the aisles with drooped heads and made no eye contact. Maybe everyone was ashamed of what they did for a living, but still, couldn't they talk to each other? Was it a crime to collect a debt?

Stepping into the aisle, he checked the cubicles to the left and right of him. Already empty.

He looked down the aisle.

No one.

How had they gotten out so fast?

Doug glanced at his watch. 11:33. That wasn't possible. It should be a couple minutes past eleven. He trotted to the building's entrance. There, he swiped his access badge.

Red.

He swiped it again.

Red.

Red.

Red.

"Damn it," he said as he pounded the glass panel of the security door. "Is anyone here?"

He hurried to the edge of the cubicles. "Hello?" he yelled over the gray panels. "Is anyone here?"

Coughing. The sound made him nauseous but he called out. "Where are you? Stand up so I can see you."

More coughing.

He hurried toward the sound. The coughing was everywhere, but nowhere. Bullshit. He needed to be more organized. Going to the row of cubicles at the south of the building, he methodically searched the entire call center. Not a single person. But still, he could hear the coughing coming from somewhere.

He glanced at his watch. 3:30 a.m.

Finding himself back at his desk, he rested. He was tired. Damn tired. He tried to do what Dad had taught him. *When you've got a problem, Son, you've got to think hard.*

Think, Doug, think. There's got to be a way to leave the building short of smashing the massive glass windows.

Jesus, he couldn't remember the last time he'd even been out of the building. Pulling his cellphone from the pocket, he checked for a signal. During the shift, all cellular calls were electronically blocked for security reasons. Banking regulations demanded it to secure customer confidential information. But you'd think late at night you could make a personal call.

No cell signal.

He grabbed the handset of the phone at his desk.

No dial tone.

Pressure built in his chest, like it was going to split. His solar plexus was on fire.

He'd never been a good thinker. That's what had ruined his marriage. He'd bought an F150 and a Waterman ski boat on credit instead of paying rent and making a baby. It had been too much for his wife. As Assistant Manager at Fryman's Paint, he made decent money, but he'd got caught with his hand in the till. He'd sweet-talked his way to a confidential settlement. No jail time, but the incident had ruined his references. And destroyed his marriage. Now he worked here. The only job he could find.

Think, Doug, think.

He ran to a nearby wall. There, the Fire Department alarm. If he pulled it, he could leave. Firemen would come. But if he pulled it, he'd lose his job. He ran his fingers over the bright red alarm, going so far as to hook his fingers behind the pull bar. Quickly he took them away. He couldn't afford to lose his job.

He returned to his cubicle.

On the keyboard was a note. It read: *Mrs. Wong is fucking your ratio.* His handwriting. But the note hadn't been there a few moments ago. Jesus, was he writing these notes to himself? He had to be. And the slime. That must be *his* slime.

The pressure in his chest was ready to explode. It did. Collapsing to the floor, Doug coughed and coughed until he thought his lungs would rip his body apart and a bloody liquid mash would pour from his chest. Finally, exhausted, he curled into a ball and slid under his desk to sleep.

Doug sat in his cube.

Staring at the computer screen, he monitored his collection accounts. At the beginning of each shift, he checked how many of his assigned customers had kept their promises and viewed his performance ratio. What was this? His ratio was better. An account on the screen was blinking an alert.

Default. No payment. Account closed.

Doug double-clicked to see the reason.

Mrs. Wong was deceased.

Good.

That bitch wasn't ever going to pay.

Doug sat in his cube.

Some calls may be recorded for training or quality assurance purposes.

Hello, my name is Douglas, ID Number 958029 of the Interstate Collection Agency of West Covina, and I'm calling on behalf of the Stockton Savings Bank. This call is about your mortgage account and this is an attempt to collect a debt.

Yes, Mr. Svensen, I understand that your wife has cancer, but that doesn't change the terms of your mortgage. We need you to bring your account current. You owe six months of payments and late fees. We require a payment of $23,849.18.

Can you have a couple more days?

(No. You and your wife are leeches on the banking system, jerkwad.)

Yes, I understand you are declaring bankruptcy. I will refer your case to the proper department and someone from the bank will be in touch about your rights as an obligor.

(You have no fucking rights. The bank owns your ass, Mr. Svensen. If you think cancer is bad, just wait.)

Thank you and have a nice day.

(Think, Doug, think.)

Doug sat in his cube.

On a yellow sticky note he had written *Svensen, Peter and Donna.* Scribbled beneath the note was an annotation.

No assets. Wife's condition terminal.

They'd broken their promise to the San Antonio Savings Bank. Jesus, what would happen if every debtor were given a break? The system would collapse. Anarchy. The miseries and mistakes of other human beings weren't his problem, were they?

Besides, he'd rather focus on good news. His performance ratios were steadily improving as he worked his portfolio of customers. And today was his ninetieth day on the job. A memo had welcomed him as a permanent employee of the Interstate Collection Agency of West Covina and reassigned him to a new, and slightly larger, cubicle. Attached to the memo was a small brass pin with three letters atop two lightning bolts: ICA.

Coughing, Doug placed the pin on his shirt collar.

He was an official debt collector.

The pain in his chest was constant now.

Doug sat in his cube.

At 11:00 p.m. he logged off the system and tore up the Svensen note. A line had been drawn through their names. Tomorrow his ratio would be better.

Doug placed his box of tissues, pad of paper, sticky notes, and pencils into the shoebox provided for his cube move.

He didn't feel quite right.

Day ninety.

From his throat to his pelvis, pressure was a live electrical wire filling him with fire. Still, he wasn't worried. A sense of calm had swept through him earlier in the day.

It was time.

He coughed, blew his nose, and accidentally kicked the plastic garbage can as he tossed the tissue away.

His head sank slackly onto his chest and he separated. His shirt ripped violently apart as his flesh peeled back and expanded. Skin, muscle, broken shards of bone, tendons were pushed aside by the creature.

The Doug better suited to this job.

The other Doug.

The Doug with no mercy.

The opposite Doug.

The Doug with no heart.

Hatchling.

Doug sat in his cubicle.

His fingers fondled the brass ICA pin. He adjusted his headset. At the other end of the telephone line, the phone rang.

The cough was gone. It made his job so much easier. After the disclosure, Doug said the words he loved to say to every loser he talked to.

Hello, my name is Douglas, ID Number 958029, and I'm calling on behalf of First Regional Bank of Southern California. This call is about your mortgage account and this is an attempt to collect a debt.

(Pay your bills, asshole, or I'll write your name on a yellow sticky note.)

Doug leaned back in his chair. His new cubicle was three ceiling tiles by four.

Things were looking up.

THE APOLOGIES

ERIK T. JOHNSON

EACH WEEKDAY, Lenore placed her mail in a wicker tray on the credenza in the violet hallway, just as Mother had done. She arranged envelopes in precise stacks, equidistant and inevitable as the numbered boxes of a calendar. On Saturday evenings she separated the bills from solicitations, charity appeals, political flyers, credit card offers, menus and other propaganda. These went into the chromium waste bin under the kitchen sink.

Sundays she woke at six. Sometimes she looked twice at her thin image in the bedroom's full-sized mirror, as if to confirm it wasn't a lost traveler who should be pointed in another direction. She then slipped into a scraggly suggestion of a robe. In the bathroom Lenore scrubbed her features in triplicate. She washed the soap into cleaner nothing. Her skin was smooth for a woman her age, but wasn't it constricted, tight as zipper-mouthed rubber?

She carefully wiped up the few sudsy splashes. She walked toward the violet hallway that adjoined the foyer, crossing a carmine shag carpet from which sewing needles lost during the Cuban Missile Crisis occasionally emerged, sharp and pointless.

Lenore gathered the week's bills from the wicker tray. From the credenza she extracted checkbook, pen, calculator, notepad, and magnifying glass. At the dining room table, she spread the bills before her in a broad, even grid with the unselfconsciously superstitious gravity of commuters lip-reading psalms in subway cars. Interpreted properly, the fine print foretold ruin, homeostasis, or mere nuisance—Thanks for All Your Hell and I Told You the First Time I'm Not Interested.

She took her time. Dates of service? Pro-rated amounts? Discrepancies: None. It went like that. When she finished she'd sit there a bit and just listen. She'd soon spend the rest of the day bustling about, cleaning and tidying things—even the clean and tidy things. But now the house was quiet. Lenore liked that. Best of all, there was no silence to break.

One Sunday in September—forty-one years since mother followed father (she by hospice, he through windshield)—Lenore was vexed to find an unaddressed, unsealed envelope hidden between bills and her Social Security check. A handwritten note slid out, paper rough and thin as FEMA toilet tissue. The cheap blue capitals shouted like vulgar welfare leeches:

> SORRY, I'M SO SORRY FOR WHAT I DID TO YOU. IT WAS SO MANY YEARS AGO BUT THAT ONLY MAKES IT WORSE. MORE TIME TO THINK ABOUT IT. YOU KNOW HOW A SKULL IS A MASK ON THE WRONG SIDE OF THE FACE? AND HOW THAT SEEMS CRAZY, BECAUSE WHAT POINT CAN THERE BE IN A HIDDEN MASK? WELL, I FINALLY FIGURED OUT THE ANSWER. BUT IT'S NO CONSOLATION. EVERYTHING ISN'T. I HAVE TRIED EVERYTHING TO REDEEM MYSELF IN SOME WAY, TO ATONE FOR WHAT I DID TO YOU, BUT THERE IS NO WORD FOR

THE IDIOCY OF THOSE ATTEMPTS, IT IS LESS THAN ABSURD, WHICH AT LEAST HAS A PLACE IN THE DICTIONARY. HOW I REGRET YOUR DOWNFALL EYES. I LOOK FOWARD TO

To what?

The handwriting was masculine. The letters were boxy cages, crafted slowly and certainly—built, erected. Yet the message ended mid-sentence, an overambitious edifice abandoned in sturdy pieces; and in the towers of each first-person "I", the pen had gouged inaccessibly minute peepholes through the paper.

No 800-Number, no manager to hear the complaint. Who had written it? Why had she received it? Surely it couldn't be meant for her. Nobody had done her a serious wrong. She tossed it in the kitchen waste bin.

Did he bite the pen that inked it?

To what?

Saturday, the gray sky swelled and foamed like the Atlantic, and the world outside Lenore's windows was rained into an educated guess. Another blank envelope arrived, damp as though washed through the mail-slot. There was nothing special about it, yet as Lenore's eyes traced its rectangular perimeter—

—a table-top white with hot light. A magician's beautiful assistant lies glimmering there in sequined still-life, engulfed by a rusted murk of sunken highway signs, the woody, brassy silt of drowned clocks. The magician hovers unseen in hushed, blindspot-blackness, waiting for the right moment to amaze. He is thunder in a top-hat—

—the vision was quick and demanding as knife/flick/throat. Just as suddenly, the thing in her hand reverted to a typical, earthly envelope. The flap had been partially sealed, by rain she supposed. Lenore's index finger worked beneath an unglued spot, gently as though seeking evasive capers at molar recesses, then swiftly retracted—mail must be opened on Sunday, even refugee messages, daring enough to have fled the safety of their bottles. She shouldn't break protocol. Little things led to bigger, then too big; it was a short step from nailbiting to cannibalism. Change could be exponential but not inexorable, if you stayed… as you were. A distant church bell rang once, staccato, the resonance cut oddly short as though frozen by sudden embarrassment.

Between Saturday afternoon and Sunday morning, Lenore was unpleasantly impatient and vaguely expectant—somehow disembodiedly constipated. For distraction, she examined the floor in the violet hallway. Decades of coming-back and going-away had undone the boards. Nails bared their twisted, rusty heads. Naked eyesores of eroded polyurethane basked under the hallway light. The parquet inlays were loose; at a toe-tap, the floor emitted the disingenuous creak of thief-in-the-night opened doors. She pressed down on the parquet repeatedly to see if she could get used to it. No, it was worse than the inevitably bony flapping of interrupted pigeons. Reluctantly, she removed her orthopedic shoes, muffling the noise to tolerability.

On Sunday, she placed the note on the dining room table, adjacent to the bills but far enough away for a unique, quarantined status that rattled her concentration. She tried to conduct her usual routines, but the unopened envelope was a task that must be dealt with to be dismissed, a finger depressed on your doorbell with unyielding solicitous pressure—

You will go mad. You must open the door. Couldn't she break custom, just once? She tore it open and out tumbled familiar, willful shapes:

> I'M SENDING YOU ANOTHER. ONE ISN'T ENOUGH. THIS WAY I AM GIVING YOU MORE. MORE WHAT? MORE NOT ENOUGH, I GUESS. I HAVE SOLVED ANOTHER PUZZLE. I'LL SHARE: I WILL DO MORE FOR THE WORLD DEAD THAN ALIVE. I HAVE NEVER BEEN GENEROUS OR KIND. BUT DEATH IS CHARITY. I'LL GIVE A LITTLE EXTRA SPACE TO THE WORLD, AND LEAVE A FEW LESS LIES AND EXCUSES. AND I AM SO IDLE LATELY, BUT DEATH IS SO BUSY. I'VE NEVER SEEN AN UNEMPLOYED MAGGOT. I KNOW YOU CANNOT RIGHT A WRONG, BUT YOU CAN MAKE IT BIGGER, UNTIL THE WRONG IS SO TITANIC THAT NOBODY SEES IT AS ANYTHING ANYMORE, A SKY-LIKE WRONG. AFTER IT'S THROUGH I LOOK FORWARD TO DYING BECAUSE

Because what? Was this a joke? Lenore held the letter up to a light bulb without revelation. Under her magnifying glass, the letters were more gouged than written. She examined the blue trenches, so bold and frail. Faint STOP-sign red streaks had run dead-ended lanes down the uplifted arms of SORRY's emphatic Y. They were scentless, untraceable.

Things like this didn't happen to her.

Therefore, they must happen to someone else. And hadn't she once been such a Someone-Else, as a child—before Father died? She didn't recall much about that life. She didn't like looking back at it; she wished she couldn't... They didn't bury him like Father.

They put him in the ground like nuclear waste. And then it was past/never vision, breaths she chose not to take, blood flew in diagonals, blotted out Lite Brite clowns when she pricked herself on sewing needles, and something worse, more terrible than the unexplained because it couldn't be described enough to lack explanation...

And then? She learned to mimic Mother's routines—face-washing, coupon-clipping, mail management, checkbook balancing, lists of lists without completion. And then? Well, everything was okay. Lenore had a gift for forging, then living Mother's life, day into day, silence after silence, as Father had excelled at wearing his 1951 nobody suit, the one he must be wearing still.

If she was someone else again, *then*... what?

This?

Because what?

That night, on schedule, Lenore went to bed at ten o'clock. No, she didn't like thinking back. It seemed unnatural; it was like grief or white teeth. She lay there for hours, eyes bared like exposed organs waiting for scalpels, thinking no, nobody owes me an apology.

She supposed maggots *were* industrious. She turned her head toward a far side of the room. Apparently—she had no memory of it—she'd placed the today's note atop her dresser. Why hadn't she thrown it away? The edges had curled inward; it had evolved into a new object that wouldn't fit inside an envelope. It would need a box—if you were to keep it.

Because what?

The next morning, Lenore sat in bed and stared at the note. The corners had unfurled slightly during the night. In the bathroom mirror, her skin seemed to cling to the hidden mask of her skull, a faceless abyss beneath her chin.

That week dragged damp gray minutes. By Friday, the house and all its hidden places were more than spotless, even inside radiator valves, vanity knob screwholes, and Metamucil bottles. But it was as though the mess had been inside her rather than the rooms, and when she thought she was cleaning it up, she was hollowing herself out. It was hard to explain.

Shopping made sense, so she went on several such expeditions. She'd intended to visit a flooring specialist to get a quote on fixing the hallway, but kept forgetting to go through with it; instead, she bought more groceries than she needed. The people in the cereal and meat aisles looked fatally misguided as children smoking cigarettes; and she found herself looking for a top-hat among the irritably bored heads in the check-out line; and when she left the supermarket, the center of each barred apartment-building window quivered with clones—pale, sexless faces following her with disinterested, elderly voyeurism. Strangest of all was that Lenore had observed any of this. She didn't pay attention to people she didn't know, and she didn't know anyone anymore.

Had it really been rain? Or had he sealed the envelope with a tentative tongue?

She went through her routines in the usual manner on Saturday. She felt calm, transparent, practically absent, more like sight than eye—definitely there yet you can't touch it.

But as bedtime approached, Lenore glimpsed herself in the bedroom mirror and froze. She was startled to see a pale, lost traveler, and Lenore didn't have directions to offer. Transfixed, she had a thought she didn't understand: It was true that she knew no one, but that also meant everyone must know her. The mirror that held her provisional image was like a window facing a cement wall, compelling you to attempt spying through it, because somewhere, years back, you learned that's what windows are for, so…

She would not look back.

She refused.

Lenore needed a reason to step away from the mirror. Somehow, if she stayed there too long it would be too late. She began looking around her figure at the tidy objects reflected behind it. She noticed the note, past her shoulder. It was still on the dresser. Suddenly, she had not exactly an idea, and she reanimated. She retrieved a sheet of expensive, cream-colored paper and a fine, blue marker from the writing desk. In her painstakingly-looped cursive, she filled one page:

I forgive you. Let's talk about it.

Lenore sat at the dining room table and read it a few times. She believed in the words. She didn't know why. They must be addressed to someone. They struck her as true. It was the first time she'd felt sure of herself since the Sunday morning of the first apology. She neatly, firmly taped the sign on the front door. It was almost outrageously public beneath the porch light. She left the doors wide open. She put the shades up and lifted the windows high. At ten o'clock she turned off the lamps and got under the covers, and quick as knife/flick/throat, the answer came to her, and it tickled all over: BECAUSE YOU CAN'T LOOK BACK AT IT.

The clock struck eleven, then midnight. A shaft of moonlight bisected the blanket where it covered her waist, precisely where a magician's blade would saw his lovely assistant in two. She was trembling and happily confused when she heard him in the violet hallway, slipping off his boots so the floorboards wouldn't make too much noise.

THE SHOE TREE

PAT R. STEINER

"I DON'T WANT you to go."

Darren Tripp glanced up at his wife from the living room couch where he tied the laces on his sneakers. "Jesus, Connie. The dog's been crazy as you-know-it for weeks straight."

Connie crossed her arms over her chest. She'd never lost the extra pounds she put on during the failed pregnancy. If anything, she'd added weight. Her face looked rounder, fleshy and gray. A moon face.

"Are you blaming me? I can't walk Elton. He doesn't listen to me."

Darren grunted, moving on to the other shoe. Blood pounded in his ears and his temples throbbed. "Not saying nothing. Dog's gone nuts is all. I couldn't walk him before, but now I can."

"What? Now you're blaming my dad? You know, I never asked for a dog. The darn thing poops everywhere."

Shoes tied, Darren sat upright. The pressure in his ears eased, but his temples still throbbed. He realized he gritted his teeth and stopped.

For the past four months, he'd been working the third shift down at the plant. Back in May, a special order had come in from overseas. China needed mining equipment. Connie's father—thinking ever of his daughter's well-being—had chosen Darren to supervise the night crews. It was a show of how much he trusted and depended on his son-in-law. Pure bullshit in Darren's opinion. The man was out to kill him, plain and simple.

It was because of the baby. Darren was sure of it. Somehow, someway, for whatever reason, Connie's father blamed Darren for the miscarriage. Oh no, it couldn't just be bad luck that the baby died. By God, someone had to be responsible. And that person had been Darren.

Every workday since then, Darren had left home at nine-thirty, trudged down to the plant, clocked in, worked until six in the morning, came back home dead on his feet, and crashed.

What was the expression? *Dog tired.* That was a good one. Hilarious. Four months straight and the damned dog hadn't known tired, barking all day long as Darren tried to sleep. Most afternoons, when Connie woke him for supper, he felt as tired as when he'd crawled into bed. Was it any wonder his body didn't react when Connie made sexual overtures? Not that she did this very often anymore; her sex drive had gone off course even before the shift change.

But that was all over and done with. Thank you, sweet-baby Jesus. They'd completed the order Friday night. China would have its strip-mining shovels, Connie's father would be all the richer, and Darren would be getting his life back come Monday morning.

"Are you listening to me?"

He stood up. "Uh-huh."

There was still the dog though.

Darren regretted buying the damned thing for Connie. How had he ever thought a puppy could replace a baby? He'd been a fool thinking that. Now he lived daily with the consequences.

From the living room corner, the television blared the latest news. He glanced at the attractive looking anchor. Another girl had gone missing. The coverage had been nonstop for weeks.

More noise.

Darren closed his eyes, willing his growing headache at bay.

"I'll get on it first thing tomorrow."

"What?"

"The backyard. I'll clean it up first thing in the morning."

"I don't care about that!"

Pressure built behind his ears. He opened his eyes and turned toward her.

"What then?"

She pouted. "I don't want you to go."

He rubbed his temples. "If you haven't noticed, I'm not a six year old girl."

"Well then, I don't want you to leave *me* all alone."

He forced a smile. "Honey, you're not exactly this guy's type either." The word 'honey' tasted bitter on his tongue. "And besides, those girls were snatched during the day."

"You don't know they were abducted."

"What else could it be? There's a lot of sick bastards out there."

"Not here."

Not here, she meant, in their picture-perfect town.

And it was, for the most part, a perfect little town. A goddamn suburban idyll. Sure, he had a crappy job, but so what? Beggars couldn't be choosers. If it hadn't been for Connie's dad, where would they be? The old man had gotten Darren his job, had doled out the down payment on their house. Hell, he had even paid the hospital bills.

Turning to her once again, he said, "Yes, even here, honey."

There was no sarcasm attached to those words, only a sense of inevitable defeat.

Outside, Elton barked.

***

Two dark-hooded figures straddled bicycles under the shoe tree.

The bad news on the television, and Connie's concern about him leaving her alone, had worked its way under his skin. His defenses went up.

The path was dark along this stretch of the park.

"Stay close, pal."

Shoe tree.

He chuckled at his lack of originality, but the name fit.

Back in May, if Elton had chosen a different tree for shit detail, Darren might not have even noticed the shoes. Most likely, he wouldn't have; he'd been distracted even before the pup came into their life. Waiting for Elton to finish up, he happened to glance up to a pair hanging from one of the branches. Faded and worn-out Chuck Taylor Converse All-Stars, laces tied together, one shoe's sole split apart from its body.

Closing in on the tree, Darren contemplated turning around or veering off through the grass, giving the tree a wide berth, but in the end, he kept to the path. What did he have to fear?

From the bikes, these were obviously kids. Probably teenagers.

Summer was winding down. Schools would be opening their doors in a matter of days. These must be summer's children wringing out every last second of vacation time. Darren remembered the associated feelings well, the empty gnawing ache, wondering where all those precious days had gone.

Get used to it, he thought. It ain't gonna get any better from here on out.

Elton tugged on the leash and barked.

"Easy, boy."

Darren double-checked the retractable leash lock. For the last few months, the terrier's only interactions with other humans had been limited to barking at the mail carrier, the garbage men, and a pair of Latter Day Saints who had woken Darren one afternoon in

June while Connie had been out grocery shopping.

He and Connie didn't need a dog-bite lawsuit to add to their troubles.

Reaching the shoe tree, Darren glanced up into its long branching arms, but the canopy was filled with shadows and he didn't see the Chucky Ts.

"What'cha looking at?"

Darren stumbled to a stop.

One of the biked figures had moved to block the walkway, leaving his partner near the tree trunk. The one in front of him had spoken the question.

Elton strained at the end of the leash, his lips pulled back in a teeth-revealing snarl. It was the Saints situation all over again. Darren felt embarrassed by the dog's behavior. He pulled on the leash.

"Knock it off, pal."

The figure by the tree said, "Nice dog, mister. Think I could take him for a ride?"

By their voices, Darren knew he'd been right. Teenagers. His shoulders and neck muscles relaxed a little. He turned to the teen blocking his path. This one hadn't laughed at the attempted joke. If it *was* a joke. Within the hood's shadows were the contours of an aquiline nose, a wide forehead, and a set of full lips: a girl.

Darren relaxed even more.

Elton must have sensed his growing ease and stopped his verbal assault. He flopped down onto the concrete path, panting from his exertions.

"You didn't answer my question."

"Question?" Darren suddenly felt sheepish again. Who was this girl to make him feel like a fool? Yet, he answered her. "Oh, that. I was looking for the shoes."

He almost added that he used to wear the same sneakers when he was her age, but stopped short. Something didn't seem right about her. If she was a girl. The hooded jacket was too large for her, concealing any view of blossoming womanhood.

The teen boy by the tree said, "Coming back to the scene of the crime? Figures. Couldn't help yourself. Seen it on the tube. Creeps like him need their trophies close. Gets'em off."

Trophies?

"Hey, I don't know nothing about those missing little girls. I'm just walking my dog."

"Any particular pair catch your eye?"

The boy's comments had put his guard back up. "What?"

"Which ones do you like the best, maybe Mandi's?"

Darren tried to recall the names of the missing girls from the news. He thought one had been named Miranda. Mandi might be a nickname.

"Really, I have no idea what you're talking about. I've been working the night shift at the plant all summer long. Maybe one of your fathers works there?" He looked at the boy then back at the girl. "What's your name, honey?"

The boy shouted, "Look out, Deb. He's trying to sweet-talk you. That's probably how he got Mandi to go with him."

The girl jerked her hands off her handlebars and stuffed them into the large belly pocket of her jacket.

Darren put his hands up and backed away. He still held the dog leash, but the lock had come loose. The leash unwound, leaving Elton prone on the concrete path near the girl.

"I'm not him. Honestly. I wouldn't do anything like that. I just told my wife, Connie… that's my wife's name. I said the guy doing this has to be a real whack-job." Sweat tricked down the back of Darren's shirt, making the fabric stick to his skin.

The boy said, "Bet he made Mandi whack *him* off before he killed her."

"Shut up, you little shit. You don't know Jack."

"And you?" said the girl. "What do you know?"

Whatever she had in the pocket—*a gun?*—stayed there.

"Nothing. I swear on it, kid. This is all a big mistake. Call the cops if you like."

"Who says we didn't already?"

Darren didn't believe her. Something in her posture told him she wanted to deal with him personally. Was Mandi perhaps this girl's younger sister? Six-year-old Miranda Something-or-another, snatched out of her backyard in broad daylight. Little Mandi, most likely dead, her body dumped somewhere.

It finally dawned on Darren that all the missing girls must have lived near the park. Lots of places to hide in the park: the creek, the surrounding woods. Lots of places to lay and wait.

Or stash a body.

It was late August. Hot and humid weather. The body would start smelling. They'd find Lil' Mandi soon. The others, too.

He glanced around at the nearest homes. Lights blazed out from every house.

He should have listened to Connie. If he had, he'd be home right now, sitting on the sofa beside his loving wife, watching the news instead of being the breaking story for the upcoming ten-o'clock report.

The Oak Creek Killer caught by older sibling of victim.

Had the media even named the killer? Watching the news had been one of the early casualties of his night shift switch.

The Oak Creek Snatcher.

Hadn't he heard Connie say this? Or had the background noise from the television worked its way into his subconscious, details bubbling up to the surface, now that he faced a threat? And this girl and her boy friend *were* a threat.

This never would have happened a year ago. Caught unaware like this. Since the shift change—hell, since the miscarriage—he'd been sleepwalking through life, shutting the world off in his drone-like existence. He hadn't cared about the world, and the world—one that included this blonde-haired, hoody-wearing teen with her lost younger sister—hadn't given a rat's ass one way or another about Darren Tripp.

Until now.

"Listen, this is a mistake."

He'd reached the leash's limit, ten feet, still within the enclosing dome of the shoe tree's canopy, well within range of a pistol.

If the girl had a gun.

Elton seemed content to stay put, glancing back at Darren when the line tugged on his collar, then back at the girl.

"It was a mistake when you showed up here."

Darren's eyes flickered between the two of them. Focus on the girl. If he could convince the girl, things might turn out okay.

"If you have a cellphone, *please* call the cops." He held his hands out in a placating gesture. "Have them take me in, question me. You don't want to do something foolish and ruin the rest of your life."

"She's gone..."

He lowered his hands. "Your sister? Mandi, right?"

She nodded.

"How old is she?"

"Five. She's starting kindergarten this year. Or would be…"

The girl's shoulders sagged and shook.

Darren took a couple slow steps toward her.

Elton's head perked and his tail wagged.

"Watch it, Deb."

"Stuff it, Zander. You don't got a say in this."

The boy mumbled.

Darren ignored him, studying the pocket bulge where the girl's hands lay concealed. She straddled her bike and would probably knock herself over if she fired. There'd be no way he could outrun either of them anyway. Working the night shift, he'd grown soft and pudgy, and slow. Darren felt ashamed for thinking Connie had let herself go when he was just as bad. At least she'd had an excuse. The miscarriage had hit her much worse.

But Darren didn't believe this girl had a gun. She would have taken it out already to let him know she meant business. He would stake his life on it.

He stepped closer. "Deb, what do you want me to see?" Back at his original position, he reached down and petted Elton on the head. He asked her again, "You wanted me to see something. Something of Mandi's?"

She nodded.

"What is it?"

He had already guessed what she wanted to show him, what had been so important to her that she would confront her sister's possible killer.

Darren held his breath as she removed her hands from the pocket.

A flashlight.

Not a gun.

She hopped off the bike and let it crash against the concrete walk. Elton jumped up, excited. When she turned on the flashlight, Elton moved to investigate, sniffing the plate-sized circle of light.

The extra light revealed more of the girl's face. Tears sparkled on her cheekbones.

"Go ahead," Darren said, "show me."

She brought the flashlight around, shifting its beam up into the tree. Branch-shaped shadows appeared beyond the light, swaying and gyrating before they came to a stop as she directed the beam onto her target.

The high-tops were gone.

In their place were four pairs of shoes.

Four sets of shoes for four missing girls.

Clustered close together, two of the pairs even shared the same branch, but the girl had centered the beam onto one set in particular. Her sister's.

"We did this the day after Mandi disappeared."

"But, Deb," the boy said, his neck arching upward, "you told me the killer put those shoes there?"

"I never said anything like that. That's a rumor."

"Then what're they doing up there? Those are Mandi's, aren't they?"

She nodded.

Darren felt a twinge of sympathy for the boy.

Shadows of shoes danced behind the real ones.

"These are old shoes," Darren said, "ones that didn't fit her anymore, ones Mandi outgrew, right?" He couldn't look away.

They were hypnotic. So surreal. Haunting.

"Mom heard about it from the other parents."

The parents of the other missing girls.

"If you look closely you can see."

Darren studied the shoes, mostly saw the treaded soles, yet he could make out words written on the sides of each.

"Mom had us write stuff for Mandi. What we wanted to say to her. What we wished…"

Her younger sister had once worn those hanging shoes. Darren moved in to embrace her, but when she noticed his approach, she cringed and jerked away.

"Don't touch me."

He couldn't stop himself from looking up into the tree. The shoes, so small and so out of place. He pictured them then; not the shoes, but the missing girls' family members, gathered under the shoe tree days ago, a cloudless blue sky dazzled overhead. The proceedings take place a short distance away, family members taking turns writing down their thoughts and prayers onto the little shoes. First the mothers, then the fathers. They tie them by the laces and, at some unspoken command, simultaneously throw the tiny shoes into the arms of the waiting tree.

The last father leaving the tree had Darren's face.

"It's not fair."

He shook his head. He knew that lack of sleep and stress could bring on hallucinations, but the *dream? vision?* had seemed so real. He shook it off and focused on the young woman.

"I know it's not."

"This wasn't supposed to happen. It doesn't make sense. She was just a kid."

He wanted to console her more, but he couldn't bring himself to do it. Anything he'd say would be a lie. Bad things happened to good people. Even kids. Even babies still in their mother's womb.

He recalled the checkup when he and Connie had found out they were having a girl. Connie had been ecstatic. She had always wanted a daughter.

Hot tears burned Darren's eyes. He went to wipe them away and the vision returned.

This time he was in his own skin.

The shoes, in his hands, were small and light. They hardly weighed anything. Using a permanent marker, he wrote a word upon each: *love* and *hope*. He kissed each shoe, whispering the two words before he told the tree, "Remember her."

He lofted the shoes into the tree, praying it would accept them.

It did.

Light as they were, the shoes hadn't traveled far, only making it to the lowest branch. But that was good enough. The tree held them snug and secure. A storm might blow them down someday, but that would be—

The girl's words interrupted, bringing him back.

"Sounds real stupid, huh?"

Darren swallowed past a dry throat. "Sounds like you loved your sister and miss her."

"I do miss her. It's just that before... he took her, I thought she was a brat. A real pain, you know?"

He nodded.

"She'd always follow me around. Pester me if I had friends over and stuff. Ruin everything. But now that she's gone, it's like there's a big chunk of me missing, a big piece of me that was Mandi. She's gone. Forever. Mandi's never coming back, and I don't know what to do."

When Darren approached her this time, she relented, allowing him to drape his arms over her shoulders. She was crying in earnest, wracking sobs.

"I lost my baby sister," she said.

Darren comforted the girl as best as he could beneath the shoe tree, while he grieved for his own little lost one.

Darren woke the next morning feeling refreshed, reborn even. Tomorrow would be his first day back on the day shift. *Thank you sweet baby Jesus for minor miracles.* Today he would take care of chores around the house and surprise Connie, who had left half an hour ago to pick up fixings for a picnic.

As he tied his sneakers, he thought about the night before and laughed. It felt good to laugh. He hadn't laughed in a long while. It made him feel lighter. He squeezed the roll of fat hanging over his belt and laughed again.

"Good one, Darren old boy."

He would start exercising again. Get back into college shape. He stood up and did a couple of jumping jacks.

Elton twisted his head sideways.

"You too, Elton. You're looking thick around the haunches, pal. Looking like that, no bitch gonna give you the time of day."

A multitude of plans entered his mind. One of them involved joining a neighborhood watch program so he could help the police find the pervert snatching those little girls.

After returning home from the shoe tree, he had unburdened all of his pent up emotions to Connie. She, responding in kind, told him about the pain and misery she'd been going through, too. Their shared tears had moved to hugs, the hugs moving on to other, better things.

He loved Connie.

"Things are looking up, Elton, my man."

Darren laughed at his own witticism before heading out, the terrier at his heels.

Remembering his promise to clean the backyard, he turned for the tool shed. As he walked through the yard, he noticed that Elton, besides shitting every-which-where, had dug holes in the lawn. The grass—what was left of it—was also long overdue for a cut.

"Bad dog," he said, not meaning the words.

Elton's misbehavior was his own fault. Working nights wasn't an excuse. He could have walked the dog in the afternoons.

"You been the bad dog, Darren. In more ways than one."

Besides being a royal pain-in-the-ass these past months, Darren had pawned all of the household chores onto Connie. No wonder the yard looked like hell. He berated himself for his sexist thoughts, although in this instance he knew he was right. Connie was terrible with tools, butchering even the simplest of home projects.

Reaching the shed, Darren removed the padlock key from its hiding place.

Good. Connie hadn't moved it.

The only valuable object inside was the lawn mower—yet another gift provided by Connie's father—but Darren had always thought the lock was overkill. Who would want to steal a second-hand lawnmower?

Elton had dug in the soil near the bottom of the doorframe.

"You been trying to get in so you can cut the lawn for me? What a good dog."

As if understanding, the terrier dug furiously at the ground near the door, barking with high-pitched, headache-inducing yips.

"Hold on there, boy. Give me a sec."

The new Darren wasn't bothered by the grating noise, at least not yet. He fumbled with the lock, the dog under his feet making the simple task more difficult. A hot sun burned overhead. The weatherman said it might hit ninety. Darren wanted the yard cleaned and the grass cut well before then. Connie would be back from the store soon. Maybe when he finished out here, they could have a second round in the sack. Make a go at a baby.

Afterwards, he'd show Connie the shoe tree. He could think of nothing more picture perfect. Nothing could go wrong today. Darren wouldn't allow it.

The lock clicked open in his hands. Free of the lock, the door opened a crack. The reek of spoiled meat wafted out from the narrow opening, making him gag.

Elton snarled at the door, pawing at it, trying to get inside.

Darren swallowed the bile burning his throat.

Something had died inside the shed, a raccoon or possum.

"Easy, boy. I know it smells bad. Back off and let me think."

For once, Elton listened, and lay down at Darren's feet, yawning. His mouth stretched so wide that Darren could have counted the dog's teeth.

The fenced backyard was deadly quiet, the neighboring families still in bed this Sunday morning or off to church services. A soft drone came from within the tool shed.

Flies.

A lot of them.

Flies meant maggots.

Darren hated bugs in general, but maggots creeped him out.

"Damn."

No way was he going to touch a maggoty dead animal. He could do it with his work gloves, but they were inside the shed.

"Better get this over with before Connie gets back."

Connie hated bugs worse than Darren. Whenever there was an insect in the house, it was his job to get rid of it. This wasn't a tiny six-legged creature, however, easily disposed of down a flushed toilet. He glanced around the yard, at Elton's workmanship. He could bury the corpse in one of the holes, but the dog would dig up the remains the first chance he got. If Darren didn't know better, he would have thought his whole backyard was already an animal cemetery. A dog's dream. A bone buffet.

He couldn't bury the poor creature.

What he needed—besides work gloves—were trash bags. A couple to three. It would take multiple layers of plastic to keep the stench at bay. Maybe four. Let the bugger maggots suffocate. He'd go back inside the kitchen and grab the whole box from the cabinet where Connie stored such things. And he could let the shed air out.

"So much for the perfect day."

Life wasn't perfect. He knew that. It was pure delusion to think otherwise. He recalled when he was younger, watching old movies with his father, how he'd cover his face with his hands if something too scary came on to the small flickering screen. Pops had always laughed, telling Darren he needed to face his fears head-on.

You keep your fingers up there and you gonna miss the good stuff.

"Pops was right," he told Elton.

The dog didn't respond.

"No comment, huh?"

The shoe tree had pried the hands away from Darren's eyes.

Seeing those four pairs of shoes hanging from its branches… he couldn't pretend he hadn't seen them. He couldn't ignore them. They existed. They demanded that he deal with them, accept them, and understand them, even if understanding brought pain.

He thought of Debbie and her family. What was a dead animal stinking up a tool shed compared to the anguish they must be going through? This was an inconvenience, a distasteful, yet minor setback to his morning. There were a lot of days left to change things around again, a lot of life to live, imperfect as it may be.

He sighed, making sure that when he inhaled he did so through his mouth. Bringing his arm up to cover his nose, he nudged the now whining dog out of the way with his foot, and then yanked the door wide open.

At first he thought he imagined them—another flashback to the night before at the shoe tree—but then Darren Tripp saw the legs attached to the sneakers and fell to his knees.

"Connie. What'd you do?"

Beside him, Elton began to wail.

GAIA UNGAIA

JOHN PALISANO

The things that haunt us
Reappear
Reflecting inside our eyes

WE TRAIPSED from the ocean and Brooke grasped my hand. My palms felt sticky inside hers as the salt water dried.

"This is the house where I grew up," she said. Her white tee-shirt clung to her, but she didn't seem self-conscious. She smiled. "I'm glad you're able to see this house. It's a big part of who I am."

I couldn't help but imagine what growing up must have been like inside and around such a place. Long trees overhung the white house and its two-story frame. Curved red wooden benches lined the side yards. She pulled me close and laughed.

Before we stepped inside, Brooke pointed to the sky.

"See those clouds?"

Bands of pink and red and blue stretched above us, as though someone painted them, capturing the most extraordinary light.

"I've never seen a storm so gorgeous," I said. "The clouds are moving in fast."

She nodded.

"I've been waiting a long time. You must be good luck."

We showered together and I barely glanced below her face. I shut my eyes two or three times and imagined what it'd be like if we were lovers. There'd be a time for us later, somewhere.

"Good to get all the ocean water off," I said. "I was feeling sticky."

Brooke soaped her face. "I don't mind the stickiness. I just don't want anyone to know where we've been."

"Really?"

"Sure," she said, washing her face. "Do you remember what month this is?"

"January."

"You've been living on the west coast too long. This is the east coast, where you're not supposed to be outside without wearing several layers. But there we were, in our bathing suits, swimming in the Atlantic just like it was August."

My temples throbbed with the first drizzles of rain.

"What's happening?" I asked.

We stood in her bedroom and dried. She'd put clean clothes out for both of us, laying them neatly across her bed.

"What are we going to see?" I asked.

"Something beyond ourselves. All the way through the world."

"The world?"

"Everything there is to see, we're going to see it."

We walked downstairs and there were small framed pictures at every step, but none had captured people. They looked like prints of paintings.

"Once I hit my late-twenties, everything changed," Brooke said. "Growing old is weird. At times, I feel like I'm still a teenager. It's like time stands still. Then I see myself in the mirror and have no idea who that person is. Everyone that was close to me years ago is now gone."

"Even your family?"

"They left all of this to me."

I wondered if they'd died. I tried to think of a way to find out more without sounding insensitive.

"Where are they?"

"They left."

At the bottom of the staircase, she turned and faced me and I smelled the peppermint from her shampoo.

"It's been up to me to take care of this house."

Behind her pretty round face, she hid something terrible. Maybe her folks had been killed, or there'd been some awful, unmentionable tragedy. Perhaps she kept the house exactly as they'd left it so she wouldn't forget them.

The living room centered around a large, fossilized tree stump. It'd been carved in such a way as to make it a chair. There were potted plants and flowers in vases everywhere. The far wall was painted edge-to-edge with a mural of people lingering in some woods. I pointed to it.

"What's that?"

"My mother was a painter."

"Was?"

"She stopped painting after we were born."

"That's too bad. It's great."

"You think so?"

"Absolutely."

There was a short table running alongside the wall closest to us. I recognized the white porcelain bowl where she'd put the seashells.

"We've been friends a really long time."

"We have," I said, nodding.

"I believed my memories and my gifts were locked away inside the rooms of this house. We tried to keep them safe, but the house becomes so empty at times. We all need other people, or else we disappear."

My heart beat steadily, as though sealed inside a small concrete tomb.

"I've only ever seen my parents when they're unearthed," she said. "Right now is going to be one of those times."

There was definitely a storm approaching. Ever since I was young, my sinuses ached whenever the barometer dropped. I suffered through allergy tests until the doctors figured out that the migraines were the result of atmospheric pressure changes. I tried to hold back a sneeze as my nose ran and my eyes watered. What I would have done for a serious painkiller... Instead, I worked my way through it—better than bowing out with a sack of ice over my eyes. I didn't want to miss whatever Brooke was about to unveil. I tried focusing on her, instead.

"Can you see it? The light's gotten dimmer. Things are going to change."

She had her thumbs on her sides, her head slightly cocked, and one hip jutted out a little, as if she were about to hitch a ride.

"The storm is coming," I said.

Our eyes met and she told me it was going to snow.

"Snow?"

"It's the middle of January, after all."

"It's too warm outside for it to snow."

A windy chill came through the door. Frosty air overtook the warm summer scents of sand and salt. The hairs in my nostrils froze stiff. Brooke seemed captivated with something outside the window as everything brightened.

I thought the sun had come out, but was wrong. Snow covered the sand. Several chunks of ice floated within the Atlantic.

"We're going to freeze," I said.

Brooke laughed.

"Don't worry. I'll make sure you're nice and warm. The house is prepared. Besides, we won't be here long."

The room turned colder; it was as though the whole place had been turned into the strongest of refrigerators. I crossed my arms.

"My mother made this," Brooke said, staring at the tree stump chair. Five roots stretched out and toward the floor, acting as legs. "Rings in the wood show you how old it was when it was made. A lot has changed since then. Sit. It's more comfortable than it looks."

"This isn't some kind of trap, though, right?"

"Gary, it's a chair. Don't worry about it. Trust me."

"I'm so cold. I don't know if I can even move."

"That will change before you know it."

"What's happening to the house, and outside?"

"We're making meaning, forcing the world around us to do what we want."

"You wanted it cold?"

"Yes."

"Why?"

"My father."

"I don't get it."

"He loves winter. It was his favorite time of year. He'll know that it's me."

"How do I play into this?"

"Energy, vibes: your desires. It will all become clear soon. Are you going to sit, or am I going to have to force you?"

I went to the chair and palmed the back. It'd been ingeniously carved, smoothed and rounded, and it was stained a dark rose color. The rings on the seat looked fresh, as if the tree were cut down only hours earlier, preserved perfectly. The illusion was remarkable.

"This thing's awfully amazing," I said. "So much detail."

"My mom did a good job. It's one of my favorite things in the world."

"Takes up a lot of room, though, doesn't it?"

"Sure does. That's a good thing, right?"

"You're probably on to something," I said. "I've been trying to make everything less cluttered in my apartment. It's so empty inside. There's hardly anything. Most of my books and pictures are digital. I have a small flat screen television and everything's wireless. My fridge is small. Even my bed."

"Why?"

"It gives me peace. I can focus on things. I grew up with a bunch of packrats. When I see piles, I start getting nervous."

"Some people find comfort being inside piles of things."

"It suffocates me."

"So, what do you think of my place, then?"

"There's a lot going on here," I said, looking around.

There seemed to be a tremendous amount of thought that'd gone into the placement of knickknacks and pictures and flowers.

"Feels like I'm in a really wonderful antique shop. Weird. I don't really feel all that cluttered in here, though. It all seems to work."

"Wonder why," Brooke said. "Many people feel smothered."

"This is different. Everything in here's spotless."

"You're right, you know. These are my family's things. I wanted them to be in perfect shape when they come."

I sat on the chair, which was much more comfortable than I'd imagined. The seat was flat, and yet, the perfect height and the perfect fit.

"Your family: they're coming tonight?"

Brooke smiled.

"You're dressed all in white, like a little girl going to a dinner."

"You, too," she said. "Only you're clothes are dark, like Daddy's."

A chill.

Was I wearing her father's clothes? Was he dead and had she dressed me up to look like him? Was this some sort of sick game? That would explain her lack of sexuality toward me. Was she turning me into her father?

The chair moved. I inched myself to the front of it.

"What the…?"

It moved again, and again, as though the legs were stretching and wanting to shove me from its seat. When I stood, it stopped.

Brooke lowered her chin. Her eyes seemed to say: *watch this.*

The cold air compressed inside of my chest and hurt my throat. My kneecaps shivered. I couldn't stop it from happening. Brooke was motionless, save for her eyes, which moved back and forth between the chair and me. The vanilla candle scent in the room was soon replaced with a lemony, fizzy-water aroma, not unlike a large vat of cold medicine.

"Are you okay?" she said.

"I think so. Ask me in a few minutes."

The sky opened, but not with brightness, or with sunlight, or with a flash; instead, everything darkened. Everything had become more visible, more hyper-real, as if the true characteristics of the world around us had been revealed. The reality I'd known—the way colors worked, the way my skin appeared—was only one small aspect of a bigger picture.

Brooke had peeled back some kind of ancient door.

"Are you still with me?"

Our eyes met in the new otherworld.

Brooke glowed. Barely visible beneath her skin, I could see her architecture: veins like little organic roadways, muscles like clouds, lungs like bodies of water, her brain like a cityscape at night exploding with millions of white bursts.

"You're here," she said.

"I am."

Through the window, the ocean waves unnaturally slowed.

Three shadowy figures approached from my peripheral and I startled. The room filled with a smell that reminded me very much of burnt popcorn.

One of the shadows reached out as they formed.

"Pop?" Brooke asked.

Her family: called from the beyond by their gifted daughter.

Shadows filled in as they gained color and substance. Before I knew it, the dark spots shrank completely away. There were areas that ultimately remained darkened, which wavered as her family stepped closer.

"It's us," Brooke's mother said. "Georgie's here this time."

Brooke smiled to the slightly smaller figure behind them. Georgie hadn't formed as fully as his parents. His shape was quite different from theirs. Smaller and more squat, Georgie stepped toward his sister.

"Hello?" said a voice unlike any I'd ever heard.

"Hello." She went to him, putting a hand out.

His was not a hand that reached for her, but some sort of flattened appendage where a hand should be.

"B-Broooke," he said, as if he had three sets of vocal chords saying the same word, each with a different timbre and intonation.

"You are my brother," she said. "But you don't look like him anymore. What happened?"

Her father nodded and said, "Georgie's not doing so well lately. He hasn't believed in himself. We need you more than ever to come take care of him."

"This isn't the way things are supposed to happen," Brooke said. "We're going to have a nice visit and then go off somewhere new."

Her father looked to me, his eyes cutting right through mine.

"You've changed things by bringing something new to the equation."

"Gary's no bother," Brooke said. "He's one of the true ones."

When her father laughed, his head threw back a bit, and I could see through the dark spots inside his throat and through to the back of his neck, where his spine reached up and touched his skull; it shimmered and glistened with electric activity.

"Of course, he's no bother," her father said, "not to you."

"B-Brooke."

"This is not working for me," she said, throwing her arm down in defiance. "I can't even look at Georgie. You've let him turn on himself. He's gone disgusting. Aren't you supposed to take care of him? How could you let him become this revolting?"

Her mother came forward. "Georgie looks fine. He's just sick."

Brooke bristled and said, "He's not fine at all. You've let him forget who he is and what he's capable of. You've let him turn into a creature from the deep, instead of a chosen soul. You should be ashamed of yourselves."

"He won't listen to us anymore," her father said. "We've tried everything, but he keeps calling for you over and over again. What are we supposed to do with him if he won't take our word for it?"

Brook turned her back to them. "I don't know. I don't want any part of this. I have to live my own life. I don't want to be chained to him just because he can't control his indulgences. It's not my fault he's lazy, and that you're lazy. It's your own fault. You need to come with us to help him. If you don't, he's going to die."

"We're already dead."

"No. We are alive. We stand together and we are alive."

Those were the words that stuck most in my head. How could these beings exist in such a form? How was Brooke channeling an alternate world where her missing parents visited?

None of it made sense.

I recalled the many things we'd shared over the years: walks through the Boston Common during college, shows at the Globe Theater in Neville, awful relationships we'd both endured, crying on one another's shoulders. Never did we step forward with our relationship as lovers. Our friendship was something that neither of us wanted to forfeit. Of course, we were perfect for one another: Of absolute course. I knew I'd lose her friendship if we tried to progress, in the blink of an eye. What if it didn't work? What if we ended up hating one another? What if we found ourselves at odds, and at opposite sides of the spectrum? I'd never forgive myself.

We had gone forward; somehow, somewhere else, we had done just that.

Flashes of her kissing me sprinkled my thoughts: Brooke in her twenties, thirties, and then her forties. Each time she leaned in toward me, her eyes shut just a bit, ready to kiss my ever-nervous lips. The world changed around her. The backgrounds—strangely familiar—flashed behind her as well. There was something unique about each one. Names popped into my head, flowing easily, as though they'd always been there and I'd somehow just unlocked them: Northvale, Norwalk, Neville, Boston, New York City. Our first real date happened while she drove us into the city in her little red car, singing along in perfect pitch to every song on the radio. We stopped in the Village, where she tried on an amazing silver dress. Our lunch at a small sandwich shop…

She was not Brooke, but someone else. She was another name, another history, but she *was* the same woman.

Warmth spread over me.

I saw our pets behind her in my mind: a black dog, a tan dog, a calico cat. I felt the heat, for we had lived someplace warm. Then the window behind her changed and held more details: the New England ocean side, train tracks, a stunning orange-red sunset. In a blink: back to the sands and warmth, to the dry heat and desert.

I could sense everything, and it was all so familiar.

None of that life had I known before this moment.

I saw a boy with blond curls, laughing, pushing model trains. I saw a girl with strawberry blonde hair. I saw them older, more beautiful. I saw the boy leaning in to kiss me, because I was on a hospital bed and his eyes were wet, but he was still smiling. I saw Brooke behind him, not looking at me, not seeing me. And then everything faded.

I was back in her living room.

Where did it all lead?

"I'm sorry," Brooke said, "but I can't go with you to take care of him. I need to live for myself for a while longer, you know. I'm not ready to stop just yet."

Brooke sounded far beyond her years, sure of herself.

If it were me, I probably would have gone with them.

"You're my sister," Georgie cried. "You're supposed to be there for me."

"The best thing I can do is make you learn to dig yourself out on your own. I don't want you to be helpless."

"It's all *his* fault, I bet," he said, pointing at me, and his true face appeared. Dozens of large pots dotted his face, the round wedges under his eyes crusted with yellowish goo. "She'd rather be with him than with us."

There was nothing I could say. I could only hope he was right!

"I want to make my own world," Brooke said. "I want to do it on my own terms and in my own way. I don't want to be what you want me to be. I've got to find my own way."

"You've already done that," her mother said. "You never listened. You never agreed with any of our plans."

"Well, look how it turned out for you," Brooke said. "I wasn't right to follow the same darkness, the same negative energy, the same intent on hate that you did. I love you all, but there's nothing down that road but isolation and sickness. Just look at Georgie!"

"He's fine," her mother insisted.

"We've been through this already." Brooke shook her head. "Now there's nothing I can do at this point. You have to do it. So, I give you this gift, if you're ready. Come with me. Start over. I've found a way where we can do just that. We can start again and you will be with me, and Georgie will be all right, and we'll be fine, and you'll be here with me and Peter."

"I don't know if we can."

"All you have to do is say the word and it will happen. There is nothing you have to do other than to want something."

"Where did you learn how to do this?"

"I was born with it—my will, my strength, my foresight. The world is mine for changing and for making. The worlds beyond are ours for exploring."

"What will you have to give up?" her father said. "There is always a trade. There's always some terrible compromise."

Brooke's eyes filled; even with the strange luminescence, I could see her cry.

"I've already given up the one thing in this life that means the world to me."

Bluish tears rolled down her cheeks as she turned to me.

Again, in flashes, I saw what could have been between us—the things that should have been: our kisses, our lovemaking, our children, our long and wonderful future; gone in a flash, sacrificed so that she might rescue her family from their dark bind.

"Brooke," her father said, his voice shocked and saddened.

She wiped her tears and straightened.

"So there it all is," she said. Brooke looked at me, and I wanted to say so much, to tell her what I'd seen, but my thoughts would not let me open my mouth. How was I expected to do anything but stand there like an imbecile? She'd shown me every hope, dream, and fantasy I'd harbored, which she'd given up to them in hopes that they'd return.

Our world unearthed.

"You've given us your loss," her father said. "My beautiful, angel daughter... I'm sorry. How could I have known? We made mistakes. Things didn't go the way we wanted, things out of our control. We only wanted the best for you and Georgie."

"I know."

Georgie hobbled over and pointed his strange appendage at me. He squinted, and I recognized the similarities he'd shared with Brooke, the way his eyelids dropped. "I knew there was something with him! She's had a thing for him and he's the reason for all this nonsense. It's *his* fault!"

"He's what's going to get you out of this," Brooke said. "He's what I've sacrificed for you. If you'll take a step forward and admit what's happened, I can make all of this disappear."

"You're a witch," he said, his throat sounding scratchy, and his eyes were the ones that filled this time. "You're nothing but a manipulative tramp. You've never been on our side and now you come in here and you insult us."

"You're going to take him away from me," Brooke said.

"You said he's already been sacrificed. Make up your mind!"

"This will all go away if you say the word. If you open up, things will change, you will be free. The sacrifice—the trade—has already been made. If you deny me this, I will lose everything."

"This is why you called us, so you can have a boyfriend?"

"More than that," Brooke said. "In *this* life, I've given him up. I've lived alone, meager and unfulfilled, while you three have indulged. All you need to do is step forward, for me."

Her brother stepped back, his mouth moving a bit, but wordless for a moment.

"I don't want to forget again," he said. "I don't want to go through it again. It was too much! I like it here. Mom and Dad take care of me. We're fine. We're okay."

"We're not okay," her father said. "We're sick. We're *so* sick. We need to change. We need to move forward. We can be brave."

"We'll forget all of this!" Georgie said. "It will all go away."

"Don't you want it to go away?" Brook said. She had never looked more hurt.

Her parents stepped in front of the boy.

"Everything we have will go away! It will all be lost..."

It was enough, I believe, that the two of them agreed. There were no words, and none needed to be said.

Words can lie; hearts cannot.

Their hearts believed.

Their hearts wanted the world.

"Wake up, sleepyhead," she said. Her name was not Brooke, but something else. "Time to get up." Her lips were on mine, as they'd been a million times.

The house: I recognized every bit of it.

Before I knew it, she was out of the room and I followed.

Voices and laughter filled the kitchen. Bright, warm sunlight permeated through every window. I went to look out and saw not the Atlantic, as I'd expected, but a grassy yard stretching far toward a neighboring house. In the living room, next to the familiar wall once decorated by a mural of trees and forest, the wall with the bay window had been painted. I recognized the curve of the beach and the reef that stretched to the horizon, rendered expertly in paint.

"Good morning, Pete," her father said. "Sleep well?"

"I don't know," I said. "I had some really strange dreams."

He was not made from darkness.

Next to him, her mother was equally solid.

Georgie stared blankly at the television.

And the woman most familiar: her arms wrapped around me from behind and her chin rested on my shoulder. Her hair was not dark, but light, and not short, but long. There was no mistaking who she was. I'd recognize her anywhere.

"I'm glad we're all together," she said.

As I looked out the window, I saw a large front lawn, and two kids playing. I saw none of the darkness, but only light. The dreams I'd had were starting to fade, and the different, yet familiar people I'd met blended into the background.

Every time I sleep, I see her.

When it could be someone else, it is not.

The details may change, but we remain the same. Our world for the making. Our world for the planting, and growing, and walking. Our world… and always, always, with her.

The things that haunt us
Reappear
Reflecting inside our eyes

AMID THE WALKING WOUNDED

JACK KETCHUM

IT WAS FOUR IN THE MORNING, the Hour of the Wolf he later thought, the hour when statistically most people died who were going to die on any given night and he awakened in the condo guestroom thinking that something had shaken him awake, an earthquake, a tremor—though this was Sarasota not California and besides, he'd been awakened by an earthquake many years ago one night in San Diego and this was somehow not quite the same. The glow outside the bedroom window faded even as he woke so that he couldn't be sure it was not in some way related to his sleep. He was aware of a trickling inside his nose, a thin nasal discharge, unusual because he was a smoker and used to denser emissions. He sniffed it up into his throat and thought it tasted wrong.

The guestroom had its own bathroom just around the corner so he put on his glasses and got up and turned on the light and spit the stuff into the sink and saw that it was blood and as he leaned over the sink it began leaking out his nose in a thin unsteady stream like a faucet badly in need of new washers. He pinched his nose and stood straight, tilted back his head and felt it run down the back of his throat, suddenly heavier now so that it almost choked him, the gag response kicking in and he thought, now what the hell is *this?* so he leaned forward again and took his hand away from his nose and watched it pouring out of him.

He grabbed a hand towel, pressed it under and over his nose and pinched again. *One seriously major fucking bloody nose*, he thought, unaware as yet that he was not alone, that others in town had awakened bleeding from the nose that night though none of them had been taking Ibuprofen, eight pills a day for over a month's time trying to fight off some stupid tennis elbow without resorting to a painful shot of cortisone directly into the swollen tendon—unaware too that Ibuprofen was not just an anti-inflammatory but a blood-thinner, which was why he was not going to be doing any clotting at the moment.

The towel, pink, was turning red. The pressure wasn't working.

If he put his head up it poured down his throat—he could taste it now, salty, rich and coppery. If he put his head down it poured out his nose. Straight-up, he was an equal-opportunity bleeder, it came out both places.

He couldn't do this alone. He had to wake her.

"Ann? Annie?"

There was a streetlight outside her window. Her pale bare back and shoulders told him that she still slept nude.

"Annie. I'm bleeding."

She had always departed sleep like a drunk with one last shot left inside the bottle.

"*Whaaaa*?"

"Bleeding. *Help*." It was hard to talk with the stuff gliding down his throat and the towel pressed over his face. She rolled over squinting at him, the sheet pulled up to cover her breasts.

"What'd you do to yourself?"

"Nosebleed. Bad." He spoke softly. He didn't want to wake her son David in the next room. There was no point in disturbing the sleep of a fourteen-year-old.

She sat up. "Pinch it."

"I'm pinching it. Won't stop."

He turned and went back to the bathroom so she could get out of bed and put on a robe. He was not allowed to see her naked anymore. He leaned over the sink and took away the towel and watched it slide out of him bright red against the porcelain and swirl down the drain.

"Ice," she said behind him and then saw the extent of what was happening to him and said *jesus* while he pinched his nose and tilted back his head and swallowed and then she said *ice* again. "I'll get some."

He tried blowing out into his closed nostrils the way you did to pop the pressure in your ears in a descending plane and all he succeeded in doing was to fog up his glasses. Huh? He took them off and looked at them. The lenses were clear. He looked in the mirror. There were beads of red at each of his tear-ducts.

He was bleeding from the eyes.

It was the eyes that were fogged, not his goddamn glasses. She came back with ice wrapped in a dishtowel.

"I'm bleeding from the eyes," he told her. "If it's the Ebola virus, just shoot me."

"Eyes and nose are connected." She hadn't grown up a nurse's daughter for nothing. "Here."

He took the icepack and arranged it over his nose, tucked the corners of the dishtowel beneath. Within moments the towel was red. The ice felt good but it wasn't helping either.

"Here."

She'd taken some tissues and wrapped them thick around a pair of Q-tips.

"Put these up inside. Then pinch again."

He did as he was told. He liked the way she was rushing to his aid. It was the closest he'd felt to her for quite some time. He managed a goofy smile into her wide dark eyes and worried face. *Ain't this something?* He pinched his nose till it hurt.

The makeshift packs soaked through. He was dripping all over his tee-shirt. She handed him some tissues.

"Jesus, Alan. Should I call 911?"

He nodded. "You better."

The ambulance attendants were both half his age, somewhere in their twenties and the one with the short curly hair suggested placing a penny in the center of his mouth between his teeth and upper lip and then pressing down hard on the lip, a remedy that apparently had worked for his grandmother but which did not do a thing for him and left him with the taste of filthy copper in his mouth, a darker version of the taste of blood. Annie asked if she should go with him and he said no, stay with David, get some sleep, I'll call if I need you. She had to write down their number because at the moment he couldn't for the life of him remember.

Inside the ambulance he began to bleed heavily and the attendant sitting inside across from him couldn't seem to find any tissues nor anything for him to bleed into. Eventually he came up with a long plastic bag that looked like a heavier-grade of Ziploc which he had to hold open with one hand while dealing with his leaking nose with the other. A small box of tissues was located and placed in his lap. When one wad of tissues filled with blood he would hurriedly shove it into the bag and pull more from the box, his nose held low into the bag to prevent him from bleeding all over his khaki shorts. The attendant did nothing further to help him after finding him the bag and tissues. This was not the way it happened on *ER* or *Chicago Hope*.

The emergency room was reassuringly clean and, at five in the morning, nearly deserted but for him and a skeleton staff. They did not insist he sign in. Instead a chubby nurse's aide stood in front of him with a clipboard taking down the pertinent information, leaving him to deal with his nose, replacing the half-full Ziploc bag with a succession of pink plastic kidney-shaped vomit bowls but otherwise treating him as though it were ninety-nine percent certain he had AIDS.

He didn't mind. As long as the pink plastic bowls kept coming and the tissues were handy.

He was beginning to feel light-headed. He supposed it was loss of blood. He couldn't remember Annie's address though he'd written her from his New York apartment countless times in the past four years since she'd moved away and knew her address—quite literally—by heart. He couldn't remember his social security number either. The nurse's aide had to dig into his back pocket to get his wallet. The card was in there along with his insurance card. He couldn't do it for her because his hands, now covered with brown dried blood, were occupied trying to stop fresh red blood from flowing.

The ER doctor was also half his age, oriental, handsome and built like a swimmer with wide shoulders and a narrow waist, like the rest of the staff quite friendly and cheerful at this ungodly hour but unlike them seemingly unafraid to touch him even after, having swallowed so much of his own blood, he vomited much of it back into one of the pink plastic bowls. He asked Alan if he was taking any drugs. And that was when he learned about the blood-thinning properties of Ibuprofen. He thought that at least he was probably not going to have a heart attack. He supposed it was something.

The doctor used a kind of suction device to suck blood from each of his nostrils into a tube trying to clear them but that didn't work which Alan could have told him, there was far too much to replace it with, so he packed him with what he called pledgets, which looked like a pair of tampons mounted on sticks, shoved them high and deep into the nasal cavities and told him to wait and see if they managed to stop the bleeding.

Miraculously, they did.

Half an hour later they released him. He phoned Annie and she drove him back to the condo and he washed his hands and face and changed his clothes and they each went back to bed.

He woke needing to use the toilet and found that both his shit and piss had turned black. A tiny black droplet clung to his penis. He shook it off. He supposed he'd learned something—a vampire's shit and urine would always be black. He wondered if Anne Rice could find a way to make this glamorous.

The second time he woke he was bleeding again. He squeezed at the pledgets as he'd been told to do should this occur but the bleeding wouldn't stop. He roused Ann and this time she insisted on driving him to the hospital herself, handing him her own newly opened box of Puffs to place in his lap. Upstairs David continued to sleep his heavy adolescent sleep. It was just as well. The boy was only fond of blood in horror movies.

The chubby nurse's aide was gone when he arrived but the pink plastic bowls were there and he used them, sat in the same room he'd left only hours before while his doctor, the swimmer, summoned an Ear Nose and Throat man who arrived shortly after he'd sent Annie back home.

By now he felt weak as a newborn colt, rubber-legged and woozy. It seemed he needed to grow a new pair of hands to juggle his kidney-shaped-pan, eyeglasses, tissues and tissue boxes, all the while holding his nose and spitting, vomiting, dripping and swallowing blood at intervals.

He felt vaguely ridiculous, amused.

A bloody nose for chrissake.

What he felt next was pain that lasted quite a while as the ENT man—another healthy Florida specimen, a young Irishman who arrived in pleated shorts and polo shirt—withdrew the pledgets and peered into his nose with a long thin tubular lighted microscope, determined that it was only from the right nostril that he was actually bleeding, and then repacked it with so much stuff that by the time it was finished he felt like a small dog had crawled up and died in there.

A half-inch square accordion-type gauze ribbon coated in Vaseline, four feet of it folded back-to-back compacted tight into itself and pushed in deep. In front of that another tampon-like pledget, this one removable by means of a string. In front of that something called a Foley catheter which inflated like a balloon. Another four feet of folded ribbon. Another pledget.

He had no idea there was so much room inside his face.

The man was hearty but not gentle.

He was given drugs against the pain and possible infection and put into a wheelchair and wheeled into an elevator and settled into a hospital bed for forty-eight hours' observation. Once again a nurse had to find and read his insurance and social security cards. The drugs had kicked in by then and so had the loss of blood. He didn't even know where his wallet was though he suspected it was in its usual place, his back pocket.

The bed next to him was empty. The ward, quiet.

He slept.

He awoke sneezing, coughing blood, a bright stunning spray across the sheets—*it could not get out his nose so instead it was sliding down his throat again, his very heartbeat betraying him, pulsing thin curtains, washes of blood over his pharynx, larynx, down into his trachea.* He gagged and reached for bowl at the table by the bed and vomited violently, blood and bile, something thick in the back of his throat remaining gagging him, something thick and solid like a heavy ball of mucus making him want to puke again so he reached into his mouth to clear it, reached in with thumb and forefinger and grasped it, slippery and sodden, and pulled.

And at first he couldn't understand what it was but it was long, taut, and would not part company with his throat so he pulled again until it was out of his mouth and he could see the thing, and then he couldn't believe what he'd done, that it was even possible to do this thing but he had it between his fingers, he was staring at it covered with slime and blood, nearly a foot and a half of the accordion ribbon packed inside his nose. He'd sneezed it out or coughed it out through his pharynx and now he was holding it like a tiny extra-long tongue and it continued to gag him so he reached for the call-button and pushed and fought the urge to vomit.

"What in the world have you done?"

It was the pretty nurse, a strong young blonde with a wedding ring, the one who'd admitted him and got him into bed. She looked as though she didn't know whether to be shocked or angry or amused with him.

"Damned if I know," he said around the ribbon. *Aaand ith eye-o.*

He vomited again. There was a lot of it this time.

"Uh-oh," she said. "I'm going to call your doctor. He may have to cauterize whatever's bleeding up in there. I'll get some scissors meantime, snip that back for you, okay?"

He nodded and then sat there holding the thing. He shook his head. *A goddamn bloody nose.*

It occurred to him much later that an operation followed by a hospital stay under heavy medication combined with heavy loss of blood was a lot like drifting through a thick fetal sea from which you occasionally surfaced to glimpse fuzzy snatches of sky. In his younger days he'd dropped acid while floating in the warm Aegean and there were similarities. He awoke to orderlies serving food and nurses taking his blood pressure and handing him paper cups of medication. None of it grounded him for long. Mostly he slept and dreamed.

He remembered the dreams vividly, huge segments of them crowded spinning inside his head with unaccustomed clarity of detail and feeling—and then he'd seem to blink and they'd be gone, just like that, his mind occupied solely by the business of healing his ruptured body. Adjusting the new packing to relieve the pressure, swallowing the pill, nibbling the food. Then hurrying back to dream.

There was something ultimately lonely, he thought, about the process of healing. Nobody could really help you. All they could do was be reasonably attentive to your needs. He began to look forward to his momentary visits from the pretty blonde nurse because of all the hospital staff she seemed the wittiest and most cheerful and he liked her Southern accent, but ultimately he was completely alone in this. He'd told Annie not to call for a while after her first phone call woke him, he was fine but he was not up to conversation yet. And that felt lonely too.

When the black man with the haunted eyes appeared in the bed beside him by the window he was not really surprised. He assumed a lot went on in his room that he wasn't aware of. He'd looked over at the window to see if it was day or night because as usual he had no idea, no concept of time whatsoever, and there he was lying flat on his back and covered to the chin, hooked up to some sort of monitor and an elaborate IV device of tubes and wires much different from his own, his face thin to emaciation, drawn and gray in the moonlight, eyes open wide and focused in his direction but, Alan thought, not seeing him, or seeing through him—and this he proved with a smile and a nod into the man's wide unblinking gaze.

Possibly some sort of brain damage, he thought, poor guy, knowing somehow that this man's loneliness far exceeded his own, and moments later forgot him and returned to sleep.

***

Imagine the seats on a slowly moving Ferris wheel, only the seats are perfectly stable, they don't rock back in forth as the seats on a Ferris wheel do, they remain perfectly steady, and then imagine that they are not seats at all but a set of flat gleaming slabs of thick heavy highly polished glass or metal or even wood, dark, so that it is impossible to tell which—and now imagine that there is no wheel—*nothing whatever holding them together but the slow steady measured glide itself and that each is the size and shape of a closet door laid flat, and that there are not only one set but countless sets, intricately moving in and out and past each other, almost but never quite touching, so that you can step up or down or to the side on any of them without ever once losing your footing.*

It is like dancing. It gets you nowhere. But it's pleasurable.

That was what he dreamed.

He was alone in the dream for quite a while, until Annie appeared, a younger Annie, looking much the same as she did the day he met her sitting across from him on the plane from L.A. with her two-year-old son beside her over a dozen years ago. Her hair was short as it was then as was her skirt and she was stepping toward him in a roundabout way, one step forward and one to the side, drifting over and under him and he wasn't even sure she was aware of his presence, it was as though he were invisible, because she never looked directly at him until she turned and said, *you left us nowhere, you know that?* Which was not an accusation but merely a statement of fact and he nodded and began to cry because of course it was true, aside from these infrequent visits and the phone calls and letters he had come unstuck from them somehow, let them fend for themselves alone.

He woke and saw the black man standing in the doorway, peering out into the corridor, turning his head slowly as though searching for someone with those wide empty eyes and he thought for a moment that the man should not be out of bed, not with all those wires and tubes still attached to him reaching all the way across the room past the foot of his own bed but then heard movement to the other side of the darkened room and turned to see the form of a small squat woman who appeared to be adjusting the instruments, doing something to the instruments, a nurse or a nurse's aide he supposed so he guessed it was all right for the man to be there. He looked back at him in the doorway and closed his eyes, trying but failing to find his way back into the dream, wanting to explain to Annie the inexplicable.

It was almost dawn when the arm woke him.

He had all but forgotten about the arm, the inflamed swollen tendon that had started him on Ibuprofen and landed him here in the first place. The drugs had masked that pain too. Now the arm jerked him suddenly conscious, jerked hard twice down along his side as though some sort of electric shock had animated it, something beyond his will or perhaps inside his dream, needles of pain from the elbow rising above the constant throbbing wound inside his face.

He guessed more drugs were in order.

He was hurting himself here.

He pressed the call button and waited for the voice on the intercom.

"Yes? What can I do for you?"

"I need a shot or a pill or something."

"Pain?"

"Yes."

"I'll tell your nurse."

They were fast, he gave them that. The pretty blonde nurse was beside him almost instantly, or perhaps despite his pain he'd drifted, he didn't know. She offered him a paper cup with two bright blue pills inside.

"You hurt yourself awake, did you?"

"I guess. Yeah, my arm."

"Your arm?"

"Tennis elbow. Didn't even get to play tennis. Did it in a gym over a month ago."

She shook her head, smiling, while he took the pill and a sip of water. "You're not having a real good holiday, are you?"

"Not really, no."

She patted his shoulder. "You'll sleep for a while now."

When she was gone he lay there waiting for the pain to recede, trying to relax so that he could sleep again. He turned and saw the black man staring at him as before, and saw that the man now nestled in a thicket of tubes and wires, connected to each of his arms, running under the bedcovers to his legs, another perhaps a catheter, two more patched to his collarbones, one running to his nose and the thickest of them into his half-open mouth. Behind him lights on a tall wide panel glowed red and blue in the dark.

By morning it was gone. All of it. Alan was lying on his side so that the empty bed and the empty space behind it and the light spilling in from the window were the first things he noticed.

The next thing was the smell of eggs and bacon. He did his best by the food set in front of him though it was tasteless and none too warm and the toast was hard and dry. He drank his juice and tea. When the nurse came in with his pills—a new nurse, middle-aged, black and heavy-waisted, one he'd never seen—he asked her about the man in the bed beside him.

"Nobody beside you," she said.

"What?"

"You been all alone here. I just came on but first thing I did was check the charts. Always do. Procedure. You're lucky it's summertime, with all the showbirds gone, or we'd be up to our ears here. You got the place all to yourself."

"That's impossible. I saw this guy three times, twice in the bed and once standing right there in the doorway. He looked terrible. He was hooked up to all kinds of tubes, instruments."

"'Fraid you were dreaming. You take a little painkiller, you take a little imagination, mix and stir. Happens all the time."

"I'm an appellate lawyer. I don't *have* an imagination."

She smiled. "You were all alone, sir, all night long. I swear."

Some sort of mix-up with the charts, he thought. The man had been there. He wasn't delusional. He knew the difference between dreams and reality. For now the dreams were the more vivid of the two. It was still one way to tell them apart.

Wait till the shift changes, he thought. Ask the other nurse, the blonde. She'd given him a pill last night. The black man had been there. And he was on her watch.

He dreamed and drifted all day long. Sometime during the afternoon Annie and David came by to visit and he told David about coughing up the accordion ribbon and what he'd learned about the color of a vampire shit. Teenage kids were into things like that he thought, the grosser the better. That and Annie's cool lips on his forehead were about all he remembered of their visit. He remembered lunch and dinner, though not what he ate. He remembered the doctor coming by and that he no longer wore the shorts and polo shirt as he took his pulse and blood pressure but instead the pro forma white lab coat and trousers. He decided he liked him better the other way.

"Sure," she said. "I remember. You hurt yourself awake."

"You remember the guy in the bed beside me?"

"Who?"

"The black man. I don't know what was wrong with him but he looked pretty bad."

"You know what your doctor's giving you for pain?"

"No."

"It's called hydrocodone, honey. In the dose you're getting, it's as mean as morphine, only it's not addictive. I wouldn't be surprised if you told me you were seeing Elvis in that bed over there, let alone some black fella."

He *hurt himself awake* again that night.

This time he was batting at his aching face—at his nose. He was batting at the culprit, at the source of his misery. As though he wanted to start himself bleeding again.

What was he doing? Why was he doing this?

His dream had been intense and strange. They were alone inside a long gray tube, he and Annie, empty of everything but the two of them and stretching off into some dazzling bright infinity and he was pulling at her clothes, her blouse, her jacket, trying to rouse her and get her to her feet while she crouched in front of him saying nothing, doing nothing, as though his presence beside her meant nothing at all to her one way or another. He felt frightened, adrift, panicked.

He woke in pain batting at his face and reached for the call-button to call his nurse for yet another pill but the black man's big hand stopped him, fingers grasping his wrist. The man was standing by his bedside. The fingers were long and smooth and dry, his grip astonishingly firm.

He looked up into the wide brown eyes that did not seem to focus upon him but instead to look beyond him, into vast distances, and saw the wires and tubes trailing off behind him past the other bed where the squat dark form he realized was no nurse nor nurse's aide hovered over the panel of instruments and a voice inside his head said *no, we're not finished yet, my accident became yours and I'm very much sorry for that but it happens sometimes and for now no interruptions please, we need the facilities, deal with your own pain as I am dealing with mine* and he thought, I'm dreaming, this is crazy, this is the drug but the voice inside said *no, not crazy, only alone in this, alone together here in this room and the nurse cannot see, cannot know, the nurse is not in pain as you and I, you'll only disturb her, you can live with that, can't you* and he nodded yes because suddenly he thought that of course he could. *Good*, the voice said, *a short time, stop hurting yourself and instead of her, dream of me, you've been doing that already but she always gets in, doesn't she.* He nodded again and felt the pressure lessen on his wrist. *Stop hurting yourself. She is not the pain nor are you. Rest. Sleep.*

The man sat back on his own bed and rested, adjusted the wires, smoothed them over his chest. The dark female figure resumed her work at the lighted panel. The man's touch was like a drug. Better. The pain was vanishing. He didn't need the call button. Or perhaps he was just living with the pain, he didn't know. One more night, he thought. One more morning, maybe.

Maybe there were things he could do for her and the boy that he hadn't done, things to make it better. But he needed to let go of that now.

He dreamed of a Ferris wheel. Only there was no wheel. He dreamed of a thousand wheels intersecting.

He stepped down and up and forward and side to side.

UNDERWATER FERRIS WHEEL

MICHAEL BAILEY

THE LANKY GENTLEMAN in the pinstriped suit and moth-eaten neck ruffle staggers forward. He holds a card for you to take:

COME RIDE THE UNDERWATER FERRIS WHEEL.

There is a mixed scent of caramel corn, candied apples, corndogs and spilled beer as Cate waits her turn in line with her son. The trailer has a sign lit with small yellowing bulbs, which works cordially with the other food trailers to light up the otherwise dark path of sweets, meats, and deep-fried foods on sticks.

She lets go of Ian long enough to dig in her purse for money.

"Large cotton candy," she says to the man leaning over the counter.

"Stick or bagged?" he says, pointing to the prefilled plastic bags of rainbow clouds lining the inside of the trailer.

In back, a man wearing a hairnet spins pink silk onto a conical cone of white paper.

She takes in the smells of hot sugar and oil.

"Stick," Cate says, and adds a couple corndogs to the order.

She turns to her son to see if he wants ketchup or mustard or both, but he's gone. The couple standing in his place look past her to the menu.

"Ian?"

She expects him at the ticket counter because he wanted more rides, not food, and he isn't there, nor is he wandering around the carny games across the promenade.

The others in line don't seem bothered that he's disappeared.

Cate holds a twenty dollar bill instead of her son and no longer is she hungry, the appetite for junk food replaced with a gut-wrenching feeling of losing him. The man leaning through the window balances a pair of hefty golden corndogs in one hand, the other expecting money. She hands him the bill, not remembering having taken the cotton candy.

"Ma'am?"

He holds her food, calling for her as she calls for Ian.

"Did you see a boy," Cate says to the couple, her hand waist high to estimate height, "blond hair, red and white striped shirt?"

Ian had chosen his outfit to match the tents he'd seen from the road when they were first setting up the carnival, she knew, because he had pestered her the entire week to go.

Shaking their heads, they take her place as she steps out of line.

Hundreds fill the food court and labyrinth of walking paths.

"Ma'am?" the man calls again.

She no longer cares about the food or the money. She holds onto the cotton candy like a beacon, hoping Ian will see the pink light and come running from out of the darkness.

"One more ride, after we eat something," Mom says.

She drags him through the crowd, making her own path. Behind them, Ian's wake is swallowed by kids able to ride the bigger rides (by themselves), drunken men stumbling around and yelling, hanging off each other, beers sloshing over plastic cups (even though Ian knew there's this place called the beer tree where they are supposed to drink), and other kids—Ian's age—dragged around by their parents.

Heavy metal music blasts from speakers hidden around the rides, and then pop music, and then what the older kids at school call dub step, and then country. The music changes as rapidly as the scenery, fading in and out as they make their way from the rides to the food court.

He has enough tickets clenched in his fist for two rides, but his mom wants to go with him on the Ferris wheel after they eat and that will eat all ten that are left.

"One last ride," she had said, meaning either the marvel of their day would soon end, or they'd be going to the stupid adult stuff, like seeing the animals, or going to the building with all the paintings and quilts, or to the place with the judged fruits and vegetables and jarred stuff, which they could see any other day by going to the grocery store.

And they still hadn't played any games.

"Step up, son," says a man who isn't his father. He holds a softball that's supposed to be tossed into a tilted basket without bouncing out. "It's easy," he says, tossing it underhand, and it *is* easy because it stays in the basket, and he wasn't even looking at it.

"You can win one of these to take home."

Stuffed animals bigger than real animals hang from their necks.

"Can we play games?"

"After we eat, maybe."

Maybe means no most times.

The man with unkempt hair and brownish teeth leans out of the booth. Three baskets are lined behind him, no one else playing his game.

"Free game for the boy," he says.

"Mom!"

"There are no free games," she says, pulling him along.

The man puts his hand to his heart.

"Honest. One free toss."

"Please, Mom?"

"A gift from me to you," the man says. "No money involved, I promise. Let the boy win something to take home. One free throw."

They stop.

A bright disc of moon shines onto them.

Ian already knows he wants the dragon. It's red and about two feet long and has a forked tongue hanging out of its mouth.

The man wanting him to win the stuffed animal is within what his mom had warned as 'grabbing distance,' holding a yellow dimpled softball like they have in the batting cages. He tosses another behind his back, which spins in midair and lands in the basket.

"One," says his mom.

"There we go! Step up to the counter here, but don't lean over, and simply toss it in."

He throws another spinning ball and makes it in, and Ian thinks he might have it down. It just takes some backspin and needs to brush the upper, back portion of the basket.

Ian takes the ball, tries to copy the technique. The throw looks similar, but the ball hits the bottom of the basket and comes shooting out.

"Good try! I think you almost have it down." He holds out another yellow ball. "One more go at it."

"That's how they work," his mom whispers to him. "See?"

"One more for the boy."

"No thank you," she says.

The man in the booth sets the ball on the counter. "Try it again. No gimmicks. I want to see the boy get one in. You can try it, too," he says, placing a ball in front of her as well.

This time his mom's the one smiling, but her teeth are much whiter. She hesitates and drops Ian's hand.

"One more," she says.

She picks up the ball and throws it underhand, but doesn't put any spin on it so it bounces back at her and she he has to pick it up off the ground.

"The boy's going to do it," the man says. "I have a good feeling about this one."

Ian takes his turn and again concentrates. He needs to throw it like last time, but not as high. Softly, he lets it roll off the tips of his fingers and there's plenty of backspin. It hits the basket in the right spot, nearly rolls out, but remains inside.

"He's a natural," the man in the booth says, crouching behind the counter.

Ian points to the dragon, but the man stands upright with a goofy smile. His prize is a cheap metallic-looking pinwheel tacked to the end of a straw that matches his shirt.

"Ah, you want the dragon," he says. "You gotta work your way up to that one by trading up from the smaller prizes."

He hadn't noticed the various prize levels until now.

"That's how they work," his mom says.

You flip the card in your hand to find the other side black. The white side, with the message about the underwater Ferris wheel, contains only the invitation to ride it and nothing more. The lanky man in the pinstriped suit is gone. You took the card and read the words and sometime in between, the man resembling a makeupless clown vanished into the crowd, his pinstriped coattails consumed by kids holding balloon animals.

Cate wanders, but not far. She doesn't want to stray from the food court because Ian can't be far and he's not prone to exploring on his own. She nearly steps onto a lone ticket, remembering Ian's longing for one final ride, and retrieves it from the ground.

***

Like money in his wallet, Ian counts the red tear-off tickets to make sure there are still ten. He lets them accordion out, the last ticket lapping a puddle of a spilled soda. He holds his mom's hand as she drags him around. It would be much easier to count them if he had his other hand. He tugs and his mom tugs back to let him know she's in control and that counting won't be very easy.

He's not even hungry, but they pass through ever-changing music and laughing and cheering and the shrill of those flipping cages on the *Zipper*, kids screaming through the fast loop of the *Ring of Fire*—yellow and red bulbs flashing in circular patterns as the coaster cycles, first clockwise, then counterclockwise—and the mesmerizing vertical array of green, white and blue bars of light on the *Graviton* as it spins like a flying saucer dreidel.

A tongue of tickets trails behind as he counts. He folds them, one onto the next, with the flip of his index finger and thumb. He gets to five when a Goth girl he recognizes from school bumps into his shoulder and jars them loose.

They stop at a path of pavement to let a medic golf cart pass, and that's when Ian notices what he thinks is a clown. He doesn't resemble the colorful clowns with the big feet and honking noses and painted faces, and he's not one of those clowns seen around the park squeak-tying balloons into poodles and pirate swords. This one's unremarkable, except for the scrunched doily thing around his neck. He looks like someone from an old black and white photograph, like the one's hanging on his grandma's wall: pictures of his grandparents' parents. He thinks of this because the man is not smiling—lips pressed in a flat line—like old people in old photographs, dressed in what he thinks is an old black suit and jacket.

And he stares, eyes not moving away.

The cart is suddenly gone, the world no longer paused. A soft tug on his hand tells him they're moving again and Ian looks at his feet for only a moment because someone's stepped on his laces and he nearly stumbles. Looking back, the man is gone, the crowd alive in his place.

"You've never had cotton candy before, have you?" his mom says.

Ian shakes his head no, although she doesn't see him do it.

"When I was your age, I loved cotton candy," she says over the noise. "Me and your father used to go to the Brendan Carnival every year when it was still around."

When Dad was still around.

She always started conversations this way, always talking about what they did as a couple before Dad died, before a non-drunk driver clipped his car and drove him off the cliffs and into the ocean where he drowned.

"Your father always liked the candied apples. He had a sweet tooth. Sometimes we'd share the... I'm not sure what it was called, but it was multicolored popcorn in these little rectangular shapes wrapped in plastic; each clustered section of color was a different flavor, like orange or cherry or grape, kind of like caramel corn but different. I haven't had that in years."

The symphony of carnival noise dulls the closer they get to the food court, the lights brighter, and the stench of puke, beer and cigarette smoke lingering, yet overpowered by Chinese food, barbeque, and deep-fried everything.

"Wait until you try the corndogs. Your father used to love those, too."

Nine tickets. There are only nine.

"Mom, we need to get another ticket to ride the—"

"No rides until after we eat. Here, this one looks good."

They stop in front of a trailer lit up in yellow bulbs and the entire thing glows. One of the smaller bulbs in the word SNACKS is missing, like his tenth ticket.

***

You attempt to follow him, but he weaves in and out of the multitude of people as if gliding over ice: a glimpse of a coattail, a pinstriped leg, night black hair. He is quickly absorbed into crowds of parents and children and ages in-between. The wind picks up and you drop the card, which flaps along the ground like a dead butterfly. It flips over and along the ground as easily as it flipped in your hand and you can read the words in a strobe-like flutter of black and white—the invitation for the ride.

Cate turns a boy around, but it's not Ian.

She calls his name again and then sees him standing in front of a game booth fifty feet away. Warmth flushes through her body as she remembers to breathe, the thought of losing Ian more than she can handle. Losing a husband is one thing, but losing their only son who resembles him so undeniably…

"Ian!" she says, willing her voice to reach him.

He turns then, but not in her direction, and her heart drops.

Running to him, she continues to call his name, jouncing shoulders against those in her path and nearly trampling people over entirely. A baby stroller built for two trips her and she falls and scrapes her knee, rises, and keeps going, somehow never losing grasp of the lone red ticket and the cotton candy she points to the sky. Ian passes in and out of view, as if projected against the throng of fairgoers from a spinning shadow lamp.

"Ian!"

One moment he's there, another he's not.

A flash of silver and the pinwheel he no longer wants falls to the ground. A gangly man leans over to pick it up—one of the carnival folk, perhaps. He's the only immobile person in the multitude and wears a black pinstriped suit, as out of place in the dark as a dandelion disguised in a bouquet of yellow roses. An aged neck ruffle strangles his throat and he smiles as she approaches.

He offers the pinwheel, but she doesn't want it.

She wants her son.

Cate looks around him frantically.

"Did you see the boy who dropped that?"

The silence tells her he's mute. He stares at her, expressionless, his face drained of both color and emotion.

"I'm looking for my son, Ian. He dropped this," she says, taking it from him, "and you just picked it up. Did you see where he was going?"

He doesn't point, nor does he say anything. He simply takes his finger and spins the cheap toy on the stick and magically reveals a card from one of his shirtsleeves. The man stands there a moment before facing the ocean peer.

He tugs on his mom's hand, but she doesn't tug back to let him know she's still in control. Glancing up, Ian finds that he's not holding his mother's hand at all, but the hand of a tall man with long arms that dangle well past his knees. He can't remember ever letting go, but he must have, and somehow grabbed this man instead. Clammy fingers curl around his own. It's the man who isn't a clown, the old photograph man he saw before.

Ian jump-startles and the man let's go.

He isn't scary because he doesn't wear a fake face like regular clowns who pretend to be happy or sad or sometimes mad. He has a normal face.

He hands Ian a card.

"Are you supposed to be a mime?"

He doesn't say anything.

"I read a story once about a mime and he never said anything, either. He would pretend to be stuck in invisible boxes and climb ropes that weren't really there. But he wore makeup and had a white face and black lips like Charley Chaplin. I don't know who that is, but my mom says he looked like Charley Chaplin."

He shows Ian the rest of the cards, which are bound together with a rubber band. His dad used to do card tricks, so Ian knows what to do. He's supposed to take a card and look at it without showing and hand it back. Ian's card is a stained joker with worn edges and a crease down the middle. The joker wears a jester hat and rides a unicycle and looks drawn in scribbles of pen.

Before handing it back, the cards are splayed before him, at least two dozen. They are all different. About half are standard playing cards of different makes, some old, some new; mixed within are handmade cards like the joker, along with some baseball cards, a library card, credit cards and a few drivers licenses from different states.

Ian hands the card to him facedown and watches as it's shuffled into the deck over and over again, and in lots of different ways. The unsmiling *carny*—his mom would call him—bends the cards and bends them back like his dad used to, and shuffles them flat in the air with his thumbs and then reverses the cards in an arc to slide them in place—what his dad deemed 'the bridge.'

He hands the deck to Ian.

"I pick one?"

The man doesn't say anything.

Expecting his card to be on top because the back looks similar, Ian lifts a three of diamonds, which looks as though someone with shaky fingers drew the number with black crayon and then smudged three red diamonds on the card with lipstick. The one after it isn't his card either, but a jack of clubs. He flips over the next card with stats printed on the back and it's a rookie card for someone who used to play on a team called the Royals; over the player's face is a smiley face sticker with the eyes scratched out. The next card is a VISA. The next is a king of hearts from a standard Bicycle deck, followed by a ripped-in-half five dollar bill with a spade drawn in Sharpie over the president's face, and then a seven of clubs, and then another hand-drawn card.

Confused, Ian hands the deck back to him.

The man wraps a rubber band around them and slides them into his suit pocket.

"What's the trick?"

The man holds out his hand, as if peddling for money.

That's how they work, his mom would say.

Three of the fingers curl until he's pointing at Ian's pinwheel.

As if on cue, a cool breeze spins the cheap metallic flower around, which Ian didn't want anyway; he had wanted the dragon but they didn't have enough money to pay for more games, even though he would have given up food to pay for a few more tosses into the basket so he could win the bigger prize. Dad would have let them play. If he hadn't died, they'd have enough money to play more games and ride more rides and really have fun.

Ian gladly hands over the pinwheel. In the process, the man who looks sort of like a clown clumsily drops it as part of a gag and they both fetch for it on the ground. Lying next to the cheap toy is Ian's joker card, which the trickster silently places into his pocket with the others.

He pulls out another card, but this time it's not one of the strange playing cards; it's a business card with a black side that reflects the moon and a white side that absorbs its light. A trade for the pinwheel, it seems. Printed on the white side is an invitation.

You hand the carnival worker five red tickets and he lets you past the chain and through the gate. A set of aluminum steps leads to a grated path to the ten story wheel. Every angle of metal is lit by long neon lights and flashing bulbs that cycle in hypnotic patterns. The cart awaits—the slightly rocking yellow one with the number eight on the side. You are alone for the ride as you were in line, the carnival empty. A mechanical click and the wheel moves. The world drops with the wind at your back. You elevate in a reverse motion with the giant silver axle as you rotate around. Rods and lights and the other carts fall as you rise. At the peak, black water rises from the pier, and for a moment you float above it all, nothing but sky and water and the thin line between. The entire lit wheel is cast against the water, appearing as though there are riders beneath the placid surface revolving horizontally, perhaps looking up to you in the stars. You see your reflection on the water, and then you free-fall fly, arms stretched outward, the wind at your face. The water rising.

COME SEE THE UNDERWATER FERRIS WHEEL.

Cate reads the card a second time and when she looks up from it, the man in the pinstriped suit is gone, like her son.

"Ian!" she calls.

She parts through people on her way to the water's edge, which seems so far away. Why would he go to the pier? Somehow she knew he'd be there, and somehow the man with the moth-eaten neck ruffle knew. He was leading her to the—

Your father and I would always ride the Ferris wheel, she had told Ian in the car. That's where she'd find him. She couldn't stop talking about it on their way to the carnival. *It was always the last thing we did before going home*, she had said.

Running takes the air from her lungs and pierces her side but she spots him at the base of the ride, gazing up in wonder. She spins him around to find his eyes glossy and terrified.

"There's no underwater Ferris wheel," Ian tells the water.

There's only the reflection of the *real* Ferris wheel.

"The card's a lie."

He walks along the planks, peering over the side to the black water. If there *was* an underwater ride, he'd at least see some kind of glowing light from below.

One last ride, his mom said.

Suddenly, his stomach aches empty and craves a corndog. He doesn't remember ever letting go of her hand while in line but he must've let go at some point and grabbed the hand of the clown who wasn't really a clown—the man with the bad card trick who gave him the stupid invitation to see something that wasn't even there.

Mom had warned him to stay close and not to wander.

Ian knew the park and could find his way around easily enough, but finding his mom would be like finding his dad's body, which the people looking for him couldn't do after he went over the cliff. Even if he found his mom, she'd be mad and they'd leave early. They wouldn't ride the Ferris wheel as their last ride like she remembered doing with Dad. Ian only had nine tickets anyway because he had dropped one. He holds them to the light, counting again to make sure.

The placid water breaks, enveloping you as you ride the yellow cart beneath the surface. Round you go as the un-reflection of the Ferris wheel above glows through a watery blur. As you come round, you see them gathered on the pier. A woman and boy embrace and it feels like home.

AFTERWORD

THE ORIGINAL IDEA for *Chiral Mad* was to include twenty short stories, similar to *Pellucid Lunacy*, the first charity project by Written Backwards. This did not happen, and here's why. Prior to an open call for submissions, twenty well-respected peers were invited to write for this anthology, as well as the twenty whose work appeared in the previous anthology. Half of the forty responded within the first few days, and most of the others in the following weeks. All were intrigued by the chirality theme and, more importantly, by the charitable cause to which all proceeds would be donated: Down syndrome. Submissions then opened to the public, and the public responded magnificently. Two hundred stories were received in a matter of weeks. After releasing a teaser book trailer, which listed accepted contributors, hundreds more piled in. The quality of stories received was at such a high level that it warranted expanding the anthology to twenty-eight stories instead of the planned twenty. All of the stories within this book were donated by the authors involved. No one received payment, other than contributor copies. Biographies of each author can be found in these last pages. Some of the names you may easily recognize; some are multi-award winning authors of poems, plays, short stories, novelettes, novellas, novels; and for some, this is their first published work. These are all amazing individuals and they span the globe. Seek them out. Much thanks to everyone involved.

Sincerely,
Michael Bailey

CONTRIBUTORS

IAN SHOEBRIDGE's wrote his first book at the age of six, based on a nightmare. The sole edition (which no longer survives) was met with "Why did you do it if it wasn't homework?" from its two first-grade readers. While his style expanded in subsequent decades, his fascination with dreams, altered states and ugly architecture continues to inform his writing. His stories have most recently appeared in the anthologies *Where Are We Going?*, *In Poe's Shadow*, and *Electric Velocipede #20*. He lives in Australia, dislikes sunlight and spiders.

GORD ROLLO was born in St. Andrews, Scotland, but now lives in Ontario, Canada. His short stories and novella-length work have appeared in many professional publications throughout the genre. His novels include: *The Jigsaw Man, Crimson, Strange Magic,* and *Valley of the Scarecrow*. His work has been translated into several languages and his titles are currently being adapted for audiobooks. Besides novels, Gord edited the acclaimed evolutionary horror anthology, *Unnatural Selection: A Collection of Darwinian Nightmares*. He also co-edited *Dreaming of Angels*, a horror/fantasy anthology created to increase awareness of Down syndrome and raise money for research. He recently completed his newest horror/dark fantasy novel, *The Translators*, and can be reached at www.gordrollo.com.

ANDREW HOOK is from Norwich England and recently sold his 100th short story. Andrew founded Elastic Press, which won the British Fantasy Society's Best Small Press award in both 2005 and 2009, as well as another six separate awards, including the prestigious Edge Hill Short Story Prize. His collection, *Nitrospective*, was published by DogHorn in 2011. Recent fiction has appeared in Shadows & Tall Trees, Black Static, and the anthologies *Classical Horror, Where Are*

We Going? and *Dark Currents*. He's looking for a publisher for two noir crime novels and is currently editing a new magazine, Fur-Lined Ghettos, with his partner, Sophie. He can be found online at www.andrew-hook.com.

GARY McMAHON's short fiction has been reprinted in both *The Mammoth Book of Best New Horror* and *The Year's Best Fantasy & Horror*. He is the acclaimed author of the novels *Rain Dogs, Hungry Hearts, Pretty Little Dead Things, Dead Bad Things,* and the *Concrete Grove* trilogy. He lives with his family in Yorkshire, England, trains in Shotokan karate, and likes running in the rain. You can visit Gary online at www.garymcmahon.com

MONICA J. O'ROURKE has published more than seventy-five short stories in magazines such as Postscripts, Nasty Piece of Work, Fangoria, Flesh & Blood, Nemonymous, and Brutarian, and in anthologies such as *Horror for Good* (for charity), *The Mammoth Book of the Kama Sutra,* and *The Best of Horrorfind*. She is the author of *Poisoning Eros I* and *II*, written with Wrath James White, *Suffer the Flesh*, and the collection *Experiments in Human Nature*. Watch for her new novel later this year from Sinister Grin Press! She works as a freelance editor, proofreader, and book coach. Her website is an ongoing and seemingly endless work in progress, so you can find her on www.facebook.com/MonicaJORourke in the meantime.

AMANDA OTTINO wrote her first poem on a piece of construction paper at the age of twelve. Today she can be found her in her quiet apartment in downtown Sacramento writing in a leather-bound notebook, sipping a glass of Zin. She enjoys unusual visualizations and finding darkness to enhance the beauty in her artwork. In the midst of writing her first novel, *Pixie Dust and Poison*, she hopes to display the inspiring secrets of a disturbed feminine mind from adolescence to adulthood. "Enchanted Combustion" is not only her first published work, it is the first short story she has ever written, and certainly not her last.

CHRIS HERTZ works on his house and his stories in Allison Park, Pennsylvania. His work (fiction—not home renovation) has appeared in The Copperfield Review, Aphelion, and *Pellucid Lunacy*. "There Are Embers" goes out to Bob Hertz, who, as a young boy, witnessed his own father set fire to the family home using his baseball cards as kindling. Some things just stick with you...

DAVID HEARN is not new to writing. In several decades he's accumulated several university awards for fiction, worked as a staff writer for a newspaper, and has even written a handful of unproduced screenplays—only recently, however, has he focused on publishing short fiction. Hearn lives in Pensacola, Florida, where he's currently at work on a collection of short stories. For more information, you can visit www.author-davidhearn.com.

BARRY JAY KAPLAN's stories have appeared in Descant, Bryant Literary Review, Central Park, Storyglossia, Brink, Apple Valley Review and many others. He has twice been nominated for a Pushcart Prize and one of his stories was included in Best of the Net 2008. His novels include *Black Orchid* (with Nicholas Meyer), *That Wilder Woman,* and *Biscayne.* He is also a prize-winning playwright and the co-author, with Rosemarie Tichler, of *Actors and Work* and *The Playwright at Work*. He lives in New York and New Haven and works for Yale University.

ERIC J. GUIGNARD writes dark fiction from his office in Los Angeles, California. His most recent writing credits include Stupefying Stories Magazine, *+Horror Library+ Vol 5* (Cutting Block

Press), The Horror Zine Magazine, and Indie Gypsy. He's a member of the Horror Writers Association and the Greater Los Angeles Writers Society. Although his passion is for fiction, he's also a published essayist and editor, including this year's acclaimed collection, *Dark Tales of Lost Civilizations*. Look for the next anthology, *After Death...*, to be released in Spring, 2013. You can visit Eric online at: www.ericjguignard.com or at his blog: ericjguignard.blogspot.com.

GARY A. BRAUNBECK's work has garnered six Bram Stoker Awards, an International Horror Guild Award, and a World Fantasy Award nomination. He is the author of over 200 published short stories and 25 books, including *To Each Their Darkness, In Silent Graves, Prodigal Blues*, and the forthcoming *A Cracked and Broken Path*. He lives in Worthington, Ohio, where nobody has ever heard of him. This depresses him. So he's on medication. Approach with caution. Find him online at www.garybraunbeck.com.

JULIE STIPES likes to think no one is watching her. But there's always someone watching her. She's covered in tattoos and piercings and her hair often changes color. Sometimes she closes her eyes and imagines a world without judgment. When she hides from public view, she often writes, keeping most of those words to herself. She is currently working on a controversial novel, *Nine Inches*. "Not the Child" from this anthology is her first attempt at horror.

GENE O'NEILL has over 120 stories published and numerous anthology placements, including *Borderlands 5* and *Dead End: City Limits*. His stories have been reprinted in France, Spain and Russia. A few have garnered Nebula and Stoker recommendations, including "Balance," a short story Stoker finalist in 2007, and *The Confessions of St. Zach*, a finalist in the long fiction category in 2009. *Doc Good's Traveling Show* was a long fiction finalist in 2010 and *Taste of Tender-*

loin won that year for collection. His stories are collected in *Ghost Spirits, Computers & World Machines, The Grand Struggle,* and *Taste of Tenderloin.* Recent collections include *Dance of the Blue Lady & Other Stories,* and *In Dark Corners.* His novels include *The Burden of Indigo, Collected Tales of the Baja Express, Shadow of the Dark Angel, Deathflash, Lost Tribe,* and *Not Fade Away.* Just released are two novellas, *Rusting Chickens* (Dark Regions Press) and *Double Jack* (Sideshow Press). SSP will also release a *Cal Wild* chapbook, *Chronicles of the Double Sparrow,* and Thunderstorm Books will release a novella, *Operation Rhinoceros Hornbill.* Gene is putting the finishes touches on the *Cal Wild* trilogy and beginning a series of promised short stories.

CHRISTIAN LARSEN grew up in Park Ridge, Illinois and graduated from the University of Illinois at Urbana-Champaign. He has worked as an English teacher, radio personality, newspaper reporter, and a printer's devil, and has been published in *What Fears Become* (Imajin Books), *A Feast of Frights* (The Horror Zine Books), *The Ghost IS the Machine* (Post Mortem Press), and *Fortune: Lost and Found* (Omnium Gatherum). He lives with his wife and two sons in the fictional town of Northport, Illinois. Follow him on Twitter @exlibrislarsen or visit www.exlibrislarsen.com.

PATRICK O'NEILL is a forty-one year old Senior Research Analyst living in Poole (Dorset, England) with wife, Nikki, and fifteen year old son, Benedict. He is a rising new talent in horror fiction. Five of his short stories have been selected for publication in anthologies this year and he aims to have his single author anthology, *Dark Hearts*, published in December 2013.

P. GARDNER GOLDSMITH is a US/UK based television writer and author who has worked in the Script Departments of "Star Trek: Voyager" and "The Outer Limits." His short stories have appeared in *Naked* (UK), and *Epitaphs* (US), and will soon appear in *Horror Library 5* (US). In late 2012 and early 2013, his first two novellas, *Bite* and *Gorge*, will be published in Europe by Pendragon and in the US by Bad Moon Books. His nonfiction book, *Live Free or Die*, was published in 2007, and subsequently selected as a "Book of the Month" by the Freedom Book Club.

JON MICHAEL KELLEY began his writing career twenty years ago as a lyricist for a small music company in New York City. On a whim, his producer called him one day and asked if he wrote anything "literary"; that since she was on "Publishers Row" she could shop a sample around for him. He told her that he had, in fact, recently finished his first short story, and he sent it along. That story eventually won him featured author in a small press magazine called Heart Attack, and he's been writing ever since. His fiction has been nominated for such prizes as the Pushcart, and has appeared in such magazines and anthologies as *Night Terrors, Best of Millennium Sci Fi & Fantasy, New Genre II, Wired Hard III, Father Grim's Storybook,* and *Tales of Terror and Mayhem from Deep Within the Box*. His first novel, *Seraphim*, was released by Evil Jester Press in the summer of 2012 amid a flurry of great reviews.

A. A. GARRISON is a twenty-nine-year-old man living in the mountains of North Carolina. His short fiction has appeared in dozens of publications, both in print and online. His first novel, *The End of Jack Cruz*, is available from Montag Press. He blogs at synchroshock.blogspot.com.

AARON J. FRENCH, also writing/editing as A.J. French, is an affiliate member of the Horror Writers Association. His work has appeared in many publications, including Dark Discoveries, D. Harlan Wilson's The Dream People, Black Ink Horror, the *Potter's Field*

4 anthology from Sam's Dot Publishing, Something Wicked magazine, and The Lovecraft eZine, where he is also co-editor. He has stories in the following anthologies: *Ruthless: An Extreme Horror Anthology*, edited by Shane McKenzie, with introduction by Bentley Little; *Pellucid Lunacy*, edited by Michael Bailey; *M is for Monster*, compiled by John Prescott; *Zippered Flesh: Tales of Body Enhancements Gone Wrong*, edited by Weldon Burge; and *Dark Tales of Lost Civilizations*, edited by Eric J. Guignard. He recently edited *Monk Punk*, an anthology of monk-themed speculative fiction, with introduction by D. Harlan Wilson, and *The Shadow of the Unknown*, an anthology of nü-Lovecraftian fiction, with stories from Gary A. Braunbeck and Gene O'Neill.

MEGHAN ARCURI lives in New York's Hudson Valley. "Inevitable" is her first publication and her first foray into horror. She does not like to be scared and is generally afraid of the dark. She has convinced herself that she leaves the hallway lights on for the kids.

PATRICK LACEY is a graduate of Salem State University and an Editorial Assistant in the healthcare industry. When he's not reading about blood clots and infectious diseases, he writes about things that make the general public uncomfortable. He lives in Massachusetts with his fiancée, his Pomeranian, and his muse, who he's pretty sure is trying to kill him. Follow him on Twitter: @PatLacey.

JEFF STRAND's novels include *Pressure*, *Dweller*, *Wolf Hunt*, *A Bad Day For Voodoo*, *Graverobbers Wanted (No Experience Necessary)*, *Benjamin's Parasite*, *The Sinister Mr. Corpse*, and a bunch more. He did not know what "chirality" meant before being asked to contribute a story to this anthology. You can visit his Gleefully Macabre website at www.jeffstrand.com.

R. B. PAYNE, assembled from stolen body parts, lives in the hope of being human. Meanwhile, he writes. His work can be found in *Monk Punk, The Shadow of the Unknown,* and the forthcoming *Times of Trouble and Expiry Date*; book reviews are at Shroud Online, and his analysis of 1930's black-and-white slasher films is in Butcher Knives and Body Counts. Contact him at www.rbpayne.com – especially if you are willing to contribute a body organ.

ERIK T. JOHNSON's work has appeared or is forthcoming in fine periodicals such as Space & Time Magazine, Electric Velocipede, Structo, Morpheus Tales, Sein und Werden, Polluto, Structo and Shimmer; and anthologies including *Pellucid Lunacy, The Shadow of the Unknown, Box of Delights, Dead but Dreaming 2, WTF?!* and *Best New Zombie Tales 3.* Johnson's work is regularly welcomed and well-reviewed by critics and fans. Most recently, his story "Water Buried" (British Fantasy Society Journal, Winter 2010), was called "perfect" by D.F. Lewis and received an Honorable Mention from Ellen Datlow in her list of Best Horror of the Year 2011. A complete and regularly updated bibliography, as well as scrawling and doodles, can be found at www.eriktjohnson.net.

PAT R. STEINER once found himself hanging from a nail pounded into a tree. Left there by his older siblings, he happily communed with the tree until his mother dragged the whereabouts of the missing younger brother from the guilt-ridden children. Since then he has had a fascination with nature (including the human variety) along with its many mysteries. His writings and art are his attempts to explain these BIG QUESTIONS as well as those more mundane. Pat's stories have appeared in many small print anthologies. He is also a recent winner of the Illustrators of the Future contest. He lives in Wisconsin with his wife and two children. Visit him at: www.patsteiner.com.

JOHN PALISANO is the author of the novel *Nerves* and the novella *The BiPolar Express*, as well as short stories in the following anthologies: *The Lovecraft E-Zine, Horror Library, Beast Within, Darkness on the Edge, A Sea of Alone, Terror Scribes*, and many others. John can be found at: www.johnpalisano.wordpress.com.

JACK KETCHUM's first novel, *Off Season*, prompted the Village Voice to publicly scold its publisher in print for publishing violent pornography. He personally disagrees but is perfectly happy to let you decide for yourself. His short story "The Box" won a 1994 Bram Stoker Award from the Horror Writers Association, his story "Gone" won again in 2000—and in 2003 he won Stokers for best collection with *Peaceable Kingdom*, and for best long fiction with "Closing Time." He has written twelve novels, arguably thirteen, five of which have been filmed–*The Girl Next Door, Red, The Lost, Offspring* and *The Woman*, written with Lucky McKee. His stories are collected in *The Exit at Toledo Blade Boulevard, Peaceable Kingdom, Closing Time and Other Stories*, and *Sleep Disorder*, with Edward Lee. His horror-western novella "The Crossings" was cited by Stephen King in his speech at the 2003 National Book Awards. He was elected Grand Master for the 2011 World Horror Convention. Find him online at www.jackketchum.net

MICHAEL BAILEY is the author of *Palindrome Hannah*, a nonlinear horror novel and finalist for the Independent Publisher Awards. His follow-up novel, *Phoenix Rose*, was listed for the National Best Book Awards for horror fiction and was a finalist for the International Book Awards. *Scales and Petals*, his short story and poetry collection, won the International Book Award, as well as the USA Book News "Best Books" Award. *Pellucid Lunacy*, a charity anthology he edited prior to *Chiral Mad*, won those same two awards. His short fiction and poetry can be found in anthologies and magazines around the world, including the US, UK, Australia, Sweden, and South Africa; some of the most recent anthologies include *Surviving the End, Uncommon Assassins, Zippered Flesh: Tales of Body Enhancements Gone Wrong, Colors, Here Be Clowns, Unnatural Tales of the Jackalope, The Shadow of the Unknown, Poe-It,* and the first volume of *Something Wicked.* He is currently working on his third novel, *Psychotropic Dragon*, a new short story and poetry collection, *Inkblots and Blood Spots,* and most recently edited the book you are about to finish reading. He holds the highest of respect for those in this anthology. You can visit his strange world online at www.nettirw.com.

14702955R00214

Made in the USA
Charleston, SC
26 September 2012